Praise for Wa...

"Downing has a keen ear . . . is a sensitive writer and can put together a good plot."
—*The New York Times Book Review*

"A lawyer and a writer of considerable skill. . . ."
—*Washington Star-News*

"Downing writes with style. . . ."
—*Miami Herald*

And Warwick Downing's

A CLEAR CASE OF MURDER

"A prime specimen of the new-style courtroom novel. . . . It is both a genuinely original detective story and the kind of legal novel that trial buffs love. Don't miss this one."
—*Armchair Detective*

THE WATER CURE

"Every time things begin to look too neat, Downing tosses in another curve . . . worthwhile . . ."
—*Publishers Weekly*

Books by Warwick Downing

A Clear Case of Murder
A Lingering Doubt
The Water Cure

Published by POCKET BOOKS

A LINGERING DOUBT

WARWICK DOWNING

POCKET BOOKS

New York   London   Toronto   Sydney   Tokyo   Singapore

An *Original* Publication of POCKET BOOKS

POCKET BOOKS, a division of Simon & Schuster Inc.
1230 Avenue of the Americas, New York, NY 10020

Copyright © 1993 by Warwick Downing

All rights reserved, including the right to reproduce this book or portions thereof in any form whatsoever. For information address Pocket Books, 1230 Avenue of the Americas, New York, NY 10020

ISBN: 0-671-76034-3

First Pocket Books printing April 1993

10 9 8 7 6 5 4 3 2 1

POCKET and colophon are registered trademarks of Simon & Schuster Inc.

Cover art by Irving Freeman

Printed in the U.S.A.

Chuck:

It's too bad Daddy died before you got
your license to steal.
You are the kind of lawyer
he'd have loved.

The jury's task, like the historian's, must be to discover and evaluate events that have faded into the past, and no human mind can perform that function with certainty. Judges and juries must time and again reach decisions that are not free from doubt; only the most fatuous would claim the adjudication of guilt to be infallible. The lingering doubts of jurors in the guilt phase may well cast their shadows into the penalty phase and in some measure affect the nature of the punishment.

People v. Terry, J. Tobriner, 61 Cal. 2nd 137; 37 Cal. Rptr. 605; 390 Pac. 2d 381.

LINGERING DOUBT

1

Those NASP guys are good, I thought. The rapport he had with them was thick enough to cut. Jurors usually wear masks; they try to look impartial; but they lit up for this young pup, even though he looked wet behind the ears.

It was a death penalty case, a double-phase trial, and we were closing in on the end of the guilt phase. We had finished with the evidence at ten o'clock that morning, and I could have used a break. But the judge—one of those Long Beach hard-asses—made us plow on with the case. She even ordered the jury back at one o'clock! And while they ate lunch, we had to argue instructions! When they came back with full stomachs—"ready for their afternoon nap," as old Charley Wallace used to say—Judge Ida "Iron Pants" Mather convened her court and launched us into final argument.

"—is truly a great country," the boy wonder from NASP declaimed. "I hope I don't sound too much like a politician, but that greatness comes from you, the people, and your willingness to accept the responsibilities of citizenship."

What a nice spiel, I thought, noting the way he stressed "people," as in *People of the State of California*—his client. He will tell them their duty is to hang mine.

"—one such responsibility is the awesome task you now perform: jury service, sitting in judgment."

All through the trial I'd been trying to decide who he reminded me of. Then I realized it was the Velvet Fog: a thirty-three-year-old Mel Torme, just as I remembered him from the fifties. It was more than his smooth, mellow voice. He had the smoothed-back hair, the friendly, smooth face, and the easy, smooth manner. Everything about the boy was smooth and mellow, so whatever he fed you was easy to digest.

"As jurors, you are literally the guardians of our way of life. Those magnificent rights our ancestors, our sons and daughters died for"—sons and daughters? Like in Iraq? Huh! Not *our* sons and daughters, I thought—"rights that protect this man from the summary justice he would get in most other countries of this world." His nice little smile conveyed the wonderful magnificence of it all. "And it is your responsibility to give him the full benefit of that protection."

His name was Keane Williams, and I admired his style— in spite of the fact his goal was to kill my client. He was succeeding, too. If I didn't get him off the track, my client—Drusus Church—could kiss this good sweet world good-bye.

The plastic ballpoint pen in my hands bent like wire when I thought about that. But I nodded vigorously for the benefit of the jurors. I wanted to emphasize my complete agreement with the last observation of the prosecutor, in spite of the feeling in my stomach. It felt out of control, as though it had been pitched out the window.

Over the years the law has been good to me, and I make more money than I need. I do three or four cases a year— little people, usually, who have been trampled on "by those with the great good fortune to have pockets lined with gold," old Charley used to say of my practice. But now and then the Justice Machine will roll like a freight train at someone who shouldn't be lashed to the rails. In spite of the folklore on the subject, it's hard for the average lawyer to stand by and watch that happen.

"I'm the prosecutor," Keane Williams continued, leaning forward just a bit. As though to say, I'm cool, folks.

2

But part of really being cool is knowing it's okay to be sincere. "I represent the people; but believe me when I tell you this: It does not matter what this man did. In our country, he is entitled to a fair trial."

I glanced over at Drusus. A young, powerful man with dark skin and an incredible mind, he appeared to be listening with more intensity than anyone else in the room. But a fair trial in Long Beach? I thought. You're kidding. Most of the good people in Long Beach—including the Filipinos, African-Americans, and Asians—were rednecks, if the truth were known. They didn't believe in fair trials. If it's fair it takes too long, which is an automatic waste of taxpayer money.

"Having said that, let's consider what this man did."

That shouldn't take long, I thought. It only took three days to put the evidence in; it can slide in fast when there's no defense. "This was a simple, sordid murder of the kind that happens far too often around here," he said.

The prick. It would have been reversible error for a prosecutor to make a comment like that under the Rose Byrd court, God love the dear sweet lady. But under Lucas the prosecutor could do no wrong.

We were so different, the lad from NASP and I. He projected well; his skills had been integrated into his image; he had taken courses in how to relate to jurors. I was an old-fashioned liberal, a wily fifty-five-year-old mule with horn-rimmed glasses that wouldn't stay on my nose, and an attitude. But the funny thing was, I used to teach those courses. He believed in the death penalty; I never have. It was as easy for me to defend miscreants as it was for him to prosecute them.

Drusus Church was not the average miscreant, either. The thing that had happened to me in this case has happened at least once to all the old warhorses that romp around in the trial courts in this land. I believed—as totally and completely as I believed in the love of my mother—in the innocence of the man I was defending. Those are the cases that grab you by the gut and won't let go.

Keane started hammering away at what the evidence,

3

during the course of the trial, had shown. The victim, Kingsley Rhoades, had operated a crack house off Anaheim at Cherry. He was known to pack a wad of cash in a purse that hung off his neck. The defendant, Drusus Church, lived in an apartment down the street from the crack house but in the same block.

On the fourteenth of April of the year before, just before midnight, Rhoades caught two .38-caliber slugs in his chest, in the alley behind the crack house. April Tillman, a young black woman—"perhaps not someone you'd have over for dinner"—had been sleeping in the alley but saw it happen. "Fortunately for her, this man"—he pointed at Drusus— "didn't know she was there."

He described what April had seen. It sounded more convincing coming from him in argument than it had from her as a witness. "A black man, big as a building. The minute she saw his face she knew who it was. Hammer. And from other testimony, we know that 'Hammer' was the 'moniker'—the street name—of the defendant.

" 'It happen so fast,' she told us, remember?" Keane asked. I thought to myself: He does that well. She did more than tell the jurors; she told "us"—meaning the jury and Keane. A bit like in "We, the people." They teach them that at prosecutor school, a course in how to put yourself on the jury's team.

I wondered what old Iron Pants would do if I objected to the tactic. The old biddy. She'd hold me in contempt, then stuff me in a pillory in front of the courthouse and invite passersby to throw rocks.

" 'Just—blam. Blam. The King fall down. Then Hammer lean down an' pull something off Kingman's neck, then look up and smile.' " A nice touch, that, I thought. Villains smile after doing something villainous. " 'Then he run away.' "

Keane gestured toward Drusus again, this time with his hand and a slight bow, as though introducing the star of the show. I watched them stare at my client and hated to think what they saw.

Drusus was dark—not an Andrew Young or Harry Bela-

4

fonte, who are considered black by most whites, even though they have skins lighter than the Japanese. Dark dark. Recognizably African, with skin like deep brown paint. When the jurors looked at him, he looked right back at them. But they won't see the youngster's natural dignity, I thought. They'll see arrogance.

"So we begin with eyewitness testimony," Keane said, pausing long enough to let it sink in. "A woman, thirty feet from the scene, who saw this man"—he turned toward Drusus and pointed—"shoot the victim, then yank something off his neck and run away.

"That is usually enough. But in this case there is more. A lot more. The eyewitness evidence we have from April Tillman is corroborated by a mountain of other evidence."

I did my best, sitting there, to look perplexed about what I knew was coming. I *was* perplexed. My whole gambit had been that I couldn't explain it. It was the big mystery.

"Three days after the shooting the police obtained a search warrant. They weren't subtle about the way they executed it, and I hope that doesn't offend you." Keane's eyes turned into hard marbles. The testimony had been that the cops kicked Drusus's door in at three o'clock in the morning and dragged him out of bed. Keane's expression implied they had to do it that way because when you deal with criminals you can't afford to take chances. "Mr. Church was in bed with the woman he apparently shared the apartment with, Vera Byrd. You met her, too. She testified for the defense.

"And as you know, the police found what they were looking for: the purse." He marched over to the table by the clerk where the exhibits had been piled, lifted out a rough-leather pouch, and held it up so they could see it. "They knew right where to look: in an enclosed bookcase, the one above the cabinet that held the sound system. It sat on that shelf like a trophy, in front of a complete set of the work of Donald Goines."

He put the purse down and picked up a five-by-eight-inch color photograph. It showed the bookcase and the books and the cabinet that held the sound system. "How

5

did it get there? Did the police put it there?" he sneered. "Sometimes that is suggested."

"Objection, Judge!" I shouted, storming to my feet. "He knows better than that!"

Keane looked at me with consternation. "You're right," he confessed. "Judge, I apologize for that remark. I didn't—"

"I understand, Mr. Williams," Iron Pants said. "The objection is well taken, however. Members of the jury, you are directed to disregard the last statement of Mr. Williams."

All those righteous-looking Baptists and Presbyterians looked properly confused but nodded "yes," as though in complete agreement. The prosecutor had planted a seed in their minds that was outside the evidence. He'd said, "Sometimes that is suggested," implying that all defense lawyers are tricky bastards who will suggest anything to get their clients off. That's what everybody thinks anyway. If they don't, they should. "Mr. Bard, would you like me to pursue it?"

I made the most of it—which amounted, in this case, to glaring at the lad, then sitting down. "No, Your Honor." I could have asked for a mistrial and raised hell—good theater, maybe, but bad tactics. Judge Ida Mather—frequently called "Iron Pants," occasionally known as "Old Chastity Belt," rarely called "Your Honor," except to her face—would have denied my motion and then explained what the prosecutor had done wrong. The jury would have heard it all over again, making it worse.

I believed his apology, too. I was used to the Nazis in Long Beach, but the NASP lawyers—for National Association of Special Prosecutors—weren't like that. They had a reputation to maintain and I knew Jim Trigge, the head of the agency. He was an old warhorse like me. I'd never met a tougher, fairer, or more ethical prosecutor than Jim. His troops waved the same banner.

"Very well," Iron Pants said. Indulgently. "Please be careful, Mr. Williams. You may continue."

Continue he did. He reminded them that the detectives

had gotten the warrant before tossing the apartment. The paper described the exact spot where they found the victim's purse, which meant the police could not have planted it unless they'd been in the apartment before they searched it.

He smiled at that. "Some buildings are burglar-proof. They have elaborate security systems designed to send alarms and make noises when burglars break in. The apartment complex where Drusus Church lived is cop-proof. A cop inside that gate *is* an alarm. Everyone in all twenty-two units, from the manager to the smallest infant, would instantly know.

"Remember that line of questions I put to Vera Byrd, the defendant's girlfriend?" His expression had mellowed from marble-hard to dead certain, and his eyes sought them out one at a time. "A cop in that building rings bells. She told us that. It's like sirens and whistles."

He paused for a cup full of water. You have to like the lad, I thought. He was considerate, funny, played by the rules, and was not overbearing—which was what made him so dangerous, because the jury liked him, too. Old Charley always said when you get one like that, spike his water. Give him something to help him hallucinate, like a drop of LSD. But I hadn't, and he'd continued to bury me.

It's odd. A lawyer will say "bury me," as though it's happening to him. But when I went home that night, it would be to clean linen sheets. Drusus had been in the county jail more than a year, waiting for trial. I don't think they have sheets in the L.A. County Jail.

"Mr. Bard is a fine lawyer and a fine man," Keane said, gesturing in my direction. I smiled in agreement, of course. "He has a job to do, and he will do it to the very best of his ability. You already know what he will say: If the police didn't plant that purse in Drusus Church's bookcase, then it must have been the person who told them where to look." He smiled at me. "I know Mr. Bard is not the kind of man who likes to deliberately mislead. And he may truly believe what he will tell us. I can sympathize with his position—but don't let his eloquence or his sincerity make you think there is a mystery here.

"This is not 'Perry Mason' or 'Jake and the Fatman.' It isn't even 'L.A. Law.' It's a simple, sordid murder, and there isn't any mystery to be solved. The police did not break in to Drusus Church's apartment without knowing, before they got there, what they would find. They had a warrant. That warrant was based on a sworn affidavit, in accordance with law. The police had information, and the information proved to be correct. For legal reasons—reasons that must not concern you—the source of that information cannot be disclosed to you. Or to them." He looked past me, right at Drusus. Drusus met his stare head-on.

If Drusus dropped his eyes, they'd have thought he was guilty. When he stared back with that look on his face, they thought it was a sneer. That bastard Keane looked at *him* with understanding, too.

"There is nothing in the evidence that even hints at the possibility that someone framed Mr. Church for this murder. There is innuendo—there is always innuendo—but no evidence."

He poured more water. The mellow fellow has a dry throat? I asked myself. Does he lie, or just have a cold? Either way, is it something I can use? "Let's see what we have at this point," he said in that smooth voice. "An eyewitness who saw the defendant shoot the victim, then took something off his neck." He sat the cup on the lectern, then moved out like a soldier on parade. "Three days later the victim's purse is found in the defendant's apartment—a purse the victim wore around his neck. That is solid, rock-hard evidence. And there is more." He let them wait while he reached for the small paper cup and sipped the water.

"We found out more about the victim, Kingsley Rhoades, than we ever wanted to know, right? He was not a nice man. At least, few of us here in this room would think so." He started to march. "They called him 'King', or 'the Kingman.' That's how the people in the area saw him. But he was no king." He stopped in front of Juror Four—a tough-looking, wire-haired retiree—and they looked at each other. You could see their minds mesh. "He was a crack dealer. He operated a crack house down the street from where Mr. Church lived. He was streetwise and tough— we have that from the witnesses who testified for Mr. Church—and all of them knew he carried money in that purse."

Keane Williams marches on, I thought, watching him stride along the floor in front of the jury box. "Did Mr. Church know? Well, what do you think?" He skated that thin ice with care. Drusus had not testified, and the prosecutor can't argue the failure of the defendant to take the stand—which was another right the courts were playing with. Those dirty old men should not play with themselves, Charley Wallace used to say. It creates the wrong impression. "Ask yourself this question," Keane said, frowning slightly, as someone might who is asking himself a question. "Wouldn't he know what everyone else in the neighborhood did?"

I watched the jurors. Most of them wore poker faces, but a couple of them nodded in agreement.

"And what of these?" Keane was at the evidence table, where he picked up the plastic bag that held the slugs the pathologist had found. "Thirty-eight-caliber bullets dug out of the body of Mr. Rhoades." He showed them to the jury.

"The police didn't find the weapon. We don't have a gun in this case that those bullets can be matched with. But our expert on firearms told us a lot. We know the kind of gun because every manufacturer of guns grooves the barrel differently. They all like to put their own distinctive twist on the bullet, and the imprint of that twist is visible to the expert.

"These were fired from a Smith and Wesson .38-caliber revolver—the kind of gun the cops wore until a couple of years ago." He placed the slugs on the table and walked back to the lectern. "I felt so sorry for that lovely girl," he said. "I have never disliked this job as much as I did during that brief period when she testified for us. You know who I mean: Leah Dempster."

Drusus gathered himself together like a panther, ready to leap. He was a powerful man, and I saw the muscle build in his neck. I gripped his shoulder, but if he charged, I'd have had as much chance holding him back as I would a berserk buffalo.

"She cried," Keane told the jury. "You know, I think she still loves him? How hard, hard, hard it must have been for her to give such damning evidence against the man she loves." He let the mood build. "Who was it that said, 'There is nothing to compare with the pain of the human heart, when it is in conflict with itself'?"

If I'd had a different judge, I might have put my hand up and given the answer: William Faulkner. But Iron Pants would not have been appreciative of a gambit like that.

"She told us who she was: his high-school girl. She didn't tell us why, or when they broke up. But she remembered when he showed her a gun; a silver gun, she said, with a short barrel. He told her he'd stolen it off a cop."

Keane took another hit of water. I wondered if a Quaalude might ruffle him up. "And Detective Barrett—I think it was Barrett, although it could have been one of the other officers—told us about 'cop guns.' They carry 9mm semiautomatics now. But two years ago they wore those snubnose .38-caliber revolvers. Nickel-plated."

He looked ready to quit. Great. That gave me approximately one minute to locate what I hadn't been able to find in the thirteen months I'd been with the case: an answer. "I won't belabor the law," he said, smiling at them. They loved it when he smiled at them. "You'll get the law from the judge, orally and in writing. You will even have a set of instructions with you when you deliberate. But do this for me." I had the impression they would do whatever he asked. "If there is a reasonable doubt in this case—which does not include imaginary or speculative doubts, incidentally; our law specifically says that a reasonable doubt must be based on reason—but if there is a doubt of that magnitude, we should let this man go.

"Without one, however—and in the face of such good, hard, solid evidence of guilt"—he started to sit down—"do your job. As awesome as that responsibility is, I'm confident you will have the courage to do it.

"Mr. Bard?"

Good God Almighty, I thought. I have never been invited up to the lectern by the fucking prosecutor. "Thank you Mr. Williams, but let's clear it with the judge."

He laughed, and—more importantly—so did the jury. Iron Pants even blessed me with a smile. "Proceed, Mr. Bard," she said.

I made my way to the lectern slowly, a deliberate contrast to the quick, youthful moves of my adversary. I wanted them to see me as older and wiser. My glasses had worked to the end of my nose, and I peered over them at the jury, then pushed them back. It's a fairly effective maneuver if it isn't overdone, designed to make the jury think I'm quaint and lovable. I can see better, too.

Then a strange thing happened. I've heard that a person's whole life can flash before his eyes in that moment ahead of certain death. I peered at the jury but saw something else: a memory.

2

I was in a hurry. I had to get to Redheads by noon to interview a witness; but there was gridlock on Anaheim. I ducked off, scooted up to Fifteenth, and turned east. The neighborhood was residential ghetto, and down the block a small dog wandered into the street. I eased off the pedal, ready to stand on the brake.

A little black kid on a skateboard shot into the street in front of me, between a couple of parked cars. I swerved to avoid him—I saw him go down—and hit the dog.

As quickly as possible I stopped, pulled over, and got out. "You *better* stop!" Some youths in black shirts and Raiders hats, on backwards, appeared in the street.

I kept looking for the little kid. "God, I'm sorry!" I could hear the dog squeaking; an elderly black woman had picked it up. She sat on the bumper of a car, cradling it. "Is the dog okay?"

"He fine." She smiled but saw something behind me that gave her alarm. The kid on the skateboard, I thought, turning around.

I still didn't see him. "Where's the boy?" I asked of anyone who would listen.

"He ain't no 'boy,' " one of the youths said. Five or six had formed around me in a loose circle.

"This gonna cost you."

"Somebody call the po-lice!"

Laughter.

The sun was high; cars were driving by; these punks annoyed the hell out of me. I was in a hurry; I'd lived in Long Beach all my life; I didn't need their grief. Then I saw the little kid and walked over to him. He had tears in his eyes, his pants were torn over his knees, and he had a thumb in his mouth. "Are you okay?"

One of the youths got between us. He was about sixteen, and his shirt was knotted above his waist, exposing a muscled stomach. "Don't say nothin'," he ordered the boy. Then he faced me, grinning. "You gots to make your deal with me, mister. I'm his lawyer."

I'd had it. "Get out of the way!"

From somewhere he yanked out a knife. An awful hatred smeared his face. It was pathological. "White motherfucker," he said, reaching toward me with his other hand. "You gonna be shittin' bricks."

I don't remember feeling anything, but I backed up. Then hands grabbed my arms, holding them tight. I thought it was to make it easy for the crazy one. "Let *go* of me!" I shouted, yanking one arm loose. But the other was in a vise. "Let *go!*"

The boy who held it was huge—more than six feet tall—very black, and muscular. Then I realized he was helping me! His body shoved between me and the boy with the knife, and he guided me back to my car.

His head was turned so that he could see what was happening behind us. He wasn't afraid in the slightest, although I could hear him breathe. He looked annoyed. "Hammer, man, what you doin', nigger?" the boy with the knife demanded. "I gonna cut *you!*"

"Huh. You got more sense than that."

Two years later, I saw the young man who had saved me again: sitting in my office, wearing a tie, and asking for a job. I recognized him instantly, but there was nothing on his face one way or the other. "Haven't I seen you before?" I asked.

There was a flicker of embarrassment in his expression.

13

"I been in some trouble, Mr. Bard. Maybe you seen me at the courthouse."

"What kind of trouble?"

"Burglary."

He had a direct way of talking that seemed almost rude; but to a lawyer who listens mainly to bullshit, it was great. He told me he wanted to go to college but had to graduate from high school first. "I'm in the adult education school," he said. "You can call down there if you want. They said it would be all right."

So I paid him to run a few errands and serve subpoenas but kept waiting for the catch. What had happened to the young gangster who saved me from that operation on the street? Would he rip me off? Was this a setup? Or had I been right to give him a chance? Then one day he came down to lay paper on witnesses I didn't need anymore because the case settled. We sat in my office and talked— and I was amazed. We were into a huge, deep, philosophic struggle about morals, language, God, and law. And this ghetto kid *understood* all that stuff!

I wanted to take him places after that, but usually he'd make an excuse. Still, we had lunch once or twice, and I'd drive him home. He would smile as he leaned into the leather cushion of my Mazda. I had the sense of appreciation: not so much that he liked zipping around in my car, but that he enjoyed the courtesy. But five months after he asked me for a job he was charged with murder.

Two rows of faces, twelve jurors and three alternates, faded back in. I didn't know what to say to them. There was nothing different in that. I never know; even if I memorize it. Something always gets in that gap between my memory and my mouth.

You'd better get started I thought, looking at them.

3

Mr. Williams. Your Honor. Ladies and gentlemen." I looked at my hands. They gripped the lectern as they would a telephone pole in a typhoon. Let go of it, I thought, turning toward Keane. Let the wind take you. " "What you mean "we", paleface?' "

The jurors were puzzled, naturally. They didn't know what I was talking about.

I moved out in front of the lectern, as though daring the soldiers in the fort to shoot. "Mr. Williams is an extraordinarily effective prosecutor," I told them. "He even has the ability—and the grace—to compliment me, which makes it hard for me to point out some of his tricks. Like the way he kept saying 'we' and 'us' while he was talking to you. As though he was one of you."

I got a couple of them to look at me. "He isn't, ladies and gentlemen. He doesn't sit in the jury box. Neither do I." My glasses started down my nose, and I pushed them in place. "He and I are advocates. We're down here in the pit. Don't let him link you with his so-called client, 'the People.' When he tries to create the impression that all of you are on one side, while Drusus Church and I are on the other, don't fall for it." Two of them smiled. "The truth is, he doesn't represent the people. He represents the cops."

I didn't need X-ray vision to see through the masks most

of them wore. They didn't like it when I said that. But my tactic—my only chance, it seemed to me—was to challenge them, make them think. " 'The People' "—I held my fingers up, putting the words in quotes—"is a legal fiction. Like a corporation. But he has clients in this case, the same as me. His are Detective Wink Barrett, Officer Tom Morschy, Detectives Dave Kincaid and Rory Danforth. His clients are the Long Beach PD."

One time old Charley Wallace told me I talk down to jurors. We were trying a case against each other that day, and I figured it was just a ploy to make me self-conscious. It worked. Old Charley was cagey; he beat me to death. Still I wondered, looking at these jurors, if I was over their heads. "I hope you understand what I'm saying," I offered, searching their faces for signs of intelligence. "If you don't, it's not your fault. It's mine."

I took a turn on the carpet in front of them so they could watch me think. I wanted them to think along with me. "You've heard Mr. Williams talk about your job, the awful responsibility of sitting in judgment. It's harder than he said. Because each of you, individually, has the obligation of exercising his or her own independent judgment."

I faced Juror Six at the end of the rail and let my fingers touch the wood. She had a pleasant, thoughtful look, and I stopped for a moment to talk to her. "When you're back in the jury room, don't treat it like a social event, where all of you are nicey-nice with each other." I turned away before she could feel discomfort. "Each of you must consider the evidence. Alone." I challenged Four with a stare. "You don't need his help any more than you need mine."

Damn glasses. They were sliding around on their own, and I pushed them up again. "And don't take Mr. Williams with you when you go into the jury room to deliberate, either," I said to Four. "He doesn't belong in there. Neither do I."

I poured some water and drank it, knowing I had their attention. "Let's start with April Tillman, the eyewitness." I placed the cup on the lectern and scratched my head. "Mr. Williams said you might not have her over for dinner." I tilted my head back and adjusted the glasses, letting them know I wanted to see with clarity. "Not a particularly sensitive comment, but true, as far as it went. The whole truth is, none of you would be caught in the same room with her." Some of them stared at their laps. "*I* wouldn't," I said, in the hope that might make it easier to admit the obvious.

"Does that make her incredible? Can you only believe people you feel comfortable with socially?" With them watching, I thought it over. "No. That misses the point anyway. The point is this: You can't believe her."

I looked at all of them as one thing. I wanted them to see me looking at the real issue. "She is a derelict," I said. "A tramp. A coke-head. You know that from the evidence we put on. She's been convicted for possession of cocaine, and her probation officer testified to a fifty-dollar-a-day habit." See what's important? I hoped my expression asked. "She will do anything for a load of coke and will say anything to stay out of jail. Why? Because it's hard to get loaded when you're locked up."

I moved back behind the lectern and held it with my hands. "Mr. Williams didn't talk about that, did he? Yet we know that his side—the cops—gave her a break. She didn't come to them with evidence; they came to her to get evidence. They found out she'd been sleeping in the alley, and found her in a jail, and let her out, then dusted her off, put a nice clean dress on her, and set her up on that stand. You heard the detectives. They make it sound like great detective work, but I'm telling you they bargained with her for testimony, and she bargained back, and they let her out of jail."

They're listening, I thought. What is more, they aren't laughing when they shouldn't, and they aren't nodding off. "Remember on cross-examination when she said she saw the flash of the gun? Well, it has to be dark to see the flash of a gun. And it *was* dark. Remember the testimony?" I fished around for a note and found it. " 'Like a moonless night in the country,' someone said." Actually, I had said that, and one of the cops agreed. "If it was that dark, how could she have seen anyone's face?"

Jurors Ten and Six barely moved their heads. Do I see some agreement here? I hoped. "Don't believe her, ladies and gentlemen. Not because you don't travel in the same circles, but because you can't trust her. Toss her testimony out.

"And while I'm on the subject of things Mr. Williams forgot to mention, what about Mr. Church's alibi? The prosecutor didn't even bring it up!" I wouldn't have either, if I'd been him. He knew it was all I had and guessed I'd talk about it, which would give him the chance to blow it into oblivion on rebuttal. "Vera Byrd, the woman Mr. Church lived with—until that night thirteen months ago, when he was arrested—was with him, in their apartment, the night Kingsley Rhoades was killed."

I walked away from the lectern, letting them see my body register anger. "Miss Byrd is every bit as credible as Leah Dempster, isn't she? Miss Byrd told you they had friends over that night, another couple. All of them heard the shooting! Drusus Church was sitting in the living room at the time, close enough for her to touch. Did you hear about that from Mr. Williams?"

When you've done as many jury trials as I have, you take cues from little nuances. Later on you find out how wrong you were—but you still do it. A couple of jurors watched the backs of their hands, and the faces that squinted at me looked skeptical. "Mr. Williams is very willing to accept as true those parts of Vera Byrd's testimony he wants you to believe. What's wrong with the rest of it? Can you find—beyond a reasonable doubt—that she lied?"

I caught a grin that quickly straightened out. Juror Seven, it seemed, was capable of coming to that conclusion. I decided not to talk about our other witness, Jim-Jim Joslin. He and his girl were the other couple. Since that night Jim-Jim had gone down on a robbery charge. He was easy to find, but my investigator hadn't been able to locate the girl. Jim-Jim testified in prison clothes. Two uniformed bailiffs brought him into the courtroom and quietly took seats in front of the rail. Their impact could not have been lost on the jury. He rubbed his wrists as he climbed into the witness box because the handcuffs had just been removed, and when he finished testifying they led him back out. As a witness he had been awful, but I don't think I'd have done any better. I moved on to other things.

"Mr. Williams made a production out of the slugs, and he's young and has that great voice—and he's sincere, too." Don't get sarcastic, I told myself. Sarcasm directed at the champion of the people doesn't play well in Long Beach. Not only that, seven of the jurors were women, and more than one looked like she might enjoy cuddling with the lad.

I walked over to the exhibits table and picked up the slugs. "They're .38-caliber, shot from a Smith and Wesson. There are at least a hundred thousand guns like it in Los Angeles County. When the police switched over to the 9mms pawnshops and gun dealers had barrels full of the .38s, and they sold them, too." I pushed the glasses up, then took them down the path I'd made the prosecution expert walk when he had testified. "All those lawmen from all those towns: Long Beach, Whittier, Pasadena, Compton, Palos Verdes: a hundred small police departments with guns to get rid of. Then add in the big ones, like Los Angeles, and add to that the ones in the private sector."

They were listening again. "These slugs could have come from any of an enormous number of guns. There is no dispute about that. Or this, either: Except for that purse, there is no . . . physical . . . evidence"—I paused between the words—"to link my client with this crime. All the rest is words."

I tried sneering at the paucity of evidence, but I don't think it worked. I've never been able to force a sneer. "No fingerprints or footprints or hair samples or fingernails or clothing or threads or anything to put my client in that alley. These .38-caliber slugs? They don't do it."

I dropped them and marched back to the lectern. "There is the suggestion that Mr. Church at one time had a .38-caliber pistol in his possession." I opened my palms and shrugged my shoulders. "That, from Leah Dempster. Characterized by their side as a 'damning piece of evidence.' Come on!" I jammed the glasses back to my skull. Old Charley Wallace had glasses that slid up and down on his nose, but instead of turning them into a prop he glued them in place. Charley died of skin cancer. "Her testimony was dramatic, I'll agree with that. She didn't enjoy testifying against her former boyfriend. She cried and held that cross in her hand, and Mr. Williams suggested she might still be in love with Mr. Church.

"So what? The fact *she* thought she was destroying him doesn't mean she was. The fact the evidence was wrapped in that theatrical package doesn't make it any better. I'll grant the evidence has some relevance, but enough to convict on? No!"

Four and Eleven glared at me like I was a Satanist and they were Christians, but One, Five, Six, and Ten were stroking their chins. "Don't give that evidence more weight than it's entitled to because of the package. Think only of what it's worth.

"Look. Suppose he stole that gun two or three years ago, like she said. Mr. Church was living with his grandmother then. But you know, from the evidence, that he was living with Vera Byrd when this happened. So—after acquiring the gun—you know he moved at least once. He might have moved several times in that period. You don't know. Things happen when a person moves; objects get lost. You don't know what might have happened with that gun. He was seventeen when he took it and, from all indications, a wild kid. Would he have kept it? Traded it? Given it away? Lost it in a move? You don't know."

Of course, *I* knew what had happened to the gun, because Drusus had told me. They would know I knew, too. They would wonder why Drusus hadn't taken the stand and told them. "Which brings up another point," I said, starting the long climb up another hill. "Why didn't Mr. Church get in the witness chair and tell you what he did with the gun?"

I began a slow stroll in front of them. "You won't like

the answer. Like so much about this case, it isn't easy or quick. He had the right not to testify, and he has chosen to exercise that right." I was standing in quicksand, reaching for something to grab. "Those rights Mr. Williams talked about, the ones our ancestors gave up their lives to preserve for us?" I stopped in front of Juror Two. She dropped her eyes. "The right not to testify is one of those rights. You will be instructed by Judge Mather that you have the duty and obligation *not* to hold that decision against him." She took a chance, looked up, and I locked on her. "You must follow that instruction as well as all the others. That is part of the awesome responsibility you have assumed, which the prosecutor talked about."

I let her go and started down the path. "The reason is simple. The decision of a defendant not to testify, in and of itself, is not evidence. And as Mr. Williams also said, your decision can only be based on evidence."

They all wore masks, and I couldn't see behind their cardboard faces. "Please. This man is on trial for his life. There is so much he must consider before he takes the stand, things that could have nothing whatever to do with giving a quick answer to one easy question. Trust me when I tell you this. Our law—and rightfully so—has taken the stance that a person cannot be given a fair trial if he has to testify. I expect you—everyone in this courtroom expects you—to follow the law."

They would try. I knew they would try. Which was all I could ask.

"In order to get where we are going, let's go over where we have been." I tried to lighten up, to sound conversational. "You can't trust April Tillman. And even though Mr. Church had a cop gun years before this happened"— I didn't even try to suggest he hadn't—"that isn't enough. Those guns are everywhere. So when you get down to the nub, this case depends on one bit of evidence: that purse."

I went over to the exhibit table and picked it up, looked at it, and dropped it. "How did it get into Mr. Church's apartment?" I walked back to the lectern, hoping some fantastic new insight would occur. Jurors Six and Ten looked hopeful, too. "I don't know," I had to tell them. "But I know this with my whole heart: There is a mystery here. In spite of what Mr. Williams has said, there is a mystery! And mystery, in law, translates to 'reasonable doubt.' "

I had to push the glasses up again. Maybe Charley had the right idea, I thought. He turned truly nasty when he started gluing them in place—until he died, of course. I took them off.

"Listen to me. Vera Byrd is not a liar. She told you the truth. And the truth is, she was with Drusus Church when Kingsley Rhoades was killed. If she was a liar, then why didn't she lie about that pouch? You heard what she said when she was asked about it, whether it could have been on that shelf for days without her seeing it. Remember the prosecutor asking her that question? Why didn't she say, 'Not possible. I'd read a book of Goines the night before, and it wasn't there.' Or 'No. I dust up there every day.' Instead she said, 'Yes, it could have. I go for weeks at a time without even looking up there.' "

I was way too intense and knew it. The jury would see it as desperation. Maybe they'd feel sorry for me, but that wouldn't help my client. I needed a miracle.

"Mr. Williams and I agree on one thing," I said. The grin on my face made me feel like a used-car salesman. "If you have a reasonable doubt, you have the obligation to let him go. You have the responsibility to acquit him. And there is reasonable doubt here. Because in the final analysis, the only credible piece of evidence against my client is that purse!"

I didn't like focusing on Drusus. He hadn't taken the stand, and defendants who don't have a way of looking guilty. But I had no choice. He'd been sitting in the courtroom with them from the beginning. Possibly one or two of them could see what I knew to be true. "Look at my client," I invited them. "Does he look stupid? You met the woman he lived with. Could she take up with a complete dolt? Why would anyone but an idiot—and credit my client

22

with sense—leave evidence that would convict him of murder on a bookshelf in the living room of his apartment?''

Lighten up, I had to tell myself. You're starting to froth at the mouth. I tapped the glasses on the lectern and tried to smile.

"I know how jaded you are. You can't live in Southern California without growing a layer of cynicism. You know all about lawyers who pull tricks like magicians on judges and juries, then laugh when they walk some murdering rapist. No one enjoys being betrayed by some slick shyster.''

I faced them honestly, which I do very well. "I'm not slick, folks. I'm not a shyster, either. And I'm telling you there is a mystery here. And mystery means reasonable doubt.

"Someone told the police that the purse belonging to Kingsley Rhoades was in Mr. Church's apartment. But that person wasn't here in court. You don't know who he or she is, and neither do I. I didn't have the chance to cross-examine that person. How do you know that person isn't the killer here? How do you know that person isn't the one who shot and killed Kingsley Rhoades, then put the purse in Drusus Church's apartment?''

I gathered up my notes without looking at Iron Pants. It was time to stop. In fact, it was time to run and hide. "There is a mystery here," I said. "There is reasonable doubt."

Iron Pants cleared her throat. The reason "that person" wasn't in court was because another judge had ruled, at an earlier hearing, that the prosecution didn't have to tell me who it was. She did not like anyone—especially me—challenging a judicial decision.

I could feel the heat from her eyes. I kept from getting sizzled by looking at the clock on the wall: two o'clock, straight up. She had made us start at one, and at this rate the jury might get it before three. "Mr. Williams, before your rebuttal argument, would you like a short recess?" she asked.

"I don't need one, Judge," the boy wonder said offhandedly. "It won't take long to reply to Mr. Bard." -

That improved her mood. "Very well. You may proceed."

He may have thought it was short. But it was the longest twenty-minute reply I'd ever had to sit through.

He started by extolling the great job I had done and saying how much he admired my skills. "He told you he isn't slick, but if anyone can get Drusus Church off in the face of this evidence, it is Mr. Bard."

I should never have given him a line like that to play with.

Then he got them to shed a few tears over April Tillman. "The evidence showed her to be homeless. He called her a 'derelict.' " His face showed how bad he felt over a lawyer who would go that far to win a case. "Whichever she was, isn't it obvious to all of us that she had the guts—the courage—to come forward and testify?"

He moved away from the lectern and stalked toward them. "How many of you have seen a person hit in the chest with a .38-caliber slug?" he asked. "It is an awful thing to watch a bullet explode into a person's body. It is terrifying. You can imagine her terror, can't you? Is it so hard to understand her unwillingness to come into a court of law and face the man who pulled the trigger?

"And yes, she's been convicted of drug usage. In the words of Mr. Bard, so what?"

As to why he hadn't talked about the alibi witnesses, he hoped I would have the taste not to bring it up. "They were embarrassing to watch, and it is embarrassing to talk about them now," he said. He commented on Jim-Jim's smirk and went over the discrepancies in their testimony. "Unfortunately, people will lie for other people. That's the way it is."

And just as I had suggested several possibilities regarding the cop pistol that Drusus had stolen, he suggested there might be reasons—very good reasons—explaining why the person who told the cops about the purse had not been forced to come to court. "The point is, none of those reasons is evidence. Ladies and gentlemen, you must base your verdict on the evidence. That evidence is this: The police had information that the purse taken from the body of Kingsley Rhoades was in the defendant's apartment. And that is where it was."

Iron Pants nodded as he talked, obviously in total agreement. I called her on it. "Let the record reflect the Court is nodding its head in the affirmative," I blurted. "I object to the Court's apparent attempt to influence the jury."

Fire shot out of her eyes. "Counsel, approach the sidebar," she ordered, motioning the court reporter over, too. If she wants the reporter there, I thought, it's serious. We huddled at the sidebar, and the judge started blasting away. The jury wasn't supposed to hear her, but her whispering had the intensity of electricity and danced like a blue flame through the room. She maintained her head had remained perfectly still and denied attempting to influence the jury. Keane agreed, of course. Then she told me if I made another such comment, she would cut off my head.

She really said that. Maybe facetiously; by that time she'd cooled off, but I wasn't about to give her a hatchet.

Back at the lectern, Keane asked the jury to recall what I said about the defendant: Does he look stupid? "Well, what of our courts? Are they any less smart?" He told them they could rely on the judicial process to protect the rights of the defendant. "That man over there is entitled to a fair trial," Keane said, pointing. "You can depend on the courts in this county and state to give him one. You can be absolutely certain that all the witnesses the defense was entitled to were here. Certainly no one—including members of our judiciary—wants to convict an innocent man."

The glasses slid off the end of my nose. They bounced on the table, then dived for the floor. I got down on my hands and knees and looked for them, but it didn't do any good. Keane waited with all the patience of a nurse at an old folks' home. For such a young man, he's seen too much, I thought, struggling into my chair. He didn't even lose his place.

"The evidence here is crystal clear, ladies and gentlemen. The defendant in this case is not an innocent man. An eyewitness saw him shoot and kill the victim, take the purse off his neck, and run away. The police learned of the exact location of the purse in the defendant's apartment—and guess what? That is where they found it."

Old Charley Wallace tried interrupting the DA one time by tipping over in his chair. He broke his wrist, and they still convicted his client. I leaned back, but the chair held.

"There is no mystery here, my friends," he said. "The only mystery is in the mind of Mr. Bard." Then he thanked them for their attention, waved the flag a bit, and sat down.

The judge read them the instructions and told the bailiff they were in his custody. They got the case at 3:07 P.M.

The jury didn't know the half of it. They never do. Who told the cops about the purse? The warrant described the person as a "confidential informant," meaning an unnamed source, a person whose identity would not be revealed. Lawyers, judges, and cops call them "C-Is."

Right after Drusus was arrested, even before his preliminary hearing, I tried to force the prosecution to give me the CI's name. I was still in the municipal court, and Judge Kevin Halloran set it for a hearing. I knew it would get nasty, because the case had been assigned to Ralph "Mad Dog" Hammond, who—according to good old Charley—believed petty theft should be a capital offense. Mad Dog had been a cop before becoming a lawyer, but law school had not broadened his vision of the world. He still operated like a cop.

At the hearing Mad Dog called Dave Kincaid to the stand. A Long Beach native and former football player at Long Beach State, Dave worked both homicide and the gang detail. He testified that the confidential informant came to him about the purse, and that the information contained in the search warrant was furnished "in confidence."

I knew Dave. I'd gone to high school with him. In a couple of months he would retire. I hated to see him go because he made such a rotten witness. But—possibly because he knew he would soon be traveling all over America in a paid-for Winnebago—he testified that day with confidence, like an insurance-company doctor.

"I been a detective fifteen years, mainly homicide, although I worked robbery, burglary, narcotics, and vice," he said, responding to Mad Dog's query about his background. "I know the neighborhood from PCH—that's Pacific Coast Highway—to Anaheim, Cherry to Atlantic, every rock, every brick. I was brought up there, went to Roosevelt High, worked it as a beat cop, seen it grow, change, get built up and torn down, ethnic change from Anglo to Oriental, black, and Hispanic, seen the gangs and drugs come in. Now the lawns don't get watered, security gates and fences in front of homes, graffiti splashed everywhere you look, zombies in the alleys."

Hammond drooled with delight over the new Dave. Kincaid knew the gangs, the drug dealers, the good people and the bad, he said. He knew Drusus Church, too: "Hammer, the one with the pretty sister. Could have made something of himself if he'd tried." Instead, Drusus became a leader in a vicious gang known as the Blades. Kingsley Rhoades was not a Blade, Kincaid said, and for several months before his murder street talk had it that the Blades resented the man's crack house in their territory. "No surprise to me when he got hit."

Shortly after the murder, Kincaid said—to get more specific might result in giving away the informant's name—a person was in the apartment shared by Drusus Church and Vera Byrd. The purse belonging to Rhoades was seen standing on a bookshelf in the living room, in front of a collection of books by Donald Goines. That fact was recited in the search warrant; and when the warrant was executed, that was exactly where the purse had been found.

I had a few questions on cross-examination, naturally. You never knew what might slip out when Kincaid testified. I asked him if he suspected Drusus of the murder of Kingsley Rhoades because he was a Blade. Didn't he know Drusus had dropped his affiliation with the gang? Wouldn't he admit that gangs engaged in "payback"—beating, sometimes killing former members who dropped out? What was the source of the street talk he had testified to? Was the informant a Blade? I wanted to do two things: prove my theory through the prosecution witness and stir the pot, hoping for fallout that would help my investigator figure out who this mysterious informant was.

Mad Dog screamed and hollered and frothed at the mouth, naturally. "He's trying to find out who the CI is!" he kept shouting. "That could endanger lives!" Absolute bullshit, of course, but delivered with commendable sincerity. Those guys believed their own hype.

My strategy at the hearing was based on the theory that Drusus had been framed. The obvious culprit would have been a Blade, but Drusus had other enemies, too. I put on evidence to support the theory. I submitted the affidavit of Jim-Jim Joslin, which stated that although Drusus had belonged to the Blades from the age of twelve, he had quit before Rhoades was killed. Drusus's sister testified as well. She said that only the good people on the block liked her brother because he banged the heads of folks who got out of line—especially if they hit on her or Drusus's mother or grandmother. Vera Byrd said the same thing. She told the judge that Drusus at one time had been a Blade, but he grew tired of spending so much of his life in jail. He dropped out of the gang, she said, and went back to school.

She also testified that the only people who had been in their apartment—from the time Rhoades was killed until Drusus was arrested—had been family and friends. "It couldn't have been any of them, sir," she said with tears in her eyes.

The law requires the judge to hold a private hearing with the cop before deciding what to do. The court reporter takes it all down, then the record is sealed. It can only be opened by another court. So Kevin took Dave back into chambers and questioned him about the informant. I had laid the groundwork as well as I could. The rest was up to Kevin. I trusted Kevin, too. If he thought there was any chance that Drusus was being set up by the CI he would order them to disclose the name or dismiss the case.

Or so I thought. But they weren't gone long enough for him to have gone through any mental gymnastics. "The identity of the confidential informant will not be disclosed,"

Halloran said when he announced his ruling. "The Court finds that the information relied on by the prosecution has a high degree of reliability. The Court is further satisfied that the prejudice to the defendant—though it may appear substantial—is minimal. Further, the public interest in maintaining confidentiality is overwhelming. We are adjourned."

The gambit had not worked. My side still didn't know who the CI was. "You be down to see me?" someone said, breaking in on my mind.

It was Drusus. That happens when you get a little older, I thought. Sometimes you forget where you are. "You bet, youngster." He tossed a cheerful grin my way, and then his guard pushed him into the back hall, where he would be taken down a special elevator to 3D.

I was drained. I wondered how long it would take the jury to get a verdict.

4

Keane wanted to joke around about our "acts," as he called them, once the jury was packed away. "You are *tough*, Jack S," he said with something like affection. "Could you use a drink?"

It's easy to stay humble with a name like mine: Jack S. (for Stanley) Bard. To my school buddies in Long Beach, from the first grade through high school, I was known as Jackass. It should have scarred me. Possibly it did and I don't know it, because no shrink peeled off the scab. All I know for sure is that my nickname brought me twenty-five of the best years anyone could possibly have.

It broke Robyn up. We were introduced thirty years ago by a "friend" who wanted to put me down. He made a real display—including braying like a jackass—when he told her my name. But when Robyn's eyes met mine, she smiled before she laughed. I can still see her smile, and I will always remember the sound of her laugh. It had kind of a nasty little tinkle, but it wasn't mean. All the young studs in town lusted after the foxy new probation officer, but I was the only one who could make her laugh. Not only that, I could do it without even trying. She crafted a logo for our wedding announcement: a quizzical-looking donkey, mooning the world.

"A drink, you say." I closed my briefcase and thought

how good a cold glass of beer would taste. But it would have to wait. Drusus had been shackled up and hauled down to the third floor, where they would keep him in the tank until the jury went home. I'd told him I'd be down. "Another time," I said. "Duty calls."

"You peeled off some beauties, Jack," Keane said, smiling with appreciation. " 'What you mean "We," paleface?' Absolute resonance!"

"Not as good as yours." I struck a pose. " 'There is nothing to compare with the pain of the human heart in conflict with itself.' Where did *that* bit of folklore come from?"

"My ass, man," he said. "Right out of my ass!"

Oh? I thought, riding the jail elevator down to 3D. I thought it had come out of Faulkner's.

The back end of the elevator opened, and I got off. You pass through a line of cages—steel-bar doors that slide open electronically, then slide shut behind you. This will remind the righteous to walk that straight line and will keep the crooks from making a break. A large cage at the end of the hall held all the uniforms.

"Hi, Counselor," Betty Bitler said. She was the best-looking uniform down there: soft black hair, deep brown eyes, smooth cream-brown skin, and a truly graceful body, like a ballet dancer. She shocked people with her beauty. And the damnedest thing: It kept the prisoners quiet. "I thought you'd be down. He's waiting."

I got her old man off on a DWI. Drunker than a bicycle he was, but the DA who tried it forgot to prove it was his car they found him in, wrapped around the tree. He didn't have a scratch on him, and I kept him off the stand. I told the jury for all they knew, he'd crawled in a stranger's car to sleep it off. "Thanks, luv," I said, walking through that cage into the next one, looking for Drusus.

A row of cubicles stretched down a hallway, bordered on one wall with concrete, the other with inch-thick clear plastic. The miscreants who needed lawyers waited on one side of the glass, and the lawyers who needed miscreants waited on the other. A long three-foot wide plank had been built into the plastic wall, a foot and a half on either side. Windows had been cut in each cubicle, then hung with heavy wire mesh so the prisoners couldn't reach through and grab their lawyers by the throat.

I saw Drusus through the glass. He still wore the cuffs. The jailers carried him as a gang member on a capital beef, which meant—according to jailhouse regulations—maximum security. They gave him the grizzly bear treatment whenever they took him out. The only time the cuffs came off was in front of the jury, or in his cage at the L.A. County Jail, where they kept him with the other grizzlies.

I walked down to the cubicle at the end, squeezing past the rear ends of two lawyers. They were draped over the dish seats on our side of the bar, so to speak. One was a huge balloon. The other belonged to a trim blond woman I'd seen in Ida's court but didn't know.

Drusus smiled when he saw me. His wide shoulders filled the space on his side of the glass, and he pressed the heel of one hand against the wire. "You all right, man?" he asked. "You aren't gonna have a heart attack and leave me without a lawyer?"

I pushed my palm against his. "Don't worry about me, youngster. I'm as tough as an old shoe. Where was your family?" He didn't have a father. His dad had been killed when Drusus was still belt-high to a grasshopper. But his grandmother was still alive, and his mother had stayed in the picture, and so had his sister.

"I didn't want them listening to all that shit," he said. "I told them to stay home."

"If this goes to the penalty phase, I want them there. Every day, so the jury can see them. Okay?"

He shrugged. "If that's what you want." His smile said something else. "The penalty phase is next, right? That's where they gonna bring up all the dirt in my life and try to put that Tommy Sherman hit on me, too?"

"Yes." I didn't want to think about what was coming. "Tommy Sherman is their hole card. They've saved the best for the last."

"Huh! Like if I kill one nigger, that's not so bad. But when you kill two, you die?"

"That's what they will argue."

"Maybe we won't get that far, Jack," he said, smiling at me. "Maybe that jury won't ever hear about Tommy Sherman. If they say I didn't kill Rhoades, then we don't even have a penalty phase. Isn't that the way it works?"

Hope springs eternal, I thought. "You've got it."

"What are my chances, man? Do you think they'll let me go?"

I tried looking confident, but he knew me too well. He saw what I thought. "There's always the chance." He nodded and looked down. "Hey. Keep your chin up." He lifted it for me and grinned. "Drusus, if you'd just tell me who the CI is—"

"Yeah. I thought I'd let Whitney figure it out, you know. Let him have the glory."

Whitney Lee was my investigator. He had tried to solve the mystery, but in twelve months hadn't gotten very far. I wasn't sure Drusus trusted him. "Any ideas?"

"Nothing for the big man. Maybe there's something I can do for myself." He spoke quietly. "Where did they put Jim-Jim?"

"I ordered him in from Folsom. If they haven't sent him back, he could still be at the county jail."

Disappointment showed in his expression. "He's gone, then. I'd know if he was still around."

"Jim-Jim doesn't know anything, Drusus," I said. "Whitney talked to him, and I did, too. He's as blown out by this as we are."

Drusus didn't look convinced. "He can do some jive, Jack. I'd like to look him in the eye."

"What bothers you?"

"Jim-Jim went down too easy on that robbery rap," Drusus said. "It makes me suspicious."

I wasn't sure I liked the sound of this. Drusus needed friends. He had enough enemies. "You aren't getting paranoid, are you, youngster? Jim-Jim is your best friend. He was with you the night Rhoades was shot. How the hell could it be him?''

"Maybe he's in it with somebody."

"Like who?"

"All those homeboys I used to run with."

In order to scratch his nose he had to raise both hands. I watched him scratch his nose. "Go on."

"When I left the gang Jim-Jim was still gang-bangin'. I had to go through him to get out."

"You told me. You even fought him, didn't you?"

"Yeah. I didn't want to, but he pulled a knife, so I broke his nose. That was like two years ago, and I didn't see him again until a month, maybe two months, before this went down." I had heard this before but let him talk on through. His tone was different this time, as though other things were on his mind. "One day I catch him standing in front of the apartment, you know, big grin on his sucker face, say he just come by to look me up, see how I was doing, high fives and all that shit." His smile was not very nice. "I like Jim-Jim and kind of miss it, you know. So we get together, and I meet the chick of the month, and everything is cool, like it used to be.

"But after the Kingman got shot and I go down, it was like he was too nice, Jack. He would come to the jail and leave messages, act almost like I might get a sexually transmitted disease from him. But he was gone when we had that hearing. Remember that? He could have testified for me, but he was gone."

"I don't think so, Drusus. He'd been picked up on the two-eleven."

"That's another thing. He only pulls three years for armed robbery. That's not enough of a hit, is it? He had a prior."

Drusus would have bet his life on Jim-Jim's loyalty before. Now there was distrust. "I pulled his file on the two-eleven," I told him. "I talked to the PD who worked it out. Jim-Jim got the deal because the case was weak. Poor identification."

"Would you have told him to take the deal?"

"I'd have jumped at it." Suddenly I remembered how the public defender had laughed over the case, as though she had jumped at it. Maybe Drusus had a point. "So you're thinking Jim-Jim?"

He saw my frown and smiled. "Yes."

"How could he shoot Rhoades when he was in your living room with you, and you heard the shots?"

"I don't mean *he* shot the King. What I'm saying, maybe a gangster shoot him and rob him. But maybe Jim-Jim was the CI."

"Would he do that?"

"I don't know. I'd like to ask him and watch him in the eye." His head dropped, and I had to lean forward to hear him. "Gang membership is this heavy-duty trip. You take oaths, and when someone in your family against a wall, you stand up there with him." The expression on his face was hard to read. "They don't like it when you quit."

"But would they kill Rhoades just to get even with you?"

"Look at the rest. Two or three thousand dollars out of Kingman's purse, and the Blades get the crack house."

"Do they have it now?"

"That's what I heard."

There were problems with the notion. There always are. "It sounds—I don't know—convoluted. Something that would take planning. Do those guys make plans like that?" It didn't seem plausible, and lawyers know the importance of plausibility. "If Jim-Jim set you up like that, he'd have to have known what he was going to do way back when he first came over to see you."

"Yeah. That's what got me thinking about it." He smiled. "Like a TV plot, you know, make it up to a friend, then kind of like betray him? Those homeboys watch a lot of TV. It's where they get a lot of ideas."

The new reality, I thought. "It still doesn't explain the purse in your bookcase."

His expression softened as though he was remembering a nice, wet kiss. "Vera got in to see me a week ago. She told me Jim-Jim's girl came over the day before the cops break in the door. Did you know that?"

35

"No."

"She said LuAnne act kind of strange. Nobody real cheerful after King killed, you know. Something like that puts a person inside himself. But she said it was more."

"What are you getting at? Do you think LuAnne might have stuck the purse in the bookcase when Vera wasn't looking?" I might have sounded a bit skeptical. "Vera didn't say anything about any of this when she testified a year ago."

"Said she didn't even think about it then. Like, how could LuAnne have anything to do with it?"

One of the problems with practicing law is trying to decide what to do with stuff you find out after it's too late to use it. I decided not to lay that problem off on Drusus. "You and Jim-Jim were real tight, weren't you, youngster?"

He smiled. I think it's because he likes it when I call him "youngster"—although it might have been memories. "We go all the way back to sixth grade. We do a lot of stuff, you know, the two of us. Even went down together on that burglary."

The way Drusus had described gang membership, eight and nine years ago when he had first joined, it had an innocence, like Tom Sawyer's gang of cutthroats. That changed with drugs and big money.

"Drusus, I'm not sure you should be thinking this stuff now. Jim-Jim isn't that smart, is he? And he's not a Judas."

"Maybe he don't like it either. But if you're in the gang and they give you a mission, that's what you do. That's why I got out."

My lawyer instincts took over. How could any of this be proved? At that point, I didn't even care if it was true. What difference did that make, if I could prove it? "I'll get Whitney over to see you. We'll get him to Folsom to see Jim-Jim."

"I wish Whitney was blacker."

I frowned at that. My investigator wasn't as black as Drusus, but he still was what white folks call black. "You'll have to explain."

"Kind of like he's been in the system too long or something."

"What about me, then? I could talk to Jim-Jim. One time you said I could think like a black."

He laughed. "Yeah, you kind of run off a different program. But it take you too long to translate or something. You wouldn't be quick enough."

"Whitney's the best we can do, Drusus. I'd never get an order for you to do it."

"The po-lice can talk to him, though. Any time they want."

"Yeah." One time we had rapped about the system. I told him how basically fair it was. I didn't try to defend it now. "You'll just have to tell Whitney how to be. I think he can get black enough."

Drusus nodded at me without looking at me. "I guess you're right. He can talk to Jim-Jim all right."

"Have you heard anything more about LuAnne? Jim-Jim's girl? We're still trying to find her."

"Vera still my girl?" he asked, softly.

She wasn't. That was what she had gone to see him about. But I guessed she hadn't told him, and I didn't have the heart. "What do you mean? Ask Vera?"

"Yeah."

My mind churned with possibilities. Could any of this be tortured into "newly discovered evidence," which could get us a new trial? But there was another problem: the eyewitness. "What about April Tillman? She says she saw you pull the trigger."

"She's a Blade."

"She is! Why didn't you tell me?"

"I don't know, man. It never came up."

"Damn." Trying a lawsuit is not like solving a crime. It helps when you can prove someone else did it, but the only time that happens is on television. "We might have screwed up."

"Yeah?" He grinned. "Like maybe I can sue for malpractice?"

The boy had all the heart in the world. Half the time he

acted like he was just glad to be alive. "Don't you remember anything?" I asked him. "What did I tell you about deep pocket?"

"Yours is deep enough for me. You still got that Mazda?"

I trip around in a Mazda RX 7. They are so hot you could get arrested just for owning one in Texas, I've heard. Although not in Southern California, where one third of the population owns hot machines. I manage to get to the next red light quicker than most, and Drusus liked riding in it. He would lean his head back and look at the sky. "We definitely put you on the stand for the penalty phase," I told him. "We might have made a mistake by not putting you on during the guilt phase."

"Keane will love the chance to cross-examine me," Drusus said. Funny the way he called the man who was trying to kill him "Keane." Although he'd watched him work for three weeks while we picked a jury, then three more days while we tried the case. I guess he thought he knew him. "He can hardly wait to bring out all that bad shit about my life. But maybe he won't get the chance. That jury just might turn me loose." The thought seemed to make him happy.

I looked at my watch. It was after four. "We've kept them out a whole hour."

"Is that good?"

"It doesn't mean a thing. If they come back quick, it means something, like they didn't even have to talk it over. But they have to pick a foreperson and go over the exhibits and instructions before they vote. They won't get a verdict tonight. The judge will let them go at four-thirty."

"You told me a hundred times, but tell me again. What do they have to decide?"

"First, whether you are guilty of murder in the first degree. If they say yes to that, then whether the special circumstance allegation is true." I kept my voice matter-of-fact, like I would if we were talking about a contract. "If they decide it's true, then we go on to the penalty phase."

"That's where they decide I either spend the rest of my life in jail, without the possibility of parole, or I die."

"Right."

He looked over my shoulder at something neither one of us could see, something on the other side of the wall. "Maybe I'd rather be dead."

"No!" I leaned toward him. I wanted to grab him by the shoulders and shake him. He was so young, and the props holding him up had slipped. "As long as you are alive, there is hope. Believe me. That's why we keep looking for the CI."

"What good will that do now?"

"It can do plenty. The penalty phase of a trial is different from the guilt phase. Maybe we can use it to show lingering doubt. And if it leads to new evidence, you have a chance at a new trial."

"About as good as the chance I have right now?"

"Listen to me, Drusus. I'm going to get you out." For God's sake, I told myself. Don't make a promise you can't keep. But my mouth was too far into it to stop. "You may lose a hunk of your life, but I'm going to get you out."

He smiled. The youngster had a really nice smile. His whole face got in it some way, even his ears, but especially his eyes. At that moment they had the sad-happy look of a patient dog waiting for more abuse. "I know you'll do everything that can be done, man. I appreciate it, too."

"Not good enough," I said. "I'm going to get you out. Then you finish college and go to law school just the way we've got it mapped, and ten years from now I retire and you keep me in Mazdas."

Drusus glanced over my head at the same time I felt a tap on my shoulder. "Counselor?" I heard Betty Bitler ask.

She smelled as nice as she looked. Funny, she never has called me by my first name. "What?"

"They want both of you in court."

"Why?"

"They have a verdict."

5

I hurried back to the courtroom, expecting the worst. If the jury had any doubts, reasonable or not, it would not have come back so fast. Only Don Quixote could have convinced himself of an acquittal, but I've been trying cases long enough to know that a trial is a bit like a beauty contest. You never really know who won until the judge announces the winner. I did my best to believe in the impossible and smiled with optimism when I saw Keane.

He regarded me with compassion.

The special guard in charge of Drusus brought him in, unhandcuffed him, and sat him down. Then the guard took his seat in the spectator area behind the bar, a smirk on his face, like an expectant hangman. Drusus never complained about the way the man handled him, but I didn't like the brown-shirted asshole. He was very conspicuous.

Ida mounted the podium in her robes, said something cheerful, like "This could be a record, Jack," and sat down.

When the jury filed in—their faces set along hard lines and none of them looking at either Drusus or me—it became harder to maintain an optimistic frame of mind. The clerk called the roll, and when asked to affirm his presence Drusus answered "Here" in a calm voice. His large hands and muscled forearms rested on the table.

"The bailiff informs me you've reached a verdict," Ida said, smiling down from her throne. She looked like Juno regarding her charges on Earth. "I must say you've been quick about it. Will the foreperson please stand?"

She did. Number Ten, Ms. Sandra Perkins, wife of an insurance executive. I'd left her on because she'd taught school, and teachers are supposed to make good jurors for the defense. She was a good, decent, strong-looking woman with nicely tailored clothes and graying hair she didn't tint. She reminded me of Barbara Bush.

"It's Ms. Perkins?" Judge Mather asked.

"Yes."

"Has the jury reached a verdict?"

"We have, Judge."

"Very well. Hand it to the bailiff, please."

Ivan, the bailiff, carried the verdict over to the bench and handed it up. "You can sit down, Mrs. Perkins," Ida said, looking it over. I watched her face to see if it registered any surprise. It didn't. She glanced at Drusus, then handed the paper back to the bailiff.

There are a lot of courts where the defendant must rise to hear the verdict, but not in Long Beach. Defendants don't have to stand up and take it like a man. I was glad for that. Drusus wasn't wearing a coat, and his powerful frame—he's six-two and built like a boxer—would have loomed over mine. Kind of ironic, I thought, that I'm his champion. He's the one with the biceps.

Ivan marched with the form to the desk where the clerk sat and handed it to her. "The clerk will read the verdict," Ida pronounced.

Ida's clerk is a small woman with large glasses. I never can remember her name. She stood up, adjusted her glasses, and turned the paper right side up. "Title of the court and cause," she said for the benefit of the court reporter. "We the jury find the defendant, Drusus Church, guilty of murder in the first degree." She looked over her glasses at Drusus and smiled at him. "We further find that the special circumstance alleged, to wit: robbery, is true."

"Ladies and gentlemen of the jury," Iron Pants said,

peering down at them, "is this your verdict?" They looked at one another, then back to her, most of them nodding. "So say you all?" she asked.

There were nods and yeses.

"Mr. Bard, do you wish to poll the jury?" Iron Pants asked me.

I don't know why the judge asks, because the jury should be polled. But they were back with a verdict in an hour. "No." I didn't want to make any of them madder than they already were.

I glanced at Keane, who sat by himself at the prosecutor's table. His expression was perfect. He didn't look at anyone, which complemented the statement his attitude made: None of us like this job, but it has to be done. Thank God for a jury with the courage to do its plain duty.

Maybe I'm starting to fry, I thought. How can his attitude say all that?

"We have some business to conduct, ladies and gentlemen, before I can let you go," Ida told them. "As was brought out rather extensively during voir dire, if the defendant was found guilty and the special circumstance allegation found to be true, we would have another trial to fix the penalty. What we need now is a date for the next trial." She smiled at them. "The lawyers and I need to discuss the timing, and while we do, the bailiff will take you back to the jury room. I hope we can have you home in time for dinner."

She nodded at Ivan, my favorite bailiff, who stood up again. He lifted weights and was strong enough to toss most defendants across the room. He thought all of them were guilty but felt sorry for them, as befitted a person with his background. He was a priest before he joined the Sheriff's Department, and he still believed in original sin. "Come with me, please," he said to the jurors, then stood by while they filed out of the room.

"Let the record show that counsel are present, the defendant is present, and we're having a discussion outside the presence of the jury," Iron Pants intoned. "The record should also reflect we've talked this over informally, and

I'm not particularly thrilled with counsel's suggestions." What does she want to do? I wondered. Start it tomorrow? "Mr. Bard, in view of the evidence in this case, it seems to me you should have anticipated the outcome. You should be ready to proceed immediately. Why do you need two weeks?"

I got up slowly. "I need a breather, Judge. My energy and resources have been devoted to the guilt phase. It takes a couple of days to shift gears."

She frowned at me. "I don't like the idea of tying the jurors up any longer than is necessary."

"No one wants to do that. But the penalty phase in this case is very complicated, Judge. As you know, the prosecution wants to put in evidence of another murder."

"I also know it isn't a surprise, Mr. Bard. You've known about it for several months."

"Three months, Judge."

"Four, Mr. Bard." Damn woman. I didn't think she'd remember that well. "Which should have been ample time. I assume you know who your witnesses are, and you've got them under subpoena?"

"They're on call. My secretary's been in touch with them."

"Do you have any problems, Mr. Williams?"

"No, Your Honor," Keane said, standing and charming her with his smile. "Any time is fine with me."

"Good. We'll have the jury report back Monday, then."

It was Thursday. That would give me three days. "Judge, there is no way I can be ready that soon."

"Mr. Bard, if you have a serious problem, I'll consider a delay. I've accommodated you in the past, haven't I?"

Ida has never even given me time to go to the can. "Sure," I lied, "but—"

"It's settled, then." She glanced at Ivan. "Bring them back in."

Ivan did. "Members of the jury, how does Monday sound to you?" the judge asked as soon as they were settled in their seats. They looked around and nodded and smiled at one another. "Any comment?"

"Sounds good to me," Seven said.

"Anyone else?" They all seemed satisfied. "Good. Mr. Bard, Mr. Williams, members of the jury, I'll see you Monday." She started to stand. "We are in recess until nine o'clock Monday morning. Court is adjourned."

When the jurors dribbled by a few moments later on their way home, I wondered if they could see my burning ears. "That doesn't give you much time, does it?" Drusus asked as the gladiator who guarded him cuffed him up.

"No."

"Your ears are all red, man."

"Yeah. They do that sometimes." I tried touching his shoulder, but the grinning guard got in the way. "I won't see you until trial time, youngster. Hang loose." I winked at him.

"Looks to me like you're the one who won't get any sleep."

As I packed up my briefcase I considered the options. I could waste the weekend getting out a writ to the appellate court, hoping they'd order Iron Pants to cool it and give me the two weeks I needed to get ready. But the court of appeals might agree with her. My best tactic was to take it in the shorts and make a record. If they voted to kill Drusus, I could have basis for an appeal.

My God, I thought, shutting my eyes. I've been a lawyer all my life. I believe in the law. Is this really happening?

Keane was in the hall with his back to me, talking to Wink Barrett, one of the detectives on the case. "Jack S," Barrett said, nodding and smiling affably.

I grinned at the tough-looking cop. "Wink."

We tolerated each other. Like Dave Kincaid and me and a lot of others around the courthouse, he'd been brought up in Long Beach a hundred years ago—or so it seemed. We had the same memories. We could close our eyes and see the San Gabriel Mountains from Ocean Boulevard, before they were hidden by a cloud of smog. We could remember the drive from Long Beach to L.A., when it was on a paved road that wound between hillsides full of dairy farms and fruit trees. I'd cross-examined Wink more times than

I could count. He told the truth, as long as it served his purpose.

"Jack!" Keane said, turning and greeting me as he would an old friend. "Hey, I'm sorry, man—I guess. You know." He stuck his hand out and gave me his best smile. "I thought your argument was excellent! I can't believe they came back that fast. I'd like to take this jury with me when I go back to Denver!"

"You did a nice job," I said, shaking his hand.

"What about that beer?"

I hated his all–American face at that moment, but thought he might be vulnerable to a suggestion or two. He sees how rotten I feel, I decided. Sometimes a prosecutor will be truly magnanimous in victory. "Sure. Let's take Wink. You see if you can get him to buy a round. I've never been able to."

I took Keane in my Mazda, and we met Wink at Redheads Bar and Grill, a real greasy spoon in Signal Hill. It's got a billiard room and bar on one side and a crummy restaurant and bar on the other. The parking lot has two producing oil wells pumping all the time—fortunately for the redhead, who doesn't have to live off the bar and grill. And the men's room has truly rotten wallpaper. It's filled with panels showing all the different ways to screw.

"Learn anything from those pictures?" I asked Keane when he came back from the toilet.

"Nope," he said. "I grew up in California."

"No kidding!" Wink said. "I'll drink to that. Three natives, all at the same table!" He hoisted his glass. We drank a toast to the three of us, and I set my glass down.

I was curious about Keane. I had heard of him somewhere. "How come you joined NASP?" I asked him. "Weren't you in San Diego and Fresno?"

"Yeah," he said, grinning. People like to talk about themselves. "I was chief trial deputy for a Chinese in San Diego and a Portugese in Fresno. Only in America."

"Didn't I read an article about you a couple of years back?" I watched him preen. "In the *Times*. About you and a handful of other guys who might take a run at the AG's office sometime.''

"Did you read that?"

"Yeah." I wondered if there was some buttons here I could push. "You'd tried some big case, and your name was out there. The politicos in your party were watching you."

"I was watching them, too." He laughed. "No kidding, you saw that? I was a delegate to the state and national conventions. But they thought I looked too young." He laughed again. "Five years San Diego, three years Fresno, I was thirty-five, but I looked too young."

"So you joined NASP to get away from it all?" I asked. *"Beau Geste,* joining the French Foreign Legion? Come on. You're too California for that."

"Do you want the truth?"

"Hell, no, he don't want the truth," Wink said. "He's a lawyer."

"Words of wisdom from a cop," I said. "Dead wrong, as usual. I always want the truth, except from about ninety percent of my clients."

Keane watched Wink and me batter each other. "Okay, the truth," he said. "I've been bitten by the political bug. I still want to run for AG. But when I make the next run at it my face will be older, and I'll have NASP in my background."

"So you're a short-timer with Trigge?" I was surprised. "I thought he only hired career types."

"For me he made an exception. You can't lie to Jim— not that I would, anyway—so I told him what will happen someday. I'm going to be the attorney general in California. He believes me."

"Modest, ain't he?" Wink said. But even though his face was higher than Keane's, he still managed somehow to look up.

"One of my many qualities," Keane said, smiling. "When I told him it wouldn't hurt NASP to have a high-placed graduate, he agreed. I committed to two years."

"Except you're away from California all that time," I said. "Who will remember you?"

"I'm out here now, aren't I? Jim gave me the West Coast beat, and I have the chance to get around, get some coverage. Although the press hasn't done diddly with this one."

"Like you said in your argument, Keane, just an ordinary killing."

We finished that pitcher of beer and started another one. I didn't think it would take long until we were singing. That's what you're supposed to do when you drink at Redheads. It's a very festive place for blue-collar millionaires who like to piss and moan about the economy and sing the songs they would have sung if they'd gone to college. I've never known why I like the place except my dad used to take me there, and Robyn would meet me there for lunch. "What a crude bunch of bastards," she told me once, "but they know how to laugh."

I didn't even have to steer the conversation toward the case. "If it's okay with you," Keane said, "I'll talk to the judge."

"You're the first prosecutor who ever asked. What will you talk about?"

"She's coming down too hard on the trial date. Let me see if I can't get her to cut some slack. Is that all right with you?"

"Sure it's all right."

"What the fuck. You want to cut this guy slack?" Wink asked. "Kick him in the balls." He grinned at me.

"What's left to kick?" I asked. "You guys cut them off a long time ago. They're in your trophy case."

"Right, cut them off," Wink scoffed. "Like that Tolken case, and that weenie-wagger, what the hell was his name? And Johnson. I could name a few others." Wink lifted his glass in a mock toast. "Here's to Drusus Church," he said, as though the verdict had made his life bearable. "The world will be a better place as soon as he's iced and on his way out of it."

"You dumb shit," I said angrily. "Have you ever had any doubts about anything?"

He grinned and clinked his glass with mine. "Doubts are for defense lawyers and other forms of weenies. You know as well as me, Counselor, your boy's long overdue for an attitude adjustment. When he's trying to hold his breath after they've dropped the pill, maybe we will have his attention." He leaned forward so I'd know he hadn't finished making his point. "If a cop had been able to shove a two-by-four up his butt when he was just a mean little pickaninny, he wouldn't be in the crack he's in now."

I tried not to react. I left the remark alone like a turd on the sidewalk, hoping Keane was as offended by it as I was. "We need a camera," Keane said neutrally, as though trying to keep two brothers from swinging on each other. "We could do a documentary on the criminal justice system at work."

"Speaking of justice," I said, "why are you pushing so hard for the death penalty? Why don't you take what you've got?"

I thought my timing was perfect. Wink had a smug look on his face, and I believed it formed a sharp contrast to mine, which showed courage and fortitude. Sir Thomas More with his head on the block.

"I'm easy," Keane said, his elbows resting on the table. But suddenly the look in his eye wasn't easy. All at once he looked like a prosecutor. Or a politician. I've often thought they wear the same face. "What do I get in return?"

"How about that honest, wholesome rush a person gets when he knows he's done the right thing?"

"Jack S," he said. "I mean, you could be my father, man. Don't try to sell a nice boy like me a line of crap."

"Listen to me, Keane." Every time I say "Listen to me," I know I'm cranking too hard. Robyn used to say, "When you hemorrhage, it will happen right after you say 'Listen to me.'" I let my face relax, like you do when your leg cramps. "I know what the evidence showed in this case. But those lie detector reports tell a different story."

"The one *I* looked at didn't," Keane said.

"You're talking when Doo-Rah and his wench sat on the

box?'' Wink asked innocently. "Except that buck I saw Vera with out in the hall before court the other day . . .'' He leered. "Probably has one of those purple dicks that drags on the sidewalk. When he buries it in her, he comes in her mouth.''

It's a test of character, socializing with Wink. "You've just titled the documentary,'' Keane said. *"Archie Bunker Meets Gregory Peck.''*

"Yeah,'' Wink said. "Starring Bullwinkle and Dudley Doo-Rah-Right.''

"Shut up, Wink,'' I told him.

He laughed. "You should see your ears, Counselor.''

I turned toward Keane. "Listen. You know damn good and well why those clowns put Vera on the box. They weren't trying to find out if she told the truth. They wanted to break her down so she'd admit she'd lied about the alibi. She *still* passed with flying colors!''

"I didn't look at the report on her,'' Keane admitted. "But I saw the one on Drusus. He didn't pass.''

"They tested him without telling me a damn thing about it, two days after they picked him up. Wink won't admit it—he might to you, but not with me around—but they'd already beaten the shit out of him.'' Maybe I've had too much to drink, I thought. These clowns are getting to me. "You're right. Drusus didn't do so well.''

"Didn't do well!'' Barrett jeered. "He lied like a Saturday night whore!''

"What did he score?'' Keane asked.

"Minus twelve.''

"Is that the one where plus six and up indicates truth, and minus six and below a lie?''

I had to admit that it was.

Keane rubbed his chin thoughtfully. "Not too close, Jack. Although it isn't unheard of for a defendant to fail even when he's telling the truth.''

"Keane, you know the literature. It's an established fact defendants try too hard. That's why the results are inadmissible!''

"An established fact?'' He favored me with a jaundiced

grin. "Come on, Father. You're rationalizing the fact your guy failed."

"But Vera Byrd passed!"

Keane frowned. "So basically you're saying we should drop the death penalty. What about it, Wink?"

"Hell, no! He done the dude, and there is aggravation up the gazzoo! He took out Tommy Sherman one month ahead of Rhoades! We should kiss that off? Shit!" His chin moved out like a hard fist. "The motherfucker should die!"

"I thought the prosecutor made that decision," I said.

"Well, it's a bit like you said in argument, old chap. I represent the cops. I like to keep them happy."

"He didn't do it!"

I felt like a fool. Both of them looked at me with surprise until Wink reached over and took my hand. "Ooo," he said. "If I kiss it, will it all be better?"

Wink was actually trying to be nice. He was helping me over a hurdle, and I was grateful for the lift. "Yeth," I said.

"That's a good boy."

We stopped talking about the case. We engaged in some serious joke-telling, and at one point I pulled out a pen and waved it around like a conductor with a baton. "Ready, Wink?"

"Sure, counselor. 'Balls'?"

"Perfect." Then I went "Hmmm," giving him the pitch. We sang "Balls" in two-part harmony:

> "Do your balls hang low?
>   Do they wiggle to and fro?
>   Can you drag them in the sand?
>   Can you drag them through the snow?
>   Can you throw them over your shoulder
>   Like a European soldier?
>   Do your balls . . . hang . . . low?"

Two pitchers later, Keane got in Wink's unmarked cop car, and they followed me over to Erin's house on the south side of town, near the campus. Wink had called her and told her I would be over.

My stomach used to be able to process large quantities of booze. But the year before Robyn died, half of it got chopped out. Wink always could drink me down anyway. He had the red spotlight on, and with him on my tail, the patrol units in Long Beach left me alone.

It's weird, my town. It's a family. Wink was a Long Beach cop, and by definition that meant a hard-nosed head knocker who believed in making the town safe for the Anglo business community. But we graduated from the same high school, and I knew his mom and dad. If he needed a thousand dollars, I'd lend it to him on the strength of a handshake, even though I knew he busted faces and lied on the witness stand about it. He'd do the same for me, in spite of the fact he thought I was a tricky, rotten defense lawyer with my head up my ass.

I aimed for Erin's driveway and got most of it. I parked on her lawn. Her porch light was on, and I staggered up the stone sidewalk. The front door opened as I arrived. She was a young thing of forty-five—plump and pretty—with a smile that lighted up the sky and black hair that was soft, like her eyes. Her head wasn't soft, though, except—according to her mother—in one respect: She thought I was okay. "Were you at Redheads?" she asked, a glass of wine in her hand.

"Yeah." I got inside and took off my tie. "Didn't Wink tell you where we were?"

"No. All he said was you needed a drink because at last justice had prevailed, and one of your 'poor innocents' had been convicted." She sat on the couch, and I sat next to her. "Drusus?"

"Yeah."

"How do you feel?"

I didn't feel a thing. "Great. Except you know what? It only took that jury one hour to decide he was guilty."

"It's nine-thirty," she said. "I thought we were going to a movie."

With her sitting next to me, a glass of wine in her hand, I

entertained another thought. "Hey, Robyn baby, let's mess around instead." I tried putting my arm around her.

"Erin." She moved out of the way.

"Oh. Yeah." I realized my mistake. "Didn't we see a movie last night?"

"No. The last one was *Thelma and Louise*. I can't remember how long ago that was."

"Was it any good?"

"*I* thought so. You said it was too much like *Butch Cassidy and the Sundance Kid.*"

She crossed her legs, and I caught a flash of her thigh. "You know what would be fun?"

"What?"

"I get the grease, and you take off your clothes, and I rub your back."

Actually, it wasn't grease. It was exotic-smelling oil from a health food store. When she was in the mood, I massaged her with it.

She looked like she might be persuaded. "Shouldn't we have dinner first?"

"Nope," I said, jumping to the conclusion that was foremost in my mind. "Let's go, Robyn."

She looked very pissed off about something. "Is your car locked?"

I never locked it when I left it on her lawn. "No. Why?"

"I need the keys."

I gave them to her. "What for?"

"Do me a favor."

"Sure."

"Go outside and get the paper."

At that point I'd have done anything. "Okay."

I had trouble with the door, but it finally opened, and I kind of fell outside. I looked all over the yard for the paper but couldn't find it. When I tried going back in the house the door was locked. "Hey! Robyn! Open—oh." I heard myself calling her Robyn—just a slip of the tongue—but Erin could get very hostile over small, insignificant wrinkles of speech, for some reason.

It had happened before. I crawled in my car. Another dry night, I thought—although two seconds later I was asleep.

6

When you're tired enough you can sleep standing up, so it's easy when you're sitting down in a car. I slept like a corpse and the next morning woke up looking at a huge, leafy tree in Erin's yard. It probably should have surprised me, but it didn't. The sun wasn't up, and the tree and me peered at each other through the early morning light. It occurred to me that Erin might wonder why I had parked on her lawn. I decided it might be better to explain later, after I knew why myself, and reached for the ignition. The key wasn't there. Then I remembered she had it and considered what she would do if I rang her doorbell.

It wasn't worth the risk. She hates waking before her alarm goes off, which wouldn't happen for another hour. I got out of the car, went over to the side of the house, and took a leak.

Her bedroom window went up. "Dammit, Jack!" she yelled. "Don't you have any better sense than to pee in my yard?"

I couldn't stop. At my age, once you start something like that, you can't shut it off. "I didn't want to wake you up."

"You are disgusting." A moment later I heard the sound of keys on the lawn. "Beat it!"

For a minute I wasn't sure what she meant by "beat

it"—but she's a woman, so sex was not always in the front of her mind. "I'll call you later, okay?"

"Do and I call the police." Her bedroom window crashed down.

I found the keys and picked them up, remembering everything that had happened the day before. I felt so bad that the flap with Erin felt good. The freeways were full. They were always full. But there wasn't much traffic on the streets in town, and I drove to the rambling old wreck of a house I've lived in all my life. It was within spitting distance of the ocean. A developer offered me half a million dollars for it once—"Mr. Bard, I would like to see this land achieve its real potential"—wonderful.

I unlocked the door to the screen porch and dragged myself in. Usually I look forward to going to work in the morning. All that hype about the excitement of facing challenging new problems gets me out of bed, because you never know when something like that will actually happen. I used to tell Robyn all about it so I could hear her laugh—and the funny thing is, we still talk, although not as much as we used to.

But I had nothing to look forward to that day. I had three days to get ready for the penalty phase of a capital murder, and there wasn't any real joy in that.

The air pushed out of my chest, and I had to sit down. What's happening? I wondered. A heart attack? I made myself breathe. It took a moment for me to realize it was mental! In some strange way my body had been persuaded to turn on me.

The damn thing had a mind of its own. It wouldn't let me move. It made me sit there and listen! "Give up, peckerneck," it said. "Do you think Drusus cares whether he spends the rest of his life in jail, or dies? Even if he does, it won't matter. It takes ten years of appeals and anguish—busywork for lawyers and judges—before the State of California kills the slugs who sit on death row anyway!

"So why do anything? Why not just offer him up to the hangman and say, 'This one is all yours. His only request is that when you finally get around to it, do it clean.' "

What is going on? I wondered. I could feel something squirming in my stomach. It felt like a small balloon. I was glad no one could see me, bent over like a gnome, my face buried in my hands, my teeth grinding. Then it seemed like the sac in my stomach split open, and all the crap inside it spilled into my guts.

God! I was engulfed with hatred. It must have been full of poison and hate. I *hated* the jury, and the judge in her robed dignity, and Keane Williams and his Hollywood approach to justice. I *hated* that blind lady with the scales. What the fuck did she know? Drusus was twenty-two years old. He had "put it together," as the kids say. He was motivated—on his way. And now? I was supposed to keep him alive for the rest of his life, so he could spend it in jail!

"Not good enough," I heard someone say. I looked up. Who had said that? "I'm going to get you out."

"Then do it!" I heard myself shout.

I lunged out of the chair and pushed it away from me, then kicked off my clothes, scattering them all over the room. I trotted off to the bathroom, shaved and showered, then put on a satin shirt and a bow tie. I made myself a cup of coffee, dumped in a shot of cognac, and drank it, letting it warm my stomach. Then I picked up all the dirty clothes, rinsed out the cup, put a grin on, and drove to work.

My office is in the old SeaFarer Hotel, on the ocean side of Ocean Boulevard, and I headed toward the old relic. She's as elegant and old-fashioned as a luxury liner and really made a splash in the twenties, when she was built. When you walk into the lobby, with its huge open cavity ringed by balconies that reach to the ceiling twelve floors above, it's like entering a fifteenth-century cathedral. It's a by-God spiritual experience. Now they get two hundred dollars a day for the rooms. They've been trying to evict me for years, but I wrote the lease—back when they needed the money—and it would be easier to move the building two feet to the north than to move me out.

Whitney Lee was sitting in the lobby when I came in,

staring at the ceiling. "Hi, boss." He heaved himself to his feet. I was told by a full-bodied woman not long after Robyn died that fat is merely stored-up energy. If that is true, Whitney is well energized. He is built like a mountain with a peak at the top and a solid base. He had a slow approach to a problem—which was the way mountains moved—but when he got to it, the problem was surrounded. He was the best investigator I'd ever had. He thought in terms of solutions and found answers to questions before they were asked. "I always know when you lose," he said. "You put on your best suit the next day."

"Damn straight." We walked to the elevator, and with Whitney in it, I wasn't sure which way it would go.

"How's my man?"

"He's amazing, Whitney." It went up, which was a relief. "Where did he come from?"

"Huh! He's all around, man. A lot of you white folks—and Uncle Remuses, like me—don't see him, though."

"You need to talk to him."

The elevator stopped at the sixth floor, and we got off. Maybe it was my imagination, but the platform seemed relieved. It lifted half an inch. "What about?" Whitney asked.

"Jim-Jim. Drusus thinks Jim-Jim might be the CI."

I could see the wheels turn in Whitney's mind as I fumbled with the keys to the office door. But the door was open, which meant my secretary, Carlotta, was already there. I looked at my watch: a quarter of eight. She never came in before nine. "What's wrong with Carlotta?" I asked, pushing into my three-room suite. "A guilty conscience?"

"Give me a break," she said, emerging from my office with two coffee cups and an empty bottle of wine. Sometimes she can take your breath away. She is tall, slender, and lustrous-looking, with long black hair and black eyes. Her Cuban–brown skin radiates warmth, rage, sensuality, competence—the whole gamut of emotion, depending on her mood—everything except fear. There isn't an ounce of fear in her body. "How do you get any work done in that pigpen you call an office? I'm amazed we have clients! If I was a client, I wouldn't sit in there. It stinks!"

It's hard to be neutral around Carlotta. "That's why I keep the glass door open," I said, referring to the door between my office and the outdoor balcony. "So I can mix in the smells from the ocean. Where's my coffee?"

"Don't push your luck!"

My three-room suite is in a corner of the old hotel. You come into a large reception room first, where Carlotta has her desk and I have my library. File cabinets, more books, and another desk are in a small room on the west wall, and my office stretches along the south wall. A wraparound balcony on the outside could be rented for more than I have to pay on my lease. One direction looks out to sea. I can spit on the *Queen Mary,* which is docked below, anytime I want. From the other you can see along Ocean Boulevard for half a mile. Once a year, for a solid week, I have the best seats in town to watch the finish of the Long Beach Grand Prix.

Whitney and I walked into my office. It was neat as a pin: no files on the floor, no mounds of paper on my desk, no clutter of books and legal pads with scribbled notes or half-answered letters on them, nothing piled on the chairs or surfaces on top of the cabinets that lined the walls. The only file to be seen—organized into three notebooks—stood on my clean desk: *People v. Church.* Carlotta must have worked all night. "Damn," I said, kicking off my shoes and hanging my coat on the rack. "How do you expect me to find anything?"

"I don't," she snapped. "I expect you to holler at me like I was a block away and give me two seconds. Then I expect to find it under your nose!"

We have a great working relationship. Carlotta turned the telephone over to the answering service, hung a sign on the outside door that said "Due to an emergency, the office is closed. Please call for an appointment," giving the number, and locked the door. Then she herded Whitney and me into my office, where we sat around a small conference table, each with a legal pad and a pen. I love her

almost as much as I loved Robyn, if the truth were known.
"Give yourself a raise, kid."

"I did."

By the time I was on my third cup of coffee the vise that
had its jaws around my rib cage had opened, and I could
breathe. At ten o'clock that morning—with cup seven—
we'd worked out a strategy. It would change. You have to
plan on the unexpected when you're in trial.

At the long day's end I knew all we needed was a miracle. But I also knew the lawyer from NASP would get all
the exercise he needed.

The issue was no longer guilt or innocence. It had become life or death. I had to persuade the same twelve people who thought Drusus was a killer that he shouldn't be
executed.

I had help from, of all places, the State of California. In
order to give indigent murderers the fair trials the constitu-
tion said they were entitled to, it had established a fund so
defense lawyers could hire experts to defend them. A whole
new industry was spawned: good people, mainly, who investigated the backgrounds of killers, then tried to persuade
twelve citizens who believed in the death penalty to make
an exception in a particular case. The process is enough to
turn your head from inside out to back in.

I'd hired a gaggle of them on Drusus's behalf: a social
anthropologist, a former warden, and a Ph.D. who had
done his thesis on gangs. They did their own investigation,
and I'd talked with them on the telephone and through the
fax machine, asking and answering questions as they gave
me reports. I spent Saturday morning in bed reading their
summaries so that Sunday, when we met at my office, I
could orchestrate their testimony.

I put the reports away and looked at my watch: a quarter
after ten. Erin would be up. I gave her a call.

"You slug," she said. "Mother is right." But she also
told me I could come over for dinner that night, if I brought
the meat.

After getting dressed and drinking another cup of coffee

I drove to the office and parked in the shade of the building where it said "Guests Only." I took the elevator to the sixth floor and found Carlotta busy at her desk. "What are you doing here?"

"I have a lot to catch up on."

Her way of being there when I needed her, and she knew I would.

The act my experts and I would put on wouldn't be worth the paper the script was written on if the prosecution proved its penalty-phase case. They had a good one. I knew I needed more time, and if Ida stayed as hard-ass as I knew she would, that gave me a day and a half.

Four months before the start of the guilt phase the prosecution had provided me with a "Notice of Factors in Aggravation." According to the notice, the death penalty was justified because not only had the defendant murdered Rhoades, but he had killed before. I kicked off my loafers—it was a relief to come to the office in golf clothes—and plopped at my desk, poring over the file.

The youngster had a record, too, which was what had kept him off the stand in the guilt phase. Had he testified, the prosecution would have brought it up. It was not a pretty story. Drusus had just had his eighteenth birthday when he and Jim-Jim Joslin got nailed doing a burglary over in Carson. It had been a gang caper, and Drusus had worn a gun in his belt. The public defender got him a deal. The three-year sentence on the burglary was halved, and the judge stayed the mandatory two for carrying a gun. He pleaded guilty. He kept his nose clean, and all he did was eight months.

There was nothing I could do to keep the jury from finding out about it now—and it would hurt. The jurors would have undeniable proof that Drusus was capable of using a gun in the commission of a crime. They would also find out he had been a member of a gang. I made some notes about the most effective way for my gang expert to approach the subject, then turned to the really serious problem: the other murder. If the jurors thought Drusus had killed twice, they wouldn't have any sympathy for him. "Carlotta! Where's Whitney?"

"Damn you, Jack, don't yell. I can hear you!" she yelled. "He flew to Folsom."

"Why? I need him!"

"You're the one who told him to go. Don't you remember anything? He talked to Drusus yesterday afternoon about Jim-Jim, and he'll talk to Jim-Jim today."

The victim's name was Tommy Sherman rather than Kingsley Rhoades. He'd been shot to death in front of the crack house on Cherry Street, instead of in the alley behind; and it had happened one month before Rhoades took his hit. But Sherman was a black man also, involved in drugs, who had been blasted with a gun the police had never found. It might even have been a .38-caliber Smith and Wesson. The bullets hadn't stayed in Tommy's body, and they'd not been found.

I shut my eyes, gritted my teeth, and told myself to relax. I'd been so caught up in the defense of Drusus for one murder I'd pushed the other one out of my mind. I'd read the police reports and given them to Whitney, then gotten busy doing other things. There is never enough time, I thought, feeling hollow in the stomach. I knew the presumption of innocence wouldn't mean diddly to the jury now. They'd already found him guilty of murder. The prosecution wouldn't have to prove he'd killed Tommy Sherman. I'd have to prove he hadn't. I grabbed the reports and jumped up, heading for the door. "Carlotta! Grab a legal pad and put your shoes on!"

"Why?"

"Because the people we are going to see expect nice Cuban girls to wear them!"

When we got to the elevator she pointed out I'd forgotten to put on mine.

Usually, defending a person against a charge of murder has nothing to do with solving it. In nine cases out of ten everybody knows who pulled the trigger. So trials often become tactical chess games where the lawyers position themselves for checkmate.

A hulking giant I'd never seen, wearing a hotel uniform, lurked near my Mazda when Carlotta and I climbed inside. I was so busy thinking I hardly saw him. The State of California had never charged my client with the murder of Tommy Sherman. Why? Wouldn't that have been a better tactic from the point of view of the prosecutor? Then it would have been "out there," so to speak, the second count of the complaint. The jury would have known about it from the beginning. Instead they buried it, making no more of it than a factor in aggravation. If the trial had not gone on to the penalty phase, this jury would never have known about it.

"Mister, ah, Bard," the uniform said, scowling at me. "This parking is reserved, sir."

"Don't interrupt."

I put the car in gear and started down the hotel drive, thinking furiously. Out of the corner of my eye I saw the uniform jump out of the way. The fool almost got run over, I thought, wondering what his problem was.

Keane Williams had not been at the hearing on the motion I'd filed right after getting the People's "Notice of Factors in Aggravation." I'd asked for a preliminary hearing on the murder allegation. The suit who showed up—it wasn't Mad Dog Hammond—argued that under the circumstances of the case, the defendant didn't have a right to one. "A person has to be charged with a crime before he has that right," he said. "Mister Church has not been formally charged with the murder of Tommy Sherman."

"Your Honor," I had argued back, "it's the murder of Tommy Sherman that could result in the infliction of the death penalty!"

The suit claimed that definite proof against Drusus for the murder of Tommy Sherman hadn't been found until after the Kingsley Rhoades murder had been set for trial. Charging the Tommy Sherman murder in an information, then adding it as a new count to Rhoades, would have caused a long delay, he said. A new preliminary hearing would have been needed, which could have postponed the trial by as much as a year. "Charging decisions are made by district attorneys, not defense lawyers," the twit had snipped. "If the DA doesn't want to squander taxpayer money, he doesn't have to."

Ida denied my motion for a preliminary hearing. I knew she would; I brought it to make a point. She denied my motion for a continuance, too, telling me four months was plenty of time to prepare. But she gave me what I really wanted: a discovery order with teeth. The prosecution had to give me their murder book on Tommy Sherman.

At that point I thought I was way ahead. I only had to defend against one murder at a time, so the well-known slop-over effect would not be working for the prosecution. But now I had second thoughts. Had I been painted into a corner? The rules of evidence would be relaxed during the penalty phase, making proof of the other murder easy. Which led me to wonder: Is there something about the murder of Tommy Sherman they are trying to hide?

"Watch out!" Carlotta screamed.

"What? Oh." I swerved out of the way of a huge tractor-trailer that was so big it should have been on a set of rails. "Those bastards think they own the road."

"Where are we going?"

"The scene of the crime." It only took a few minutes to drive to the corner of Cherry and Anaheim. I was smiling again. "Have you read the police file on Tommy Sherman?" I asked her.

"Yes."

"Did anything about it strike you as peculiar?"

"Not really. It seemed awfully long. Even longer than what they gave you on Kingsley Rhoades."

I am on to something, I thought. "Forget Rhoades. We're talking Sherman. The first officer on the scene interviewed an eyewitness, Salvadore Mira, who saw it happen and called the cops. That's the first report in the file. Then there are two follow-up reports by the detectives who worked the case: Kincaid and Rory Danforth. Right?"

"Yes," she said, watching the road.

"Those guys tried to find other witnesses but didn't have any luck." I pulled next to the curb. "The next thing in the book is the evidence log and the autopsy. Right? Up to that point, no case."

We got out of the car. I hated what I saw: human waste. The street was not crowded, and some of the people were dressed well enough, but the rest looked like beggars I had seen in Katmandu. Carlotta held her pad in one hand and locked her purse in the car. "Go on," she said, interested.

"Then it gets good. There's a statement from a second eyewitness—Larry Walker—who positively identifies Drusus as the guy who killed Sherman. Except that interview took place five months after the shooting. Rory Danforth took the statement from Walker at the county jail. He got it the day before Walker went on trial for an aggravated robbery!"

"What does that mean?"

"It means Walker wanted a deal. He was trading information for a light sentence."

"Did he get a light sentence?"

"No." I looked for Salvadore Mira's address on Cherry Street. "They tried him anyway, and he got convicted."

"Jack, that's two eyewitnesses," Carlotta said. "Isn't that a pretty good case?"

"Why two?" I asked. "What was wrong with the first one?"

I saw the address. We walked on the sidewalk in front: Carlotta, who would stand out in a crowd of beauty queens, and me. Next to her I'm like Woody Allen thinks he is: invisible. Nobody would see me even if the two of us were the only people on the beach.

"Money, man? A coupla bucks? You know."

A skinny Filipino—black hair, brittle eyes, cheeks that barely covered the bones in his face—had his hand out. "Do you live around here?" I asked.

"Sometime."

"Where?"

He shook his head, looked at Carlotta for a minute—long enough for his mouth to open in wonder—then shuffled off.

Three or four bungalows—stucco-faced, with worn paint on garage doors, splashed with gang graffiti—stood across the street. The grass had worn off the yards like holes worn in a rug. Scruffy half-dressed toddlers who didn't know how poor they were paused in their play to inspect us with the total concentration of kids. Then they continued their war game, or whatever it was. Two of them charged the littlest one, who ran, either squealing with delight or screaming in terror, I couldn't tell which.

The house we stood in front of was wedged between a couple of torn-up apartment buildings. An old convertible on blocks sat in a corner of the yard. "Is this where it happened?" Carlotta asked.

"Right over there," I said, pointing. "The eyewitness who reported it said the victim came out of that apartment building with two other guys. It was dark—three o'clock in the morning."

"Is that the crack house?" Carlotta asked, referring to the apartment.

"It's in there somewhere."

She seemed to light up. "I saw *V. I. Warshawski* the other night on video. Want to feel my muscle?"

"Another time." I pulled out the diagram in the police report. "We're standing about where the witness was."

"He was in a car, wasn't he? Just sitting?"

I nodded. "Let's see if he's home."

We walked up the driveway. Salvadore Mira obviously had kids. A walker—new, with half the paint scraped off—was tipped over in the yard, along with a couple of soft-rubber fake baseballs and a plastic bat. The front door—next to the driveway and over a chipped concrete platform—opened as we approached. A woman checked the screen door—it had a few holes—to make sure it was locked. "Yes?" she asked.

"Hello," I said, smiling and probably scaring the shit out of her. She was short, a little heavy, with beautiful black hair and even teeth. "I'm looking for Mr. Mira. Is he in?"

"I sorry. I no speak Onnglase." She started to shut the door.

"Español?" Carlotta asked, moving next to me.

We could hear movement in the background, and I caught a glimpse through the screen of a man on a couch. When those Spanish guys see Carlotta they sit up. *"Quién está,* Dolores?" he asked brightly. "Someone to see us?"

"Sí," she said, fading momentarily out of the way. "They ask for you."

"Let them in."

Dolores unlatched the screen and pushed it open. Both of them watched Carlotta as we entered their living room. I was invisible on the beach. Salvadore—early thirties, beginning to thicken around the middle, wearing an undershirt and black cotton pants—got off the couch and sucked in his stomach. He smiled and brushed at his hair. "Please. Make yourself welcome."

Carlotta acknowledged him with a smile but held her hand out to Dolores. "Señora Mira?"

"Yes." They touched. Carlotta smiled, and Dolores did her best to smile back.

"Dolores. Offer them to sit down."

"Yes. Please sit down."

Salvadore tried but was unable to take his eyes away from Carlotta. She sat on a chair near the television set as demurely as she could, but it is hard for Carlotta to sit demurely. I pulled a chair away from the dining room table, and Dolores sat down next to Salvadore on the couch. "Where are the kids?" I asked.

"Oh. At their grandmother. How do you know?"

I told them how cleverly I had deduced they had children. We laughed: Carlotta first, then Salvadore, then Dolores. The women exchanged some talk about babies. Carlotta can't stand them, she has told me, but I wouldn't have guessed that from her expression. And while Salvadore watched Carlotta, I watched Salvadore. I let him know I was a lawyer investigating a case, and—his gaze still draping all over Carlotta—he wondered dreamily if it was the same case this big black man had talked to him about a couple of months before.

"Whitney Lee?"

"Yeah. Really big mon."

I told him it was, that Whitney was my investigator, but we'd been very busy, and I hoped he didn't mind going over it again for me. He took a deep breath and smiled at Carlotta. "I don't mind."

He had seen the whole thing. They were new to the neighborhood then—"Kind of needed a cheap place"—buried under a pile of debts. He pointed with his head at his wife. "She signed some damn piece of paper when they took her mother to the hospital," he explained, and he'd been working two jobs ever since. The mother had since died, but they still had all those bills to pay. "I kind of baby-sit at Benny's Storage—you know, big chain-link fence all around the yard, and a gate you need to know what numbers to punch in and it will slide open. But sometime when I come home from there I sit in the car before going inside." Dolores's hand slid over his. "Maybe I fell asleep, I don't know. All I know is I saw these black guys come pouring out of that apartment."

"Did you see who they were?"

"I saw the one who did the shooting." He laughed nervously and rubbed the bottom of his chin with the top of his hand. "He didn't see me, though."

"And?"

"They kind of surrounded this one guy, like two of them were blocking him, when the big one—he was big, mon, like a fighter—said something like 'Sorry, mon,' and shot him. Twice. Right in the chest." Salvadore continued to grin, but his eyes had glazed. "I don't know. I seen lots of things, but I never saw anybody shot before. Like a hammer in the chest. He didn't leave the ground or nothin', but it was like a hard punch, you know. Dropped him."

"What did the others do?"

"Scattered. One of them was a kid. He just ran. The other—lots of hair, man, one of those Afros, you know?—he didn't run, exactly, but it was more than a walk. The big guy did the shooting, he was real cool. He turned around and walked away."

"What did you do?"

"Waited a couple minutes, then went inside the house and called the cops." He glanced at Carlotta, pulled in his stomach, and looked tough. "You know. I don't need that sh—stuff. Not in front of my own damn house."

"Had you ever seen any of these people?"

Salvadore stiffened up. "You gonna call me as a witness, right?"

I didn't have any subpoenas with me. "I don't know. Listen to me. Would—"

"I don't need that, man. Lose a day, two days, three days of work sitting around in a courthouse and get fired. You know."

"Your employer can't do that."

"Why? It's against the law?" He laughed. "You don't know my boss."

"Who is he?" I asked. "Maybe I do."

Salvadore stood up. He had that "first things first" look on his face I'd seen before. "This is no good, man," he said, watching Carlotta with regret. "You're one of them defense lawyers, right? I got to think about it."

"Listen to me," I said. "A man's life—"

Carlotta got between us. She seemed to grow there, like Venus making an appearance on earth. "Jack, Mr. Mira doesn't want to talk any more," she said. "He's been really nice." She held her hand out to Mrs. Mira. "Señora. Thank you so much."

"But—"

"Jack, you Anglo prick, don't push!"

That broke everybody up but me.

I was still grumbling as I unlocked the Mazda and got in. "What the hell did you do that for?" I demanded, jamming it in gear and shoving out of there. Then I thought it over. "Thanks."

"Do you mean it?"

"Yeah." I'd said "Listen to me" twice, which meant I was about to get hostile. "Whitney talked to him and probably has it all anyway. Tell him to put a paper on him, okay?"

"Do you really want him to testify?" Carlotta asked. She

had her legal pad open, scribbling away. " 'Black man—big—looked like a fighter.' Those were his words." She looked at me. "That sounds like Drusus, Jack. Is he something we don't know?"

"Don't you get it?" I asked her. "Salvadore saw it happen. He said he saw the guy who did it. And he's easy to find. Yet the prosecution hasn't even named him as a witness!"

"How do you know that?"

"They have to give me a list of witnesses, and he isn't on it." I gunned it around a corner. "They've lined up three people to prove up the murder of Tommy Sherman: the pathologist who did the autopsy, the con who went down on the agg rob, and the cop he talked to. Salvadore Mira isn't on their list!"

"Thank God," Carlotta said, still scribbling.

"You don't get it." I had to honk at some punk who tried to push me on to the sidewalk. "What if the cops showed Salvadore a picture of Drusus?"

She stopped writing long enough to look at me. "Would they do that?"

"Yes! They want to make a murder case! When will Whitney be back?"

"Tonight. He's flying back from Folsom. He wants you to pick him up at the airport." She looked at her watch and went back to her pad.

"How the hell can you write on that thing the way I'm driving?"

"I'm balanced right."

At 2:47 P.M. Keane called. He'd have been great on radio. When he talked—mellow and smooth—I could see his face. "What you asked about Thursday? I mean, assuming you remember what you asked about. You were kind of in the bag." I saw a photogenic grin.

"You'll have to remind me."

"The pill. You wanted me to quit on the pill."

I was all ears. "Are you willing to drop the death penalty?"

"You will never meet a nicer fellow," he said engagingly. I could see him giving the camera a profile shot. "It would also give me a chance to see my folks. They still live in San Diego, and I like the beaches down there."

Some lawyers feel cheated when it looks as though a trial will settle. Not me. I felt great. "You have a deal," I said with enthusiasm. "Have you called Ida?"

"Judge Mather?" he asked, then laughed. "I forget how everyone around here is on this first-name basis. I haven't said anything to her."

"Why not? She'll raise hell if you don't tell her as soon as you can. If it's going off, she'll want to call the jurors, and—"

"Jack, I need a little something in return. I mean, this deal is open for negotiation."

"What's to negotiate?" I asked. "He's been found guilty of first-degree murder with special circumstances. He goes to the slam for the rest of his life, with no possibility of parole! Do I have to agree he spends it in a dungeon?"

"Hey, easy, old buddy. When he sets up his house I'll even make sure he has his own TV."

I thought I knew what he wanted, and it pissed me off. "We don't have anything to give you."

"Yes, you do. The right to appeal."

"Don't take that away," I said. "Leave him with something to live for."

"Look, here's the deal, Jack. I really hope you'll take it, because I've had a hell of a time persuading Wink and the rest of the Long Beach PD to go for it. On Monday, all he has to do—on the record—is change his plea to guilty and admit the special circ. Then we let the jury go home. Okay?"

What is going on? I wondered. "He can't do that, Keane. He says he didn't kill Rhoades, and I believe him." I had a glimmer. "You want more than the right of appeal, don't you? All that would cover is trial error. Are you afraid of new evidence?"

"Jack. Father. God. I'm making a good-faith offer here. I know you think he's this saintly creature, but ask him. Okay?"

7

I took flowers over to Erin's along with two twelve-dollar-a-pound steaks. She looked great. She has green eyes—turquoise green—a pug nose and a face that kind of blooms. "Mouse called," she told me.

Mouse is my twenty-eight-year-old daughter. "What about?"

"I don't know. She was crying."

My sweet little girl married a lawyer from Tuscon—a nice enough guy—but he does divorces and meets women with needs he doesn't always have the class to leave alone. "I'll have to call her."

The slug had dragged himself home the night before with lipstick on his shirt, in the bag. Mouse wanted to kill him. She asked me if finding lipstick on his shirt was enough for the battered-woman defense.

"Are you afraid of him?"

"No! I hate him! Isn't that justifiable homicide or something?"

"It would be murder, Mouse." I've never been able to reason with my little girl, but she understands consequences. "Twenty years in the bucket. You could be out before your fiftieth."

"You're on his side!"

It was a relief to hang up, pour myself a scotch, and talk

70

to Erin. I told her everything that had happened that day.
She has a way of listening like no one I have ever known,
with total honesty. It enables her to hear more than the
talker saw. As I nuked the potatoes in the microwave her
face puckered, and she asked some questions. "Salvadore
Mira saw the person who killed Tommy Sherman?"

"That's what he said."

"This happened before Drusus was put in jail, didn't it?"

"Yes. Sherman got shot in March, Rhoades in April.
Drusus was arrested three days after Rhoades was killed."

"Well, after the first man was killed—Sherman?"

"Right."

"Did the police talk to Drusus then? I mean, this witness
described a big black man who looked like a fighter.
Wouldn't they have questioned Drusus about it?"

I let the implications of her question roll around in my
head. Whitney could turn it into a clue and possibly work
out a piece of the puzzle. I would turn it into a line of
questions, transforming the witness chair into a hot seat for
the cops.

After dinner I left for the airport to go pick Whitney up.
Erin told me she'd leave the light on until midnight, but
after that I'd have to sleep alone. So I moved right along.

I never worry about getting Whitney into the passenger
seat of my sports car. He holds onto the roof, swings his
butt over the leather, and drops. Getting him out is the
problem, but that would come later. We jumped on the
freeway and flew toward Hollywood, where he lives.

"Drusus is wrong," Whitney said, his eyes glued to the
road. "I hope the airbag in this thing doesn't have a hole
in it."

"I'm just trying to keep up," I told him. "Jim-Jim is not
the CI?" I asked. "How do you know?"

"Nothing is absolute except numbers, man. But I stayed
with the boy two hours, long enough to know where he
sweats when he lies. He's got a few secrets, but that ain't
one of them. Sweet Jesus."

We were cruising at about ninety, and I made one of my
better moves. I slid between two pickups before the cow-

boy in the old Dodge could block me. "If Jim-Jim isn't the CI, does he know who the informant is?"

"We talked about that. He could, but I don't think so. Holy shit."

I slowed from ninety to fifty in the space of a few yards, which moved Whitney forward in his seat. I'd tried running a bluff on some native who wouldn't be bluffed. You get philosophical about those minor confrontations in L.A. "The CI was supposed to have known Drusus would whack Rhoades before Rhoades got hit. Did you ask him about that?"

Whitney moved into my lap. "Aren't you a bit close to that big fucking truck?"

"I don't know what's wrong with that guy." I honked, and the truck swerved away. "Did you ask him?"

"He says he'd heard some of the OG's talking about—"

"OG?"

"Original Gangster. Gang talk. Any one over the age of twenty is an OG. There aren't many left by that time because most are used up, dead, or in prison."

"Go on."

"A couple of OG's talked about Rhoades and his crack house, but Jim-Jim never heard anything about hitting him. Rhoades had muscle of his own. He also had some Blades on his payroll—Drusus and Jim-Jim used to work for him when they should have been in school, and they liked it. Good dope and good money."

"But didn't the Blades want it for themselves? Drusus told me they own it now."

"Next exit, man, if we live that long." He climbed off my lap, but his eyes were locked on the road. "When Rhoades went down the operation fell in their lap. They're trying to run it, but it won't work. They don't have the smarts or the supply connection. Slow down, okay?"

I dropped it to eighty. "Better?"

"Not much. Rhoades had the right kind of a head. He had an MBA from Stanford. Did you know that?"

"No."

"There's more to running a crack house than you think.

It's a business, like a shoe store only more complicated. You have to buy the raw material, manufacture the product, and retail it. It takes someone in charge who is smart and tough." He wiped some sweat off his forehead. "The Blades are tryin' to run it by committee. Turn off at Silver Lake."

"I know how to get there." I had to get in the far left lane to pass a line of farmers who were gawking at the tall buildings or something. We cornered onto Silver Lake at a pretty good clip. "What do you think, Whitney? Did the informant make the whole thing up?"

"Let's start at the beginning, Jack. How do we know there was an informant? What if the purse was planted there by the cops when they searched the place?"

"Not possible," I said. "The search warrant, remember? They got the warrant before they did the search, and it described the exact spot where the purse was found." Suddenly I thought of what Erin had said. "Did the cops come over to the apartment to question him about the killing of Tommy Sherman?" Maybe they *were* there, I thought.

"They weren't," Whitney said. "I've been over that with Vera and Drusus ten times. Next corner, man." He looked relieved about something. "They couldn't have planted it then anyway, Jack. Rhoades was still alive. It was still hanging from his neck."

You don't pull in front of someone's house in Hollywood. You go up a cow trail and wind around another one—asphalt trenches, dug into the hills, that run between buildings—until you finally find a place to park. I found one a quarter of a mile from where Whitney lived. It's a small apartment—more of a cliff dwelling, ready to slide into the street. I parked, turned off the motor, and rolled down the window. "Want to come up?" he asked.

It was 11:30. I could still get to Erin's if I hurried. "No." I focused on what we'd been talking about. "We're still nowhere on the CI then. Right?"

"Right." Whitney looked at me patiently. "I've checked everything I can think of, Jack. Gang members with grudges, old girlfriends, people with an angle. Maybe it's time we faced up to the fact.''

"What are you talking about?"

"The prosecution is right, my man. Drusus did them both. He was working for Rhoades when he killed Sherman and was taking the operation over when he did Rhoades. He had the smarts to run the crack house and would have staffed it with Blades." He sounded like a buddy telling a friend his wife was running around on him. "He probably knows who the CI is. But if he told us, we'd learn the truth—and you wouldn't be anywhere near as enthusiastic."

I hung onto the wheel of my car. "I don't believe it."

"Your trouble is you've been defending these guys too long." He started to unlatch the door. "Drusus is an intelligent, personable guy with ambition and heart. He's so slick you don't see the con. Either that or you want to believe in him so bad you won't look for it."

"No." My feeling about Drusus was too straight. The world wasn't that cockeyed—yet. That would be too much of a betrayal. "He wants to be my partner someday. He's got more than heart, Whitney. He's got—I don't know the word. . . ."

"What you think you see is soul," Whitney said, struggling to get out of the car. It never takes as long as I think it should, considering the obstacles. "I'll see you in the morning, Jack S," he said.

It was easier holding a conversation with Whitney the next morning in my office than it had been the night before in my car. He could concentrate better. He listened carefully to Carlotta as she read her notes of our interview with Salvadore Mira. Then he looked at his watch. "I'll have to sneak up on him," he said. "I talked to him before, and he knows what I look like. If he sees me coming, he'll lock the door."

"You didn't tell me about that, by the way," I said. "Why not?"

"It wouldn't have done any good, Jack. You were in trial."

I frowned. "Madalena?"

"Yes."

Madalena Sanches had been my client in a product liability case. She was ten years old when she got tangled up in a towel—one of those huge cloth ribbons—in a public restroom. It wound around her throat somehow, literally hanging her from the wall. Most of her brain died, but none of her body did. I sued the towel company. "We made a lot of money on that case. You'd better get going."

"Will Salvadore be out of bed?" Whitney asked, leaning forward. "It's Sunday morning."

"*Sí,*" Carlotta said cheerfully. "Didn't you see all those crucifixes in there? He's baby-sitting with a beer can right now, watching a game on television. Dolores is at Saint Theresa's on Atlantic."

"What if he tells me Drusus did it?" Whitney asked me, pushing to his feet. "When I talked to him before, after he told me what the killer looked like, I decided not to take a chance on getting the wrong answer and quit asking questions." He looked down at me. "Do I subpoena him anyway?"

"He won't give you the wrong answer." I smiled up at him. "But if he does, save the subpoena. We'll use it on somebody else."

An hour later Whitney called. Salvadore had not wanted to talk to him, so he put the paper on him to get his attention. "He definitely does not want to testify," Whitney said. "He says he'll lose his job."

"Threats?" I asked angrily. "I wouldn't put it past those guys." Whitney knew what I meant: the cops. Defendants aren't the only ones who intimidate witnesses.

"I don't know."

"Cut to the chase, man. Did you show him a picture of Drusus?"

"Yes."

"And?"

"He doesn't think so. It could have been, though. You know. 'They all look alike.' "

I took in a yard of air. I could feel it feed my body. It

felt great. "Did you ask him if the cops showed him any pictures?"

"Yeah, I did that, too."

"And?"

"They showed him a mug-shot folder—you know, six mug shots stuck in slots in a file jacket. One of them might have been the shooter, he said—lighter skin than Drusus—but he didn't think so."

"A mug-shot lineup! The prosecution should have told me! That's the first *I've* heard about it."

"Or me. I thought I'd swing by the police building. It's Sunday, and they use part-timers on holidays. I might con a clerk into letting me look through their file."

When I hung up I saw Carlotta standing in the doorway. "Good news?" she asked, smiling at me.

"EEEEE-YYEEOOWWW!" I shouted, throwing a fist in the air. "Now it makes sense!"

"What?"

"The reason they didn't charge Drusus with killing Tommy Sherman in the complaint. The eyewitness ID was no good! So they bring it the only way they can: as an aggravating factor!"

"But they have another eyewitness, don't they?"

"Yes. In a prison suit! He's at Atascadero on an agg rob beef, and he's got a rape prior!" I rubbed my hands in glee. "I hope he's got beady eyes."

"Why?"

"I'll see if I can't get him to stare at the women on the jury."

It's hard to sleep the night before the battle begins. Usually I put on my pajamas and crawl in bed and give it a try. But after tossing and turning and then lying as rigid as a board, I'll put a movie on the VCR and twitch and doze. At five A.M. I'm out cold. When the alarm goes off at seven I'm sleeping so hard I can't hear it.

That night was different. It started the same: When I got back from the office at ten I brushed my teeth and put on my pajamas. But I didn't get in bed. I turned off the lights and sat in the recliner in the living room, staring at the wall.

What am I fighting for? I asked myself. When we had *voir dired* the panel, a couple of prospective jurors—upon learning that the alternative to death was life without possibility of parole—said they might vote to execute out of kindness. They could not imagine anything as awful as a young man having to spend the rest of his life in a cage. They had been excused, naturally. But were they right?

Sometimes it's hard to make yourself believe in what you do—which could account for the undeniable fact that our economic system is such a resounding success. It gives ninety percent of the population something really important to believe in. Money. I'm part of the ten percent that needs more. It's un–American, and I don't know how or why it happened to me, because I was brought up right. My mother made me scrub behind my ears, took me to church, and made me join the Boy Scouts. In spite of that, turning the quest for money into a noble purpose never took.

Whitney was wrong about the man I called "youngster." He'd done a lot of living in that Long Beach ghetto when—like a moth coming out of a cocoon—he started coming out. Up to that point in his life he had survived. His extraordinary quality—whatever it was—had not been destroyed. The world I lived in needed Drusus Church. I could not let him down. Or let him die.

I shut my eyes and let my hands coil into fists. I prayed.

8

I swung by the office to pick up the file. Carlotta hadn't come in yet. Poor kid, I thought. She'd put in two sixteen-hour days on the weekend and was probably bagged.

I drove to the courthouse, looking in vain for the mountains that used to loom up over the valley. You hardly see them at all now, though it used to be the rare day when you didn't. On cold days the farmers would light smudge pots to keep the crops alive, and the San Gabriels would hide behind the smoke. Now the only time you find them is when the Santa Ana winds blow hard enough to move the smog out to sea.

I parked in the underground parking garage next to the courthouse, flashing a permit I'd boosted from the DA's office. I've gotten to know the guard. He waved at me, and I waved back. He thinks I'm a helluva guy, for a DA. At a quarter to nine I struggled into Ida's courtroom, as worn as an old tomcat who had been chasing little pussies all night. I waited for the drama to begin.

No one was there, which seemed strange. I spread the contents of my briefcase all over the table reserved for the defendant, which makes it easier to lose what I'm looking for, old Charley Wallace used to tell me. Keane came in a few minutes later, scrubbed and wholesome as a newly picked apple. He grinned when he saw me. "You're looking dapper this morning, Jack S."

"I try."

"Great tie, man. Dolphins or killer whales?"

I hadn't looked at it when I put it on. Now I did. "Uh-oh. Dolphins." A death-qualified jury—which means twelve citizens and two alternates who can drop the pill—usually doesn't have any vegetarians. This one was no exception. Several of them were eaters of raw red meat—prosecution favorites—but there weren't any nice, quiet types who liked bean sprouts and tofu. Dolphins could turn them off. "Could they pass for sharks?"

Keane shook his head. "Sorry, Charlie. Not enough teeth." He sat down on the edge of my table. "Have you talked to your client?"

"If you mean about your so-called offer—no. I haven't had a chance."

"Good. I'd like to sweeten it."

I tried not to react. "How?"

"If he changes his plea to first-degree murder, I will drop the special circumstance." He smiled, letting the significance of the offer sink in. "Then he has a future, Jack. He doesn't go down on an L-WOPP. He could be out in under twenty-five years."

"Why would you do that?"

"Don't be so suspicious, old buddy," he said, which made me even more suspicious. He'd never called me "old buddy" before. "It's possible my side has had a change of heart. I've been working on them. I've watched your guy, too, when he wasn't watching me, and I like him."

"What kind of fairy tale is that?" I got up. "Have you found out something exculpatory? What is going on?"

The prisoner entrance door opened, and Godzilla marched in with Drusus in tow. He was shackled at both wrists and ankles and had to shuffle. His head was down so he could watch his feet.

"Hey. I'm just a fair-minded prosecutor," Keane said, getting off my desk, "who would like to spend a few days in San Diego with my folks and renew old friendships and maybe do a little politicking. But if you want to duke it out and risk your client's life, that's okay.'' He gave me one of those Lone Ranger looks that DAs practice when they brush their teeth, then moved over to his table and started arranging files.

Godzilla yanked harder than he needed to get the irons off. Drusus rubbed his wrists, but other than that he didn't react. He nodded at me and smiled with what looked like affection. "Yo," he said.

"Yo?"

"I've been reading *Bonfire of the Vanities*. That's the way us black guys are supposed to talk.'' Godzilla pushed him into his chair, then sat on a bench behind the rail with his hand on the butt of his club as though ready for an escape attempt. Drusus glanced at him, then looked at me kind of dreamlike. "How are you doing?"

Some court-watchers had taken seats in the courtroom, and Whitney Lee stuck his head in, saw me, and waved at Drusus, then disappeared. That was a signal to let me know all my witnesses were under subpoena. "We need to talk, Drusus." I didn't like his expression. It was spacey, the way druggies look when they are so high nothing can touch them. "I'll ask the judge if it's okay to use the attorney conference room."

"Sure."

Ida didn't have her robe on yet. She sat behind her desk, smoking and reading the paper. "Good morning, Jack," she said, laying it down and looking at me over her glasses. "You aren't going to ask me for a continuance, are you?"

"Would I come in the morning of trial and ask for a continuance?" I asked. She didn't offer me a chair.

"You knew we weren't starting until two o'clock, didn't you?" she asked.

"That's" why nobody's around. No." I sat down anyway. Age has its privileges.

"Well. There's been a delay. Ms. Perkins, one of the jurors, lost an uncle Saturday, and the funeral is this morning. She feels she can go on with the case, but it will be a short day. Didn't my clerk call you?"

I don't think Ida knows her name, either. "Probably," I lied. It's never a good idea to blame the clerk. "But the message didn't get passed on." I told her Drusus was in court, that I needed to talk to him about something that had come up and hinted at a plea bargain, and asked her to authorize the use of the attorney room.

"Sure." She smiled and picked up the paper as I stood up. "Good luck."

"Can I tell that guard to unlace him when we talk?"

"You can tell him I think that would be nice, but his regs may not allow it, and I'm not going to take on the Sheriff's Department over it."

It is always so friendly in a courtroom before the shooting starts. I bumped into Keane in the hall between the judge's chambers and the pit. "Did you hear we don't start until two?" he asked. "The clerk just told me. What is her name, anyway?"

The court-watchers were gone, and Godzilla had started lacing the chains around Drusus. The brown-shirt didn't like it when I told him what the judge had said, but he untied him and stood by. I wondered if he would make the youngster hurt more later. I summoned Whitney out of the hall—he told the witnesses he was baby-sitting to wait in the cafeteria on the sixth floor—and Drusus, Whitney, and I gathered around a table in one of the attorney conference rooms. We shut the door on the Hulk, who stood guard in the hall.

I decided to put the offer out there and get Drusus's reaction without talking about my suspicions. If he was as guilty as Whitney thought, he'd snap at it. "Keane says he likes you," I said. "He's made an offer we need to talk about."

"My grandmother here?"

"She's upstairs drinking coffee," Whitney said.

"Here it is," I said. "If you plead guilty to the murder of Kingsley Rhoades, they'll drop the special circumstances. You'd still get life, but it wouldn't be life without possibility of parole. In twenty years you'd be eligible for parole.

You'd probably be out of the slam in something like twenty-two years."

I had wanted to watch Drusus, but Whitney's expression was more interesting. It registered astonishment. I held my hand up so he wouldn't say anything.

"Do that again?" Drusus asked.

I said it over; longer this time, spelling it out in more detail. It would depend on whether the judge would allow it, I explained, but—since it was coming from the special prosecutor—I knew she would.

"How could that happen? I've already been convicted!"

"She can set that aside and take your plea."

"What they want to be so nice for?"

"If you plead guilty, case closed. They don't have to worry about appeals."

He thought it over. "I'd be out in twenty-two years?"

I nodded. "Could be less. Depending on the legislature, how crowded the prisons get, how well you do."

He stared at his hands. Whitney watched, too, although he wasn't as obvious about it. "I didn't kill him."

"What about Tommy Sherman?"

"I didn't kill him either." His head jerked up and stared at me with surprise. He had not expected me to ask that question. "Don't you believe me?"

Whitney cut in. "Jack does. I don't."

Drusus looked at him, then looked away. He shrugged. "I can't say it any different. I didn't do either one of them."

"Do you know who did?"

"No."

Like the mean cop in the nice-cop, mean-cop two-step, Whitney loomed over Drusus. "You been shittin' me, boy. I was in the Sheriff's Office. I've been trained on a polygraph. I know the man who tested you, and he's good. I've been over the charts with him. You lied, dude. You just plain lied."

"I don't lie."

Some of the steam went out of Whitney, but he still looked like a volcano ready to erupt. "Here's what those guys are going to show the jury," he said. "There's a connection between Sherman and Rhoades: you. You were an enforcer for Rhoades and did Sherman on his orders. Then you turn around and ice Rhoades because the Blades wanted to take over his business."

"I was not in the Blades when Sherman was hit, man. I met Vera and started going to school and dropped out of the gang. I fought the line. I broke Jim-Jim's nose." He rested his forearms on the table. "Who do you work for, Whitney?"

"Not for you, boy. I work for the lawyer."

Drusus looked at me with pain. I wondered if he would ever trust me again. "Do you think I killed them, Jack?" he asked.

"No." But I dropped my face, and I don't know if he believed me.

"What do you want me to do?"

"I can't tell you what to do, youngster. You'll have to decide. But I can tell you what I think." I outlined my suspicions. Whitney frowned as I talked, but he agreed with me. They could be hiding something, I told Drusus. Maybe they were trying to buy their way out of a bad deal. "But once you change your plea and admit guilt, that's that. You won't go to death row, and you'll be out in twenty, but you'll never get a new trial, either."

"So it's a good offer?"

I nodded. "The alternative could be the pill."

"Then the smart thing would be take it, right?" He started sitting up, and his eyes had that spacey look. I didn't say anything, and neither did Whitney. We watched. "I can't, man." The expression on his face grew peaceful, and his eyes seemed to regain their focus. "All I got is the truth. That's all I got left. I can't let go of the only thing I got left."

The prosecution would go first. The defense would follow with evidence of mitigation, then the prosecution would finish with rebuttal. My plan was to drag the trial out as long as I could to make time for Whitney. While Keane and I duked it out before the jury, he would roam the sidelines, hunting for what had to be out there.

I would start with a motion or two, to create some excitement and jam things up. But the feathers and dust would settle, and I'd have to get serious. The first hurdle would be the prosecution's case in aggravation: the murder of Tommy Sherman. If we didn't blunt it with evidence—and a theory—of our own to explain the two kills, it would be thumbs down.

The next jump was our case in mitigation. My plan was to open the youngster up, to let the jurors take a long, hard, critical look at Drusus Church. I would develop his background—all of it, including his gang involvement. But if it went right—and you never know how it will play, it's like improvised theater—our witnesses would show he had turned his life around and was on his way out of the ghetto when calamity struck. Then Drusus would mount the stand like an offering, and there was no doubt that Keane Williams would do his best to carve out the youngster's heart with cross-examination.

It was a risky tack. Drusus would maintain his innocence, which meant telling the jury, "You guys fucked up." That isn't what jurors like to hear. They want to believe in the righteousness of what they've already done. They like defendants who admit the error of their ways, feel awful, staggering remorse, and beg for mercy. They don't want to deal with lingering doubt.

Drusus knew that as well as anyone. But all he wanted to do, that morning before the war, was see his grandmother.

9

The court-watchers were back, and most of the players were in the courtroom, waiting for the ceremony to begin. Iron Pants trotted in, hiked up her skirts, and mounted the throne. "Good afternoon, gentlemen," she said. "Well. It appears everyone is here. Did all the jurors show up?"

"Yes, Judge," Ivan said. "They're in the jury room."

She sat down, arranging something on the bench. "Excellent. Let's get going. Ivan, why don't you—"

"Your Honor, I need to make a motion out of their presence," I said.

She didn't look pleased. Neither did the special prosecutor. Five minutes ago I'd told him what I was going to do. "Very well."

"I want to make a *Hitch* motion, Judge," I said, ambling up to the lectern. "I don't have that citation, but I'll get it if you need it. I'm asking for sanctions against the prosecution for intentionally withholding material evidence. I can't think of any statutory way to bring it. You see, the problem—"

"Mr. Bard, why don't you just tell me what they did?"

She knows me too well, I thought. It was like the way a person can recognize the melody after hearing a few bars. She knew I was stalling for time. I gave her my most lovable smile. "As the Court is well aware, the prosecution at this stage of the proceeding will attempt to prove the alleged murder of one Tommy Sherman as an aggravating factor. We had a hearing about it four months ago. Mr. Williams, who came in later as a special prosecutor, didn't handle the proceeding for the People, but he is nevertheless bound by the orders issued to the same extent as everyone else."

I paused for a glass of water and let her drum her fingers on the desk. "Mr. Bard. The jury is waiting."

"I feel it's necessary to present the background, Judge, just to put this in context. And also"—I blessed Keane with my lovable smile, too, although he didn't smile back—"because I don't think Mr. Williams, personally, is responsible. He may not even know what happened then."

She sighed. She looked at her watch. "Please continue."

"It has come to my attention that significant exculpatory data in connection with the murder of Tommy Sherman has not been disclosed to me. This is in direct violation of the duty of the prosecutor, under *Brady v. United States*. As interpreted by—"

"Mr. Bard, I am well aware of the authorities. Please tell me what you believe has been withheld and what you think I should do about it."

I pushed the glasses back and brought my head down. I felt like Winston Churchill. "As a result of that hearing, the prosecution gave me a copy of their so-called murder book on Sherman. They represented to me that it was all they had. The fact is, Judge, that it isn't."

I paused for what might have been dramatic effect, if she'd been receptive to a bit of drama, but she wasn't. She iced me with an appropriate judicial stare, informing me she'd heard all this before. "Please continue."

"Thank you. The book contains a police report indicating there was an eyewitness to that incident. I have learned that a mug-shot photographic lineup was shown to that witness. However, there is no report of it in the murder book." She frowned, touching the rim of her glasses. "There is a real possibility that my client's photograph was in that lineup and that the eyewitness did not identify my client as the perpetrator. That information—clearly exculpatory—isn't in the murder book either."

Ida sat up. "As I recall, a rather strict discovery order entered at the hearing you referred to, didn't it?"

"It did, Your Honor. It put the prosecution under a continuing order to provide the defense with police reports, reports of experts, witness interviews, and exculpatory material. If I can have a moment."

"You may."

It took more than a moment. Old Charley was probably smiling from up there somewhere as he watched me search for the goddam thing. I finally found it. Someone had put it with "Pre-trial Orders" instead of "Discovery." "Let me have this marked and entered as an exhibit," I said, handing a copy of the order to the clerk.

"Yes. Defendant's exhibit A." She glared at both Keane Williams and Wink Barrett, who sat at counsel table for the prosecution, Williams as the lawyer and Barrett as advisory witness. "This is a serious allegation, Mr. Williams. How do you respond, sir?"

The boy wonder stood up and opened his hands. "I hardly know what to say, Judge. I admit it's a serious allegation, although I had no knowledge of any of it until approximately ten minutes ago." He was talking her language and knew it. He offered her a smile and a shrug. "Just before we convened Mr. Bard was kind enough to tell me he would make this oral motion."

"You're not suggesting that Mr. Bard was—well, lying in the weeds with this, are you?" she asked.

"I'm not suggesting anything, Judge, believe me," he said with great sincerity. "I'm merely trying to explain my situation. I've had five minutes with Detective Barrett but no opportunity to find out anything else about it." He can charm the birds right out of the trees, I thought. An understanding smile blew off Ida's face and perched on his arm. "If I may add this rather obvious comment: Neither the police nor the prosecution is perfect. Mr. Bard was given a forty-eight-page file on Tommy Sherman, the so-called murder book. Some reports might inadvertently have been left out of it."

"You are right," Iron Pants said, smiling at him. "The People aren't perfect. What do you propose, Mr. Bard?"

"We need a hearing," I said, putting my belly into it. "The mug-shot folder is all I know about. Who knows what else they've got I haven't seen? I also believe sanctions should be applied. This Court should not allow the prosecution to make a mockery of its discovery orders. I think you should show the prosecution that you mean it when you tell them to do something."

She sat up straighter, and the line of her lips stretched out like a wire. Good, I thought. If her nostrils start flapping, I've got her. "What do you suggest in the way of sanctions?"

"I think you should preclude the prosecution from putting on any evidence at all about the alleged murder of Tommy Sherman."

"Mr. Williams?"

"Judge, I'm as upset about this as anyone, believe me." He certainly looks upset, I thought. "I'll say this, too: If *I* find out that the prosecution has deliberately and knowingly held exculpatory information back, I'll come in here and ask you to apply those sanctions. My boss—I'm talking about James Trigge now, who is the head of the National Association of Special Prosecutors—would not have it any other way.

"But there's no indication of bad faith here." He gestured toward Wink Barrett, as though to say: "Look at this man. Would he lie?" "As serious as this may be, at this stage of the game I just don't think anyone needs to open a vein and bleed." He smiled up at her. "I think we can avoid a hearing, too. Detective Barrett tells me he thinks he saw a mug-shot folder in the police department file." A halo appeared over Wink's head. "He is very willing to sit down with Mr. Bard at the Long Beach PD office and open up the file. If a photo lineup is there, I'll make sure Mr. Bard gets a copy and finds out who it was shown to and what they said."

"Why wasn't it included in the murder book?" Ida asked.

"I don't know, Judge," Keane said. "Detective Barrett informs me he thought it was."

She relaxed. The line of her mouth softened. "And your position, I take it, is that this prosecutorial failure should simply be overlooked?" I had the peculiar feeling she was flirting with him.

"It certainly isn't being overlooked, Judge." He smiled at her. "I mean, here we are, talking about it. But it seems that all there is here is the inadvertent failure to provide some discovery material—we don't know whether it's exculpatory or not—and I don't know of any case that holds what Mr. Bard asks." He has class, I thought. It probably comes from experience with beating them back with a stick. "He wants to exclude proof of an aggravating factor on that basis. I just think that would be too severe.

"As a matter of fact, I don't even see the need to delay here." He glanced over at me. "I mean, the jury is waiting to get started, and the defense has some witnesses in the hallway. I would be quite willing for them to put their case on first. Let *them* strike the first big blow instead of the People. That ought to be sanction enough. Mr. Bard and I can get together on this other thing tonight." He smiled at me. "Possibly over a beer."

Iron Pants looked hopeful. "Do you really think this situation can be resolved that simply?"

"I do. Mr. Barrett believes it's over there. All that needs to be done is to make a copy."

"Mr. Bard, what counsel says is very sensible. Why don't you take care of it this evening, rather than waste valuable court time?"

The self-proclaimed future attorney general of California was worth his salary, I decided. His side had screwed up, yet I was the one who was on the defensive. "Judge, it needs to be resolved now," I said. "Before either side starts. It could have a real impact on my opening statement and the strategy I employ, all of which has a direct bearing on effective assistance of counsel." I saw a hand go up in the air and realized it was mine. "Who knows what else they have—through inadvertence—forgotten to give me? It's conceivable, for example, that the Sherman homicide connects with the Rhoades homicide. If they *do* connect, there could be a serious question as to whether the jury should reconsider the guilt phase." I glanced at Keane. "We can't settle that over a beer."

"If it please the Court, may I make a suggestion?" Williams asked.

"Yes. Please do."

"Perhaps we should send the jury home, Judge, and bring them back tomorrow." There he goes with that "we" con, I thought. Now he's bonding with the judge. "I don't like to do that to jurors, either, because God knows they give up enough." They vote, too, I thought, which all of us—including God—knew. "But that would provide both Mr. Bard and me the opportunity to go over the police file with the officers and make certain he has everything he's entitled to have. We could report back to you at three o'clock, and if Mr. Bard still thinks he needs a hearing, we'd have time this afternoon to come back into court and argue it."

She looked for all the world like she was thinking it over. Maybe she was. "Very well," she said. "I'm very concerned that the jury is going to get the wrong idea—or perhaps it's the right idea—of justice. But I don't suppose it can be helped." She nodded at Ivan, who went to get them. "We'll excuse them for the remainder of the day. But Mr. Bard, barring something rather extraordinary, we will start tomorrow morning at nine o'clock."

It was there, all right. Six mug shots, booking numbers blanked out, in a file folder; of black guys mainly, although one looked more Puerto Rican than black. Drusus's picture was bottom right. On the back of the folder were three sets of initials, with dates: "AD, 3/19"; "SM, 3/21"; and "LW, 6/15." "What's all this stuff?" I asked, pointing to the initials and dates.

We were standing around a counter on the second floor

of the Police Building: Whitney Lee, Wink Barrett, Keane Williams, and me. The contents of the file the record clerk had brought up were scattered all over the place. Most of the stuff Whitney and I recognized, except for some scraps of paper with notes, two three-by-five cards, and the mug-shot lineup. "Procedure," Wink said, responding to a question of mine. "Whenever the mug-shot folder is shown to a witness, we make the witness put his initials and the date on the back."

"What about a report?" I asked sarcastically. "There's nothing in the murder book about a lineup at all."

Wink kept his cool. "Danforth and Kincaid worked Sherman," he said. "Ask them."

"So the lineup was shown to three people, right?" I asked, excited over the discovery. "Who were they?"

"You're asking the wrong guy. The 'SM' probably Salvadore Mira. Sherman was killed on March eighteenth, right? So they put together a lineup and took it to Mira a couple days later. I don't know who 'AD' is." He rummaged through the file. "Got a three-by-five here—that's Danforth, he writes notes on the damn things, sticks them in the file, confuses everybody—got a name Archie Dock and an address. Maybe that's the 'AD.' Want it?"

"Damn right." I felt pretty good. "Who is 'LW'?"

"Got a June date. *I* don't know."

"Larry Walker," Keane said. "You know, I can use this too. Walker is the eyewitness we have who makes the case. Danforth must have showed him the mug-shot lineup when he talked to him in June."

It's always a noble, uplifting feeling to know you've contributed to the cause of justice by helping the prosecution make its case. "Maybe I can help you some more," I said. "Who is Archie Dock?"

"Beats hell out of me," Barrett said.

"I guess we have a hearing, then," I said, amicably. "You guys are hiding another witness."

"Old Rory ain't gonna like this." A telephone stood on the counter, and Wink picked up the speaker and punched in some numbers.

"What do you want now?" we all heard a voice cry out in anguish.

Wink punched the conference-call mode, which—with Rory Danforth shouting angrily—we didn't need. His voice, ricocheting around the room, was loud enough to echo off the walls. He let it be known he was on vacation and didn't appreciate being bothered by a bunch of shitbirds. That meant Keane Williams. It especially meant Keane Williams, although it included everyone in the Long Beach PD and all the judges in the Superior Court.

"What's with Rory?" I asked.

"I laid a subpoena on him," Keane told me. "He's on standby, and it spoiled his trip to Hawaii. I may need him."

"Sure I'll tell you who Archie Dock is," he shouted. "Is Whitney there?"

"Yeah, man."

"Dock is a little puke who has a CYA record as big as your ass. You know him?"

"Might if I saw him."

"We got a mug shot on him somewhere. Like Salvadore said, there were two people with Drusus when he shot Tommy Sherman. One was Larry Walker, the other was Archie Dock. Kincaid and me made up the mug-shot folder after we talked to Salvadore, and the first person I showed it to was Archie. He ID'd Drusus as the hitter."

Whitney glared at me. "Let me ask him some questions."

"Be my guest."

"Rory, how come you had Drusus in the lineup?"

"Because—oh, yeah. Salvadore's description of the hitter: big black guy, looked like a boxer. That fit Hammer to a T."

"Then how come you didn't make some arrests? Like Archie Dock and Larry Walker for complicity in the murder, and Drusus for the murder?"

"What? You think Archie said like, 'Oh, yeah, you mean the guy me and Larry held so Drusus could shoot?' " He laughed. "He just said he saw it happen. The last I heard, it ain't a crime to be a witness. It's a mistake—like being a cop—but it ain't a crime."

"How come you didn't pick up Drusus?"

"We wanted to make sure we had a case before arresting his ass. That meant more than Dock, and we couldn't find Walker. So we showed the lineup to Salvadore a couple days later—the guy was never home—and all he would say was 'could be.' Then we get the word that both Drusus and Archie Dock are out of town." He laughed again. "Drusus came back, but Dock never did. You know what I think?"

It was fairly obvious what Danforth thought, but Whitney asked him anyway. "What?"

"I think maybe Dock got fed to the fish. I think your boy Drusus extincted a witness."

Keane Williams grinned at me. "Still want a hearing?"

"Rory," I said, aiming my mouth at the telephone. "Jack Bard."

"Yeah. I recognize those soft, low tones. How you doin', Jack S?"

"How come you didn't do any reports on this?"

"Why should I? Can't use any of it." I had a vision of him about to take a bite out of the telephone. "More paperwork now than I can handle. I don't have a secretary."

"How come you waited until June to show the lineup to the other guy? Walker?"

"Couldn't find him is why. Then he got popped on that agg rob, and I went down to the jail to talk to him. I got nothing the first time. He responded with curse words when I asked him about it, if you can believe that."

"When was that?"

"I don't know." Whitney showed me a scrap of paper with a note scribbled on it: "Larry Walker busted 5/6. L.A. county. Go see."

"May sixth?" I asked.

"Yeah, sounds right."

"And no report."

"I don't write down every tiny fart. Just only when somebody has a movement."

"Okay. Then what?" I asked. "Walker changed his mind and wanted to see you?"

"Yeah. It come to him he was about to be tried for a crime—he's not real bright—and he thought he could make a deal."

"What did you do?"

"The usual. I told him if he'd give me something to go to the DA about, I'd see what I could do, but it wasn't up to me to make a deal. Then he spilled his guts."

"Did you talk to the DA?"

"Yeah. Mad Dog." I had a vision of Danforth picking his nose. "Ralphie says, 'You got his statement, right?' and I says, 'Yeah,' so he says, 'So then we don't need to deal with the puke.' "

"Rory, Keane Williams," the boy wonder said. "Who is Ralphie?"

"Ralph Hammond. Mad Dog. He's the reason they had to bring you in." He seemed to spit. "I kind of like Mad Dog, you know? He ain't a fucking politician, for one thing, and don't try to get along with pukes. For another, he won't ever mess up a man's vacation."

"Give me a break," Williams said angrily. "You have your job, and I have mine. Okay?"

"Rory, Whitney," Whitney said.

"I recognize your voice, dude."

Whitney's brown face turned black, but he didn't lose his composure. "How long did you look for Archie Dock?"

"I'm still looking, dude."

"Where?"

"Records search, mainly. His name don't come up, though. I tell you, he's gone."

Wink looked at all of us. "Any more questions?"

"Rory," Williams said, smiling one of those you-know-I-gotcha-big-fella smiles at me. "Two things. First: Did you show Walker the mug-shot lineup?"

Danforth took his time answering. "Yeah, seems to me I did. Is that in my report?"

"No."

"Well, it shoulda been. He ID'd Drusus Church. Bottom right, right?"

Williams beamed. "Thanks."

"What's the other thing?" Danforth asked. "I mean, is there anything else I can do for you, sir? Other than vote for you?"

"Just tell me what you want for Christmas."

I decided not to ask for a hearing.

That night, on the way home, I picked up a bottle of brandy. It was a test. If I opened it, I knew I'd get royally drunk. It was either that or pick out a corner and hide.

I wanted to forget all about Drusus. How had he become my problem? I wondered. I had Mouse and Erin and Robyn's ghost and Carlotta and a ton of clients who would ante up the dough before I talked to them. Drusus hadn't paid me a dime. Neither had his girlfriend or mother or grandmother or any member of his family. His mother tried to give me five hundred dollars, but I didn't take it. It wouldn't even have paid the overhead for two days.

I should have turned him over to the Public Defender, I thought. Instead I'd let myself get embroiled in a problem that would probably add a few new pimples to what was left of the lining of my stomach.

Whitney had surprised me after the session with the cops. No "I told you so" to add some bounce to the doubts that had started to rattle around in my head. Instead, the Mountain came away from his shouting match with Danforth like a hungry panther. At first I thought it was because Danforth kept calling him "dude," which—in Long Beach, at least—has come to mean "nigger." But that wasn't it. He got a mug-shot photo of Archie Dock. I didn't know why Whitney wanted it until we got outside, when he asked, "How did they know Dock and Walker was in on it?"

A very good question. Salvadore Mira's description of Dock had been something like "a tall black kid who ran," and Walker's description was equally vague. Yet Danforth and Kincaid had gone right to Dock and had known about Walker. Had the CI whose name we couldn't get given them some dope on the Sherman kill, too?

I didn't know. It made my head ache. I went into the

kitchen and opened the bottle. Then I put the cork back in and stuck it in a cupboard. I thought of calling Erin, who might be willing to help me through the night, but found a corner and curled up in it, staring at the wall.

After a while it got interesting. I started thinking weird shit, like: Can dogs tell lies? What would people be like if they couldn't make stories up to keep themselves entertained? Do humans shoot each other and then make movies about it, or make movies first and then act them out in real life?

This wasn't the first time I'd huddled in a corner the night before a trial. But it only happened on the cases I didn't make money on, the ones I cared about. I asked myself: Why am I like that? Where did I go wrong? The answer was one I'd heard before. As old and ugly as I've become, I still need to look at myself in the mirror. I like being able to face the Erins of this world, and I like being able to tell my daughter and her kids what I do for a living.

How can a doctor refuse to operate on a patient because he doesn't have Blue Cross? I'd probably have been a disappointment as a doctor, too. But my faith in my "patient" had taken a beating that afternoon. A heavy situation can fog up a person's glasses. Had Drusus really murdered Tommy Sherman? Had Salvadore Mira simply made a mistake?

"I can't, man," I heard the youngster say. "All I got is the truth." One of those rare feelings of bliss blew through me. He's innocent, I thought. It was a rush, the sudden, inexplicable faith that falls on a born-again Christian or lands on you when you know you're in love. He didn't do it. He can hammer, but he doesn't kill. And I'd promised to get him out.

It felt like I was inside a warm, soft bubble. I barely got into bed before falling asleep.

10

When you know the defendant has to testify, the question becomes when. Do you showcase him because he's good or bury him because he's bad? I hadn't yet decided whether to wedge Drusus in between other witnesses—like hiding him under a pile of rocks—or put the spotlight on him.

There was still time to make up my mind. I watched the jurors file into their seats, solemn-faced, eyes averted, as though Drusus had AIDS and they might catch it if they looked at him. Given the worst-case scenario, he wouldn't go on that day. It would take at least one day for the prosecution to put on its case in aggravation, and they had the first act.

Ordinarily, I would have wanted to showcase a defendant like Drusus. He was articulate, open, and, I believed, innocent. He also had the true gentleness of a man of huge strength. The problem I had was this: He would deny it. He would not show remorse because he hadn't done anything wrong. He would look them in the eye and tell them what they didn't want to hear.

"Mr. Bard?"

I looked around but didn't see anything. Am I hearing voices? I wondered.

"It's me, Mr. Bard."

"Oh." No-name. She can sit right in front of a person and not be seen. "Yeah."

"Carlotta? Your secretary? She'd like you to call before you go back to your office tonight. I—I think she wants you to pick something up." She smiled. And then damned if she didn't disappear.

"Are counsel ready to proceed?" I heard Iron Pants ask.

We were. Keane Williams wore a dark—almost charcoal—brown suit, as befitted a prosecutor with such a heavy responsibility. I wore lighter brown and a striped green tie with no dolphins. Wink Barrett, lounging next to Williams in the attitude of lead counsel, had on a pinstriped gray top-of-the-line thread system from Sears, and Drusus—wearing only a soft gold-colored cotton shirt—looked like what he might have been in another life: a king.

"Very well. The record will show that the jurors are assembled and present, the defendant is here, and the lawyers are here. We are in session." Iron Pants turned toward the jury. "We are about to begin the second phase of this proceeding," she said, as though talking to old friends. "You already have an idea of what to expect, but in just a moment I will read you a preliminary instruction. Later, of course, after all the evidence is in, you will get your final instructions." She glanced at the papers in front of her. "What I tell you now is designed to give you a clearer picture of the total court proceedings and how this phase fits in."

She smiled. Ida has a very nice smile, I thought. She could be such a bitch that it always surprised me when she flashed that wonderful smile. "First," she went on, "let me convey to all of you my appreciation for your cooperation and service. There have been delays followed by vague explanation, and you haven't complained. There may have been a few grumbles, but I didn't even hear that. Then yesterday you arrived in the afternoon and waited around for perhaps an hour, only to be sent home." She raised a shoulder. "In spite of that you have returned today and appear very attentive. It is your willingness to serve, to conscientiously play your part, that allows our system of law to work."

She adjusted her glasses. Her nose must be different than mine, I thought, because her glasses would stay in that position until she adjusted them out of it. Probably a deformity of some kind held them in place. A wart, I thought. It's only people with perfect noses that have trouble. "Are you ready?" she asked, holding the papers she would read from in her hands. The jurors looked at one another and at her, nodding. "The issues presented at this, the second phase of the trial, are quite different from the ones you previously wrestled with, so please listen carefully."

She began reading:

"It is the law of the State of California that the penalty for a defendant found guilty of murder in the first degree, in any case where the special circumstance alleged has been found to be true, shall be either death or confinement in the state prison for life without possibility of parole. You have found the defendant guilty of first-degree murder and have found the special circumstance to be true. Therefore, you must now determine which of those penalties shall be imposed on this defendant.

"In determining which penalty to impose"—she looked up, departing from the script—"and to remind you of your choices, they are: one, death, or two, life without possibility of parole." Her face bent over the paper. "I'll start over here. In determining which penalty to impose, you shall consider all of the evidence which has been received during any part of the trial in this case. Therefore, you shall consider the evidence which you have already received during the first, or guilt, phase, as well as any evidence you may receive during this, the second, or penalty, phase." She looked up. "Do I make myself clear?"

The mood of the jurors changed. It was no longer old friends getting together for a drink. It had become serious. Two of them had their eyes closed—clamped shut was more like it. The rest watched with intensity. Ida had solicited responses and gotten some: a few affirmative nods of the head. "Good." She continued to read. "You shall consider, take into account, and be guided by the following factors if they are applicable. Some of these may not apply, but I'm giving you all that might possibly apply, depending upon the evidence that's later produced.''

She isn't a bad-looking woman, I thought; and for a Deukmeijian appointment—gentrified aristocrats, most of them, bent on protecting themselves from riffraff—she's not a bad judge. As she began ticking off the so-called factors in aggravation and mitigation I wondered what was going through her woman's heart.

The fingers of her left hand counted the factors. ''The circumstances of the crime of which the defendant was convicted and the existence of any special circumstance found to be true.'' Her index finger flipped up. ''The presence or absence of other criminal activity by the defendant''—her middle finger joined in—''apart from the crime for which he has been tried in the present proceedings, which involved the use or attempted use of force or violence or the express or implied threat of force or violence.'' A couple of jurors appeared dazed, but the rest of them pretended to understand. She raised her fourth finger. ''The presence or absence of any prior felony conviction, apart from the crime for which the defendant was tried in the present proceedings.''

I stopped listening. Out of the corner of my eye I watched one of the jurors shift her gaze from the judge to Drusus. I wondered what she saw. He sat with an alert, dispassionate attitude, like a medical student watching an operation.

''The age of the defendant at the time of the crime.'' Ida had used all her fingers and waved her hand. Drusus turned his face to me. His eyes softened, and he smiled. But when she started up again he resumed that odd attitude of intellectual involvement.

I fought an urge to shout obscenities, like the crazies you see charging up and down the streets crying out in anguish at who knows what. The prosecution wanted to kill this man! What had gone wrong with the world?

Keane had made a point of leaving his offer open until

court started that morning. He had been confident we'd take it, especially after the disclosures at the police department. A friendly war-ace attitude—pip-pip old chap and all that rot—had kept the two of us on speaking terms, but that morning the atmosphere changed. "Jack, I like you," he'd said ominously. "Please. Take the deal. I'm very good at what I do, and once we start the offer is withdrawn. I play Pac-Man for keeps, and I'm telling you. It will get ugly and you'll get blown off the screen."

"Then give me a big kiss now," I'd said. He didn't think that was funny.

"—any sympathetic or other aspect of the defendant's character or history that the defendant offers as a basis for a sentence less than death, whether or not related to the offense for which he is here on trial." She was about done with her recitation. "And finally, you must disregard any jury instruction given to you in the guilt phase of this trial which conflicts, in principle, with anything I have just told you."

She laid the paper down and looked at them. She has nice eyes, too, I thought. You would never guess that an attractive woman with a lovely smile and nice eyes, who is a judge in the Superior Court in Long Beach, could be such a bitch. Of course, I thought, not everyone feels as I do. Her children might even call her Mommy. "At the end of the trial you will be getting more instructions," she told them, easing that burden somewhat with a show of teeth. "What I have read to you are those which hopefully will help you at this stage of the proceeding."

She turned toward the pit. "The attorneys will now be afforded an opportunity to make an opening statement, just as they were during the earlier phase. However, this time it will address this new issue of penalty rather than the previous issue of guilt. Mister Williams?"

"Thank you, Your Honor."

Keane no longer looked like Mel Torme. This time around he was wrapped in a different image: the penetrating, rock-hard honesty of Spencer Tracy. At least that was the way he looked to the over-forty folk. I don't think anyone plays the part of an honest lawyer now. Once he started speaking I knew he'd been there before. This was obviously not his first death-penalty case.

"Members of the jury, Mr. Bard"—he glanced a harsh moment at Drusus but didn't acknowledge him—"as Judge Mather told you, we now begin the second phase of this trial. Although it's a different issue, it gets proved up the same way. The laws of evidence still apply—the law itself still applies—but the evidence my esteemed counterpart and I will put before you is aimed at another target."

That's a nice comparison, I thought. He does a good job. Put a few more lines in his face, and when he runs for attorney general I might even vote for him. His voice had undergone a subtle change, however. He was still a warrior, although not a knight in shining armor as before. Now he was a battle-hardened veteran of modern war, someone the People could count on to do whatever it took to win.

"It works like this," he said, moving out from behind the lectern. "The People will be allowed to put on evidence to prove as many factors in aggravation as we can. Of course, we've already put on a lot of that evidence. Everything you've heard to this point." He smiled bravely at them. "The brutal shooting of Kingsley Rhoades and the cold-blooded, calculated way he did it should now be used by you for a different purpose. Don't think of it now as proof of murder. Now it's proof of an aggravating factor as it relates to this new issue: penalty."

He even stood straighter, I thought. He moved on the balls of his feet, walking pantherlike toward the panel. "That isn't all the evidence you will get from me on this issue of penalty. I will show you other factors in aggravation, too." With one hand on the rail before Juror Number Ten he turned his face toward Drusus and looked at him without pity. "Among other things, I will show you how he murdered another man."

I decided to nip that personal pitch in the bud. "Objection, Judge. *He* won't show the jury anything. The evidence could."

"He's right, Mr. Williams," Iron Pants said apologetically. "I must ask you to phrase your statements with more care."

That gave this torch the chance to blaze with more passion. "Very well." He turned his back toward me. His manner invited the jury to share in his contempt for me, for the defendant, and for anything that stood in the way of justice. "When the prosecution has finished presenting its evidence, Mr. Bard will be given the opportunity to prove factors in mitigation."

Some prosecutors get so close to the jurors that they scare them. Come on, baby, I said to myself, trying to send a little message to his brain that would encourage him to get in their face. But he knew where the line was. He radiated vengeance layered over with a coat of righteousness. He let the jury know they were Christians, the same as he was, and you knew if you were a Christian, you had nothing to worry about.

"When the evidence is in," he continued, walking away from them, "you will get another set of instructions from the judge. She will tell you how to use those factors that have been proved. How to apply them, under the law, to the issue of penalty. That's when you will decide what penalty to impose on this defendant." He tossed his head at Drusus but didn't look at him.

"Obviously, neither side will try to prove or disprove all of the factors the judge read." He returned to the lectern. "I'll tell you the ones I think you need to remember, and Mr. Bard can either add to or subtract from that list." His knuckles showed. "You should remember those factors you already know about, the ones having to do with the murder you already know he committed." He paused, giving them time to absorb his words. "There may be a little new evidence offered regarding that crime, but not much. What more do you need?"

He looked ten years older, a whole lot wiser, much more mature. "You will discover that Kingsley Rhoades was the defendant's second victim, not his first. He shot and killed another man—Mister Tommy Sherman—about one month before murdering Rhoades." His mouth drew a hard line.

"I hope it is clear to you that this new evidence of another murder won't be offered for the purpose of finding him guilty of that murder. Instead, you will use it as it relates to this new issue of penalty, to assist you in deciding which of the two penalties to impose."

I could have kept that out. He was explaining the law, which is up to the judge. But if I screamed and hollered over it, the judge might explain it in the same words. Then how would I look? "Tommy Sherman was also a black man," the champion of the People continued, "who died after being shot twice, in the chest, from a pistol in the hands of this defendant. You will get the details from an eyewitness. That eyewitness is presently in prison, but he'll be here, in this courtroom, to tell you what he saw. He will describe in detail how this defendant shot and killed another man in cold blood."

The jurors didn't move. They maintained their impartial attitudes, but I would swear their faces turned to stone. "You will also discover that this defendant—who was not even twenty years old when he was arrested for the murder of Kingsley Rhoades—has a record. That will be a part of our proof, too. He committed a burglary when he was eighteen and served eight months in prison because of it. Interestingly enough, you will learn that he was armed when he committed that burglary. With a gun. Two factors in aggravation, you could say, for the price of one: a felony conviction, and more on this point of the use of force and violence, or implied force and violence."

Californians are more sophisticated than jurors in other states, I've been told. That's because in La-La land they've been bombarded with show-biz technique. It's hard to know if that's a cultural advantage, but at least they learn the difference between a bad act and a good one. The NASP prosecutor was a very good act. The inflections in his voice, the expressions in his eyes, the attitudes of his hands and body conveyed his message with more eloquence than words: The man should die. He does not deserve to live.

"Of course, to prove a man committed a burglary with

a gun and spent eight months in prison for it—you might think, so what? But after you meet the family that was invaded by the defendant and his partner, and learn of their terror, and possibly experience as they did the awful danger and fear of confrontation with a man who would as soon kill them as look at them . . ." His voice trailed off. He brought his head around and examined Drusus like a fruit farmer confronting a medfly. "What more do you need?" he asked, sitting down.

Iron Pants waited a dramatic moment, then looked at me. "Mr. Bard?"

I kind of stumbled up, if that's possible. I still wasn't sure what I would do. There is a real danger in not following the prosecution's opening statement with one of your own because an uncorrected first impression, like a statue made out of clay, gets hard if you don't get your fingers in it right away.

But for one thing, I didn't want to tip my hand. The Long Beach Police Department might arrive on Salvadore Mira's front doorstep with a mug-shot folder and fuck him up. "If it please the Court, I'll reserve the open."

Ida gave me one of those perfectly impartial judgelike looks. "The defense has reserved its opening statement," she announced for the benefit of the jury and the record. "You may make one at a later time, Mr. Bard, if you choose to do so."

She nodded at Keane. "Mr. Williams, please call your first witness."

11

Dr. Graham Wallotan, the prosecution's first witness, climbed back on the stand. He nodded familiarly at the jurors, as though confident they would remember him. He had testified during the guilt phase, then regarding the body of Kingsley Rhoades; now he would discuss the corpse of Tommy Sherman. "You are the same Dr. Wallotan who testified earlier, are you not, sir?" Keane Williams asked.

The well-fed crew-cut pathologist who wore glasses with steel rims looked like what he was: an engineer, trained in anatomy instead of physics. His approach to the field of medicine was like that of a physicist who has become a rocket scientist. "I am," he said, settling himself comfortably into his chair and smiling.

"And you are a deputy medical examiner employed by the coroner of Los Angeles County?"

"That's correct."

"This jury has previously heard your qualifications, and you've already been accepted as an expert in the field of human pathology. Dr. Wallotan, on March nineteen of last year, did you perform an autopsy on . . ."

He had. His testimony followed the report I had in my hand: two gunshot wounds in the chest, either one of which would have been fatal in that both passed through the victim's heart. One of them also tore a hole in Sherman's lung. Neither bullet was recovered.

Williams started a line of questions I could have objected to but didn't. If I had, he'd have called in another expert. "You have had experience with trauma caused by the infliction of gunshots, have you not?" He smiled ironically at the obvious understatement.

"Yes."

"Can you state, in your opinion, whether the wounds you observed in the body of this human being, identified to you as Tommy Sherman, could have come from a thirty-eight-caliber weapon?"

Wallotan obviously was ready for the question. "I can. From the visual observations I made, which included an examination of the point of entry of the projectiles and their point of departure, and an evaluation of their relative impact—that is to say, the explosive effect of their intrusion into the body—in my opinion, they could have been made by a thirty-eight-caliber weapon."

"You don't mean, of course, that they necessarily had to have been inflicted by a thirty-eight-caliber weapon, do you?"

"Not at all. But it was something larger than a twenty-two magnum, for example, and smaller than—well—a cannonball."

He accompanied his remark with a thin little smile, but there was very little laughter, and Williams froze him with a glance. What Wallotan had not realized was that the special prosecutor's attitude had changed. Keane had given no hint of conviviality as he had the first time around, but Wallotan hadn't picked up on the difference. This time Williams was deadly serious, as though conditioning the jury to do what he would later demand of them. He pulled three large photographs out of a file and purposefully strode toward the witness. "Will you identify these photographs for us, sir?"

Wallotan did. They had been taken at an operating room at the medical examiner's office just before the autopsy of the man identified to him as Tommy Sherman. One was of his nude body, stretched full-length on a gurney. Another showed Sherman—still on the gurney—from the waist up, and the third was a close-up of his face. Sherman had not been a bad-looking fellow: young, muscled, nicely styled hair, clean complexion. His skin was the color of treated redwood, and although his eyes were closed, he seemed to frown. He had one hole under his left nipple and another in the center of his chest. The photographs were admitted in evidence and passed to the jurors. "Your witness, Mr. Bard."

I played with Wallotan on cross-examination. "You indicated on direct that the bullets that killed Mr. Sherman were larger than a twenty-two and smaller than a cannonball. Do you recall that testimony?"

"Yes, I do." His manner had grown serious, to match that of the special prosecutor.

"Of course, if a cannonball were to pass through someone's chest, there wouldn't be anything left to examine, would there?"

"It's doubtful. That may have been a poor choice of words."

"Oh?" I asked. "It may have been a poor choice of words?"

"Yes."

"Then why did you choose them, sir?"

He appeared suitably embarrassed about it. "I don't know."

"Were you trying to be amusing?"

Williams glared at me but didn't move. "I'm not sure," the contrite witness said.

"Well. Are you sure of anything? Withdraw that," I said quickly, before he had a chance to tell me all the things he was sure of. "Is it that you've examined so many bodies and seen so many people with holes in them that it's become humorous?"

"Objection, Judge," Williams said contemptuously. "Argumentative and calls for a conclusion."

Good, I thought. "It goes to the credibility of the witness."

Ida did not look amused. "I'll allow it. But please move on, Mr. Bard."

I didn't have much to move on to. I tried to suggest that the shooter must have been a short person, based on the height of the victim—5'10"—and the location of the entry wounds. The good doctor fielded my suggestions with the obvious. It would depend on where Mr. Sherman had stood in relation to the murderer and how the killer held the weapon, he said. If Mr. Sherman had been on his toes, for example—not an uncommon reaction when faced with a sudden threat—or leaning backwards in avoidance, the weapon could quite easily have been held by a taller person. Or if the killer had "shot from the hip," so to speak, the entry wounds and the angle made by the projectiles as they tore through Mr. Sherman's vital organs would have been consistent with a tall killer.

To the prosecution's witnesses, victims always have names, even though defendants don't. That's to personalize the tragedy to the jury and depersonalize the monster who did it. The defense witnesses are usually just the opposite. They speak reverently of the defendant and tend to regard the victim as a mere caricature whom no one will miss. "What a great and wondrous game," old Charley Wallace used to say. "I wonder if any of the magnificent posturing we engage in makes a particle's worth of difference to the jury."

I got Wallotan to agree that the distance between the end of the barrel and the point of entry had to have been more than two feet. "In other words, the person who pulled the trigger wasn't on top of the victim, was he? He might even have been thirty or forty feet away. Correct?"

"There was nothing on the person of Mr. Sherman, or in his clothing, to suggest otherwise," Wallotan said. "He wore a thin white shirt—quite clean, I might add, as though recently laundered—and there were no traces of lead or powder or any discoloration whatever on it. At least that I could see with the naked eye. I did not suggest that it be examined under a microscope, but it may have been."

"What about his skin?" I asked.

"There was no stippling or tattooing to his skin."

"And that suggests to you that the muzzle of the weapon was more than two feet away?"

"Correct."

The prosecutor should have objected, because Wallotan had not qualified as a firearms or ballistics expert and should not be giving opinions on such subjects. I hoped his mistake would loop around and smack him in the eye. I always like to tighten things up as much as possible because you never know where you might develop an inconsistency. I made a note to myself: "Get eyewitness to agree that muzzle of gun *next* to Sherman. Maybe killer put it in Sherman's ear!" The doctor—with the solemn dignity of a funeral director—departed from the stand.

One of the uniforms who responded to the call got up next. I didn't know him, but as one of the officers that had rolled out to the scene that night, he had been included on the witness list.

Most of the cops in Long Beach are Anglo in spite of the fact that more than half of the citizens aren't. This guy was typical. He had short blond hair, stood over six feet, and looked like he'd played football in high school—not very long ago. He sat at attention and—except for the fact that his uniform was blue—appeared young and idealistic, like Canadian Mounties in movies I'd seen as a kid.

"Your name please, for the record?" Williams asked.

"Kevin Finley, sir."

"A year ago on March nineteenth, what was your occupation?"

"I was a patrol officer with the Long Beach Police Department."

This may have been his first time in the chair, but he had obviously taken a class in how to testify. He looked over at the jury as he talked—they teach them to do that, and it takes some of them two or three months to get over it. I checked him out like a quarterback watching movies of a rookie cornerback, figuring out how to take him apart. I wondered how far Ida would let me go with him.

He identified the photographs taken by Wallotan as the man whose body had been on the sidewalk on Cherry

Street that night. As he did so he continued to face the jury and charm them with game-show-host affability. Williams couldn't do anything about it. He got what he needed from the witness—a cop at the scene who saw the body—and turned him over for cross-examination.

"Good morning, Officer Finley," I said.

"Good morning, sir."

"You are quite sure these are photographs of the man you saw that night—rather, that morning?"

"Oh, yes, sir, no question." He smiled at the jury.

"What time did the call come in to go to that location?"

"Approximately oh-three hundred, sir. That is, three o'clock A.M."

"And that was when the dispatcher, the Long Beach dispatcher, told you to go to that location?"

"Yes, sir."

"These pictures are of a naked man. Was the man you saw on the sidewalk naked?"

Finley smiled agreeably. "Not at all, sir. He had clothes on when I saw him."

I fumbled with what could have been a report. "Light brown slacks and a bright red cotton shirt?"

The witness looked uncertain, but only for a moment. "I believe that's right, sir."

"Believe? Aren't you certain?" I demanded, waving the paper.

"Yes." He blushed slightly but looked me in the eye, then smiled at the jury.

"Light brown slacks and a red cotton shirt. A grimy red cotton shirt. Right?"

"Yes, sir."

I nodded and placed the paper on the lectern, as though his statement confirmed the report. "The dispatcher sent you to that location because of a telephone call about a shooting?"

"Objection, Judge. Hearsay."

Ida looked pained. "I'm going to allow it," she said.

Finley smiled at the judge, then at me. "Do I answer the question?"

"Yes," I said.

"A man—a Spanish fellow—called nine-one-one and reported a shooting."

"Now this Spanish fellow. Did he see it happen?"

"Objection, Judge," Keane said. "How can this witness testify as to what another witness saw?"

"Mister Williams, sit down. The rules of evidence are relaxed at this stage of the proceeding, and I see no harm to either side here." She glanced at Finley. "Overruled."

Finley glanced at Keane, as though for guidance.

"Do you need help with your answer, Officer?" I asked him.

"Oh, no, sir. That's what he said, sir."

"So you believe this Spanish person saw it happen, right?"

"Yes, sir."

"Do you know his name?"

"No, sir."

"Does the name Salvadore Mira ring a bell?"

He thought a moment. "No, it doesn't, sir."

"Could that have been the name of the Spanish fellow who you believe saw this happen, and who called nine-one-one?"

"Judge—" Keane started.

"Yes. You've gone too far, Mr. Bard," Iron Pants said. "That question will not be allowed."

I smiled as though she had ruled in my favor. "Thank you. Officer Finley, did you see a Spanish person on the scene?"

"I—I can't recall."

"Did you interview anyone on the scene? In particular, did you interview a person by the name of Salvadore Mira?"

"No, sir. I didn't do either."

"I see. You just—well, stood around?"

"I stabilized the crime scene, sir."

"Why? Was it in danger of tipping over?"

He smiled good-naturedly. "That's just an expression, sir."

A Lingering Doubt

I was tempted to ask him why he kept looking at the jury, but my sense was they liked him better than me. I'd gotten some good stuff out of him and let go. "Save your grandstanding for clear losers," Charley Wallace cautioned. "You might impress some sucker with bucks even as you go down the toilet. Otherwise, quit when you're ahead."

Thanks, Charley.

On redirect the special prosecutor—still in his new role as a slashing advocate of justice—gave a lesson in the art of advocacy. I smiled through most of it and blushed through the rest. "Officer, during his examination of you Mr. Bard picked up a piece of paper. Did you see him do that?"

"Yes, sir, I did."

"That happened when he was asking you questions about the clothing worn by the victim in this case, Mr. Sherman, didn't it?"

Oh, dear, I thought. I'd better interrupt. "Objection, Judge. Leading."

It didn't do any good. "I'll rephrase, then," Keane Williams said. "When, in the course of your testimony, did Mr. Bard pick up that piece of paper?"

Kevin Finley looked my way and smiled in distress. He knows I tricked him, I thought. "I believe when he asked me what Mr. Sherman had on."

"Did you think Mr. Bard had a report of some kind in his hand, a report that described the clothing worn by Mr. Sherman?"

"Yes, I did."

"Do you know Mr. Bard personally?"

"No, sir, I don't."

"But you know his occupation, don't you?"

"Yes, sir, I do. He's an attorney."

"When you are asked questions by attorneys in a trial, what is your expectation of the attorneys?"

"Objection, Judge," I said, trying to sound righteous. "Aren't we a little far afield here? What difference does any of this make?"

"Mr. Williams?"

"Your Honor, the rules of evidence in this phase are not as exacting as they are in the guilt phase. I believe Mr. Bard may have led the witness, through a tactic, to make a misstatement. This won't take long."

Ida has never forgiven me for dumping her in the *Henderson* case when she was a DA. "You may proceed."

Finley didn't know what to do, so Williams helped him out. "Officer, were you expecting trickery or chicanery or tactics on the part of Mr. Bard?"

"No, sir, I was not."

"When you answered the question posed by him regarding the kind of clothing worn by Mr. Sherman, your testimony was based on your expectation of Mr. Bard's honesty, rather than your memory?"

I could have objected, but it wouldn't have done any good. I felt foolish, like the villain in the melodrama who says "Curses. Foiled again."

Finley sighed. "That's right, sir."

"Officer Finley, do you remember what Mr. Sherman's body had on that morning when you saw him lying dead on the sidewalk?"

He looked like Tom Cruise doing his absolute best to tell the truth. "I can't honestly say, sir. But it wasn't a red shirt. I believe it was light in color."

"Have you ever been examined by Mr. Bard before?"

"No, sir."

"Perhaps you'll be more careful if you are again."

"Most definitely, sir."

"Thank you. No further questions."

I couldn't read the expressions on the faces of the jurors, but I imagined I could feel their vibes. They didn't hate me. They wanted to know how I'd handle it. "Officer Finley," I said, standing up but not going to the lectern, "Mr. Williams has characterized my holding up a piece of paper as trickery or chicanery. Did you hear him do that?"

"Yes."

"Would you agree, sir, that perhaps it could also be characterized as testing your credibility as a witness?"

We got into a verbal wrestling match that filled at least

three pages of transcript before Iron Pants cut it off. Finley will be a better man, I'm sure. I personally don't expect to change.

Tommy Sherman's mother was next. Why do murder victims always have mothers? I watched a large woman wearing a corset climb painfully into the box. My liberal do-gooder heart did a small flip. It was obvious she had arthritis and had spent much of her life on her knees cleaning other people's kitchens.

She was ready to cry when she took the stand, and in no time at all the special prosecutor had her weeping buckets. He showed her the photographs of her son that had been taken at the medical examiner's office. As she identified his remains she managed a few hateful glares at Drusus. "The only thing worse than a mother is a grandmother," old Charley said. I let her go without asking any questions.

A jury trial is not structured like a three-act play, even though it has some moments of drama. I knew what the prosecution would do next. I knew how I would attempt to prevent it. I even knew how the judge would rule so that, in the end, it would get done.

I decided to drag it out as long as I could. The special prosecutor wasn't fun anymore, nor was his advisory witness, Wink Barrett. It was as though I was being punished for my part in turning down their magnanimous offer. They looked over me and under me, but not at me. I had become a piece of wood they needed to see around. To tell the truth, it felt better that way: more natural. Like most liberals—even though most of us won't admit it—I really enjoy open hatred.

There was also a practical reason for trying to toss as much gum between the gears of justice as I could: Whitney Lee. He needed all the time I could give him. Giving the system lockjaw is always more fun when you can feel righteous about it.

"Approach the sidebar?" Williams asked after helping Tommy's mother off the stand. The tears in the courtroom hadn't even dried.

"You may," Ida allowed.

In a whispered conversation Williams explained the problem. His next witness—who had actually seen the defendant gun down Tommy Sherman, he claimed—might refuse to testify on the grounds that it could tend to incriminate him. "I have been empowered by the district attorney's office to request this Court to grant him immunity for any crime he may have committed at that time. However, I believe this should be done out of the presence of the jury . . ." blah blah blah.

Iron Pants hates delay. I saw her mouth harden, but she knew she wouldn't get any help from me. She will go with the prosecutor, I thought, knowing he will get it done as quickly as possible. "When do you suggest I tell the jury to return?" she asked, her face down so the jurors wouldn't even know who she was talking to.

"Tomorrow, Judge," I said in a low voice. "I anticipate a fairly long argument."

"With all due respect to Mr. Bard's position, Your Honor, I don't believe we need to lose the rest of the day." Spencer Tracy couldn't have done it any better. "If they're back here by two-thirty, I can almost guarantee we'll be ready for testimony in front of the jury."

"Do you anticipate a *Green* type situation?" she asked.

"Yes. Complicated by *Williams,* but easily cured. Granting the witness immunity won't take any longer than it takes to bring him in, lay a foundation, and say the words." When he whispers he sounds more like Henry Fonda, I thought. "We don't need briefs, or much argument either, unless some new law developed overnight. I've been through the procedure several times. I'm sure Mr. Bard has, too, and it is my understanding the Court has more experience along these lines than either Mr. Bard or myself, having conducted the hearings both as a prosecutor and as a judge."

As I watched Ida beam at him I considered anointing his head with oil and lighting it. Every judge likes to hear others acknowledge how experienced they are. "I am familiar with the procedure," she admitted glowingly. "Mr. Bard,

I agree with Mr. Williams," she whispered. "It is eleven o'clock now. Surely all of this can be finished by two-thirty."

"He'll need a lawyer."

Keane ducked his head low, like the quarterback in the huddle. "Three lawyers—members in good standing of the Long Beach bar—are waiting in the hall," he said. He had thought of everything. "Any one of them can confer with the witness and advise him of his rights."

"Who are they?"

He gave names: a kiss-ass, a dodo, and a pretty good lawyer. "Jack, choose one," Iron Pants ordered.

I picked the dodo. If I got lucky, she might make a mess of it.

We went back to our tables. "I'm sorry, ladies and gentlemen," Ida announced, blessing them with an understanding smile. "It appears we will have a short delay. What it will mean for you is a long lunch. What it will mean for the attorneys and the Court is a working lunch. Please don't discuss the case with anyone; not even among yourselves. And please return to the jury room at two-twenty P.M. today. Until that time, remain away from the courtroom area." She nodded at Ivan. "You are excused until two-twenty."

We waited until they were gone.

I knew I wouldn't make a liar out of the boy wonder, so I made it easy for him instead. If we weren't going to start until 2:30, I decided I could make better use of the time than arguing a point I couldn't win. They brought Larry Walker in through a side door and led him to the witness box.

A thin man with sunken cheeks and hollow eyes, he smiled when he saw Drusus, as though they were friends— which they were not. "Hey, man," he said, raising his cuffed hands in a wave. "Don' worry 'bout nothin' from me, man. They tryin' to run a bad scene here, but I ain't gonna say shit."

The court reporter had stood up to stretch, but when Walker started talking she plopped back in her chair and frantically rolled paper in her little gadget. "Are we on the record?" I asked, watching her fingers catch up with all the conversation. "Judge, we aren't on the record, are we?"

"Of course we are, Mr. Bard."

"I ask the remarks we just heard be stricken, Judge. The man hasn't even been sworn!"

"Denied."

The court reporter waited patiently for the next bit of drama. Walker raised his hand and took the oath. But it didn't even take five minutes for Williams to lay the foundation, ask a couple of questions, and have the man refuse to answer. Gladys Zabriski, attorney at law, was directed by the Court to confer with Walker and report back when ready to proceed. Being a dodo-head, it took her exactly the same amount of time it would have taken either of the others. They were back in fifteen minutes.

He still refused to answer on the grounds it would tend to incriminate him, and Keane made his little speech. Two seconds later Iron Pants granted him immunity from prosecution. With it went his right to refuse to answer, because he could no longer incriminate himself. Poor old Larry didn't quite know what to do. He still refused to answer questions about what he'd seen, so Ida threatened him with contempt. Another short recess while dodo-head told him what that was all about.

I shouldn't call Gladys names. She was a microbiologist before going to law school and even wrote a book on the subject. She's a very good scientist, I've heard, but there has to be some slippage in her brain. Why else would she give up what she had to be a lawyer?

"If it please the Court," Gladys said before Ivan brought Walker back in. "I've advised him of his rights, but he has indicated he still won't testify. May I also add something?" she timidly asked.

Iron Pants glared at her. "That is entirely up to you."

Ida cannot abide a timid lawyer, especially when the lawyer is a woman. "If I may say this?" Not a good start, Gladys, I thought. Ida will land in the pit of your stomach.

"I have not advised him one way or the other on the question of whether or not he should testify."

"Then what have you been doing?" Ida demanded, leaning over the bench.

Gladys got smaller. "I've told him what to expect?" Her statement came off as though asking the Court for help. She sounded uncertain about what she should do.

Iron Pants glared sternly at the shrinking woman, then looked away. "Very well. There isn't much I have to threaten him with unfortunately. He's in prison on an armed robbery, isn't he, Mr. Williams? A fairly long haul?"

"Eleven years, Judge."

"Is it your position that the *Green* case applies?" she asked the prosecutor.

"It is, Judge."

"What is your position, Mr. Bard?"

I was tempted to save time and waive argument but took a pass at it. "*Green* only applies where a witness is available to testify but won't. Where the witness in effect says, 'The hell with you guys, I'm not going to say anything, and I don't care what you do to me.' " I pushed my glasses back. "*Williams* held that the *Green* rule does not apply when the witness—even though present in court—refuses to testify on the grounds of self-incrimination. The *Williams* court said, 'Look. When someone claims a constitutional privilege, then—even though he's physically present in court—he's unavailable.' "

"I know that, Mr. Bard. But the witness here has been granted immunity," Ida said impatiently. "It appears to me he *is* available. Please address the issue."

"Judge, we all know what Mr. Walker's real problem is," I said. "If he testifies, when he goes back to Pelican Bay someone will shove a darning needle, or the sharpened handle of a toothbrush, through his ribs. His real reason for refusing to testify is that if he does, it will kill him. Doesn't he have the right—the constitutional right—to save his own life?" I watched her eyes roll around in her head. "He's unavailable, Judge. The *Williams* case applies, and the special prosecutor should not be permitted to '*Green*' him.''

"Rebuttal, Mr. Williams?"

He complimented my ingenuity but pointed out that since the *Green* case had not been overruled that morning, it was still the law.

Ida agreed, naturally. "That didn't take long, Mr. Bard," she said, getting up after making her ruling. "We will start promptly at two-thirty. We are in recess."

I turned toward the counsel table and saw Drusus, who was looking at me. "We've got them just where we want them," I said.

He smiled. "You mean, like, overconfident?"

"Right."

Godzilla didn't need to tie all that chain around him just to take him down to 3D, but he did. Drusus had a peculiar light in his eye. "You know something, Jack? I think I get it."

"I'll be right down," I told him. "Don't say a word."

He continued smiling but looked strange, like he was about to become one with a cloud. I didn't like his expression at all. "No. You're supposed to see Whitney, right? Don't worry, man, what I got will keep. You go on and do what you have to do."

"What's going on, Drusus?"

"Nothin', man. Really." He started shuffling away. "See you in court."

When I got to the office Carlotta gave me a number. "It's Whitney. He's got something really hot."

"What?" I sat down and started dialing.

"Archie Dock."

12

Whitney. Are you there or aren't you?"

It took a moment for a whispered reply. "I'm here man."

"Where?" I looked at my watch: almost one o'clock. In an hour and a half I'd be back in court.

"My car. Watts. Tryin' not to look like a cop."

"Why should that be hard? You're not a cop."

"I used to be. Kind of like an accent, man. It's hard to lose the look, especially when you're doin' a stakeout."

I envisioned him sitting low in his car—a classic cream-colored 1985 Lincoln Continental—sighting his target over the line of the long hood, like Daniel Boone taking aim down the barrel of a rifle. "Archie Dock?"

"Yeah. I had him on the phone, but he hung up."

"Fill me in."

He did. For three hundred and twenty dollars—enough to keep his contact blasted for the rest of the day—the onetime family man ex-reliable informant had arranged for Archie Dock to call him up. Dock had done so two hours ago but hung up when he found out what Whitney wanted. But some background sound had leaked over the wire before the click and buzz, enough to let Whitney know where the call had come from. "Ivories, that black-ass jazz joint off the old Compton road? Lenny Piersall comes by every morning he's in town with his horn, him and Venus X jam around and laugh, tryin' to make each other feel good, which both of them need since they got clean. They just give all that music away."

"Are you sure it was Dock who called?"

"If it wasn't, it was somebody who knew his date of birth, where he lived a year ago, and the names of his folks."

"Is he in there now?" I asked.

"I would be if I was him. But I don't know."

"Why don't you go in and see?"

"I'm kind of conspicuous, you know, don't want to get him runnin'. I want him where I can sit on him. Shhh." I heard soft movement, as though he shifted his weight. "It's Archie. I'm checkin' out." He hung up.

I sat for a moment, staring at the telephone, deciding what to do. Lawyers have a different perspective than detectives because a fact is worthless to a lawyer unless it can be proved in court. I now had good, solid, reliable information that Archie Dock—who had witnessed the shooting of Tommy Sherman—was in Watts, within thirty miles of Long Beach. What should I do with it? File an affidavit with the court and move for a continuance? Did I want the prosecution to know where he was? They could have a cop pick him up. All my side could do was lay a subpoena on him.

The problem was this: How bad did I want him? What would Archie Dock do for my case? According to Rory Danforth, Dock had put his finger on Drusus. Hadn't I already done enough for those guys by giving them the mug-shot folder with Larry Walker's initials? Should I give them Archie Dock, too? "Carlotta!"

"Shit!" I heard her cry out. It sounded serious, so I dashed for the door and looked into the reception room. "You are a hard man to work for, Jack S," she said, punching stuff into her computer. "Do you know that?"

"What's wrong?"

"You made me hit a function key when you yelled. I could have lost a whole day's work!"

I don't think Carlotta is aware of the impact of her presence on male hormones. She is stunning. She had on a loose-fitting yellow blouse and designer jeans, and her black hair was coiled on her head and around her face with haphazard carelessness. The effect turned my old man's heart into mush. "I need a motion for continuance," I said brusquely, retreating into the safety of my office. "Archie Dock. A witness we didn't know about until yesterday." I waited for her behind the barricade of my desk.

She is bilingual, computer literate, modem-qualified, able to type at 120 words per minute and take shorthand faster than I can talk. She is equipped with the generosity to fix me coffee when I need it and the grace to accept mine even though it tastes awful. I wouldn't want Erin to know, but I am absolutely, totally, horribly and indecently in love with Carlotta. It would be worse than incest, however, if I were to crawl into her bed. It would be the worst form of betrayal. So I handle my feelings by yelling, which forces her to keep a distance but allows me to get close enough to smell her perfume. She runs my professional life, too, and together we make a good living. "How soon do you need this?" she asked a few minutes later, after I told her what I wanted it to say.

"Before two-thirty. You'll have to bring it to court." I grabbed my briefcase and headed for the door.

"Jack. Is something wrong?"

"No."

I drove back to the courthouse. Before moving for a continuance I needed to challenge Drusus with more talk. What would Archie say? Could we take a chance on him being there, or would he hurt us? I didn't think I would file the motion because it was too risky. But we'd be positioned right. Being a lawyer is like shopping at the supermarket. You try to get in the right line.

I went to 3D, and Betty Bitler brought Drusus out. We faced each other in the privacy of the row of cubicles, talking low enough so no one else could hear, but loud enough—over the din on his side of the clear-plastic wall—so we could hear each other.

A patient, generous smile spread over his face when he

saw me. I knew it wouldn't last, and it didn't. "I knew Archie," he said later. "Real thin, younger than me, a Blade. Everybody thought he was slow. That's why they called him Zero."

"Does he tell the truth?"

Drusus shrugged those huge shoulders. "That depends on who's asking the questions. You know."

I leaned as close to the wire mesh as I could get. I laid it out to him in whispers, trying to judge his reactions from what I could see of his ear. I told him that Danforth claimed Dock—along with Larry Walker—saw him shoot and kill Tommy Sherman; that Danforth and Kincaid had put together a mug-shot folder the day after that killing and shown it to Dock; and that he had fingered Drusus. Then he'd disappeared—"until today. Whitney just found him. Do we try to make a witness out of him, or don't we?"

The youngster was as old as God. The expression on his face showed he knew I had some doubts, but he didn't hate me for them. It was as though he understood and forgave me. "You're losing a lot of money on me, aren't you?"

"What are you talking about?"

"Maybe I ought to get the public defender, Jack, you know? Fire you so you can get off the hook."

"Are you crazy?"

"No, man. Just that, you know, you kind of like lost confidence in me, and the public defender—well, they're used to working for people they don't believe in."

"You didn't kill Tommy Sherman, did you?"

"No."

"Or Kingsley Rhoades?"

"No."

Who the hell had that polygraph machine been wired to? I wondered. "I believe you, kid. But there's a lot I don't get. Like how come you didn't tell me about Archie Dock a long time ago? Or Larry Walker? I keep getting blindsided by the prosecution. All this new stuff keeps coming out!"

"We never talked that much about Tommy Sherman. You were doing some other case about then." He wasn't angry about it, just stating a fact. "Kind of like he wasn't important anyway because we had to get ready for the guilt phase.''

He was right. My God. Suddenly I felt like the preacher I'd represented who had gotten drunk and run over a child. I'd spent nine tenths of my time on Rhoades. The murder count on Rhoades had been formally charged, which allowed me to neglect the one against Sherman. I saw myself in a totally different light: not as an embattled crusader for justice, but as a lazy lawyer who might have cost a decent man his life. I had made an unconscious decision to make my own life easier. Why get ready for what I may not have to do, I had decided, especially when I'm not making a dime?

In other words, I'd blown Sherman off. It was my fault we hadn't talked about it. Not Drusus's. "We'd better talk now."

In the space of fifteen minutes he totally rattled my confidence in myself as a lawyer and as a man. For the first time I learned that Drusus had packed a bag and taken a quick trip to Texas right after Sherman had been hit. "Why?"

"The word on the street was I'd done it. So I got lost."

"How long were you gone?"

"Maybe a week. I kept remembering things you said, like how the law isn't perfect, but the machinery is there. You said if a person stands up to what is wrong, most times he can face it down." He smiled at me. "So I came back."

I remembered the conversation he was talking about. We'd had it in my office three months before Drusus wound up in jail. He had told me about friends of his who had run away from crimes they hadn't committed, only to become fugitives. Their lives had gone from bad to worse, and they blamed it on the system. I had won a case that day and was all pumped up and waving the flag. I told him the system takes heart, but if you don't run, the chances are it will work for you; that the machinery, which has been honed over centuries of human history, is designed to get to the truth.

"Okay. When you came back from Texas, what did you do?"

"Moved right back in with Vera, man. I went back to school and just waited for the trouble to start."

"How come you didn't tell me about any of this then?"

"There wasn't anything to tell. I didn't get busted or even hassled on account of Sherman. Then two weeks later they come storming in my house and bounce me out of bed. But that's when they arrested me for killing the King-man! Total surprise, man. I didn't know anything about that at all."

He must have seen the questions in my eyes. I wasn't satisfied with his explanation. If I'd been him, at some time or another I'd have brought this up.

"Jack, I know you better now than I did then," he said, as though reading my mind.

"What?"

"We rapped some before I got arrested, but you were a big lawyer with a Mazda, and the way it felt to me, I was just a dude from the ghetto. Kind of like I couldn't talk about anything real close to me, you know. I didn't want to impose."

"In other words, you're black, and I'm white. Right?"

"Not that so much. You were somebody, and I wasn't."

I looked at my watch. Carlotta would be coming over in a few minutes with the motion. "What about Archie Dock? Will he help us or hurt us?"

"Archie told the police he saw me shoot Sherman?"

"Yes."

"Why would he do that? Why is somebody so anxious to put it on me?"

"Who?"

"I don't know. The Blades, the cops, whoever killed Sherman in the first place. Somebody put all that gossip out there on the street that it was me, but it would really surprise me if it was Archie."

"Why?"

"He's the man who called me up and told me about it."

* * *

The penalty phase of a death penalty case is a different lens to look at jurors with. By that time they know the lawyers pretty well, and the lawyers know them. I'd been with these people in a courtroom for almost a month, performing, trying to look good. But I'd watched them as much as they'd watched me, speculating about twitches and tics and mannerisms and trying to guess what was in their minds. At 2:34 Ivan brought them in from the jury room. As they took their seats in the jury box I noticed that none of them would look at Drusus. A couple of them smiled at the judge, but most of them kept their eyes on their feet.

Maybe they need to make up their mind before they can look at him, I thought hopefully. If they know they're going to kill him, they'll look his way when no one is watching, with lips curling down and expressions like schoolteachers who have caught a student cheating on a test. What will they do if they know they're going to let him live? Smile?

Ida made her usual announcements for the record as everyone got comfortable. Then: "Ladies and gentlemen, during your absence a witness—Mister Larry Walker—was called by the prosecution and sworn in. He will be recalled now." She nodded at Ivan, who went to get him. "For reasons you needn't be concerned about, a lawyer has been appointed to represent him." She glanced toward Gladys Zabriski, who stood up and smiled at the jurors as though she was being introduced. Iron Pants hid her feelings, and Gladys stood there as though wondering whether or not she should sit down.

Walker shuffled in, a chain running between the bracelets around his ankles and handcuffs over his wrists. Ivan guided him to the witness chair. Walker was sweating, and his thin, pointed face searched through the jury as though looking for someone who might recognize him. "Mr. Walker," Ida said after he was seated, "you have previously been sworn in. Are you ready to testify, sir?"

"No. I got nothin' to say." That morning he had been cocky and defiant on the stand. In front of the jury he showed fear.

"Well. Your court-appointed lawyer is present, and you can confer with her any time you wish. Do you understand?"

"I don't understand nothin'." He stared first at Gladys, then at the judge. "She don't know nothin' either. She ain't no lawyer!"

Ida glanced at Keane Williams, who stood at the lectern looking like Excalibur, King Arthur's sword. "Proceed, Mr. Williams."

The prosecutor had a report in his hand. I had a copy of it in mine. He was about to *Green* Larry, and there wasn't anything I could do about it. First he would lay the groundwork. "Mr. Walker, your being here isn't your idea, is it?"

"It ain't my idea at all. I don't want to be here, I'm bein' forced against my rights, and they got chains all over me, and I been brutalized and kicked in the stomach."

"You weren't in chains on March eighteenth of last year, were you?"

"I don't know nothin' about any March eighteenth."

"Did you know Tommy Sherman?"

"I don't know what you're talking about."

"Is there something about my question you don't understand?"

"Yes. The whole thing."

"Did you know Tommy Sherman?"

"I refuse to answer on the grounds it will incriminate me."

"Your Honor, will you order the witness to answer the question?"

Iron Pants looked at him sternly. "You have been granted immunity from prosecution, sir. I direct you to answer the question."

Williams waited. "Your answer, sir."

"I ain't sayin' nothin'."

"Your Honor?"

"Mister Walker, you must answer the question. If you refuse, you will be in contempt of court and punished accordingly."

"Huh! What are you gonna do? Put me in jail?"

"Proceed, Mr. Williams."

Exuding a religious zeal, Keane Williams attacked. "On June fifteenth you were interviewed by Detective Rory Danforth of the Long Beach Police Department, weren't you?"

"I ain't sayin' nothin'."

"No comment?"

"That's right, man. No comment."

"That interview took place here in the Long Beach courthouse, didn't it?"

"No comment."

"Incidentally, you're serving time for aggravated robbery, aren't you?"

"What if I am?"

"You have eleven years left on your sentence, so being held in contempt of court doesn't mean a thing to you, does it?"

"That's my business."

"A few days or weeks tacked on to the end of your sentence, so what, right?"

"Objection, Judge," I said. "Leading."

"Your Honor, he's obviously hostile," Williams said. "Request permission to lead the witness."

"Yes. Granted."

There are times when I realize I should have been a prosecutor. I'd just succeeded in making it easier for those guys again.

"Mr. Walker, you told Detective Danforth about a murder you'd seen on March eighteenth, didn't you?"

"No."

"No? You are under oath, Mr. Walker. Are you aware of the penalty for perjury?"

He sat there saying nothing.

"Would you like to talk to your lawyer?"

"That won't do me any good."

"Answer the question, Mr. Walker," Iron Pants said.

"No comment."

He had finally figured out—after being herded in that direction by the prosecutor—that his best answer was "no comment." If he denied it, he could be prosecuted for perjury and have years more added to his sentence. As far as the prosecution was concerned, it didn't matter. They could either *Green* him or impeach him. Either way, the statement he gave Danforth would come in.

"You told Detective Danforth that you saw Drusus Church shoot and kill Tommy Sherman in the early morning hours of March eighteenth, didn't you?"

"No comment."

"You told him it took place on Cherry Street a few doors north of Anaheim in Long Beach, right?"

"No comment."

"You even drew him a diagram, didn't you, showing him where you were standing, and where a fellow by the name of Archie Dock stood, and Mister Church, and Tommy Sherman?" He picked up a paper and got ready to walk to the witness box.

"No comment."

"Let me show you this diagram and ask you if you can identify it." Williams walked up to the witness chair. "I'd like this marked for identification purposes as People's next in order, Judge. Twenty-seven, I think."

"For identification purposes only at this point," Iron Pants said. "Number twenty-seven."

"Do you recognize this diagram?" Keane asked, laying it in front of Walker.

He wouldn't look at it. "No comment."

"You drew this for the detective, didn't you? Look. Here." Keane stuck his finger on the paper. "You even initialed it for him in the left margin."

"No comment."

"Your initials are 'LW,' aren't they?"

"I don't know." The face he turned toward the prosecutor was that of a wolf caught in a trap.

Williams took the exhibit back to the lectern with him. "On June fifteenth, in an interview room in this courthouse where you met with Detective Rory Danforth, you were also shown a folder with several photographs in it, weren't you?" He picked up the mug-shot folder we'd found at the Long Beach PD.

"No comment."

Williams strolled back up to the witness box. "And Detective Danforth showed it to you, and you identified this picture here—the bottom right—as a photograph of the man who had shot and killed Tommy Sherman?"

"No comment."

"And after that you initialed the folder on the back, didn't you?"

"No comment."

"What did you say your initials were?"

"I didn't say."

"That's right. You didn't say. Or was it no comment?"

Walker's eyes lit on Drusus. It couldn't have been worse. He looked terrified, as though he knew he was a dead man who hadn't been killed yet. "This is bullshit, man. Total bullshit."

"Ask that the answer be stricken," Williams said.

"Why should it be, Judge?" I asked, struggling to get up. I was mad as hell. "He was badgering the witness!"

Ida smiled like she would at a child who was having a tantrum. "Very well, Mr. Bard. I'll let the answer stand."

What a favor. What did the answer prove?

The prosecutor played him another fifteen minutes, going into details: the number of shots, what was said, five feet away from the victim, not more than ten feet away from Drusus, plenty of light. All the questions were asked in the same way—"Isn't that what you said to the detective?"—and answered with "No comment."

"Thank you so much, sir," Williams said when he was done. "He's your witness, Mr. Bard."

I did what I could on cross, which wasn't much. I made him admit that in addition to the agg rob rap he'd also been convicted of rape. Then I tried to get him to agree with me that he was a liar who would tell the cops anything to lighten his load. But he refused to see himself that way. Still, I got him to agree that Danforth came to see him first, right after he'd been picked up on the agg rob beef.

I finished with a string of questions I knew he wouldn't answer, just to get them out where the jury could see them—like when did he find out the cops were trying to make a case against Drusus, hadn't he tried to make a deal for a light sentence, and didn't he lie to Danforth hoping it would do him some good? Then I let him go.

"Call Detective Rory Danforth," Williams said.

No one would question whether Danforth told the truth, even if they thought he lied. He was a big, red-faced, honest-looking, old-fashioned cop, and you knew that whatever he did was right. He boomed out his answers in apparent anger, like someone from Operation Rescue drawing the line in front of an abortion clinic. In spite of that, he made a good witness. He infused his testimony with small details: the crack in the face of the clock on the wall in the interview room, the way Walker sat so no one in the hall could see him, the baseball game he'd been following that day.

"Was anyone with you?"

"No, sir. My partner, Detective Kincaid, was at the dentist, which necessitated that I do it alone."

"As a consequence of that, did you do anything different?"

"Yes." He eyed the jury. "This type situation, you can't always depend on the person you interview to remember what he said when he comes to court. When *two* people are there it isn't critical because it isn't just my word against his. So I did some extra. I got him to draw me a picture, and I got him to initial a couple of items."

Keane showed him the diagram. "Can you identify this document?"

"I can. When Walker was telling me what went down when Tommy Sherman was shot, I acted like I couldn't understand too well and had him draw out what happened at my request. I had him put down where people was standing when the defendant shot Tommy Sherman."

"And this document is that drawing?"

"Yes, sir."

"Move for the admission of People's Exhibit number twenty-seven."

Keane showed him the mug-shot folder. "Did Mr. Walker identify any of the photographs in this photographic lineup as being the person who shot and killed Tommy Sherman?"

"Yes, sir, he did."

"Which photograph did he identify?"

"Bottom right."

"And you saw him do that?"

"Yes I did, sir. No question. I even had him initial the back of the folder and date it. All of that is in his handwriting."

I could have objected to the way the witness expanded on his answers, but what good would it have done? It would have painted the wrong kind of picture for the jury—that of crusaders who have to fight tooth and nail to get the job done.

"Do you see the person in this courtroom whose photograph was identified by Mr. Walker as the man who shot and killed Tommy Sherman?"

"He's sitting right over there next to his lawyer," Danforth said with obvious satisfaction. "The defendant. The big man in the yellow shirt."

Danforth stayed on the stand another twenty minutes, hammering nails in Drusus's coffin. By the time I got him on cross-examination, half the jurors had stolen those quick, hard looks at Drusus with their lips curled down like the sentence of death. So I flashed my most charming smile all around the room. "Good afternoon, Officer Danforth," I said cheerfully.

"Counselor."

Sometimes it's hard. But you stand up there and do your best, knowing it amounts to less than a fart in a windstorm. That's when you get desperate and take chances. I took a big one. "You testified that you showed the mug-shot folder—this thing here"—I picked it up from in front of Keane—"to Mr. Walker?"

"Yes, sir."

"You also showed it to an individual whose name was Salvadore Mira, didn't you?"

"That's right. I did."

"And he initialed it on the back and dated it. Correct?"

"Correct."

"The murder took place on the eighteenth of March, and you showed it to Mira on the twenty-first of March. Right? Three days after it happened?"

He smiled. "Right again, Counselor."

I folded it up and put it back on the prosecution table, carefully working out the wording of my next question. I might already have opened the door to a flood of questions that would bury Drusus. I wasn't sure it mattered. He looked dead anyway. "Mira was not able to make a positive identification of anyone in this folder as the person who shot Sherman, was he?"

"Not positive, no. But—"

"Then your answer is no?"

"To that question it's no. But—"

"Detective Danforth, that question is all you've been asked. Now, you've testified enough in court to know all you're supposed to do is answer the question you've been asked, haven't you? Withdraw that." I glared at him righteously but wished I'd never started the game. "You didn't file any reports, did you, concerning the showing of the folder to Salvadore Mira?"

"No, I didn't."

"Mr. Walker wanted to make a deal with you, didn't he?"

"They all want to make a deal."

I started breathing again. He was trying so hard to screw me over that he might have screwed up. "Yes. They all want to make a deal, don't they?"

"That's right. That's why we don't deal with the pukes." He smiled at me, thinking he had scored with the jury.

"And the reason you don't deal with the pukes is that you know you can't trust them, right?"

He thought for a moment. "That's part of it. That isn't all of it, though."

"But it's part of it. And the point is, you know you can't trust them when they want to make a deal. Right?"

He did what a lot of righteous-looking cops can do and get away with. Right there in the middle of the stream he climbed on another horse. "Wrong. You can trust them as much as you can anyone else."

"You can? You can trust a man who is faced with the prospect of going to prison for several years, and who wants to make a deal, as much as you can trust the average man off the street?"

Danforth smiled knowingly, his eyes shrouded in hard cop cynicism. He exuded complete confidence in himself. "Believe it," he said.

I looked for a friendly face in the jury box but couldn't find one. So I shrugged my shoulders and opened the palms of my hands, then started to sit down. "In other words, don't trust them when they want to make a deal, except when they tell you what you want to hear?"

"Objection, Judge," Keane Williams said. "Argumentative."

"Sustained." Ida watched me slide my chair close to the table. "Mr. Williams, do you have any other questions?"

"Yes, I do, if it please the Court."

The boy wonder's first question was like an electric prod. It brought me out of my chair screaming. He asked Danforth whether the mug-shot folder with Drusus Church's picture had been shown to an individual by the name of Archie Dock. "I object, Judge!" My thighs slammed into the table, bouncing it toward the bench. "Oww!" I cried out, hoping someone would feel my pain. "May we approach?"

Ida's expression did not include sympathy. "You may."

The conversation at the sidebar turned hot as the sun, and Ida sent the jury out to keep them from listening. The prosecutor wanted Danforth to tell the jury that Archie Dock had also identified Drusus from the mug-shot folder as the killer of Tommy Sherman. He claimed he could do it because, when I'd asked Danforth about the folder, I'd opened the door!

I could feel the hair on my head turning white, but she finally agreed with me. She ruled that too many doors would open if she allowed it, that the prejudicial effect outweighed the relevance. Thanks, God, I thought. Tell her I'll never call her Iron Pants again.

But the lad from NASP still managed to stick it in me. With the jury back in place—where, once again, they were exposed to Danforth's obvious contempt for the limitations of courtroom truth—he said, "Detective Danforth, Mr. Bard used the phrase 'positive identification' when he questioned you about showing the photographic lineup to Mr. Mira. Did you notice that?"

"I did."

"Did Mr. Mira make any kind of identification of the photograph of the defendant?"

"Mr. Mira said it could be, but he wasn't sure."

Ida sent the jury home. As they filed out of the box I tried to see what was in their minds. There was no way to tell, of course. Their blank faces got in the way.

13

"Jack!" Carlotta whispered excitedly as I trudged into my office. "Ralph Hammond! He's in the library."

"Hammond? Here?" I couldn't believe it. Most of the deputy DAs in Long Beach were pretty good guys who tolerated me in the same way I tolerated them. We worked together, so we waved at one another in the courthouse halls and shared dirty jokes. But I hated Mad Dog Hammond's guts, and he hated mine. If I saw him bleeding in the gutter, I wouldn't help him up. I'd kick him. "Why can't he wait in the reception room like everybody else?"

"He was afraid someone might see him."

I didn't even take off my coat. The corner office of my three-room suite has been converted into a library, and I banged through the door. "Mad Dog!" I said. "What are you doing here?"

Hammond had a reputation in the Los Angeles District Attorney's Office as the toughest of the tough. He was so bad they didn't even like him downtown. He was tall and looked like a cadaver—or like Abe Lincoln, his mother would say. He had a heavy brow and unruly hair over his sunken cheeks. He also lifted weights in his spare time, which—judging from the man's physique—was considerable. I could see muscles rippling under his coat.

"Please don't call me 'Mad Dog,' okay?" he suggested

in his friendly voice—friendly for him. It sounded like Darth Vader. "I don't have rabies. Shut the door."

I felt like throwing him out. He was in my office, and not by invitation, and he could by God ask rather than order. But it's easy to get in a fight with Mad Dog, and I wanted to find out why he was there, so I shut the door. "I haven't seen you since the preliminary," I said, taking a chair by the table. He stayed on his feet.

"You know, that clown really got under my skin."

"Ralph, you've been pulling that stunt on defendants for years. It's time you found out what it feels like."

"The queer started coming on to me, honest to God, like I was a queen or something."

I laughed. Mad Dog had run what he called a "mind-fuck" game on Drusus. Only he'd lost. When no one is watching, Hammond will mouth insults and flash obscene signs at the defendant. Usually the tactic is saved for jury trials, so the bad guy—who reacts by puffing up in anger, frothing at the mouth, and glaring around like a maddened bull—will look like a chained, savage animal to the jurors. But he decided to exercise his skills at the preliminary hearing held against Drusus. A sweet young reporter from the Long Beach *Sentinel* was sitting in the courtroom that day, and he wanted her to see him as the defender of all that is true and just.

Drusus didn't react right, however. He smiled pleasantly and probed, so to speak, where Hammond was vulnerable! Mad Dog was the one who couldn't handle it. He blew up, challenging Drusus—who was handcuffed—to fight. "Take the cuffs off him! I'll kill him! I want him bad!"

The reporter knew a story when she saw one. She reported the flap in the *Sentinel,* and the next day it got picked up by the Los Angeles *Times.* Because of the publicity the district attorney disqualified the office and brought in NASP.

"Sit down, Ralph. The door is shut. No one can see you. Of course, I've got the place bugged—"

"You kill me." But that was exactly what he was thinking. He walked over to the French door that led to the balcony and opened it. "These digs must cost you a ton. If *you* can make it in private practice, I wonder what I could do." He looked outside. "Let's do our talking out there."

"Fine," I said, then encouraged his paranoia. "What are you going to do about the battery pack I carry in my pocket?"

"Take off your coat and leave it in here."

I grinned at him. "I will if you will, Mad Dog. Let's take everything off." It had worked for Drusus, maybe it would for me. "A great big guy like you. I'll bet you could show me a lot, honey."

He had more demons circulating around in him than the average bear. He blushed and blanched and stared and dropped his eyes, and his jaw came out an inch, then went slack. "Just coats," he said, pulling his off and waiting for me to take off mine. We draped them over a couple of chairs, then filed onto the balcony and shut the door. "Great view of the street," he said. "What would you charge me to watch the Grand Prix?"

"Let's get it over with, Ralphie. Why are you here?"

I thought for a minute he was going to pick me up and pitch me over the balcony. But he got his face under control, and his fingers quit their twitch, and he turned away as though he hated saying what he had to say. "I'm just gonna lay this out for you once, asshole. I heard you got hammered in court today. Believe me, even with a social worker like Williams dealing, it will get worse before it gets better." He gritted his teeth. "I don't like this a fucking bit."

"Don't like what?"

"Offering you a deal. I know you'll take the son of a bitch, and it makes me sick."

"We don't have any cases. What are you talking about?"

"Drusus Church. That puke. God!"

I laughed. "Get off my back, Mad Dog. He isn't your case. You came apart at the preliminary, remember? Don't you read the newspapers?"

"That turd-bird from NASP ought to wear a wig, you

know that? No shit, he isn't even an American. He acts like a British barrister."

I had a hunch. "Does Keane know you're here?"

"Fuck no. He would pass gas if he did. He isn't man enough to take a shit." He spat over the balcony. "I heard he wants to be the AG, lining up support! He couldn't even be dog catcher."

"How can you offer me a deal, Ralphie? It's his case."

"Believe me, I can do it."

What is going on? I asked myself. Can the DA take it back from NASP? Is that the way Jim Trigge operates? "What's the deal?"

He looked like he might throw up. "Manslaughter, but he's got to plead to it. Eleven for the manslaughter, five for the prior, two for the gun add up to eighteen years. They give him credit for time served, he's out in eight."

"What?" From a death-penalty case to an eighteen-year lock! "Why?"

"Take it or leave it," Hammond said, ramming the door open and yanking his coat off the chair. He raised his nose and smelled the air, nostrils flaring as though offended by an odor. "You have until Monday, and you do the deal with me. I hope you leave it." He blew through the door into the reception room as though he couldn't possibly stand being around me another second.

Carlotta rushed into the library anxiously, as though afraid of what she might find. "Jack?"

"Yeah." I stood by the table, trying to sort things out. "What time is it?"

"Five-thirty. Are you all right?"

"Friendly sort of fellow, isn't he?"

"The way he left, I thought he might have taken off your head!" She laughed nervously, and it did my old heart good to know she was worried. Either that, or she doesn't like messes. "What happened?"

"Tell you later. Can you get Keane Williams for me?"

"I'll try."

I sat down and tried to figure it out. It had been Hammond's case through the preliminary hearing. Had he done something while the case was still his that he wanted buried?

"Jack, line three," Carlotta said.

I picked up the telephone and punched the button. I could hear the sound of a shower in the background. "Uh-oh," I said. "Are you at your hotel?"

"Yes, sir," Keane Williams said in one of those business-like voices that asks, "How may I direct your call?"

"Mad Dog Hammond was just in here and made me a plea offer. I thought I'd better find out who's in charge."

"Is he the hot dog I inherited the case from?"

"Yes."

"I don't know what he said to you, Jack, but it doesn't mean a thing. He has no authority. It's my case, and whatever he said, disregard."

"You sound pissed."

"I am pissed, as a matter of fact. Like I told you in court, fella, we're done talking. Anything else?"

I noticed that he didn't hang up. "So there's no chance of a plea bargain with you now. Right?"

"Jack, I made you a good-faith offer, and I know this will sound hokey, but I did it out of the kindness of my heart. Your client is bad, but I've seen worse. You turn me down and okay, that's all right, I don't score every time I ask. It's the way you did it that burned me off."

I asked myself what he was telling me. That all I needed to do was apologize? "I'm sorry if I made you mad."

"Damn right you made me mad," he said angrily. "You accused me of hiding something. Like you were challenging my integrity."

A lot of deputy DAs are like that, I thought. If you call them a son of a bitch, as Owen Wister said, you'd better smile. But there were more angles to this one than that. Maybe political ambition had complicated his soul, but he wasn't that simple. "So are you still pissed off?"

"Look. If you want to plead him out—I mean, you'd have to get on your knees"—he laughed as though to say, "You're forgiven"—"I'd listen. Okay?"

* * *

It was after nine, and as I waited in my office for Whitney I watched a steamer put out to sea. It lit up a piece of ocean, but in half an hour—from my perspective—it would only be a speck.

When I gave up the view to sit at my desk he was seated across from it. His chair was too small, even though it was the biggest one in the room other than the high-back swivel chair I sat down in. His knees were spread apart, and his huge thighs seemed to anchor the world in place. I hadn't heard him come in. "How did you do that?"

He smiled with satisfaction. "Just something I know how to do."

He had come over to tell me what happened when he caught Archie Dock, but I started talking first. The expression on his face registered pure amazement, like Edison's when the damn thing talked back. "He could be out in eight years?"

"Yes."

"What you gonna tell Drusus?"

There are times when I'd rather butcher hogs than be a lawyer. "That he'd be a fool not to take it."

I was beyond the minor stumbling block of whether or not Hammond could make the offer. As Charley Wallace would have explained, were he alive—God rest his beautiful old head in a down pillow—that was a political problem. If the Los Angeles District Attorney's Office wanted to cut the deal, they would yank the case away from the righteous grasp of NASP and Keane Williams.

Whitney looked like he might fall asleep. He does that to throw the opposition off guard. It meant he was thinking. "From a capital beef to manslaughter," he said. "They gonna have a very tough time runnin' that one over the cops. Why would he make an offer like that? It doesn't sound like Mad Dog!"

I'd been trying to figure it out since Mad Dog had stomped out earlier that evening. I trotted out my best theory. "How's this: Mad Dog did something bad—very bad—when he had the case. You know, a DA Dirty Harry, the hell with the law, just put the bastards away." I watched

Whitney for a reaction. "Maybe they're afraid of an appeal, worried that whatever he did will come out."

"This case stinks!" Whitney's voice was up a notch. "Wouldn't it be great if the smell could be traced to Hammond?"

"Can you find out?"

He looked at me in surprise. "How would I do that?"

I stuck a finger in my ear. "You're good at those things. You just proved it, the way you snuck in here." I examined a little piece of wax on my finger, thinking: My ears generate a lot of wax. Getting old is hard on us fastidious types. "I could plead it down to breaking and entering."

"Uh-huh." He laughed. "Like break into Mad Dog's office and steal his file?"

"Actually, I was thinking more along the lines of make copies. He'd miss the file."

"Are you serious, man?"

I hesitated. It came to me that maybe I was. "No." I let it rattle around in my head again. "I don't know," I said, as honest as I knew how to be. "I have to believe—as bad as Mad Dog is—that even he thinks Drusus did it. But if I thought the prosecution, or the police, was trying to take him down for something they know he didn't do . . ."

"Do you know something, Jack? It's why I like you. You talk nasty, but the truth? You're too good to be a lawyer. You are also the most naïve son of a bitch who ever lived."

"Bullshit." But it started me thinking. A vision of Charley Wallace grinning at me drifted into my mind. "Remember old Charley?"

"Yeah. He thought you'd been warped, too."

Occasionally I have to ignore the person I'm talking to in order to keep my conversation with the person going. "According to Charley, the successful man will figure out who has the power to levy the taxes, and get on their side, and live a good life."

Whitney grinned. "Yeah."

"Old Charley said if you're on the right side of the tax collector—and it doesn't matter who; the feds, the Church, the Mafia, they're all basically the same—and pay your taxes, life will be beautiful and good. Because once you let the collectors know how sincere you are, they will lower your taxes. And if things go wrong, you can go to work for them."

Whitney was not in the mood for an interlude. He looked at his watch. "How much time do we have on the offer?"

I stood up and opened the glass door onto the balcony to let the ocean air in. It was dark out, and I could see the lights of Avalon, across twenty miles of ocean, in the Channel Islands. There were some specks out there, too, although I didn't know which one was the ship I'd watched earlier. "Five days. Monday. A lot can happen."

"Will the trial last that long?"

I nodded a yes. "Keane's got enough stuff for one more day, and my witnesses will take at least two. Add to that the usual delays, hassles, and arguments that make of the common law the wondrous instrument for the determination of justice that she has become."

"I'm hungry, man. When do we eat?"

"After you tell me what you know about Archie Dock."

Whitney leaned forward, reached in a back pocket, and pulled out a tape. He popped it in a small portable recorder and jumped it back and forth, searching for the conversation. "It's on here somewhere." When he found it, I couldn't understand it.

"What did he say, Whitney?"

"That's gonna take some work." He shut it off. "The little sucker. I had to sit on him."

"Is he still alive?"

"Yeah. Most of him. He got away before I was done."

"Did he see the shooting?"

Whitney settled back in his chair and nodded a yes. "Said it was early in the morning, nobody on the streets. Just him and Larry Walker led Sherman outside, which was easy, because Sherman was all used up on drugs. Then Drusus came out and hit him. Said Kingsley Rhoades gave the order because Sherman had been stealing from him, so he had to be taught a lesson. Like pure business."

"To kill him, you mean?"

"Yeah."

I slumped in my chair. "Then he saw Drusus do it?"

"At first he said Drusus. But Drusus told you he heard about it from Archie, right?" I nodded. "I jumped him about that," Whitney continued. " 'Archie, that don't wash,' I said. 'If Drusus did it, how come you had to call him up on the telephone and tell him to split? Wouldn't the boy have figured that out by his own self?' " Whitney watched me, making sure I understood what he'd done. I nodded again. "Archie didn't come back with an explanation in time. He knew I had him in a lie."

"Then what?"

"I leaned on him hard enough to break his leg. Told him he'd better tell me the truth. He said, 'I ain't lyin' man.' He said, 'Drusus too smart, and King skeered of him.' He said, 'King told us to spread the truth on the street, get rid of Drusus, and that's what I warned Drusus about.' " He looked at his feet. "Kingman thought Drusus would get mashed right away by the po-lice, but the youngster split. What Dock heard, he said, was when Drusus got back, he took him out."

"So he heard Drusus did Kingsley Rhoades, too?"

"Yeah."

A piece of fog blotted out the lights of Avalon, and there wasn't anything more out there to see. "Do you believe him?"

"No."

"Why not?"

"He didn't explain in time. But the other thing is this: If that's the way it was, King would have had Drusus taken out. And for sure your boy wouldn't have come up on him in a dark alley."

"Did Archie say anything else?"

"No. The boy's an artist. He was cryin', you know, so I eased off a little, and damn if he didn't break loose and run off."

"Did you put a subpoena on him?"

"Sure I did, just like you said." He leaned forward. "It's

here in my pocket somewhere. He laughed about it on the way out the door."

"You got him served, though, didn't you?"

"Legally he's been served. I put the paper on him, and it don't matter he threw it back at me. But don't worry, Jack. He won't be there."

"God, I hope not."

"I'm really hungry, man." Whitney pushed himself to his feet. "If we don't eat, I'm gonna pass out."

I got up and started looking for my shoes. "You haven't seen a pair of loafers, have you?"

"Jack, if Mad Dog has something to hide, what he'd do is clean up his files, right? I mean, will you concede that Mad Dog would run anything bad in his file through the shredder?"

"Yes."

"But when something happens in court and a court reporter takes it all down, like at a hearing or a trial, the DA can't clean that up, can he? Mad Dog wouldn't have those keys, right? They're in somebody else's pocket?"

"Right." I was in the reception room on my hands and knees. How had they gotten under Carlotta's desk? "So what you're saying is . . ." It occurred to me what he was saying. "Whitney, you're a genius."

He smiled. "I've been telling you that for years."

14

Before bringing the jury in that morning, Keane had winked at me as though to say, "Isn't this great sport?" But the witness he had on the stand—a matronly-looking black woman who told what happened the night her house was burglarized by Drusus and his pal Jim-Jim Joslin—was beating me to death.

I longed for the open hatred of the day before. It's more trustworthy than pip-pip, cheerio, and all that rot.

"And then?"

"My husband, seemed like he couldn't get out of there quick enough. He just ran."

Keane frowned. "Let's back up a moment, Mrs. Greer. You told us you heard this noise in the house sometime after you'd gone to bed, and you woke up your husband. Is that right?"

"Yes, sir."

Keane spoke with great sympathy, as though to warn the jury not to find anything the woman said amusing. "And he ran?"

"He sure did." There was anger in her voice, not aimed at Keane, but—so it seemed—at her husband. "He just climb over me and run out the room and away."

"Is it fair to say that he appeared frightened?"

"Huh!" she snorted, a wry smile on her face. "You could surely say that!"

"Do you have children?" Keane asked quickly.

"Yes. They was in another room."

"And so your children were in another room when you heard this noise, and your husband ran off?"

"Yes, sir."

"What did you do, Mrs. Greer?"

"I ran in there to where they was at."

"Were you concerned for your children at that time?"

"Of course I was." She looked at Keane with a questioning expression, then glared angrily at Drusus. "I was very concerned for my children."

"How many children did you have at that time?"

"Two girls. One was seven, and the other was almost five."

"Both in the room?"

"Yes, sir."

"Was either of them awake?"

"Lucille. She was sitting up in her bed. She had the covers pulled up to her chest."

"And was Lucille the seven-year-old or the five-year-old?"

"Lucille my oldest child. She was seven."

"Can you describe her expression for the jury, Mrs. Greer?"

"Her eyes was open as far as they could go, and her mouth had a shake to it. She was terrified. I could almost hear her heart."

I could have objected. You either hear a thing or you don't. But this was clearly no time to get technical.

"What did you do?"

She glanced again at Drusus, making no effort to mask her rage. "I shut the door soft as I could. I put a finger over my lips, kind of a warning, you know, but Lucille not about to make any noise. I pick up my baby—I could feel she knew something's wrong soon as I pick her up—and we get in a corner behind Lucille's bed."

"Your baby?"

"Rhonda, my five-year-old."

"Could you hear anything?"

"Oh, yes. Even with the door shut." Drusus sat up straight, but his eyes were averted. "Sound like something tip over, then it was just as still as death."

"What happened next?"

"I could hear sounds like feet, you know, running up the stairs. And somebody yell, 'That's cops, man!' or something. And then the door break open, and this big man standing there with a gun in his hand."

"Do you see that man in court?"

"Yes, sir. He sitting right over there with his head down." Her voice vibrated with contempt and rage. "That's him, right over there."

Drusus looked up. His eyes met those of Mrs. Greer. What I saw was an expression of sadness, but I don't know what the jurors saw. "You feel bad about it now, don't you, boy?" she sneered.

"What was your state of mind at that moment, Mrs. Greer, if you can recall?" Keane asked.

"I don't know." Her voice was shaking, and one hand covered her face. She cried a moment, then pulled out a tissue and wiped her eyes. "All I know is, he'd have to go through me to get my girls."

"Were you frightened?"

"I don't know."

Keane nodded at her and folded the file on the lectern. "Your witness, Mr. Bard."

What a rotten place for him to stop, I thought, getting up. I knew what had happened next—Drusus shut the door and ran down the hall, looking for a window to crawl out of—but I didn't know how the witness saw it.

"Hello, Mrs. Greer," I said.

"Hello."

Words, images, and fears were hurtling through my mind. I didn't know how to play this one at all. "You must have been terrified."

"Yes, sir, I was."

"And your daughters. Are they okay now?"

"They both in school. They don't talk about it anymore, if that what you mean."

"Are they here?" I asked, deciding on a tactic of sheer avoidance. "Perhaps in the hallway, waiting to testify?"

"No, sir. Mr. Keane said they didn't have to come."

"Do they have nightmares about this?" I asked, knowing it was open-ended, but wanting to let the jurors know of my real concern.

"No."

"I'm so glad," I told her. "They are good, strong, healthy children, then?"

She smiled. "Yes, sir."

I considered doing some grandstanding, like asking her to accept my client's apology, but it was sticky enough. I thought of asking to see pictures of the girls, but one of them might have only one eye. If Keane had set a trap for me—something about the husband, who might have died of a heart attack—so far I'd avoided it. The best thing for me to do was stop. "Thank you for your testimony, Mrs. Greer," I said, and I sat down.

Keane knew how to play his part, I'll have to say that for the lad. He got up, which attracted the jurors' attention, then looked at me in such a way that the panel could see the expression on his face. It was cynical, as though to say, "I have some reservations about Mr. Bard's sincerity."

Pip-pip, old chap, I thought, without noticing. I followed Mrs. Greer when she left the stand. It was easy for me to watch her with respect, because that's what I felt for her. "Your next witness, Mr. Williams?" Iron Pants asked.

"Call Officer Waddell."

Officer Baxter Waddell of the Compton Police Department took the stand. He was a large, carefully dressed, mustachioed, and graying black man. I was delighted to see him there. I tried to look horrified—within appropriate limits, naturally. If you're too obvious about such things, the prosecutor will get suspicious.

Keane ran through the preliminaries quickly, then got down to the meat. "Officer Waddell, do you recall the early morning of September nineteenth, nineteen eighty-six?"

"Very well."

"You were on duty at that time, in the city of Compton?"

He was leading him all over the block, but I didn't care. "I was."

"In the course of your duties that night, were you dispatched to a burglary in progress?"

He was. He gave the time and the address, and the circumstances. Some unknown person had called it in. He and his partner, a white officer by the name of Lucas Trimble, responded. "When you say 'responded,' were the sirens and overheads activated?"

"Oh, no. Me and Lucas didn't work that way. We came up quiet, you know, try to keep everybody's emotions under control. We didn't want no hostage situation to occur."

"What did you do?"

Waddell explained they called for backup, then parked two doors down from the two-story Greer residence. They saw signs of suspicious entry—an open front door and screen door ajar—so Lucas went around to the back of the building, and Waddell took a deep breath and rolled through the front door. "I didn't hear anything for a minute when a black youth stuck his face around the corner. I had my weapon drawn, and he immediately put his hands in the air. But the other larger youth ran up the stairs. I saw him pull a pistol from his belt and remember thinking to myself, 'Trouble.' "

Keane went over it again with Waddell, cleaning it up. Waddell had landed in a hallway and couldn't see anything when he first dived in, he explained. He had his gun out, and when Jim-Jim looked around the corner it was right in Jim-Jim's face. Waddell quickly moved into the open, in time to see Drusus run up the stairs. The youth had a gun out, but it wasn't aimed at Waddell, so he didn't shoot. He remembered, too, that something was said about "cops."

"Then what did you do?"

"I didn't know who or what was upstairs and did not want to make the situation worse than it was by yelling orders. So I secured the youth in front of me—I handcuffed him to a chair and told him the place was surrounded, and that for his own safety he should stay where he was. Then I went up the stairs."

"Please go on."

"I encountered a hallway at the head of the stairs. All doors were closed except for the one at the end, which turned out to be the master or main bedroom." He cleared his throat. "I heard noises from that room, then heard my partner call, 'Gotcha! One move and you're dead.'" He paused long enough to wipe some perspiration from his lip. "I heard some scrambling sound, and I ran to the room and rather carelessly ran through the door. I saw a large, well-muscled youth trying to get back inside a window he had just tried to crawl out of."

"Was there anything in his hand?"

"No. But he had a pistol stuck in his belt."

Ah, the pistol. Keane suddenly realized his mistake. At least that is what I thought I saw in his expression. But he smiled in my direction as though nothing was wrong. "I take it the youth was arrested?"

"Yes. He was."

"And do you see the youth in court?"

"Yes, sir, I do." Waddell identified Drusus.

"How would you characterize this situation, Officer?" Keane asked. I could have objected on any number of grounds, but there was no point. I didn't need the jurors regarding me as an obstructionist.

"I would say volatile and dangerous in the extreme."

"Thank you. Nothing further." He sat down.

"Mr. Bard?"

I peered over my glasses at the witness as I wandered toward the lectern and smiled, hoping he might smile back. He didn't. "How are you, sir?" I said.

"Fine."

"My client didn't offer any resistance did he, Officer?"

"No." The witness brushed a speck of dust off his trousers. "I had the drop on him from one side, and Lucas had him covered from the other. I suspect he knew he was caught."

"He'd been drinking, hadn't he?"

"There was a faint odor of alchoholic beverage about him."

"Did you see anyone else inside the house?"

"Yes. A woman and two young females—little kids— came out of one room, and a man appeared from somewhere. The woman kind of tore into the man, I remember. That was Mister and Missus Greer."

"Mister Greer had locked himself in the bathroom, hadn't he?" I asked.

"That was my understanding."

"So he wasn't much help, was he?"

Waddell frowned at me, then looked away. "I felt sorry for the man."

"And the woman and the children, I'm sure you felt sorry for them, too," I said.

"You are right, sir. I felt sorry for them, too."

"Now this gun or pistol you saw in my client's belt. Did you check the chamber?"

I knew the answer, so it didn't hurt to ask the question. "Yes, sir."

"It was empty, right?"

"That's correct."

"And you confiscated the weapon, didn't you?"

"I did."

"What kind of weapon?"

"It was a thirty-eight-caliber special."

"A thirty-eight-caliber special," I repeated, putting a look on my face like I was trying to see it in my mind. "Isn't that the so-called cop gun?" I saw Juror Six lean forward.

"You could call it a cop gun. Most officers used them in those days."

"It was a revolver, wasn't it? Made of nickel, or nickel-plated?"

He thought a moment. "Yes."

"Now, about this revolver, which you confiscated at that time from the defendant. Did you give it back to him?"

Good old Waddell did what I'd have done. He sneered.

"A weapon seized in the commission of a crime don't go back to the defendant," he said.

"So your answer is no, it was never returned to him?"

He stared at me with no expression. "That is my answer, sir."

"You arrested the defendant for this burglary on September nineteenth, nineteen eighty-six. Correct?"

"Correct."

"So the defendant could not possibly have had that weapon in March or April of last year, when either Kingsley Rhoades or Tommy Sherman was murdered with a so-called cop gun?"

Keane gave me a look of supreme patience, and so did the judge. But he didn't object, which is what I wanted him to do. I wanted him to make me do it right, to force me to nail it down, which I was prepared to do over and over, until it echoed in the courtroom like an advertisement. "I can't say nothing about when those gentlemen you mention was murdered," Waddell said. "But for sure, the defendant did not have that gun in March or April of last year."

"The gun had been confiscated by you before those gentlemen were murdered?" I asked, still waving the same red flag.

But the boy wonder knew better than to charge. "If those murders took place when you say they did, the answer is yes, isn't it?" the witness replied testily.

"Thank you, Officer Waddell," I said. "No further questions."

15

Never let yourself believe you know what a jury is thinking, Charley Wallace used to tell me. Never assume that because they laugh, they think you have said something funny. Never make the mistake of believing that when they cry, they feel sorry for the person you want them to feel sorry for. They could all be smelling the same onion. And never conclude they are "with you" after a particularly brilliant performance or agree with your invincible logic.

Good advice. When I gave my opening statement that morning before lunch, my temptation was to gloat over Waddell's testimony. Wouldn't the jurors remember the huge production the prosecution had made of the gun? Leah Dempster, Drusus's high school girl, had cried when she told them about it: how he showed it to her and told her he'd stolen it off a cop. Well, what do you think of that evidence now? I wanted to ask them. Rhoades and Sherman were shot with what might have been a cop gun, but you sure as hell know it wasn't the one Leah Dempster told you about—because Officer Waddell confiscated that one before those guys got whacked! I wanted to urge the jurors, implore them, order them to take another look at what they had done, to reconsider the awful mistake they had obviously made.

But old Charley's face got in the way. I heard him say,

"Jack S, don't be stupid. People's minds don't work that way, my boy. Except for Juror Six, the rest of them would tune you out." Old Charley grinned and kept right on talking. "They've already made up their minds about that miscreant you represent, laddie. If you challenge them with it, they'll just say to themselves, okay, so he stole *two* guns." Good old Charley. "Do you know what happened in Italy after Columbus proved the world was round?" he said. "Nothing. Not for twenty years. Those Italians still knew it was flat."

So after the prosecution rested and Ida asked me if I wanted to make an opening statement, I said, "Yes, if it please the Court," and I got up and walked to the lectern with no clear idea of what to say. I decided to put some stuff out there in the most edible form, hoping they would take a bite or two and, in their own time, transform it into a lingering doubt.

"We've come a long way," I said, holding on to the lectern. "We've been together about a month now, and you've convicted my client of murder. Soon you'll have to decide what to do with him. You've seen him in court, and you've met him through the eyes and minds of others—all the people who have testified about him—and you may think you know him. I am going to suggest to you that, perhaps, you don't."

I needed a refrain. Martin Luther King wasn't the first to use the technique, but he was the best. "I'm going to suggest to you—I believe our evidence will show—that the person you think you see isn't Drusus Church at all. The person you think you see is a large young powerful black man with one of those awful, pitiless hearts that permits him to murder and rob. The person you think you see is an animal who doesn't deserve your consideration or mercy."

I wandered away from the lectern with a thoughtful look on my face. When I was getting started I had practiced that look in front of a mirror. "I'm going to suggest to you that the person you think you see isn't like that at all." I looked them over with all the sincerity I could muster. What a game. I used to practice that one, too.

"You will hear from two teachers: one from his high school days, and another who knew him later. She teaches a course in remedial English at the adult high school Drusus Church was enrolled in when he was arrested for the murder of Kingsley Rhoades. They will tell you some things about this young man's mind that may surprise you. You will discover he has a searching, insatiable, unquenchable desire to learn. I don't know why. Possibly so he can figure himself out." I gestured toward Drusus and saw his easy smile. Perfect, I thought, except the killers on the jury will think it's an act.

"You'll see him through the eyes of his mother, his sister, and his grandmother, too. Maybe you'll discover he does not have the heart of a murderer."

Keane rose slowly. "Your Honor—"

"Mr. Bard," Iron Pants said. She'd been frowning at me like a parent who knows she shouldn't spank the kid but doesn't like him pissing on the living room floor, either. "This is not argument."

"I'm telling them what I believe the evidence will show, Judge."

"I'm telling you, sir, this is not argument. Confine your remarks to the evidence and that does not include impressions."

The hell it doesn't, I thought. But I nodded my understanding and scratched my ear. "The person you will see, through our evidence, is a very complicated young man. Among other things, he is the direct result of his environment." Drusus's face tilted as I talked about him. He looked interested, but nothing more. "What is it like, growing up in a tough ghetto neighborhood?" I asked. "You'll have the chance to get a glimmer, a small insight, into that jungle, through our evidence. For one thing, if you are like Drusus Church, you make enemies."

I rested my left hand on the rail but didn't look at Juror Two. I could feel him shrink away from me. I decided to stay there long enough for him to realize I wasn't going to bite. "That is what his mother, his sister, and his grandmother—and others—will tell you. You may already have guessed my client belonged to a gang. But you will find that in that neighborhood, you don't make enemies when you belong to a gang. You make friends. In fact, you join a gang—usually when you're very young—to survive." Juror Two softened a little. He massaged his jaw. "Where you make enemies is when you quit. And that is what this young man did. He made enemies out of gang members because he quit."

I got back behind the lectern and leaned toward them, trying to see into their minds. I couldn't, and their expressions didn't tell me anything either. "He also made enemies because he wanted everyone in that neighborhood to know they had better not fool around with his family. He loved his little sister and his grandmother and his mom, and he was big enough, and strong enough, to take care of them. Drusus didn't allow people to bother his family, to hit on them, get in their faces. He would punish those people."

Now for the sticky part, I thought. Don't confront this jury with my belief they made a mistake. Just tell them he wouldn't use a gun. "But not with a gun. He didn't have to. You already know his moniker—his street name—was 'Hammer.' You will find, through our evidence, that he was kind of a policeman on the block. But he didn't enforce the law with a gun. He used his fists."

I was doing it again: searching faces and trying to decide who believed me, who didn't, who I should work on and who was a lost cause. All I knew for sure was that they were listening, that no one had fallen asleep.

"You'll hear from Drusus, too. He will take the stand, and he will be put through the test of cross-examination, and you will have the chance to see him yourself. The murder of Tommy Sherman? He will tell you he had nothing to do with it. But he won't deny the burglary in Compton. You will find out, however, that it wasn't quite what you think." I tried teasing them a little but didn't want to say too much. No point in giving Keane time to get ready.

"You will hear about him through our experts, too. A social anthropologist will help you see the world through his eyes, so you can understand why he may have acted in ways that seem wrong from our perspective but could be necessary for survival in the ghetto. A man who has studied gangs will tell you—among other things—of the inevitability of belonging if you have the luck to be born into a ghetto, as well as the consequences of quitting."

I took a deep breath, because I hated telling them about our last expert—not out of shame, but because of what it said about our society. "We also have a former warden. He will tell you that if Drusus Church is allowed to live, he would probably be a good influence in prison. He can do good there, possibly save a life, because of his constructive attitude."

I looked at Ida. She had one of those old-fashioned Mona Lisa expressions, but her eyes were on Drusus. "When you get this case, ladies and gentlemen," I said, trying to sneak it in when it looked like I could get away with it, "I do not believe you will vote to execute. I believe our evidence will be more than enough to convince you that this young man's life should be spared." I sat down.

Iron Pants looked at the clock on the wall: twenty minutes before noon. "Mister Bard, let me suggest that we break now for lunch."

The old lady was going to give me a break? "I would much appreciate it, Judge. And I have a further request."

Give them an inch and they'll take a mile, her face said. "You may ask, sir."

"I hadn't expected to go on this quickly, Judge. Can we start up at two?"

She looked over at the jury as though asking them how they felt about it. "Will that be all right with you, Mister Williams?"

He looked impatient, but that was all Mr. Nice Guy—in front of the jury—could afford. "Whatever you decide, Judge."

She nodded, gave her usual admonishment to the jury, then said, "We're in recess until two."

I got back to the office as quick as I could. My beeper has a setting on it that works like an electric prod; I use it when I'm in court. I had enough juice in me to light up the building. The signal I'd gotten from Carlotta was the equivalent of red alert.

"Hi, Mouse."

"Daddy, can I stay with you? That son of a bitch!"

At that moment she looked more like Robyn than Robyn had after her second miscarriage. What a tangle. "What happened?" I asked, my heart and stomach wilting with pity. Whitney sat in the chair near the library. He nodded a quick "Hi," then looked away, knowing he'd have to wait his turn. "Let's go in here, Mouse. Then you can tell me all about it." I pushed her into my office. Carlotta hadn't even looked up when I came in the office. She kept on typing as though she hadn't seen me.

"I'm sorry, Daddy," Mouse said after I'd shut the door and opened my arms to her. She snuggled into my chest. "I know you're in a trial and you don't need this."

"Wrong," I said. "You are the most important creature on this planet. God might not know that, but I do. What happened?"

"Just hold me a minute, okay?"

"Okay." I could feel her body as it warmed in my arms and relaxed.

"This isn't incest, is it?"

"Mouse!" She giggled, nestling more comfortably against my chest. But I could feel her tears soaking through my shirt. "It's trust," I said, so grateful for that moment and the knowledge that she trusted me. What kind of monster can betray that trust? "I'll kill him if you want," I told her.

"Good!"

It took a few minutes to get the story. Clark—when she'd married him she told me he was named after Clark Gable, not Clark Kent—was in trouble with the Arizona State Bar Ethics Committee. He was under investigation for stealing money from a client. When she first found out about it she'd wanted to do everything she could to help—until learning what he'd used it for.

"Another woman?"

"Another life! A condo on Lake Tahoe I've never even seen!"

We were sitting down by this time, in chairs in front of my desk. "Business?"

"Hah! I've seen pictures of some of the women he takes there."

"I'm glad it's women."

"Oh, Daddy, don't be so old-fashioned!"

We talked a few more minutes when she caught me looking at my watch and got up. "You run on home, hon." I fished a twenty-dollar bill out of my pocket. "I don't have any daiquiri mix," I said, handing it to her. "We'll talk tonight."

"I love you, Daddy."

"You should. Beat it."

Carlotta didn't think she should, though. Carlotta told me it was time for Mouse to grow up. She told me it was time for me to grow up, too. "You guys are cos," she said, pounding away at the word processor after Mouse had gone. "Codependents. Disgusting!"

Sometimes I think I know why Carlotta is so beautiful. She has transformed herself into this spectacular creature searching for someone to trust.

Whitney lumbered into my office. "Have you heard anything more from Mad Dog?" he asked, settling into a chair. It held.

"No. We have until Monday."

"What does Drusus say? Does he want to take the deal?"

"I haven't talked to him about it. He doesn't know about it yet."

The big man quit picking lint off his pants. "You gonna? I mean, don't you have to tell him about it? Legal ethics—which is a crock of shit."

"Oxymoron, Whitney. Not a crock of shit. I'll tell him after he testifies."

Whitney shook his head. "Meaning you want to keep that throb in his voice when he talks to the jury?" He found more lint. "Jesus. I'd hate being a lawyer."

"Yeah. Am I gonna have any witnesses this afternoon?"

"Can you start with Sal? He's getting real tight. I don't want to have to sit on him."

I nodded, making a note. "Who else?"

"Elizabeth Gorman and Angela Price."

The teachers. "How will they be?"

"Price'll be good. Gorman has trouble remembering him, but she doesn't believe in capital punishment."

"She'll be okay, then. Who else?"

"The family. Too bad they can't sit in there and listen."

"It's almost better this way. The jurors have seen them in the hall, and they'll know who they are when they testify. Experts?"

"On call—except for the warden, whatever his name is. You have to schedule him in advance. He'll be here Friday at two o'clock. He's got a flight out at five."

There was a time when I felt pressure over witnesses. It could be that the numbness I get in my gut during trial means I still do. I looked at my watch. "Anything on the Mad Dog angle?"

He avoided my eyes. "I got some hooks out, man. You don't want to know."

"I don't?"

"No. Except it ties in with the CI, and I'm getting nowhere on that."

"What have you done?"

"I made me a list of everyone in Drusus and Vera's apartment from a month before Kingsley got killed until two days after Drusus got arrested. Seventeen names. I talked to all of them except LuAnne Jones, and I don't have a clue."

"LuAnne?"

"Jim-Jim's girl."

"What are you trying to tell me?" I asked. "No CI? The cops knew exactly where to look for that purse before they blew over the door! How did they know?"

"Huh!" my man said, a startled look on his face. He lurched to his feet. "Maybe I been askin' the wrong question."

16

"Would you spell your name please, Mister Mira? For the court reporter." I smiled at Salvadore in a phony attempt to get him to smile back at me.

"M - I - R - A."

"Where do you live, sir?"

He gave his address on Cherry Street. Then suddenly he looked around him, at the jury and the judge and the spectators behind the bar. I recognized the expression: stage fright. Salvadore Mira had never had a microphone in his face. He was scared.

"Mister Mira, on March eighteenth of last year, were you living at that address?"

"Yes, sir."

He will be putty in the hands of the boy wonder, I thought. I'll have to tie it down as tight as I can. "You were working a couple of jobs back then, weren't you?"

"Objection, Judge. Leading," Keane said.

"Sustained."

Keane had seen the same thing. I realized he wouldn't make it easy. And on cross-examination he would have the right to ask leading questions of this piece of clay. He will be able to form poor old Salvadore into a statue for the prosecution. "Were you employed on that day, sir?" I asked, trying to convey to the witness: I am your friend.

Those guys—the judge and the nasty DA—are your enemies.

"Yes, sir."

"How many jobs did you have?"

"Two."

"A daytime job and a nighttime job?" I asked.

"Objection, Judge," Keane said, standing. "Not relevant."

I knew what he was doing, and if Ida had a brain in her head, she'd have known, too. The man who wanted to be the AG was sending a tough message to the witness. It said, watch yourself, buster. You are not on the side of law and order. "Sustained," Ida said.

"Judge, don't I get to respond?"

She glared at me. It's too bad those glares don't make it into the record. "Very well."

"This goes to the competence of the witness, Judge. It shows that the man is absolutely and completely capable of seeing what he saw and hearing what he heard. What he does for a living—how hard he works and so forth—is relevant to that issue."

Sometimes I really think Ida tries to be a judge instead of a prosecutor. "All right, Mister Bard," she said. "I'll allow it."

Keane knows how to play the game, I thought. As he sat down he looked angrily at the witness, but not at the judge. The translation: That was *your* fault, man. You are doomed. "So you have one job during the day and another at night?" I asked.

"Yes, sir," Salvadore said, his frightened eyes on Keane.

I should have asked him if he was afraid of the lawyer for the People. He'd have said, "That little prick? Hell, no, mon!" And then he wouldn't have been scared. All that Spanish macho that makes those guys such great Marines would have kicked in. "Tell us about the daytime job first, if you will, Mister Mira." I glanced toward the jury, trying to get him to do the same thing.

"I sell shoes."

It got easier the longer I kept him up there. The jurors laughed a couple of times, and he was finally able to look at them. He relaxed a little bit also. His posture didn't convey the rigid stance of a person in front of a firing squad. "And so that morning, after getting off your night-time job and driving home, you were sitting in your car?" I asked, repeating everything he'd said. It's dull, but it works. That way you never leave the jurors behind you.

"Yes, sir. Just sittin'. Kind of tired."

"Will you describe for the jury where your car was parked?"

He did. He had parked in his driveway, in front of the sidewalk. As he sat in the driver's seat he had a clear view of the apartment buildings down the street.

"But it was dark, wasn't it?" I asked, poking around to give him something to disagree with. When he did, it would make him a more credible witness.

"Not too dark. There's a streetlight across the street, and one on my side of the street maybe halfway down the block."

"Then you could see clearly?"

"Objection, Judge," Keane said, standing again and glaring at Salvadore. "He is leading the witness!"

"Yes. Sustained. Rephrase, please, Mr. Bard."

"How well could you see, Mister Mira?" I asked pleasantly, assessing Salvadore's expression. Good, I thought. He knows I am his friend, and the movie star isn't.

"Pretty good."

"Well enough to see people's faces?"

"Yeah."

I walked over to the exhibit board. It was a large chalkboard, three feet by five feet, mounted on a pedestal and facing out like a screen. A tablet of three-by-five-foot sheets of paper had been clipped to the top, and I folded the top sheet back, exposing the second one. "This is a diagram of Cherry Street between Anaheim and PCH," I told him. Earlier there had been a stipulation allowing me to use it. "It isn't drawn to scale. But it's been taken from the police reports, and it shows the houses and apartments along the block. Can you come over here, please, Mister Mira?"

"Sure."

As I questioned him he dutifully made X's at the right places: where he'd parked his car, where the streetlights were, then the apartment the men had come out of. His breathing shortened as it came back to him. With him standing in front of the board I asked him to describe what he had seen.

"They came out here," he said, putting a line on the paper. His eyes were lighted by the memory.

"What did they do?"

"Two guys was kind of like holding up this other guy who was between them."

"And then?"

"They stopped when this other man—the big man—came out."

"Going back to the three men. When the other man—the big man—came out, were the three men walking at that time, or did they stop, or what did they do?"

"They stopped and kind of turned around."

" 'Kind of' turned around?"

"I mean they turned around." He faced me and tried to smile. "They was all the way turned around, so I couldn't see their faces."

"But could you see the big man's face?"

"Yes, sir."

"So they were facing the big man at that point?"

"Yes."

I asked him to show with a mark the approximate location of the three men and to estimate the distance between them and his car. He did: forty feet. The big man was fifteen or twenty feet further away.

"And then?"

"It was kind of like a signal. These two guys let go the one in the middle and moved away." Salvadore's expression was that of a man who sees it again. "Then the big man says something—'Sorry, sucker' or something—and lifts a gun and shoots. Twice." Salvadore flinched with the memory, touching his stomach. "Then they go away."

"Who went where?" I asked. "Can you indicate?"

He did, with lines. The big man turned down Cherry

toward PCH, walking away. The youngest one—tall, thin, very dark—ran across Cherry and disappeared between a couple of houses. The other man—Salvadore remembered he wore a large Afro—walked right by his car. Salvadore didn't even look at him.

"Then what did you do?"

"Went in my house, sir. I called the police."

"Did you go outside to see the man who'd been shot? To see if you could help him or anything?"

"No."

"Why not?"

"Wasn't nothing I could do. The cops said stay inside."

"Did the police come?"

"Yeah. Two uniformed cops in about two minutes."

"Did you talk to them?"

"Yeah. One of them. I told him everything."

Now for the marbles, I thought. "Mr. Mira, did you get a good look at the man who did the shooting?"

"It was pretty good. I mean, it wasn't broad daylight."

"Was it good enough so you would recognize him if you saw him again?"

"Yes, sir. I'd recognize his face."

"Do you see that man in the courtroom now?"

He looked at Drusus. I couldn't breathe. He frowned. "No."

I breathed again. But I wanted it cleaner, always a risk. "With the Court's permission, can Mr. Church stand up?"

"Yes," Iron Pants said.

"Mr. Church, will you please stand?"

Drusus got up. With curiosity he gazed toward Salvadore Mira. "Mr. Mira, please look at this man carefully. Is he the man you saw?"

Mira frowned at me, then shrugged his shoulders as though to say "the hell with it" and leaned forward, staring at Drusus. Finally he settled back in the witness chair. "He ain't the one," he said. "He's big enough, but he ain't the one."

"For demonstration purposes, Your Honor, may I ask

the witness to say 'Sorry, sucker,' to see if there is voice identification?''

Ida frowned but said, "If you wish, sir."

She had more sense about it than I did. "Mr. Church, please say, in a normal voice, 'Sorry, sucker.' ''

"Sorry, sucker."

I looked at the witness, who frowned with uncertainty. When I saw his expression I didn't want to ask the question, but it was too late. "Was that the voice?"

"It could have been."

Oh, dear, I thought. "But you don't think so?"

"Objection, Judge. Leading."

"Sustained."

"Are you able to say with certainty whether that was the voice you heard on that night say 'Sorry sucker'?" I asked.

"No. Is all I can say is, it could have been."

"But you can say with certainty that this man is not the man who did the shooting that night?"

I'd hammered at him too long. It was starting to come apart in his mind. "No, I don't think he was."

When will you ever learn, laddie? I could hear old Charley say. Don't you know enough to quit when you're ahead? I nodded at Drusus as though that settled the matter, even though my persistence had just unsettled it. "You can sit down, Mister Church." I turned to the witness. "Now, you were contacted by the police—a couple of detectives—later, weren't you, Mister Mira?"

"Judge. I protest counsel's continued use of leading questions!" Keane said angrily, hamming it up to the hilt.

"This is minor stuff, Judge," I said. "I'm just trying to save time."

"Ask questions correctly, Mr. Bard. That will save time." She made a mark on the legal pad in front of her, as though giving me a demerit. "Sustained."

I smiled at everyone. I even turned around and smiled at the few spectators in the courtroom. "After the shooting that early morning on March eighteenth, were you contacted by anyone from the Long Beach Police Department?"

"Yes, sir."

I began phrasing my questions correctly, dragging them out like roads to nowhere. It was infantile and stupid and didn't do any good, and I stopped when I looked at Keane and noticed how much he enjoyed my tantrum. That got me back on the track, and I started acting like a grown-up again. Salvadore testified about being shown the mug-shot folder, not recognizing anyone, and never being contacted by the police again.

Then I tried to put him in the right frame of mind for the boy wonder. "Mister Mira, are you afraid to tell the truth here?"

It was the right question. "No."

"Are you aware of the fact that you are testifying here for the defendant, Drusus Church?"

"Sure."

"Are you aware of the fact that you will soon be cross-examined by the prosecutor, Mr. Williams?"

"Yeah." He looked toward Keane with something like anticipation.

Sit down, laddie, I heard old Charley say. "Very well. Your witness, Mr. Williams."

Keane worked him smoothly. He started by showing him a picture—a mug shot—of Larry Walker. I had to admire the tactic, because Keane couldn't lose. If Mira identified Walker as one of the men who were there, then the *Greening* of Walker—the statement he'd given to Rory Danforth identifying Drusus as the shooter—would get a huge boost in the eyes of the jury. And if Mira couldn't identify Walker, then the jury would know the man's recollection couldn't be trusted. "Yeah, that's the guy with the Afro," Salvadore said. "He walked right by my car." I stipulated as to the identity of the person in the photograph, shrugging my shoulders as though it made no difference.

Then Keane went to work on the voice identification, playing with Mira's answer: "It could have been." The pitch was the same, the accent was the same, practically everything was the same, wasn't it? "They're a lot alike," Mira admitted. When Keane was done, Mira's "It could have been" was transformed to "It probably was."

169

It was easy, after that, for Keane to get Salvadore to question his own memory. Three o'clock A.M., no moon, no stars even, right? You couldn't see very well, could you, sir? You were bone-tired, too, and when this happened it woke you up, didn't it? And it happened so fast. I'll bet your heart rate jumped from eighty beats a minute to over two hundred in the space of five seconds, right, sir? Yeah, it got pumped, Salvadore admitted.

"Then you could have made a mistake in what you saw, right?" and Salvadore admitted that he could have. "But you didn't make a mistake in what you heard. Did you, sir?"

"No. I heard him all right."

Keane knows when to quit, I thought, watching him sit down.

It's times like that when you'd like to let your mind drift with the clouds and speculate on the nature of truth. Instead I had to call my next witness. "Elizabeth Gorman."

Gorman—a black woman, early forties, wearing a green suit and a severe expression—conveyed the impression of neatness and order. Everything about her was in place. Whitney had told me of her trouble remembering Drusus, but when she saw him she nodded and—for the barest part of a moment—looked surprised. Her testimony was a wash, naturally. It gave both Keane and me ammunition for argument. She taught "History Through Literature" at Roosevelt High School and remembered wondering how and why he got into her class. She remembered being impressed with the young man's intellect, even though his grades— D's and F's—were awful. "He just let others drag him down," she said.

I put in evidence one of her report cards so the jury could see the comment she'd written on the back: "You have a fine mind, young man. Do you ever intend to use it?"

Angela Price got up next. The large, obese young woman might have had trouble pushing herself away from the table, but there was nothing wrong with her head. Blond, blue-eyed, and cheerful, she taught remedial English at the Long

Beach Adult Education High School and had no trouble recognizing Drusus. "He was one of my very best students," she said. "In the space of five or six months—that is, from mid–November, when he joined us, until mid–April, when he stopped coming—I would say he made enormous progress. His writing skills especially showed marked improvement." She even agreed with me that he frequently challenged her intellectually, never inappropriately, but in such a way as to cause her to rethink her own attitudes.

But she was a wash, too. Her attendance records showed Drusus did not go to class from March 17 until March 27. Keane asked her if she knew where he was, if he'd offered any explanation for his "disappearance," if he ever seemed in need of money. I objected to that one, but Ida let it in! "No, my impression was that he was not poor."

I tried sticking it back to Keane. I got her to agree with me that Drusus didn't wear gold chains, or flash wads of money, or dress in obviously expensive clothes, all the time trying to find truth from a perch on that cloud in the sky. I'll never know if it was too high or too low.

Drusus's family testified next. They were no surprise. They'd been sitting in the hall along with the other witnesses, where they'd been waiting—except for his mother, who had to work—from the first day of trial. I knew the jurors had seen them and probably knew who they were, so in a way it was like introducing the friends of friends.

All of them had different last names, but their love and concern for the man next to me couldn't have been more real. Drusus smiled at them as they talked about him, and— at last, I thought—his gentleness was out there where the jury could see it. Even Juror Four seemed uncertain. Tiki— Drusus's half-sister, two years younger—recalled the times Drusus had stepped in and straightened out people who wanted to mess with her. She talked of playing with him, too, how he'd take her and her friends to the park, and she and her playmates would know they were safe. Mrs. Gold, his mother, seemed to blame herself and all her husbands for her son's problems. And Mrs. Cattle—arthritic, black eyes alive with emotion—told the jurors how he would spend nights with her and make sure she took her medicine, and of the awful mess he made of a man who ran off with her purse.

Keane was properly sympathetic but got them all to agree they'd do anything to save his life. He didn't add, "Even lie, right?"—but he would argue it.

We adjourned. Drusus would go on in the morning. I wondered who the jury would see.

17

When I got home Mouse was in the bag. That was okay. She's like her mother was: a classy drunk. But the kitchen was a mess. She'd tried to make herself a chocolate angel-food cake from scratch, but half the ingredients were on the floor. That was okay, except she'd skidded on the stuff—egg yolks, I think—and fallen in the middle of it. Her clothes, bare arms, and face were smeared with goo.

That is what I found at seven that evening when I trudged through the door. A pitcher of margaritas was next to her. Her back leaned against a leg of the kitchen table, and she was humming to herself. "Hi, Daddy," she said when she saw me. "Want a drink?"

Mouse learned a long time ago that her daddy was a lawyer, so she quit paying attention to his words. I knew my words wouldn't do much good at that moment. I also knew I was pissed. It was terribly insensitive of me; my little girl had just been betrayed by her husband. I should have gone to her and wrapped my arms around her soggy, egg-drenched body. But I could not. "Stay right where you are, my little darling," I said. "I'll get us some help."

"Okay, Daddy," she said, pouring herself another drink.

I called Carlotta. Carlotta laid down a condition: Once she got there I had to leave. "Okay." I called Erin, who said, "Good for Carlotta!" She told me I could come over as long as I brought a bottle of wine, something pleasant to say, and no family baggage. She was not in the mood for my problems.

That sounded great to me, because I wasn't either.

But fifteen minutes later, when Carlotta arrived on the scene, I hesitated. Mouse was still sitting in the kitchen, humming to herself, and I noticed that Carlotta had hooked up the outdoor hose. "Beat it, Jack," she said to me, aiming the nozzle in the direction of my darling little girl. "A promise is a promise. This won't hurt her. But you don't want to watch."

"Don't worry," Erin said later. I don't remember driving to her house, but there I was, pouring her a glass of wine as she made us a salad. "Tough love."

"Huh! Tough shit!"

By eight-thirty that night I was half in the bag myself. It doesn't take as long as it once did, which is an advantage of having part of your stomach chopped away. I was having one of those wondrous moments where all I could do was feel gratitude for the women in my life. It started, for me, with my mother, tough, cheerful, and warm. Then Robyn and her world-class ass. I told her she still had it two days before she slipped away. She smiled, weak, tired, worn out with pain; but she had the heart to bless me with her smile.

I let my body hum like a cat with thankfulness. Erin might kick me out of her life at any moment, but she seemed to like having me around. Mouse still had my influence to overcome, but she'd clear that hurdle soon enough. And Carlotta had her beauty and her spunk—and her troubled heart. I wondered if the little frozen spots would ever melt. What an arrangement. At that moment Erin and I were huddled into each other on the couch. We were—or at least I was—feeling the peace, and the comfort, of shared love.

Carlotta called. Erin handed me the telephone. "Give yourself a raise, kid," I said.

"Can't," she said. "You can't afford it."

"Why not?"

"I've hired your daughter."

We buzzed back and forth about that for a while. Then she told me the real reason for her call. "Whitney is at the office. Says it's important."

One advantage to having my office in the SeaFarer Hotel is that the lobby is always open and a bellman is always on duty. I parked in the "Guests Only" lane and waved away a valet who wanted to park it. "It's in my lease," I told him, pocketing the keys. "Don't worry."

A huge wedding reception was being tossed in the Lighthouse Room. Guests in tuxedos and elegant dresses were spilling all over the lobby. I caught a glimpse of an elderly, tough-looking man with a buzzard eye and proprietary manner wearing a scarlet cummerbund. He looked like the pirate who was rich enough to afford the splash. I wondered what *his* daughter was like.

Whitney was reading a short story by Karl Hansen in *Omni* when I opened the door. "This guy is good," he said, tucking the magazine under his arm and following me into my office. "Science-fiction porn. Really weird stuff." I knew I'd never see the magazine again.

I opened the liquor cabinet, pulled out two small glasses, and filled them both with brandy. It's something of a ritual with Whitney. When he has to open up my office after eight we always share a glass. Among other things, it gives me the chance to see how much he drank before I got there. "Cheers."

"Good on you, boss."

He seemed to be having trouble deciding how to bring up the subject, whatever it was. He didn't even sit down. "I think I've got a feel for Mad Dog's problem," he said, draining his glass. "But we can't talk about it here. Let's go downstairs and mingle with the guests."

"Why? Do you think there's a bug?"

"It wouldn't be the first time."

I grinned but started for the door. "You're getting paranoid, Whitney."

"Like you in the courtroom."

We found a love seat in the huge lobby, about a quarter

of a mile away from all the gaiety. It overlooked the bay. I watched the pirate watching us as we strolled across the lobby floor. "You have piqued my curiosity, as they say," I said, sitting down.

Whitney grunted. His eyes were half closed, which meant he was totally aware of everything within a radius of fifty feet. "Boss, my ass is hangin' out on this one. Some others are, too."

That meant he wanted some assurances, so I gave them to him. "Total quiet, Whitney. Absolutely no burn." He nodded with understanding. Whatever he told me was totally confidential. Before using what he told me in any way I not only had to check with him first but had to get his permission.

A fancy man with black hair and pearly teeth crossed the lobby floor toward us. He had just been talking with the pirate. "Good evening, gentlemen," he said. "How are you? We got a private party here, and Mister Hightower wanted to know could I see your invitation?"

"We aren't guests," I said, recognizing the name. Among his possessions, Hightower owned the Signal Hill Police Department lock, stock, and barrel. "I'm a tenant here at the hotel." I fished around for a card and pulled it out. "Jack Bard. This man and I need a clean place to talk."

The man looked at my card. "So you're an attorney. Look around you, Mr. Bard. Do you see any other tenants here? If you gentlemen don't mind, how about the bar?" He smiled with his mouth, but nothing else joined in. "Mister Hightower would be happy to buy your drinks."

Whitney pulled out his billfold and yanked out a couple of twenties. "For the bride, man. We won't be long. The bar's real noisy."

The elegant young killer examined Whitney a moment, then folded the money next to my card. "You gonna get any closer than this?"

"No, man. No need."

"How long will you gentlemen be?"

Whitney glanced at me, then said, "Five minutes max. I got to make a living, you know."

"I'll see if Mr. Hightower will allow." He walked away.

"You know that guy?" I asked.

"Just one of Hightower's shields, man. Probably has more notches than Billy the Kid." He snorted. "Drusus fightin' in a court for his life, and that goon out lapping it up. Make sense?"

What a grand and glorious gift is life, I thought. "No."

"Let's get down on it, man. You remember that hearing you had in court with Mad Dog? Where you tried to get the prosecution to give up the name of their confidential informant?"

"Yeah. Evidence Code 1042(d). I did it in Muny Court, because I thought old Kevin Halloran would be fair."

"There was that *in camera* bit, remember? Where the judge talked to the cop, and nobody there but the court reporter?"

"Go on." The record of that conversation had been sealed. But it was what Kevin had based his decision on.

"I saw a copy of the transcript of what was said. Don't ask me how, okay?"

"Don't worry, Whitney. I don't want to know." Hightower's shield gave Whitney a wave. It poisoned my gut that we had to have his permission, but it wasn't worth trouble. What a country. "Did you make a copy?"

"No way. I barely got it read, but I know what it said."

"What?"

Whitney could talk like a ventriloquist, without even moving his mouth. He tossed his voice as far as me—two feet away—but no further. "All that stuff you did that day, you know, tryin' to show the judge all the people who might want to frame the kid? All the testimony you put on about Drusus's enemies, him an ex–Blade and the people in the 'hood he beat up on to keep it nice for his family? It made an impression." He waited to make sure I was with him. "Judge Halloran wanted to make real sure the kid was not being set up. He made Kincaid prove to him the CI wasn't from that set."

"Who was the CI, Whitney?"

"Vera Byrd's mother."

I stared out the window. "Vera's mom? I didn't expect that."

"Here's what Kincaid said the old lady told him. She came over to see her daughter two days after the Rhoades hit. All kinds of tales floating around the streets then, the woman said. One was that Drusus knocked over the Kingman, getting even over something. So Vera's mother paid a visit to make sure everything was okay."

"And?"

"She saw the purse on the bookshelf. The bit about the purse was ripped off Kingman's neck, you know, that was on the streets, too. Vera's mom knew what it looked like, apparently. Kincaid didn't get into that, but maybe she'd seen it around his neck. So she told Kincaid she saw it, just sitting out there in front of those books by Goines like a trophy. She didn't let on to Vera anything about it."

"But she told the cops? Why?"

"She been tryin' to get Vera away from Drusus a long time. But if Vera knew it was her who told the po-lice, that would be the end of it. Said the only way she'd tell it is if she could stay completely out of it."

I sank into the cushion. "So Drusus did it after all?"

"Hold on, man. You want to hear the rest of the story?"

"Yes!"

"I tried to get a line on Vera's mom." The fancy man in the tuxedo peeled away from a knot of guests and walked toward us. He smiled nicely at Whitney, but something about the way he held the palms of his hands seemed to say, your time is up. Whitney nodded at the man and started to stand. "There ain't no such person, Jack. Vera doesn't even know who her mother is."

I got up, too, trying to understand what it meant. "You mean there isn't a confidential informant? No one?" It didn't make sense. At all. "What is going on?"

"You tell me."

* * *

A Lingering Doubt

You never know whether you're right or wrong about the jury, but the attitude I seemed to pick up on as Drusus climbed into the witness box was curiosity. There was one exception: Juror Twelve. Mrs. Carroll, a heavy woman in her middle thirties, held one hand over her face like a shield, as though to protect herself.

Drusus was my first witness that morning. I wanted to put him on while the jurors were fresh, while their minds were clean, rested, and receptive. I believed in the youngster and hoped he would print them with that odd quality of decency and respect he had stamped on me. Was I just another sucker? Or was there truly something different about this man?

He has presence, I thought, watching his movements from my station behind the lectern. There was a naturalness about him, a frankness. He made a good entrance, like Richard Burton coming on stage, or Sean Connery's first appearance in a movie, or O. J. Simpson taking a chair in a high-school auditorium. There was no way to hide his musculature because shirt sizes weren't large enough for his shoulders. He wore a long-sleeved light green cotton tent buttoned at the cuffs. On him it looked small through the back.

I waited until he was settled in. "Your name?" I asked.

"Drusus Church."

"You are the defendant here, correct?"

"Yes, sir."

I took my time. I wanted the jurors to feel him, not just know him; to sit next to this powerful yet truly gentle man long enough to feel comfortable with him. In spite of the fact he was on trial for his life, I wanted them to know how easy he was within himself. I hoped to point out that the youngster actually was the way most of us wish we were, with no need to rush into conversation, not the kind of person who is terrified by silence. So I took my time. Maybe some of the jurors will appreciate the confidence he has in himself, I thought. Maybe later, when they face one another in the jury room, they will ask themselves: Is he a killer?

"How old are you, Mister Church?"

"Twenty. I be twenty-one in two months."

"You were arrested on April eighteenth last year, weren't you, sir?"

"Yes."

"And since that time you've been in jail?"

"Yes, sir."

There are two schools of thought about letting the jury know your client is in jail. A lot of jurors—a lot of citizens—think cops never make mistakes. They assume that people in jail are automatically guilty. But we were in the penalty phase. They'd already found him guilty. Now I wanted them to empathize with his condition. "How do you like it?"

His wide, sloping shoulders lifted as he tilted his head. He obviously hadn't spent much time thinking about it. "It's all right. They do their best."

"Do you mean the guards, your jailers, do their best?"

"Yes, sir."

I adjusted my glasses as though reading significance into his answer. I cleared my throat. "You don't mean you'd just as soon be in jail, do you?"

He smiled. "No, sir. I miss my freedom."

With some defendants you can't finish with them quick enough, but I had the sense that we were off to a good start. I thought he would wear well, and at that point I wouldn't have minded leaving him up there all day. He knew in a general way what I would ask him, but we hadn't rehearsed it. I wanted his responses to be genuine, not studied, even when it came to cross-examination. "Mister Church"—I looked up at Ida—"may I address the defendant by his first name?"

"It's Drusus," the youngster said. "Sure."

Iron Pants looked down at him from her throne. "Mister Church, the question was for me," she said pleasantly. He glanced at her quickly, then looked at his hands, smiling with an easy embarrassment.

She thought it over. I did, too, thinking I'd screwed up. Why had I asked? I should have gone ahead and called him by his first name until Keane objected, then argued the question. But Ida surprised me. "You may."

Keane acted as though he didn't care. He sat stiff-backed in his chair, bent toward a legal pad, taking notes. He faced more toward the jury than the witness, which is what they teach them to do in prosecutors' schools. It sends a message: the People have their eye on you.

The youngster was a pleasure to question compared to most of the miscreants I've tried to restore to society. Drusus's answers were direct, delivered in a soft but powerful voice, without fear. He described his life with his mother, grandmother, and half-sister, many of the places he'd lived, and some of the things he'd done. He remembered visiting in Long Beach before moving to the community at the age of eleven, and not liking it. His then-stepfather "knocked me around some" and kept pushing him outdoors, where kids stood in line, it seemed, to beat him up. Until that time he'd lived in Vallejo with his grandmother. He hadn't known his real dad very well. The man was in prison until Drusus was seven or eight. Then, when they let him out on parole, he got himself killed.

I showed Drusus a picture of a nine-year-old boy wearing a coat and tie and staring into an open coffin. The photograph, in color, showed a brightly lit room with high-backed pews in the background and yellow walls. The boy had a tear in his eye. "Can you identify this photograph?"

Drusus looked at me with a touch of disappointment. He hadn't known I had the photograph. "Yeah."

"What is it?"

"That's me at my daddy's funeral."

"Do you mind if I show this photograph to the jury?"

His face closed slightly as he looked away from me. I hoped the jurors would see that he didn't really want to share his private life with them. "I don't mind."

I offered it in evidence, then requested permission to let the jurors see it. None of them looked at it very long, and all their expressions were hidden behind private veils, but it seemed to me that all were touched by it—except Juror Twelve. She refused to look, as though to protect herself from seeing something that could get in the way of what she already knew to be the truth.

Drusus and I had talked about the risk of the next line of questions but decided to take it. The problem was that we would "open the door." Once opened, there was no closing it. I didn't really know what Keane would try to drive through that open door when he took the witness on cross-examination. That's what makes lawsuits a bit like crapshoots. "Did you belong to a street gang?"

"Yes, sir."

He told the jury he was eleven years old when he "jumped in." When asked why, his answer was simple: "Survival." Did he like it? "Not at first. I was scared all the time, and all my homeboys wanted to do was take bites out of me." What about later? "It got to where it was— don't know how to say it—cool. Exciting and fun. I liked it a lot. My homeboys were my family." He looked at me with simple honesty. "You learn the rules, you know, the code. After that, people—at least in my neighborhood— respected me."

"And was that important?"

"Yes, sir. When you're fourteen years old and you're feelin' all kinds of things in your heart, you know, about girls and life—" He stopped, as though afraid to say any more.

"Go on."

"You know." His voice had a really superb resonance. It filled the room with life. "TV and images, and you see people all around who have it all. And you're black, and you want what it look like everybody else can reach out and take." He looked behind me at one of the court-watchers. "That's when respect kind of like a religion. You can't let anybody dis you, but as long as you're willing to stand and everybody knows it, then when you walk on the street it feel good."

"Dis you?" I asked. "What does that mean?"

"Like, offer you disrespect. Then you got to stand."

To that point Keane Williams had not even looked at Drusus Church. As he leaned over his notepad with his torso more toward the jury box than the witness his attitude suggested he would turn his back on the witness if he could. But when Drusus used the word "stand" he glanced at him with coldness and made a note. Quickly he turned away again. It was almost as though he were talking to the jury, telling them by his expression, "Don't let this killer fill you with his hype. He is a scourge, and he deserves to die."

I thought about approaching the sidebar. But my feeling was that the jurors were looking past Keane at Drusus. I left it alone, but I also kept away from the word "stand." On cross-examination Keane might try to turn it into "duel," "fight," or "kill." That's what I'd have tried. Iron Pants would have some decisions to make.

"Did there come a time when you wanted out of the gang?"

"Yes, sir."

"Why?"

"Seemed like too much of my life caught up in the wrong thing."

Then we went over other aspects of his past life: the fact he'd been sentenced twice to youth camps, once to a term in the California Youth Authority, and once, as a convicted felon, to prison. "All that happen after I join the gang. Maybe I'm slow, but it took some time before I'd see the connection. I didn't want that for my life. Then I notice something else. I don't see very man OGs—that's for 'Old Gangster' or 'Original Gangster,' meaning people who been in the set long enough for status—around. A lot are dead, and others gone to prison. So when come my time to be an OG I didn't want it."

"Why?"

"Too risky. More to life than that. I met Vera, and it seem like we fit, you know, we were right for each other. I start thinking about kids, family, a nice place to live. Things like that."

"But they were out of reach, weren't they?" I asked.

"No, sir. Hard to get there, but I come to see where there was people who would help me if I'd let them in.

Vera got me enrolled in that adult high school, and you give me a job, Mr. Bard."

"Then you worked for me?"

He smiled. My tone had made it sound like I wanted to know. And how could I not know? "Yes, sir."

I stopped, looked down at my notes on the lectern, and tried to let the jurors feel the respect I had for my client. I kept still a moment in the hope they would pick it up, too. Then I went on with the examination. "You heard Mrs. Greer testify about a burglary in Compton, didn't you?"

"Yes, sir."

"Did you commit that burglary?"

"Yes, sir."

"Why?"

"Jim-Jim and me on a mission, but we messed up." A wry little smile. "We went to the wrong house."

"You'll have to explain."

He did. At Camp Fitzpatrick Drusus had gotten to know a gangster in a rival Blade set from Compton. They'd "dissed" one another and stood, then had to spend a week each in the "box." That was the term used for the isolation cells at the camp. But as often happens, after sharing the experience they had respect for each other. "Then after we're out, we see each other sometimes, you know, make faces, but the respect doesn't go away. Then one day I'm on the street in my neighborhood, and this bomber turns the corner, and it's on me."

" 'Bomber'?" I asked.

"That's a big car, kind of like a throwaway car. Usually stolen. It get used by gangsters when they do something wrong."

"All right. Go on."

"So when I see the car runnin' right at me I thought: uh-oh. It look like a drive-by, with me the target. But this boy's face pops up, and he's got something in his hands"— Drusus grinned—"only it's a fire extinguisher. He squirts me good, then runs away."

"This was a game?"

"More like a prank, you know. I've read how Indians used to do the same thing. They go up to an enemy in his territory, and then all they do is touch him, kind of for the excitement of it. They called it counting coup."

Good, I thought, hoping all the jurors had seen *Dances with Wolves*. But I didn't want to get too far afield. Let Keane come back if he wants. "Then, when you broke into Mrs. Greer's house, did you think you were playing a prank on that other person?"

The question was about as objectionable as questions get, but Keane made no move. He maintained his posture that anything the witness said was beneath his contempt. "Yes, sir," Drusus said. "Jim-Jim said he'd help out, and we thought we'd go throw a scare at the boy."

"The gun you carried with you. Was it loaded?"

"No, sir."

I considered asking him what he had in mind, but he'd have told them he intended to put the barrel in the boy's ear and pull the trigger. I hoped Keane would think I was setting him up and not ask. "Obviously it didn't work out that way. What went wrong?"

"We had the wrong address."

"How did that happen?"

"What I think is—"

"Objection, Judge." Keane, on his feet, drew a line after all. But he still did not appear to notice Drusus. It was as though Keane were a Jew and Drusus were a Palestinian, and they had unwittingly found themselves at the same dinner party. "What the witness thinks is not evidence."

"Sustained."

Does Keane know what I'm trying to do here? I wondered. Is he that good? "How did you obtain the address?" I asked.

"From a person in my set who knew the boy."

"But it was the wrong address?"

"Yes."

"Did this person who gave you the wrong address know the right address?"

"Objection! That's hearsay on hearsay. Mister Bard—"

"Thank you, Mr. Williams. You may leave Mister Bard to me. The objection is sustained."

He knows, I thought. He won't allow obvious evidence of treachery within the gang. I put an expression on my face that clearly said, "I won that one, right?"—then moved, as though in triumph, away from the lectern.

I walked over to the far side of the jury box and stood in such a way that the youngster's eyes had to go past all of them. "Drusus, how do you feel about what you did to that household that night?"

Keane considered objecting but decided not to. I wished he'd go ahead, because I would then have the chance to respond with anguish.

"I feel bad."

"Will you elaborate, please?"

He looked at me with frank, open eyes. Then they squinted, as though blinking away a momentary twinge of pain. "Don't know how else to say it. I didn't know that woman, or her daughters or her husband either. We scared 'em bad. *They* didn't know what we was after. They hear all that noise at night, see me with a gun, and it turn their daddy into a buster, so they see that, too. I feel bad."

" 'Buster'? What does that mean?"

"A buster"—he rolled his right hand, thinking of the best way to define the term—"a person who lost his heart. A coward."

I let the jurors watch him. It seemed to me at that moment that they liked him. "What I don't understand, however, is why you should feel bad. You went to prison. So you paid. Why does it still bother you?"

Drusus spoke without hesitation, almost in anger: "That isn't the kind of thing a person can pay for."

I nodded slowly but thought: Shit. I hope that answer isn't too good. "Drusus, did you kill Tommy Sherman?"

"No, sir. I did not."

A good place to stop, I thought, glancing at my notes. Then I found a question I'd forgotten to ask. "Do you know April Tillman, the woman who claims she saw you shoot Kingsley Rhoades?"

"Yes, sir."

"How long have you known her?"

He shrugged. "Long time, Mr. Bard. She's a Blade."

You're on your own, youngster. "No further questions." I sat down.

18

Keane wasted no time in going for the throat. "You're a gang member, right? You're a Blade?"

"No, sir. Not now."

"You *were* a gangster, then. That's the correct term, incidentally, isn't it Mister Church? Gangster?"

Drusus smiled as though he would like to help. "Sometime what they say is 'gang banger.' "

"I see," Keane said icily. "Whatever you call yourself— gangster or gang banger—you won't try to deny that's what you were the night you broke into Mrs. Greer's house, will you?"

"No, sir."

"So we know, then, that you were a Blade approximately one year before the Tommy Sherman murder. Isn't that right?"

"Yes, sir."

"Are you used to calling people 'sir,' Mister Church?" Keane asked, smiling at the jury. "Somehow I wouldn't expect that of a Blade, or a former Blade."

I could have objected but didn't. "No, sir, I'm not," the youngster said mildly. "Mister Bard said I should show respect."

The simple honesty of the reply jolted Keane for the

barest part of a moment. "Then you talked your testimony over with Mr. Bard, right?"

"Yes, sir. We talked about it."

"I thought so. But let's stay with your conversion, your alleged conversion, your fierce desire to get out of the gang. You testified about this sudden feeling about the right way to live. Correct?"

"Don't know if I said 'sudden,' sir."

Keane stared at him harshly, as though he had just about had it with his attitude. "All right. In any event, this sudden feeling hadn't fallen on you when you broke into the Greer residence and brandished a gun at them, had it?"

"No, sir."

"And right after that you went to prison, where you spent the next eight months. Right?"

"That's right, sir."

"So all the time you were in prison—for eight months after that burglary with a firearm—you and Jim-Jim were gang members then, too, weren't you?"

He looked at the backs of his hands. "Jim-Jim was. But within me, kind of inside myself, I was pulling back."

"You were pulling back." He made it sound like a lie. "Then this sudden transformation or awakening in your soul—is that how it happened? You woke up one morning and the sun looked different, and you knew—from that day on—you would seek a better way?"

I could have stepped in but decided not to. Drusus could take care of himself. "No, sir. It didn't happen overnight. It was kind of slow."

"Jim-Jim stayed on as your friend, though, didn't he?"

"Yes, sir."

"As a matter of fact, he's still a gang member as far as you know. Isn't that right?"

"Yes, sir."

"He was your alibi earlier in this trial, the fellow who sat where you're sitting now and tried to tell this jury you were with him the night you murdered Kingsley Rhoades?"

"That's right, sir."

"So you were with this gangster friend of yours the night Kingsley Rhoades was killed by you. Right?"

Drusus's face hardened, and he looked away from the prosecutor. "I didn't kill Kingsley Rhoades."

"This jury says you did. That's already been determined as a fact. Are you telling this jury that they have failed miserably in the exercise of their judgment and that they have convicted an innocent man?"

"I ain't tellin' the jury anything, Mister Williams. All I'm saying is, I did not kill the Kingman."

"A very good answer," Keane said quickly, taking the floor away from the youngster. My adversary in the pit had a lot of technique. When the witness looks good, create a disturbance so the jurors will look at you. Then pepper the witness with questions until you get him to look bad. *That's* when you step back and let the jurors look at the witness. Keane and I must have read the same book. "A very good answer," he said, repeating himself. "I've observed, Mister Church, that your answers are very good. Right?"

Drusus looked surprised. He opened his palms to the prosecutor and raised his shoulders. "I don't know."

"You *do* know, however, don't you? You've worked on your answers, haven't you, sir?"

Drusus looked toward me, so I looked at my feet. "No," he said.

"Oh. I see. You haven't anticipated in the slightest degree that you would be cross-examined?"

"Yes, sir, I've known that."

"But you and your lawyer haven't done anything at all to prepare you? You haven't discussed any of this with your lawyer?"

"Like I said before, sir, we talked about it."

"Then you admit going over your answers and rehearsing them with your lawyer after all, don't you?"

Drusus showed a good-natured grin, as though he was being teased by an expert. "What do you want me to say, sir?"

Keane sneered with contempt. "A very good answer."

He lowered his head like a bull. "Tommy Sherman was murdered on March eighteenth, wasn't he?"

"Yes, sir."

"And you left Long Beach the next day, didn't you?"

"Yes, sir."

Williams jerked his head toward the jurors as though to include them in on this discovery. "So you don't deny running away from the neighborhood immediately after Tommy Sherman was murdered, do you?"

Drusus gazed without expression at the man in the suit behind the lectern. I hoped the jurors would not interpret his eyes as dangerous. "Yes, sir."

"Then you did run away!"

The jurors were watching, many of them critically. Drusus took a deep breath. "Yes, sir, I did."

"And before leaving you didn't let your teacher, Angela Price, know anything about it, did you?"

"No, I didn't. I didn't—"

"Then your answer is no?"

"Yes, sir."

"You were gone—how long? A week? Ten days?"

"About a week, I think, sir."

"That would be long enough for the investigation into that murder to lose its push, right?"

Drusus smiled a bit cynically. "I don't know the answer to that, sir."

Keane said nothing for a moment, allowing the jurors to watch the witness in the hope he looked bad. Then: "You know Larry Walker, don't you?"

"Yes, sir."

"He's someone you've known a long time, and not someone you've gotten to know since the trial started?"

"That's right."

"He'd been your friend for months, even years, before Tommy Sherman was murdered, right?"

"Larry and me never very tight, sir."

"But you don't deny knowing him, do you?"

"No, sir."

"He's a liar, I take it?"

"What he said about me was a lie." Drusus spoke in anger.

Keane regarded him with cynicism. "Just as April Tillman lied about seeing you kill Kingsley Rhoades, right?"

The muscles in Drusus's jaws were working. He looked at his hands. "Yes, sir."

"So she's a liar, too?"

Drusus relaxed and smiled. He looked over Keane's head and might have read the clock on the wall at the far end of the courtroom. His head rocked back and forth as though to relieve tension in his neck. "I can't say if she's a liar, sir. All I know is me."

"A very good answer." Keane spoke with anger and contempt. He let the jurors see him at his angriest, breathing deeply, barely controlled emotions, with nostrils flapping like those of a bull about to charge. I made a show of looking toward him and smiling, deciding to cut in on his act. Keep it up, I said to myself, and I'll offer Kleenex for your dripping nose. "This boy at Camp Fitzgerald, the one who stood up to you, do you remember that?"

"Yes, sir."

"You've stood with others, haven't you?"

"Yes, sir."

"On the streets as well as at camp?"

"Yes, sir."

"And you've challenged them, haven't you, to do their best? To take their best shot?"

I got up quickly. "Approach?"

"Judge, this is tactical," Keane said. "He's interrupting—"

"Mister Williams, you and Mister Bard may approach the bench."

The flap at the sidebar didn't last long. Ida said the door was open. I objected for the record, of course, which might make a difference on appeal but wouldn't save the youngster from the heat. Keane got back to the lectern in record time, but I made him wait while I smiled at him, then sat down.

The next ten minutes went by in a blur. Keane touched all the jurors' pressure points, punching up the images of the awful, mindless violence that forms the average citizen's notion of "gang." I fiddled with my hands. One time when a client of old Charley was getting hammered into dust, the grand old fellow made a paper airplane and sailed it at the prosecutor. I considered it.

Keane saved his best line of questions for the last, naturally. "Who is Leah Dempster?"

Drusus had kept his composure through the previous onslaught and kept it now. "She was my girlfriend."

"She testified during the guilt phase, didn't she?"

"Yes, sir."

"She told the jury about a gun—a cop gun—you'd shown her, do you remember that?"

"Yes, sir."

"You don't deny that you had such a gun and that you showed it to her then, do you?"

"No, I don't."

"You stole that weapon off a policeman, didn't you?"

"Yes, sir."

"Stealing a weapon off a policeman: a fairly typical gang mission?"

At that point Drusus was willing to agree with anything. "Yes, sir."

"A prank?"

"Yes, sir."

"How many cop guns did you steal, Mister Church?"

"That was the only one."

"A very good answer. How many weapons did you own?"

Drusus took a deep breath, his eyes sliding off me, then back to the prosecutor. "I don't know."

"So many that you can't count them?"

"It depend on what you mean by 'weapon.'"

"Oh," Keane said in a mocking tone. I was on my feet, ready to object if he kept on. "No further questions."

On redirect examination I had him explain why he had left town after Tommy Sherman's death: "The word on the street was the po-lice wanted me. They thought I'd done it.'' Hearsay, but it cut two ways, so Keane didn't object to it coming in.

"But didn't you tell this jury you didn't kill him?"

"I didn't kill him, Mr. Bard.'' His eyes had locked on mine, and to me he sounded truthful. I don't know what he sounded like to the panel.

"Then why did you run away?"

He slumped down as though his shoulders were too heavy. "I just got scared.''

I let the jurors examine him, hoping they would see what I saw. "No further questions.''

Keane didn't have any more, either. We broke for lunch.

When I called the office Mouse answered the telephone. "Law office of Jack Bard,'' she said.

"Hi, Mouse.'' Memories started chasing around in my head. "You sound like your mom.''

"Oh, hi, Daddy. What did you expect?'' Muffled tones. "Wait a sec.'' Carlotta's voice in the background. "Whitney's waiting for you at Redheads,'' Mouse said. "Okay?''

"Okay. You be home for dinner?"

"You're having dinner at Erin's, Pops. I'm living at Carlotta's until I get an apartment.'' I could hear the phone ring. It sounded like a newsroom. "I love you, Pops. Gotta go.''

Not everything about getting old is bad, I thought, hanging the telephone on its hook. I had a lump in my throat and tears in my eyes, and it felt good. That's the kind of thing that would have embarrassed me when I was young and tough.

Whitney was on his second cheeseburger when I walked into Redheads. "I only eat this much when it's on somebody else's expense account,'' he said when I sat down across from him.

I ordered coffee and a grilled cheese sandwich. They make one cauldron of coffee a day, and by the time noon rolls around it is strong enough to dissolve pennies. The grilled cheese sandwiches are full of grease, like they've been boiled in deep fat, then hung out to dry. Knowing what to expect makes it easier to wait for your food.

"I heard some stuff about Keane Williams," Whitney said.

"What?"

"He wants to be governor. The cat's a politician."

"Attorney general," I said, correcting him.

"Yeah, like the Duke. A stepping-stone."

"He might be good at it."

He put the rest of the sandwich in his mouth and swallowed, all in one motion. I thought of Jonah entering the whale. "Jack, the plot's gettin' too thick," he said, wiping off his fingers. "I can't figure out why Dave Kincaid would tell a bald-faced lie to the judge. Don't he know he's gonna get caught?"

His question brought back the revelations of the previous night: Whitney's reading of the transcript of the *in camera* hearing. Now we knew who the confidential informant was: the person who had seen Kingsley Rhoades's purse in the youngster's apartment. Kincaid had told the judge it was Vera Byrd's mother, which made sense to the judge, because she didn't know that Vera Byrd didn't have a mother. "What makes you think Kincaid will get caught in a lie?" I asked.

"Won't he?"

"That isn't the way it works, Whitney," I told him. I'd been thinking about it, too. "For one thing, maybe he didn't lie. Even if he did, he could still get away with it."

"Man, what are you talking about?" Whitney had finished off the cheeseburger as well as all his fries and pickles and was looking around for something more to eat when his eyes lit on me. From the tone of his voice I wasn't sure what to expect. "How could he not lie? Ain't no *way* he can get away with it!"

"What if some black grandmother came to him and told him she was Vera's mother?" I suggested. "All we know is Drusus was set up. What if it was like that?"

Whitney thought it over. "Huh." He slumped into the booth. "You know what the trouble is? Anything is possible. The first thing all ready to come out of my mouth, I'd say shit. It wouldn't be possible for what you just said. But you know what? About the only thing those kids *do* when they aren't blowin' each other to pieces is watch television. That's where they get their ideas. They see some new way to trick somebody on TV, some fast way to tear up an enemy, they try it on."

"So it's possible, right?"

"Yeah. But not likely. I think he lied. Because if he's any kind of cop, he'd verify his information, and then he'd know."

"What would he do to verify it?" I asked.

"He'd get some identification from the woman, like a driver's license or social security number. Then he'd run it."

"Let's say he did all that. She comes back clean. Here Kincaid is with what looks like hot information: a purse that could disappear in five minutes. What would he do?"

"How come you're tryin' so hard to make Kincaid out like he didn't lie?" Whitney asked. "You make me think you've known him too long."

You struggle with all kinds of doubts—self-doubts—when you try a case. I'd struggled with that one, too. "Dave and I go all the way back to high school," I said. "But if you think for one minute I would sacrifice my client to *that* kind of—"

"Yeah. Okay." He grinned at my anger. "Buy my own cheeseburger, right?"

"Right." I watched Annie take care of somebody else. "Hey, Annie!" I yelled. "Where's my food? I'm in trial."

"Go to McDonalds, then!" she hollered back.

I drank some of the coffee she'd poured when I first came in. "I think he lied, too. But here's what I can't get out of my mind: When the cops went in, they knew exactly where to go. How did they know?"

"Yeah." The Mountain leaned on the table. "So somebody had to tell them, right?"

"That's also what I think. But the real informant could be someone whose identity they knew they'd have to give up. Mad Dog would have seen that. He might have told Kincaid to cook up a phony one.''

Whitney frowned. "How does that work?"

"The cops—a lot of them—think everybody's a confidential informant. But if the CI really ought to be a witness in the case, like he saw or knows something that could help the defense, then the judge will tell the DA he has to give up the name. They scream and holler, naturally, because it can mean burning a good source of information. So what? Convicting some poor slob of something he didn't do isn't very nice either."

"Does the prosecutor ever say, 'Hey, Judge, I ain't gonna burn this guy anyway'? Does that happen?"

"There are times when justice prevails," I said. "When that happens—about once every ten years or so—the judge will dismiss the case. Then the cops and prosecutors go to work, and usually at the next election you have a new judge."

"Huh," Whitney said, peering at me. "So what you think now is the real CI is still out there?"

"Right."

"What does that do for us, man? You make it sound like it doesn't do any good what we know. Do I just keep on looking?"

Annie came over with my sandwich and poured me another cup of the fluid that looked as lethal as the black hole. The grilled cheese looked like a huge, square old-style Mexican tortilla chip, cut in half, that someone had softened with hot water. "Thanks, Annie."

"You gonna eat that?" Whitney asked as I picked up one half of it.

"I'm going to try. How much of this can we bring out now?"

"What do you mean?"

"I mean this: Can I file a motion now—today—telling the court that we know the CI is bogus?" I watched him as I chewed the grease-slogged bread. "We don't have a copy of the *in camera* transcript, and the record has been sealed. I'd have to file your affidavit to the effect you'd seen all that stuff, and how and why and so forth—and the shit would be in the fan."

"So I'd have to blow over my source, right?"

"Probably. We might be able to do it *ex parte* and *in camera*—"

"How about you speak to me in English?"

"I mean we might be able to do it without letting the prosecution know about it. But I don't think so. They'd find out soon enough. And even if we did, your source would get blown."

"Huh." I watched him wrestle with himself. "I'd be out of work, man. Probably in jail. Take some people down with me who don't deserve it." He took one of my fried potatoes. "They still get caught in this lie, won't they? On appeal?"

"That's only a maybe," I said. "And it's three years away."

"The man lied! Vera Byrd doesn't have a mama!" Angrily he inhaled another french fry. I did not want to get in his way. "How come it's just a maybe?"

"Because it won't come up as an issue for the Court of Appeals unless I bring it up."

"You'd bring it up, wouldn't you?"

"Bet your sweet ass. I could directly ask the appellate court to verify the identity of the informant. But Mad Dog has got to know the score. He's out there scrambling around right now, trying to figure out some way to cover his butt, and in three years he could make it."

"So what you're saying is, we don't have this thing won yet."

I couldn't eat any more of that cheese sausage. "I'm saying more than that." My next life, I'd like to be a person who never gets confronted with moral or ethical canyons. A preacher would be nice. "The deal they've offered still looks pretty good."

Whitney started moving out of the booth. "You talked to Drusus about that?"

"Not yet." I pushed the remains of my plate at the big man. "I might need your help."

"How did he do today?"

"The jury watched him pretty hard. Keane beat him up bad about having been a gangster. I don't know."

"So you have until Monday to take that deal, right?" I didn't say anything. "This stinks too bad, Jack." He pushed himself the rest of the way out. "I'm no lawyer, so I don't have to tell him he should be smart. It stinks too bad."

There was a huge snarl of traffic on the freeway, and I was fifteen minutes late getting back. I ran down the hall, trying to work up a sweat. Maybe Ida would take pity on me if she realized I'd risked a heart attack.

When I rounded the corner I realized something was wrong. My first expert should have been sitting in the hallway in front of the courtroom. If you aren't ready to go, Iron Pants will remove your head from your shoulders, I told myself—when it occurred to me that no one was there. Drusus's mother, grandmother, and sister should have been waiting there, too. I yanked on the door to the courtroom only to discover it was locked.

Fire drill, I wondered? Bomb scare? That didn't play, because there were people in the hallway, milling around in front of the other courtrooms. I found an open one and charged back into the private hallway behind. It was used to bring prisoners in and gave access to the judge's offices. I hustled into Ida's reception area. "Jack!" Keane was the first to greet me, even before no-name—Ida's clerk—who sat there with her usual intelligent look. Keane seemed shook up about something. "Judge Mather is waiting for you." He held the door to her chambers open.

Iron Pants didn't even have her robe on. She was talking to Ivan, the bailiff, when I came in. "Well. I didn't think you'd go this far," she said when she saw me. But she was smiling, so I decided I wasn't going to jail for contempt.

"Sorry I'm late, Judge. What is it?"

"Your client's been stabbed, Jack." She nodded at the court reporter, who started coiling paper into her little box. "Let's go on the record. We need to decide what to tell the jury."

19

I stood there like the fool in a bad dream. "What?"

Ida sat behind her desk and nodded at the court reporter. Keane gazed at me with what looked like concern, which was a part of his repertoire. "We'll give you a minute to collect yourself, Jack, but then we need to—"

"Where is he?" I demanded. "How bad? *What happened*, for God's sake?"

"Nobody knows, Jack," Ivan said. "Hey. Take it easy."

"Where is he?"

"Saint Mary's, on Tenth and Atlantic. The emergency ward."

"Ida, I have to talk to him," I said, striding toward the door.

"Just a minute, Jack! Now, just a moment!"

I stopped. "Judge, it is absolutely crucial that I be with my client," I said. "He might be charged with another crime. He might be dying. He might be under the influence of a painkiller, spilling his guts. I really need to—"

"All right. Do you want a mistrial?"

The court reporter was taking it all down. I almost said "Yes!" because a mistrial would mean time, but I held back. I could agree to something in the heat of the moment that could destroy us. "I don't know, Your Honor. I need to see my client first and think about it. He's a tough kid.

Maybe all he needs is a Band-Aid. But at the present time—as I stand here and try to talk—I can tell you I am extremely upset and in a great state of mental agitation. I am not competent, at this moment, to make a decision that could bind my client's future. The record should be clear on that."

She nodded. "Very well. Mister Williams, do you have a comment?"

"Judge, there are double jeopardy implications here. As the lawyer for the People, I have to be very careful."

She nodded again. "Mister Bard, I'm going to ask you to wait a few minutes longer. I would like to call the jury in and tell them to return tomorrow at ten o'clock." She nodded at Ivan, who started to leave.

"Hold it," I said. Ivan stopped. "I don't want to sit there without my client, Judge. The jury might think all kinds of things."

Her face clamped together in anger but softened as she thought about it. "True." Women really do make better judges than men, I thought. She heard *my* problem instead of hers. "Let's do this, then," she said. "Will both of you waive your presence in the courtroom? I'll return the jury and tell them something unexpected has happened—without any further comment—and that they are to report back tomorrow at ten. If neither of you is there, they won't have anyone to blame or not to blame. Does that sound fair?"

"It does to me," I said.

"Keane?" Ida asked.

He thought it over slowly. I had the sudden realization he was looking for advantage. I don't know why it pissed me off, but it did. I'd have done the same thing.

"It would be simpler if Jack asked for a mistrial on the penalty phase," he said. "I won't oppose it."

So that's what he wanted from me. From his point of view, where was the high ground in that? "I'll ask for a mistrial," I said, "as long as it's understood we start the whole thing over. Guilt phase, too."

"Get real, Jack," he said. "The guilt phase has been

decided. You're only entitled to a mistrial on the penalty phase.''

Ida made a calming gesture. "Gentlemen, this is what I propose to do. I'll excuse both of you now and direct you to return tomorrow at nine in the morning. I will then put on my robe and my best judicial manner and talk to the jury without you fellows there to interfere." She smiled, so I knew she was being witty. "I will tell them they are excused for the rest of the day in order to accommodate an unexpected development, and to report back tomorrow at ten. Do you consent to that procedure?"

"I do, Judge," I said. There are times when she really is a judge.

"Agreed," Keane said.

"Anything else?"

"I can't think of anything," I said, starting to open the door.

"Jack." Ida motioned to the court reporter, indicating we were off the record. "You really care what happened to that young hoodlum, don't you?"

"Yeah."

"I'm sorry, Jack. I hope he's okay."

I didn't go to the hospital right away. I had the sense to call Carlotta first, from a pay phone on the first floor. She knew Drusus had been stabbed. The Court had called, looking for me. She'd sent Mouse to the hospital to baby-sit. "Have you heard anything?"

She had. Mouse called and told her that Drusus was in the operating room and that she'd call again when there was more to report. "If your beeper had been on, you'd know all this," Carlotta told me.

"Bull shit. I was stuck in freeway traffic."

"If you weren't so old-fashioned and had a car telephone, you'd have known then."

"Damn it, Carlotta, I'm hooked into too much of the world already! I hate having a telephone in my *house!*" A Filipino woman was trying not to listen as I yelled at my ice-cold, red-hot Cuban secretary. "I'm going to the hospital. I want to be there—"

"Whitney has to see you," she said. "Can you come by here before you go there?"

"Yeah."

"He'll meet you in the lobby."

The "Guests Only" parking lane was filled with fancy cars, so I pulled up to the doorman and gave him a ten-dollar bill. "I may need it real quick," I told him.

"You're covered, Jack."

Whitney was sitting in the same love seat we'd been in the night before. If we hadn't had lunch together an hour before, I'd have thought he'd slept there. "Are you still worried about a bug?" I asked, sitting down.

"You'd be worried, too, if you took off them blinders you got on. I'm telling you, Jack. This thing has turned evil."

My man Whitney usually knows how to keep his cool, but I wondered if he was losing it. The feds use bugs, I'd heard, on high-profile cases. But the State of California, on a rinky-dink run-of-the-mill murder? I refused to believe that the justice machine had come to that. "What are you talking about?" I asked, deciding to humor him.

"I think the cops killed Kingsley Rhoades," he said. "They were the ones who ripped that purse off Kingman's neck. Then, when they searched Drusus's apartment, they planted it."

"Come off that crap, Whitney. They're bad, but they aren't that bad. Besides, we've been down that road."

"Jack, some things have happened you don't know about. I quit looking for an enemy who could have set the kid up and went back over where I been, this time with a different question. I also found LuAnne Jones."

I stuck my feet out there where I could see them. The search warrant had described the exact location of the purse, which meant—to me—that whoever put the purse on that bookshelf in Drusus's apartment had to have known it was there before the warrant was executed. That let the cops out. "Okay. What did you find?"

"The new question was this: Did the cops come to you before the Kingman got hit? If they did, what did they want?"

I shrugged. "Probably some of them said, 'Sure. They were looking for Drusus.' "

"That's not what I was after, though."

"What were you looking for?"

"I wanted to see if the cops knew what it looked like in Drusus's apartment before they went in. It wouldn't take much—just a description, enough for a warrant."

"And?"

"Vera Byrd talked to Dave Kincaid while Drusus was gone."

I sat up. "Where? In the apartment?"

"No. At the beauty shop she works on Pacific Boulevard. But he wanted to talk to her another time, in the apartment."

"Did he?"

"No. She laughed and giggled with him—you know, she thought he was hitting on her, but he's a cop, so she didn't want to piss him off. But she wasn't about to let him in *that* door."

"When Drusus came back, did she tell him?"

"No."

"Why not?"

"She says people hit on her all the time. She doesn't like to make a big deal out of it and get everybody upset."

"So Kincaid tried to come over." I slumped back in the chair. "That isn't very much."

"Yeah. But I also found Jim-Jim's girl, LuAnne Jones. She's been working in Long Beach all this time, too. Living in Hollywood, but hitching rides over here to work." He gave his head an ironic little twist. "I just talked to her."

"And?"

"She told me about a big white cop who came by to see her two days after Kingsley Rhoades was killed." He glanced at me, making sure I was with him. "The man had already talked to Jim-Jim, she told me, and that's how he found out about her. She lived in San Pedro then, working in one of those fish houses on the wharf as a waitress. Did you know they picked Jim-Jim up?"

"No." I glared at my investigator. "There's no record of that! Why didn't Jim-Jim tell us?"

"Jack, he's a gangster. Talking to you or me, like talking to the man. He won't say anything he isn't asked."

"Huh."

"So she told me this white cop said he needed to verify Jim-Jim's alibi. Said Jim-Jim told him he was with her at Drusus and Vera's apartment, but he needed to know for sure. She said, 'Well, now you know, because that's where he was.' But the cop said, 'Oh, yeah? Well, I don't even know if *you* were there.' And she says, 'Ask Vera, or Drusus,' and he said, 'All you'll do is call. I need some proof.' So they sat there, and then he said, 'I got an idea. You tell me what the living room looks like, how it's furnished. That's something I can see for myself. Then at least I'll know you were there.' "

"So she did?" I asked.

"Yeah. Drusus and Vera the only people she knew who had a complete set of those books by Donald Goines, and she remembers telling him where they were."

I couldn't move. I felt totally betrayed. These were guys I'd known all my life. "Do you realize what you are saying?"

"Yeah. That a cop hit Kingsley Rhoades and stole his purse. That they got enough of a description to do the warrant and then planted the purse in the kid's apartment when they searched it."

Some plastic grocery bags had gathered around a pier in the harbor. The water had a film over it. If somebody tossed a match in there, it would go up in flames. "You know, I'd almost rather find out it was Drusus."

"You, maybe, but not me." Whitney spoke with scorn. "I grew up around here, too." He turned toward me and stared, his expression challenging mine. "Where do we go from here, boss?"

I thought it over. "We go slow."

Whitney faced around toward the lobby. "Okay. I understand that. They can make LuAnne look like a fool."

"Right. Find out which cop. What did LuAnne give you?"

"She said a big guy, middle-aged. That could be any one of them: Wink, Kincaid, Rory Danforth."

"I need to know why she wasn't suspicious, too."

"Man, what was to be suspicious about? She didn't think anything of it. She just thought a dumb white cop."

Maybe I was trying to hang onto old illusions about my hometown. "Try telling that to a jury," I said. "I also need to know why it's taken so long to find her. How come she didn't get in touch with us?"

"I don't know, Jack, but it isn't sinister, man. She just lost touch. She moved to Hollywood—she don't have a car or driver's license—and she's taking acting lessons, you know, and her last name is 'Jones,' which don't make it easy. I just got lucky when I found a LuAnne Jones working as a tour guide on the *Queen Mary*."

"Still, she heard nothing?"

"You don't know what it's like, Jack. People want to know all the time why black folks that make it move out of the ghetto and forget. I'll tell you why. They cut that part of their life out, man, the same as anybody else that blocks out pain. It's like amnesia, what black people do sometimes. They want out!"

My chin settled on my chest, and my eyes ground shut. When they opened they were staring at my hands, which were holding my stomach. "Can you talk to her without scaring her?"

"Yeah. She remembers Drusus. She likes him. She'll help."

"You'll need some photographs to show her. Do you have any?"

"Shouldn't be too hard. I'll get them out of your high school yearbook."

"Ho ho. What about the newspaper?"

"You know, the PD has this public relations department

now," he said. *"They* might have some pictures. I'll tell 'em I'm a fan." He started to move. "Anything else?"

"Try to find a witness who saw her talking to whoever she talked to. Something. If it's a shouting match, we lose."

"I hear you all right." He was close to the edge of his seat.

"After you know which cop, work on motive. Some particular reason to do Rhoades, and to put it on the youngster."

He got up. "How soon you need all this stuff?"

"The sooner the better Whitney. You know as well as I do what can happen to a hot witness. They get cold feet."

"You're gonna take them on, aren't you?" Whitney asked.

"You're damn right I am." I thought of "the law"—and still loved the creature, in spite of all the wrinkles in her face. Maybe because of them. "If you can't trust the cops, who can you trust?"

"So now you know what the view is from the ghetto." He popped me on the head with something like affection. "Good on you, Jack."

"Thanks." I let my head ring without telling him about it.

"You okay?"

"I'm okay. Go do it."

He started walking away. "One other thing, Jack. Drusus is at risk. If they whacked Kingsley and think we might find out, they could set him up in that jail."

I knew I was at the right place when I saw Godzilla. He looked disappointed, and I assumed it was because Drusus wasn't chained to his wrist.

The next people I saw—sitting in the hospital's hall, where they had dragged up chairs—were his mother, his grandmother, and his sister. "Hi, ladies."

Part of being a white liberal is not always being able to communicate. The only way I could talk to Mrs. Gold, the youngster's mother, was with her on the witness stand and me behind the shield of a lectern wall. It would have been awkward visiting with her on the street. The same with Tiki. They would smile at me and say "Hello," and then it would stop.

But I could talk to Mrs. Cattle, the kid's grandmother. She and I were the same age. She was all stove up with arthritis, and I'd had a bout with cancer. It was as though a lifetime of fear had worked through her bones, locking them up, and a lifetime of anger had festered in my stomach, screwing it up. So in a way we had something in common. "How you doin', Mr. Bard?" she said while the other two smiled at me and nodded, then looked at the floor.

"About as well as can be expected, considering my good looks," I said, putting my hand on her arm. "How's Drusus?"

"He doin' fine. He smile when he see us"—she smiled when she thought about it, even though it brought tears to her eyes—"but that man over there won't let us in, so we don't know much."

"Is he in there?" I asked, leaning my head toward the door Godzilla stood near. The door was closed.

"Uh-huh."

"Did they bring him in on a gurney?"

"You mean one of them tables on wheels?"

I nodded. It's a problem that cuts both ways. She knew what the word meant, but life had taught her to play dumb.

"Uh-huh. He look strong enough to push it his own self, but they had someone doin' it for him."

"Okay. Anything you want to tell him?" I looked at the others, too.

They were touching at their eyes. They shrugged. "Jus'— you know," Tiki said. "Hope you're all right."

Godzilla got in the way when I tried to open the door. "I need some identification, please."

"What?" He knew who I was. He'd seen me every day for the last two months. But if I got sarcastic, he'd probably take it out on the youngster. "Sure," I said, watching him grin, and smiling back at him. "What do you need?"

"A bar card, a driver's license." He realized it wouldn't be any fun. "You're his lawyer, ain't you?"

"Yes."

"Go on in."

There were two beds in the room, one of those cloth screens that can be yanked around for privacy, and a couple of chairs. Drusus was alone in the room. He'd been rolled up into a sitting position and grinned when he saw me. An ankle bracelet chained him to the bed. "Hi, youngster," I said, shutting the door behind me.

"You come by to see me? Thanks man." He sounded a little goofy.

"Your mom, grandma, and sister are in the hall. They came by, too."

"I thought I heard something out there." Painfully, he reached his left hand across his body and took mine. The right side of him was covered in bandage. "I like this," he said, looking out the window at a couple of palm trees and the yellow air. "I'm in a bed with clean sheets. Feel like a human, you know, instead of—"

"What?"

"Was gonna say 'nigger.' Sure glad I didn't say *that*."

I pulled up a chair. "What happened?"

"Nothing I can't handle," he said. "I'll take care of it my own self."

"Drusus, damn it, what are you talking about? I need to *know*. Don't worry; telling me is the same as talking it over with yourself. There's the attorney-client privilege. Whatever you tell me *stays* with me. It doesn't go past me without your say-so."

He smiled at me. "I know all that shit, Jack." As he laid his head back he seemed to think it over. "I just got attacked, is all. But I seen it comin'."

"Where did it happen, youngster? When?"

"After we ate lunch. I was in the bubble on two-D with about ten others, we were all waitin' for the men with chains, you know, lace us up and take us to court."

"The bubble on two-D? Is that a cell?"

"Kind of like a cell, only no furniture or anything."

"Go on."

"Three dudes from a Blade set in West Central. I saw them flashing signs, you know." He seemed impatient over their incompetence.

"So there were others in the bubble when it happened? People who saw these guys come at you?"

"Yeah, must be six or seven others. They all turn their backs, you know, so I wait in a corner for these bad-asses to bring it on."

"Why did they come at you?"

"Just natural enemies, man." He looked out the window.

I'd been assessing the damage to his body, and—except for the bag of blood over his head that was emptying into his veins—no tubes. A wrap around his throat, bandages on his right shoulder and back, wrapped around his torso, a mummy wrap on his right hand. I wondered if he could walk. "They all have knives?"

"Only one of 'em. I got hit a couple times up here with it"—he touched his shoulder and back with his left hand—"then took it away from the boy and threw it on the floor. I didn't use it on anybody."

"Why not?"

He shrugged. "By that time I didn't need it. There was only three of them." He smiled.

"Were they arrested?"

"Yeah. Guards come swarming in, you know, start beating heads like they got to subdue a riot, even though everything over when they get there. I'm on one side, and everybody else on the other side."

"Did they beat yours?"

"No."

"How bad were you hurt?"

"Not bad, really, just squirted blood all over, you know. Cut a vein. The dude went for my throat, but the cut that did most of the bleeding in my hand."

The door opened. A light brown black man, possibly forty, and a short, heavyset woman came in. "Drusus Church?" the man asked.

The youngster craned his head around. It hurt, but he could do it. "Yes, sir."

"Sir, you'll have to leave," the woman said to me.

"I'm his lawyer."

"That don't matter at this point, sir," she said, flashing a badge. "We're from the Los Angeles Sheriff's Office, and we need to talk to Mister Church here."

"Fine. But I have a right to be here." I smiled to show her how reasonable I could be.

"Not unless he wants you, sir, and I doubt if he does." I stared at Drusus, who calmly watched the female officer. "He hasn't been charged with anything, and he hasn't asked for a lawyer. You'll have to leave."

"Drusus, tell these guys you want your lawyer here, okay?"

He grinned. "I'll talk to you later, man."

"Drusus—"

"Jack, I'm in jail all by myself, man. I have to do this on my own."

The female officer held the door for me as I went out. I'm worse than Whitney, I thought, wondering if she was part of the problem.

20

According to legend, choirboys have angelic faces and appear to be thinking lofty thoughts, when in actuality they are plotting mayhem and rape. At nine o'clock Friday morning I waited like a legendary choirboy for Keane and Wink Barrett to show up in court. Drusus sat next to me. A soft-colored sport coat draped over his wide shoulders. His left arm fit through the sleeve, but his right arm, hugging his chest, hung in a sling. The empty right sleeve had been pinned to the pocket.

Whoever bandaged him up should have been a plastic surgeon. It was obvious he'd been in a wreck, but in spite of that, he looked good. The deadliest jab had landed under his right ear, slicing some muscle in his neck. It had been sealed, stitched, and covered over with an orange flesh-colored square patch that looked innocuous, like a scar or a birthmark. However, his right wrist and hand were wrapped in gauze the size of a boxer's glove. They hung from the belt-loop sling around his neck, under his coat.

Whitney sat behind us, next to Godzilla. In a way, what we had was our guard watching over theirs. Godzilla frowned over the situation, but it didn't appear to bother Whitney.

Keane and Wink banged through the door from the main hallway into the courtroom. They had been laughing about something but stopped when they saw us waiting. "Good morning, Counselor," Wink tossed at me, his eyes on Drusus. "Hey, kid," he said in a bantering tone. "I hear you broke a couple noses."

Drusus immediately looked at the floor. His face gave away nothing, in spite of what I knew he felt. He knew everything: the plea offer from Mad Dog Hammond, that the informant on the so-called search was supposed to have been Vera's mother, and how the cops found out what the inside of his apartment looked like without going in. "It's hard for him to talk," I said, hoping the venom in my stomach didn't show up on my face. "He got hit in the throat."

"What happened?" Keane asked eagerly, like a fellow employee after some juicy bit of gossip. He put his briefcase on the counsel table.

Never for one moment think the DA is your friend, old Charley Wallace used to say. The good ones are slicker than jailhouse snitches. "It's in the reports," I said, doing my best to keep it light. "Haven't you seen them?"

"No."

"It's in the paper, too," Wink said. The respect that one athlete has for another lined his voice. "Your boy made the news."

"So come on, guys. Tell me what happened." Keane propped his butt against the edge of his table and looked at my side like old friends.

I didn't know what he was after. Maybe just gossip, although the turns we'd taken so far prepared me for anything. You never let your guard down in trial, because your brother at the bar—if he's worth his salt—won't quit swinging until the verdict is in. I'd even done it a time or two myself, though only to the deserving. You stroke them and get them going, and sometimes they will give away the store.

It crossed my mind that these guys might be looking for some way to charge Drusus with an assault. "I think they're still trying to sort it out, Keane," I said. "Somebody put a knife in Drusus. The investigators found a shiv—one of those all-blade things, you know, about eight inches long—on the floor in the holding module." I told him what he could read in the investigator's report but tried to make it sound like more. "They found Drusus there, too, with some cuts in him." I stopped, as though that was the end of it.

"Come on, man. Is that all?"

"What more do you want? Everybody was questioned, nobody saw anything. One of those deals where nobody knows what happened."

"Yeah." Wink grinned. "Nobody knows. Eleven peanuts in that bubble, waiting to go to court. I don't know where the slicer had the knife—maybe up his ass. Had to go through three searches that morning before seeing a judge, and searched again before being loaded into the bubble." Except for the word "peanut," you could still hear admiration in Wink's voice. "What I heard, blood dripping off the walls." His eyes even seemed to shine with the stuff. "Hope your boy don't have AIDS, Jack. If he does, ten newly infected peanuts—including two young African-American male subjects with broken noses. Happened in the space of about five seconds, give or take a couple. And not one person interviewed saw any of it. Amazing."

Keane watched Drusus, who sat comfortably but did not appear to be aware of the fact anyone was talking about him. "How does he feel?" he asked me.

"He feels okay," I said. "He's a quick healer."

"Are you going to ask for a mistrial?"

"I don't know yet."

No-name came in. "Hi," I said. "Is the judge back there somewhere?"

She blushed. She isn't used to all that attention. "Yes, Mister Bard. She sent me out to get you."

"Him, too?" I asked, jerking a thumb at Keane.

She smiled. "Him, too."

When we walked into chambers Iron Pants put the paper down and looked at me. "How is your client?"

"Fine, Ida. He's here."

"Really!" She smiled and glanced at Keane. "Well. The

report I had was, he'd lost a huge amount of blood and needed a transfusion. I didn't expect him to be out of the hospital."

I smiled at her. "What can I say?"

"Well, what are we going to do? Do we need to go on the record?"

"That would probably be a good idea," I said.

"Can we do it in here?" she asked. "It's hot, and I don't want to put on my robe unless I have to."

Everybody is so friendly, I thought. "Sure," I said. "I'll go get my client."

A few minutes later the conference table in Ida's chambers was ringed with bodies. Ida, at the head, nodded at the reporter. "It's Friday, May seventeenth, we are in chambers, the time is nine-seventeen A.M.," she intoned like a cantor. "Present are Jack Bard, the defendant Drusus Church, Whitney Lee, a private investigator, Keane Williams for the People, and Wink Barrett of the Long Beach Police Department. We are here to decide what to do with the jury in view of a recent development. Mister Bard, can you bring us up to date?"

I had plopped a pad on the conference table. "As the Court knows, my client was stabbed yesterday. He lost a lot of blood but received a transfusion and—except for some patches and bandages and a sling—looks and feels fine. He is able to communicate with me and is in complete possession of his mental faculties." I stopped and peered at Drusus, who sat erectly with the alert intensity he showed whenever the shooting was going on. "I am satisfied he is physically and mentally capable of going forward with the trial. However, we believe a mistrial would be the best course, as long as it means starting the case over from scratch."

"Are you serious?" Ida asked. "You want us to relitigate the guilt phase?"

"Yes."

She looked tired. She picked up a cup of coffee and held her hands around it, next to her chest. "Mister Williams, it's my understanding that the People believe a mistrial con-

215

cerning the penalty phase only would be appropriate. Is that still your position?"

"It is, Judge."

"I must say, Mister Bard, that I find your position illogical in the extreme. If a mistrial is the right course, why should it go behind the penalty phase? That is the only portion of this trial that could have been affected by the incident involving your client."

"Because it would not be fair for my client to have to face a brand-new jury when it would have to assume he was guilty of the murder of Kingsley Rhoades."

"But he has been found guilty of the murder of Kingsley Rhoades!"

Keane glanced at me with something like a sneer. "Judge?"

"Yes, Mister Williams."

"They're trying to take tactical advantage here. It would be unfair to the State and an uneconomic use of judicial time to be compelled to do the guilt phase again."

Ida nodded her head in agreement. "Mister Bard, I am quite willing to declare a mistrial as to the penalty phase. All you have to do is ask for it."

I glanced at the youngster. He will make a great lawyer, I thought. He has a chess player's eyes. "We do not want and will object to a mistrial as to the penalty phase only," I said.

"God damn it, Jack!" She glared at me in exasperation, then looked at the court reporter. His hands hadn't moved. "Shit."

It was hard not to laugh, but I've had practice. I stuck my hand in the air like a kid in a classroom. "We're off the record, aren't we, Judge?"

"Yes."

"Then it's okay for me to call Keane Williams an asshole?"

It wasn't as funny as it might have been, because he knew I meant it. Ida sighed, then nodded at the court reporter. "We're back on the record," she told him, "You were saying, Mister Bard?"

"Actually, I don't know what else to say. As Mister Williams pointed out yesterday, there are double jeopardy implications if you order a mistrial without the defendant's consent." You always tread on thin ice when you throw a red flag at a judge, so I waved it as gently as possible. It's when you tell them what they *can* do that your ground is as firm as cement.

She was back in control. "I am quite concerned over the perception this jury will have of your client, Mister Bard. There was an article in the paper which some of them— inadvertently—may have read. It seems to me they might well conclude he is a troublemaker."

"That's a chance we are willing to take."

"Mister Williams, in your opinion, what will happen if I declare a mistrial, over the objection of the defense, as to the penalty phase only?"

His smile did not include me. "A difficult question. The defendant will holler 'double jeopardy,' and the Court of Appeals could agree."

"Do you know what you're doing, Jack?"

What did she expect me to say? Something like, "Your Honor, I don't have a clue"? "I'm certain, Judge."

"I don't understand your position! Can't you see I'm trying to help your client? You know you aren't entitled to a retrial of the guilt phase!" She'd have been a great singer, I thought. She has one of those strong voices that can make you ache. "Why are you in such a hurry to push on with the penalty phase? Isn't half a loaf better than none? We're talking a one- or two-month delay. I don't wish to sound crude, but your client has the time, doesn't he?"

"There are factors at work here I can't disclose."

"Well, I am quite frankly concerned about what you are doing," she said testily. "I don't like to suggest this, but there could be a competency of counsel issue."

I cleared my throat and kind of ducked. "Judge, I always worry about the people who hire me."

"There are a couple of things that concern me, too, Judge," Keane said. "Can I speak to them?"

"Please do."

"I think the prosecution, and the court, are being jock-eyed into a no-win situation by what I will characterize as a deliberate defense strategy. Who will decide if the defendant is 'incapacitated'? Will it be you, Judge, or Mister Bard? We are going to have a situation where—if things don't go his way—he can say 'Whoops! Mistrial time! Let's start over, Judge, because the defendant is incapacitated!' "

I laughed. "Mister Williams is giving me credit for strategy," I said. "That means something planned and thought out in advance." I decided to take the old self-deprecatory tack. "This Court knows me better than that!"

It didn't work. She didn't even crack a smile. "What do you suggest I do, Mister Williams?"

"It should be made crystal clear to the defendant that he will have to live with his decision. He should know that under no circumstances will he get another bite out of the apple. If he comes in later crying for a mistrial, he gets a towel for his tears, but nothing more."

Good, I thought. He went too far. "I am not prepared to decide at this time that under no circumstances will they get a mistrial. But I appreciate your point. Do you have anything more?"

"Yes." He gave us the benefit of his most thoughtful frown. "I'd also like to go on record—just so if it comes up on appeal, the record can show it was my concern, too—as agreeing with the Court, in that I don't think the defense has considered the impact the sight of the defendant will have on the jury. His arm is in a sling, his hand is heavily bandaged, he has a dressing on his neck. There was an article in yesterday's paper about a fight in the jail and a stabbing involving this defendant. If *I* was on that jury, I'd think to myself: 'The man is so violent he even gets in fights when he's locked up!' "

Iron Pants nodded with approval. "I totally agree."

Keane swung his head at Drusus and stared at the youngster with deep sincerity. "Because of that, Judge, I'm going to ask for a direct expression from the defendant. It's possible he doesn't really understand he can have a mistrial if he wants one. Now, I don't doubt Mister Bard's word on the subject for a moment, but to be safe . . ."

I bristled. He was trying to drive a wedge between me and my client. "Smile, laddie," I heard Charley say, so I smiled. "Good idea," I said to Keane. "Ask him."

Keane glanced at the judge for approval. She nodded. "Mister Church," Keane said, taking quick advantage of the chance to ask some questions. "You've suffered a serious injury, haven't you, sir?"

Drusus moved his left shoulder. "Not too bad," he said in a low voice. It obviously hurt to talk.

"Well, you were operated on, weren't you? And if you hadn't been, you might have died?"

"They stitched me up, give me some blood."

"And at the present time, how do you—strike that." Keane covered up the change of direction with a smile. "At the present time, sir, you look like you've been in a fight. Will you agree with that?"

"I got some bandages on me. Could have happened a lot of ways."

"Right. But one of those ways is in a fight?"

"Yes."

"If the jury thinks you've been in a fight—I mean, you're literally on trial for your life here, and one of the questions is whether or not you are a violent person. You don't want them to think you've been in a fight, do you, sir?"

"A little far afield, aren't we, Judge?" I suggested.

"Yes, Mister Keane," Ida said. "I think I'd better do the questioning. Mister Church, are you aware, sir, that if you want a mistrial at this point, I will order one for you?"

"I know that, Judge."

"However, you must agree to it?"

"I understand. My lawyer explained all that to me."

"And have you considered how it might look—how you might look—to the jury if we continue?"

"Yes, ma'am, I have."

"Do you want a mistrial?"

"If you mean start the whole thing over, yes, ma'am, I do."

"I don't mean that. I mean as to the penalty phase."

"Then no, Judge." He smiled across the table at Keane and Wink. "Let's get it on."

It's hard to stage a trial. You know that much of the time the jurors have to guess at what you're doing, and all you can do is hope they are guessing right. What I knew at that point in the trial was this: The prosecution had put on a very good case for death. They had drawn the picture of a gangster, a gang-banger, a Blade who had murdered twice in the space of a month. Before that he'd committed a burglary while carrying a gun, which he had characterized as a gang mission done as a joke. Some little escapade. The jurors might ask themselves later: What about all the other capers he'd done?

The only certainty when you try a lawsuit is this: You really don't know. I couldn't crawl into the minds of the jury to see which way they were leaning. Salvadore Mira had told them, "He's not the one," but is that what the jurors heard? Would they buy into the "proof" that the youngster didn't have a gun when Rhoades was killed? Were they having second thoughts? Or—after watching Larry Walker sweat—were they more convinced than ever of Drusus's guilt? And if I put my experts on, would they take that to mean, "See? Even those guys think he did it. Otherwise they wouldn't go to so much trouble to ask us to forgive."

That's why I watch horror movies at night. They are easy for defense lawyers to sleep through.

At 10:15 the jurors filed into the courtroom and took their chairs. Their faces were masks. I wasn't even sure if anyone saw the difference in Drusus, who sat beside me as though he were a spectator rather than the main attraction.

In chambers we had worked out what the jury should be told about the delay. When Iron Pants smiled at them as they settled in their chairs I could see their eyes drift toward my man. Iron Pants greeted them, then said: "As some of you may have heard, there was an altercation among some prisoners yesterday, and in the course of it

Mister Drusus Church was injured. You are advised that Mister Church did not initiate or start that altercation. You are also advised that you are not to consider the altercation, or Mister Church's injury, as evidence in this proceeding, or for any purpose whatever. Do any of you have any questions?" She waited long enough to make sure that no one did. "Very well. Mister Bard, your next witness."

Now and then I space out during a trial. It's fun. I watched myself amble to the lectern. "Call Sarah Perkins," I heard myself say.

Sarah was a prim-looking, white-haired woman with a back as stiff as a steel rod and a chin that was always up. She was dying of cancer. The jury didn't know that, of course. All they saw was a white woman in her late fifties who had a cheerful, wide-open face.

Sarah was a social anthropologist, and she told the jury what that meant, distinguishing it from a whole array of other anthropological disciplines: linguists, physical anthropologists like Jane Goodall, archeologists who dig up remnants of the past. "I study living groups, their cultures, the way they organize themselves and why—that sort of thing. I study the behavior of people who live within those groups. I attempt to articulate the organizational patternings and try to observe the relationships between individual behavior and organizational patterns." She listed her degrees, mentioned the papers she'd authored, and otherwise prepared them for her pitch.

My defense against the death penalty charge was lingering doubt, yet here I was with a team of experts who would explain that a ghetto boy—or at least this particular one—couldn't help but be a killer because he never had a chance. In other words, I had to ride two horses. "Look, you guys," my side had to tell the jury, "he didn't kill anyone. But if he did, keep this in mind: If you'd come from that environment and had to deal with all his problems, you probably would have done the same thing."

Sarah detailed what she had done to understand and describe the defendant in terms of her discipline: the interviews she had conducted with family members, schoolteachers, probation officers, and youth camp personnel; the reports she had read; her long talks with the defendant. Then she went into her findings.

She listed the instabilities in the life of Drusus Church: a father he never knew because of prison, murdered shortly after his release; the broken homes he lived through because of his mother, who was compelled to make a life for herself and her children, and who used and was used by men in the process; the number of schools he was forced to attend.

"How confusing it must have been to this young child," she declared in her remarkably clear voice. "If one were to enumerate all the opportunities for betrayal, from his perspective, they would add up into the hundreds! No sooner would he come to trust in something lasting than the ground would shift, as it were. Another earthquake, another betrayal."

Sarah did a good job. She always does a good job. But when she was done, I didn't recognize the portrait. The trouble was, it had to be painted. This jury had already convicted Drusus of murder, and I had to assume they believed he was a killer.

Keane's cross-examination was predictably brutal. He started by asking her how long she'd spent on this case.

"I should say well over a hundred hours," Sarah replied.

Keane next learned—to his apparent horror—that she charged seventy-five dollars an hour. "And so your fee will be in excess of seven thousand five hundred dollars?"

"Yes."

He also asked her about the victims, Kingsley Rhoades and Tommy Sherman. "Did you spend any time at all studying the lives of either of these men?"

"No."

He followed with questions that compared the background of Drusus with that of others from the ghetto who were success stories. He wanted her to explain the difference. "As bad as you have pictured the environment of the defendant, you've seen plenty of cases where an individual from an equally bad environment did not kill two people in the space of less than a month?" I objected like a stuck pig, which prevented Sarah from answering, but the jury still heard the question.

I didn't eat any lunch. I watched the seagulls and the people who fed them on a piece of beach near the courthouse, wondering which species needed the other the most. I don't remember getting back to the courthouse.

"You may call your next witness, Mister Bard."

Dr. William O'Rourke got into the box. Short, thin, intense, the fingers of his right hand were blotched yellow with tobacco stain. He burned with zeal for some secret cause, like a revolutionary or an unpublished poet.

He told the jury that he was a professor in the department of political science at California State, Long Beach. An urbanologist, he had been awarded grant moneys from various foundations with an interest in reducing the impact of gangs on cities. He had studied gangs extensively through interviews with gang members, residents, city officials, merchants, policemen, etc. He had published several papers, was co-authoring a book, and had otherwise developed an expertise in the subject of gangs.

What the jury didn't know was that O'Rourke had belonged to, and escaped from, membership in a gang in his youth. His interest in the subject grew from a desire to understand his own twitches.

He was a volcano erupting with words and ideas. I had to slow him down, make him go back and forth, and hope the jurors would hang in. Getting it out of him was like scraping the wax off a stencil; the words—in bold relief—were down there, but you had to be patient.

Given the background of Drusus Church, O'Rourke said, one would have to expect that he would join a gang. In fact, he would have to have been abnormal—different—weird—not to have done so. The ironic fact was this: It was because of Church's psychological wholeness or togetherness that he became a gang member.

In explaining what he meant, he took a stab at defining the concept of "multiple marginality." "All of us are a part of many societies," he said. "Family, school, church, our own circle of friends—each of them a separate circle. What happens to a healthy young person who finds himself at the edge—way out on the periphery—of virtually all of the societies he is a part of?

"He is *in* a family—but barely inside its walls. Either because the family itself has marginal existence, or because—due to the dynamics of the family—he is more or less an outcast. He is in an educational institution, but not really. He's been bounced around so often it's impossible to cope, or, for other reasons, he doesn't fit. The same with church; he attends now and then, but his participation is marginal.

"Where this multiple marginality occurs, what will a healthy-minded young person do who knows that 'out there' there is something he can belong to? Especially when we factor in the obvious impact of racism and poverty. Ironically enough, if he's normal—if he's healthy—he'll join a gang. And why? Because the normal, healthy young person wants and needs stability and structure. Those needs can be met by gang membership. A gang is something he can be a part of, not marginally, but internally. That's who his 'homeboys' are, that's the significance of his ' 'hood,' that's who he is."

O'Rourke described some of the gang rituals: "jumping in"—a joining ritual, but not like a fraternity with a formal initiation. In gangs you hang out with gang members, go kicking with them, and at some point you will have to prove yourself to them. "You have to show them you have heart and courage," O'Rourke said. "They don't make it easy on you, either. They really do test you. They want to see what you're made of."

In Drusus's case, he "jumped in" at the age of eleven. And *because* of the young man's character—not because of a defect—he proved to them he had the heart. What did Drusus get? Status, respect, protection, and freedom within his 'hood—the things all of us want that are so often denied to persons who suffer from multiple marginality.

Nobody cried, I noticed, at the conclusion of his direct. Keane least of all. "Doctor O'Rourke, you make gangs sound like innocent little boys' clubs," he said. "Did your investigation and study of gangs include crime statistics?"

"Yes. Of course."

"Perhaps you can tell us, sir. How many murders were committed by gang members in Los Angeles County last year?"

So my side took another shower. Keane also walked O'Rourke through another gang ritual: the bonding, joy, and brotherhood involved when these "boys" went off on missions. "Often, criminal behavior is involved in such missions. Correct?"

"I would say usually," the good doctor agreed.

"So that particular ritual involves anything from gang graffiti to rape to witness intimidation to robbery to murder, right?"

O'Rourke had a low boiling point. I watched his ears get red. "It can. But Mister Williams, if I may say something?"

Keane shrugged his shoulders. "Go ahead."

"It is quite wrong to conclude that gang members spend all their time doing drive-by shootings."

Big help, I thought.

As the barbecue continued I let a picture of old Charley appear in my mind. He stuck his tongue out at the special prosecutor, then got right in his face and gave him the finger. When Keane dropped a paper on the floor and bent over to pick it up, old Charley kicked him in the ass. "Way to go, Charley," I said.

"Pardon me?" Iron Pants asked. "Was that an objection?"

"No, Your Honor." Damn him anyway. I watched him moon the nice woman. "Not an objection, Judge." I cleared my throat. "I'm not sure what it was."

"Well." She regarded me with a peculiar understanding. "Perhaps this would be a good time for a recess."

There have been times—in spite of the fact she is married and the mother of two children—that I have seriously considered offering my hand in marriage to that woman. She would laugh at the proposal, of course. But it would be a nice laugh.

* * *

The rest of the afternoon was predictable. For my next witness I offered James Best, a former warden who would describe the life-style of a man in prison for the remainder of his life. Keane objected because of the *Thompson* case, so we had to clear the courtroom and go to the mat. The defense lawyer in the *Thompson* case tried to use a former warden to detail for the jury what an execution was really like, right down to the involuntary evacuation of the man's bowels, which happens when a person gives up the fight for life. It took some time, but I finally persuaded Iron Pants that there was a difference between what I wanted and that.

So James climbed on the stand—all 260 pounds of him. Former wardens and guards are like ex-football players. They muscle up for the job, but it turns to fat when they retire. He described the sixty square feet—the size of a large bathroom—that would be Drusus's home for the remainder of his life, whether he was executed or not. Of course, that space would be shared with another inmate.

I don't know why so many people get the notion that prison, for a true lifer, is a country club. But a lot of them have it, and when Keane took Best on cross-examination he did what he could to encourage that particular misconception. Through his questions Keane had Drusus sitting in his cell and watching television while waiting for a conjugal visit. When Drusus tired of TV Keane trotted him out to the exercise yard, where he ran around in circles and lifted weights.

I took Best on redirect. Keane was whispering with Wink and not paying a whole lot of attention. I asked the one-time warden if he thought Drusus would do well in prison, and he said, "Yes." I asked him why he thought so. Keane heard that one, thought it over, squirmed a bit, but didn't object. "He appears to have a very constructive attitude," Best said. "Such men—who know they are there for the rest of their lives—want to make it as easy on themselves as possible. They usually exercise a positive, stabilizing influence on other inmates."

It can be very depressing. I'd done what you have to do

when you put on a death penalty defense: give the jury reasons to vote for life rather than death. As I watched Best leave the courtroom I thought to myself: If that doesn't persuade them he did it, nothing will.

"Your next witness, Mister Bard?"

"Approach?" I asked.

We huddled at the sidebar—Keane, the judge, and me—and in whispers I told her the testimony had gone faster than I thought it would, and I was out of witnesses for the day. "I thought this was all you had," Keane whispered in a voice loud enough to carry through the room. I wondered if he wanted the jurors to hear. "You didn't talk about anyone else in your opening statement."

"Who knows?" I whispered in an equally loud voice. "I might get lucky over the weekend and find the guy who did it."

"Gentlemen, keep your voices down!" Iron Pants ordered in a tone that didn't go out of our circle but cut like a knife within it. "Jack, do you have any more testimony or don't you? If not, I assume the defense rests."

"I'd like to leave it open, Judge," I whispered. "It's almost four o'clock. It's very possible that I'll have one or two more witnesses."

"Surprise witnesses?" Keane asked in a low voice. "I think I'm entitled to know who they are."

Drusus had started to sag, and Ida could see it. "We'll argue that on the record, if necessary. I'm going to send the jury home now."

She did. She told them to return on Monday at 9:00 A.M., and we waited for them to file out of the room. "Will there be anything further?" she asked when they were gone, looking at Keane.

"Nothing further," he said.

"We are in recess, then." She banged her gavel down, hiked up her skirts, and made her exit.

Godzilla seemed to have softened, but not by much. After he laced Drusus up he didn't yank him around with quite as much joy. I waved at the youngster as he shuffled out the door. "We got 'em just where we want 'em," I said.

He grinned.

"What have you got up your sleeve, Jack S?" Keane asked, packing up his briefcase. "I'm letting you get away with murder, you know that?"

Don't "Mr. Nice Guy" me, I thought. "You're letting *me* get away with murder!" I had the sense to adopt his bantering tone. "Come on. You're killing my guy!"

Wink stood next to Keane, waiting as the prosecutor stuffed a couple of books in his bag. "I was watching the jury," he said. "They're gonna make mincemeat out of that fuckin' kid, Jack S. They're licking their chops."

I almost said, "Wait until Monday." But they were watching too closely, as though looking for a clue. So I tossed out a red herring, just for the hell of it. "You're probably right," I said. "I'll have to win this one on appeal."

21

Keane called me Saturday morning. At home. I don't know how he got my number. "How hard are you going to make me work this weekend?"

"I don't want you to work at all," I said. "Relax."

"Does that mean you'll take our offer on Monday?"

He sounds like such a nice man, I thought. The politician everyone can trust. " 'Our' offer? I thought the only one on the table was *your* offer. You told me to ignore the other one."

He laughed as easily as an old college roommate. "Hey. It doesn't matter to me. I'm getting rumbles from different corners, if you know what I mean. If these guys want me to cut a deal, I'm easy."

My stomach headed off in one direction, but my brain tried to keep me on course. "Then it's official?" I asked. "You are offering that manslaughter package with a lock?"

There was a moment of silence. "Don't tell me," he said, that TV anchorman's smile still in his voice. "We are being recorded even as we speak."

"No."

"Then let me talk to you frankly."

I thought of old Charley. When they say "Let me talk to you frankly" you know they intend to lie. "Sure."

There was another moment of silence. "Jack, old buddy,

I have some heavy-duty shit I want to lay upon you," he said jovially. "How about we get together for a beer this afternoon at Redheads?"

"Sounds serious," I said, trying to keep my feelings out of the way. "Is your conscience gaining on the rest of you?"

He must not have heard. "What's a good time? Three o'clock?"

"Good enough."

I called the hospital to make sure the youngster was still there. He was, but he'd been pronounced well enough to go back to jail. He could be leaving at any time. If a stray Sheriff's Office van had room, they'd load him in it and take him downtown. But he was still in the same bed, so I hung up and drove on out.

A different Godzilla stood by his door. "I'm sorry, sir. No visitors," the neatly uniformed Samoan said.

"I'm not a visitor," I said, pulling out my bar card. "I'm his lawyer."

"Mister Bard?"

"Yes."

He looked at my driver's license and then at me. "You can undress in there, sir," he said, pointing to a room across the hall.

"Undress! What for?"

"Regulations, sir. Put on the hospital clothes you'll see in there."

A few minutes later, wearing a robe and slippers, I was patted down and allowed through the door. "You may need these," the giant offered, handing me a pad and a ballpoint pen.

Drusus was dressed in orange jail fatigues that were too small; the cuffs reached only part of the way down his arms. He grinned when he saw me—I look better in a suit—but didn't say anything. He was sitting in a chair next to the window, a chain running between his ankle and the bed. If he decided to run away, he'd have to drag the bed down the hall with him. He'd been staring outside at the street and a blue sky that hadn't had time that morning to fill with fumes. A couple of magazines were in his lap. "Looks nice out," he said.

"It is." I pulled up a chair and sat down next to him, feeling puny. "Thanks for not laughing at my body."

"I am on the inside, man."

"How are you doing?"

"Fine." His smile was big, wide, full of life and even joy. "See?" He lifted his right shoulder like a boxer and jabbed with his hands at the window. "Don't even hurt. It feels good just to feel good."

"You are amazing, kid."

He laughed. "Yeah. I am."

Is he cracking up, I wondered? How can anyone go through what he has been put through, and feel so good that it's contagious? I smiled, too. "You know, this is the first time since Whitney laid it out for me that I've had anything in my stomach except hate," I said. "What's happening to you is harder on me than it is on you. I don't get it."

"Maybe because your grandmother never read you the Bible."

"The Bible! You mean an eye for an eye?"

"That's not the best part, man. I'm talking about how it's better to give than receive." Oh, dear, I thought. But if that's what he needs, amen. "Got some good shit in there," he said. "Like, I saw Vera this morning. She came up to see me, but they wouldn't let her in." He shook his head slowly. His eyes seemed to see other things. "Then a little later I watch her out there on the sidewalk"—he gestured with his head—"holdin' hands with Pac-Man, this boy used to spend all his days playing video games." I cleared my throat. "I'm glad for her," the youngster said. "I'm glad for him, too."

"Why did she have to walk down that sidewalk?"

"She do that so I can see."

"Are you serious?"

He shrugged. "Yeah. You know, she didn't turn around and wave at me, but she used to work here. She knows how the place is laid out and knew I'd be looking." We watched a pigeon land on the windowsill. "That could eat me up, except for the Bible. But if you can switch it around, like it says to do, you fill up over it instead."

"What about those homeboys that stuck a knife in you?"

He grinned. "You got to survive. That's why I make myself feel good. Helps me to survive."

"If you were out, and free, what would you do?"

"What do you mean?"

"The cops framed a murder on you. If I were you, I'd want to blow them up. Keane, too. He's got to be in on it. And April Tillman, for her lies."

"I don't need to blow up anybody," he said. "That shit they do to me? It will eat them up someday." He smiled, but he seemed to feel bad about it, too. "It's easy to see when you're in jail. That's the trouble. It could eat me up on the outside."

"But you'd try not to let it, right? You'd turn the other cheek?" I had trouble believing what he said.

He laughed. "That isn't what I mean."

"Then what do you mean?"

He rubbed his mouth. "I won't let any man hit me in the face if I can stop it. But if I have to knock a man down, I'll help him back on his feet. And I'll show him some respect."

I don't know why. I felt unsure of myself, maybe like Satan with a cross in his face. I wanted to get away. "Keane called," I said. "I'm going to—"

"Jack, some things I got to tell you about myself." The pigeon started flapping its wings, then flew away. "That's how I want to be." We watched it fly over to a rain gutter on top of an old wing of the building.

"Free?"

"I don't mean that, man. I want to be whole. True to myself."

I looked at his eyes, but they were clear. If I were to diagnose his expression, I would list it as "not remarkable." I still wondered if he was okay in the head. "Is that what you wanted to tell me?"

"Huh-uh. That just came up." He sat with a calmness

that was extraordinary, it seemed to me. Especially because it made me realize how bad I needed a cup of coffee. "I killed a boy one time."

It took a moment before the sounds made sense. "Wait a minute. Do you mean Rhoades or Sherman?"

He rolled his head over to the left side, stretching the muscles. "No, wasn't anybody in this case. But when I took that polygraph test?" He looked at me. "You know where I am?"

"Yes."

"All I could see was that other boy's face."

Not older than God, I thought. They were the same age. "You don't need to tell me this, kid," I told him. "I don't need to know."

"See, when you kill somebody, it kind of change your perspective on life. Know what I mean?"

"No, I don't." At that moment I didn't want to know, either.

"That's what this is all about." He lifted his bandaged hand and touched his neck. "The boy I killed was a West Side Blade from the same set as those dudes in the bubble." He sounded wistful, as one might who remembers a missed opportunity. "I shot him in the throat and watched him fall down. I don't like to see it." His eyes started closing, then opened wide. "Alive one minute and dead the next. The fool. Come wearin' his colors in my 'hood, then challenging me with his face, one of those 'do or die' looks. He thought I'd run."

"Couldn't you just have hit him?"

"Yeah. But I was fourteen, and he was an OG with a big reputation who thought he could dis me. So I shot him in the throat." He stared out the window. "Like, you said to me just now, 'You are amazing,' and I know it's true? That boy was amazing, too. Just like me. He had a heart that pumped blood and muscles that looked good, and he used to laugh and get crazed about sex and shit, and he had brains, and a mama. I took that away to keep my respect."

I felt a rush of sympathy for the youngster and put my

hand on his arm. "Drusus, that was in the past," I told him. "Forget about it. It was stupid and wrong, but you were a kid, and it was warfare, gang stuff." I tried to make him feel okay about it.

But he didn't need me. "I don't want to forget. It's what makes me appreciate what I got, even here." He looked at my hand. "I'd like to make it up to somebody, though. Maybe if I could be a lawyer someday."

He didn't even need my hand. I sat back in my chair, rubbing my face. "Do you want to take their deal?" What a crazy fucking world, I thought. "Go down on a manslaughter for the wrong guy?"

"No. See, I won't have the chance to make it up if I go to the big cage."

"Why not?"

"Survival." He looked over my head. "I'm dead if I go to prison, Jack. County jail is one thing, but the joint is something else."

I talk tough when I'm really a sweetheart. That's part of my image. Through another person's eyes, Redheads is probably just an ordinary bar and grill, but to me it's out of a Hemingway novel. When Keane stood up as I walked through the door I thought: lights, camera, action. My life is a movie starring me, playing myself, in the lead.

"Hello, sweetheart," I said.

It wasn't very good Bogart, but Keane's a Californian and recognized it. He was nice enough to laugh. "Hey. Have you been drinking without me?"

We started our negotiator's dance where each side waits for the other side to bring it up. He told a couple of jokes that would have eliminated him from any political consideration whatever if a cameraman had been around; one about a Polish lesbian, and another that linked Dan Quayle with Anita Hill. I laughed, but I was surprised. For a guy with political aspirations, he told the wrong kind of jokes. "Jim was right about you, you old bastard," he said affectionately, filling our glasses with beer from the pitcher on the table.

"Jim Trigge? What about him?" I smiled as I remembered losing the only case I'd ever enjoyed losing.

"He said I'd have my hands full."

I told him about my case against his boss: a moot court exercise at Hastings College of Law, before NASP was formed. It had been a course in legal ethics for practicing lawyers, featuring—according to the hype on the mailer—two renowned advocates, one for the defense and the other a prosecutor, both of whom were known for their dedication to and belief in the system. "He kicked my ass—turned every one of my numerous tricks against me—but we made our point."

"Which was?"

"About what you'd expect of a course in ethics. How the procedure is more important than the result, because if you don't protect the procedure, it won't take long until all the results are haywire. You know, the end does not justify the means and all that stuff nobody believes anymore except lawyers. But how the procedure allows for the clash of ideas, and how that clash of ideas usually produces the truth." I lifted my glass in a toast. "To NASP, Keane. To Jim Trigge. To everything I know he stands for."

"I'll drink to that," the boy wonder said, looking me squarely in the eye.

I tried not to choke on it. Annie brought us another pitcher. It occurred to me I only had half a stomach and had better slow down. "How's your campaign going, by the way?"

"Who knows?" But he was preening, so to speak. His face glowed with something extra. "I stay in touch with the local pols."

"That's a pretty small audience, isn't it?"

"True. But I've got a great case coming up in Redding I should get some mileage out of." It occurred to me that his candor with me—taking me into his confidence—could be his method of softening me up. He never asked me to keep it to myself, as though he knew he didn't have to say that to a friend. "It'll make the media, I'll see to that. Entirely circumstantial, where the only witnesses are the killers who moved bodies around the house to fit a bullshit story." He poured more beer. "Blood spatter is all we have, but the police did a great job protecting it. We have this guy MacDonald, and it's amazing what you can get out of blood spatters."

"I've heard of him."

"He charges two thousand dollars a day. Can you believe that?"

I made the right kind of face. "Why be attorney general when you can have so much fun with blood spatters?" I asked, aware that my tongue got caught on the "s" sound. I set my glass down.

"Attorney general! I want to be the czar of California, not just the top cop." He blessed me with that charming 1960s Mel Torme schoolboy smile. "Attorney general first, like old Eddie Meese, then take over, man." He touched my glass with his.

"Do you think you'll make it?"

"I don't know about czar, but AG is do-able. Unless something gets in the way." When he looked at me I had the eerie feeling that Drusus Church was a potential obstacle. He broke it with a grin. "I'm as active as I can be in the party—you know, go to banquets, contribute, give speeches when I can, raise a little money. I know some movie stars, too, which is what you need out here in the Far West. Glamour, image, something you can tape and splash on a screen. But whether they'd back me as far as the governor's mansion is another question." He picked up his beer and drank some of it.

"People versus Drusus Church," I said. "Is it in the way?"

"What?" He acted surprised. "Hey, I've already won the hard part, remember? How could it get in the way?"

I might have said too much. I had to keep my word to Whitney; and the hint I'd dropped yesterday about winning on appeal could have been a tip-off. "I don't know. It's just that you seem so eager to get my client to plead guilty. I've been trying to figure out why."

"You were born and raised in Long Beach, right?" he

asked. "Went to school here, knew a lot of these guys—
I'm talking about the detectives—in high school?"

"Yes."

"Do you like those guys?"

"No." I took a small sip of beer. "I love them in a way.
We're part of the same family. But I don't like them."

"Would you protect them if you could?"

"What are you talking about?" My voice turned up a
notch. "You know, Whitney has a theory. He thinks the
cops planted that damn purse in Drusus's apartment. He
thinks the cops killed Kingsley Rhoades. Hell, the man was
a big drug dealer! The way they think, they'd have been
doing the country a favor!"

"That's the way most people think."

"Is that what happened?"

"Take it easy, Jack. You're getting loud."

I smiled. "Sorry." I pushed the beer glass away. "Hey,
Annie!" I yelled. "Get over here!"

She acted like she hadn't heard, naturally. I got up. "If
you see her before I do, order me a cup of coffee."

I went to the bathroom, took a leak, and stared at the
wallpaper. Some of the poses of the fornicating couples
were nice, but others were grotesque. All that athleticism,
I thought, wondering if two people could really get into
those positions. When I got back to the booth I found a
mug full of coffee. "Annie has a message for you," Keane
said. "It is, and I quote: 'Shut the fuck up.' "

I picked up the coffee and let some of it burn my lip.
"What's going on, Keane? Why are you willing to drop
this down to manslaughter?"

He opened his hands in that wide-open gesture that used
to mean "I'll level with you." I'm not sure what it means
now. "I'll get as close as I can," he said. "There could
have been some bad advice. Some things were done because of it. If the story were known, it could hurt the reputation of one of those guys in your family. You know, the
Long Beach family. But if your guy takes the deal, the
story won't get out." His hands closed. "You know, Barrett, Danforth, Kincaid—they feel about you the same way

237

you feel about them, Jack. They can't understand how you think the way you do. But they don't know why. Each of them would give you the shirt off his back."

"Very touching. Before I cry, let me make sure I understand, okay?" I waited for him to nod. "Somebody I know and love got some bad advice. Who was it, and what was the bad advice?" I let him watch as a light turned on in my head. "You really are worried about an appeal, aren't you? Something that will come up. Something that's out of your control. Right?"

"You said it," he said ambiguously. "I didn't."

"So I'm supposed to sell my kid down the river to save someone from embarrassment?"

"Hey. Have some more coffee." He smiled. "You're getting loud again."

"You're supposed to be loud in Redheads."

"You aren't selling him down the river, Jack. You'd be making him one hell of a deal. Let's make an assumption here for the sake of argument." He paused, thinking carefully. "Something that no doubt has crossed your mind anyway. Let's assume some irregularity at the *in camera* hearing—before I got into the case—when you wanted the name of the confidential informant. Okay? You know as well as I do that nothing is certain in law. We aren't engineers. We don't deal in numbers that add up to exact amounts. Who knows what kind of spin could get put on a so-called irregularity, from a nanosecond case out of Long Beach, when the Supremes or the Court of Appeals looks at it two years from now? There is no way to predict what an appellate court would do with it."

"So that's it," I said. "Mad Dog screwed up something at the Motion to Disclose!"

"Let's say, for the sake of argument, that he did."

"Make me a better offer, then. A two-year sentence with credit for time served. Something Drusus can plead to, then walk away."

"I'm trying to keep my cool."

"Go ahead and lose it."

"Use your head, Jack. You know whatever we do has to get past Ida."

He called her Ida. Possibly he knew her better than I thought. "That's a great place to start. What do you plan to tell her now? How are you going to get her to vacate a jury conviction so he can cop to a manslaughter?"

"I'd tell her what I've told you, Jack. You know. Put it in legalese. I would hint at the possibility of procedural error and tell her it's a negotiated plea to avoid the expense of a new trial. I'd also add my impressions of the defendant. Stroke him up." He looked at me over his beer. "She'd do it."

"Have you already asked her?"

"We've talked around it."

My hands were shaking. They do that when they want to grab a witness, or a judge, or a lawyer around the throat. "Here's my problem, Keane," I said, smiling. "Drusus tells me he didn't do it. He didn't kill anyone."

The boy wonder might have picked up something in my face. "Anyone?"

My turn with the open palms. "I'm talking about Rhoades and Sherman. He didn't kill either one of them."

"Get real, Jack. You know better than that."

"That's what he tells me. So what can I do?"

"Twist his arm off, for Christ's sake. He's risking the pill!"

"What about you? You guys have your necks out a lot further than you're letting on."

He laughed. "Are you comparing the pill to having your neck out?"

"Maybe. What if Whitney is right?" I continued to smile. "Did one of my old chums kill Rhoades? Is that the bag of snakes you're afraid the Court of Appeals will open?"

There was enough beer in the mug to refill Keane's glass and top off mine. He filled the glasses carefully, then set the pitcher down. "Just for the sake of argument, let's say you're right." He rested his elbows on the table and stared at me. Hard. "Let's say it was Wink. Do you think his life, his reputation, should go down the tubes because he did some street justice?"

"Do that again?"

"Your client is a killer, Jack. We both know that. If he didn't kill Rhoades, he killed Sherman. If he didn't kill Sherman, he killed Rhoades. So what difference does it make if he pleads to manslaughter? Wouldn't that be better than to destroy a really righteous cop?"

"That's what I thought you said." I picked up the glass of beer in total shock. "Now what I need to figure out is this: Are you serious?"

"Do you want to take a poll right now of your friends in this bar? Do you want to sample the attitudes of the people in downtown Long Beach? You think you believe in democracy, right? Let's have them vote on it." He tossed off a mouthful of beer. "They don't *care* if the right guy hangs for the wrong crime—as long as the right guy gets hung. It doesn't matter if he didn't do this one, when they know he did that one. But they *do* care about the police. They know what the cops are up against. They know how tough, thankless, and dangerous it is to be a policeman in this town."

"Yeah. Thanks to Clint Eastwood," I said. "Because the fact is, the cops in this town, the detectives, make seventy bills a year, work forty-hour weeks, and don't do overtime."

He looked appalled. "Is that what you think?"

"That's what I know."

"You have a problem, fella. And part of your problem is you're out of step—completely out of step—with reality. What *they* know—I'm talking about the public, the voters—"

"Yeah," I said, interrupting, "the TV audience."

He started over. "What *they* know is, cities are a dangerous place. And what they want from the police and prosecutors is action. Drusus Church? A gang-banger. They know, and *you* know, he is part of the reason that cities are a dangerous place. They are right, too. Get rid of the punks! Babies get killed in drive-bys. So do old people. *Stop* them!

Stop it from happening. *That* is more important because *lives* are more important than the Fourteenth Amendment!''

I felt old. "Is that the law you would uphold if you became attorney general?"

"Get real."

"I want to know. I thought we drank a toast to the Fourteenth Amendment."

He shrugged with impatience. *"You* did, apparently. I thought we were drinking to NASP."

"The presumption of innocence?"

"Still applies, Jack, in the right kind of case."

"Who decides which case is the right kind?"

"The public! That's the new jury system. That's the law I want to uphold. I want it clean and quick, and so do they."

"I'm really ill."

"Well, don't throw up on the table, old man."

"Does Jim Trigge know what you're doing?"

He didn't blink an eye. "In the first place, I'm not 'doing' anything. In the second place, Jim and I have had extensive discussions about this case."

Et tu, Trigge? "So what you're telling me is, forget the law, right? Tell Drusus Church to plead guilty to a crime he didn't commit so he can save the reputation of a cop?"

"It isn't that simple, and you know it."

"Go ahead, then. Complicate it for me."

He took a couple of very deep breaths. "Let's suppose this. Let's suppose the police know, without any doubt, that your client murdered Tommy Sherman. Now I want you to really get that part: They *know*—and there is no mistake—he whacked Tommy."

"Is that what they know?"

"Hold on." He stuck his hand out as though to slow down traffic. "I'm giving you a hypothetical set of facts, like a law school exam."

Sure, I thought, touching my cheek. "Go ahead."

"Assume they also know they don't have a case against Church for whacking Tommy, because a badly confused witness—Salvadore Mira—made a mistake. Are you still there?"

"I'm here."

"Now add this in. There is a drug dealer on the streets—a heartless scumbag who deserves to die—but they can't make him. They've tried, lots of times, but he's too smart and too ruthless. Now. Are you ready for the question?"

"Ready."

"How bad are the police if they decide to kill two birds with one stone?"

This time a light really did turn on in my head. "Is that what happened?"

"Easy, big fellow. Remember: This is purely a hypothetical exercise."

"Sure, but I need to understand the facts before I try to answer the question. We are supposing that the cops killed the bad drug dealer and framed it on a gang-banger, because they knew the gang-banger had gotten away with murder in another case. And the question is: What's wrong with that?"

"You've got it."

I felt like I was in an airplane cabin where the pilot had forgotten to turn off the pressure. It seemed like the air in the room was pushing in on me. "What's the answer?"

"I'll give you mine. The gang-banger doesn't deserve to die. Give him a few years."

"The cop?"

"Give him a medal."

"What if the cops made a mistake? What if the gang-banger didn't kill either one of them?"

"That's a different set of facts, Jack."

I reached for my billfold. "I've got to go."

"This is paid for, old fellow." He watched me struggle out of the booth. "What's your answer?"

I put a ten-dollar bill on the table. "Thanks, but no thanks."

22

I thought about calling Jim Trigge but didn't. Keane was too slick. He'd have that angle covered. I considered going to Ida as an officer of the court but didn't do that either. Keane would be ready for that one, too. He'd turn it around, or deny it, or admit part but not all, and I'd be the one who smelled. I thought of some fancy legal maneuvers, too.

The legal maneuvers stayed in my mind.

On Monday morning the smog in Long Beach got an early start. By the time I trudged up the courthouse steps I could feel it on my teeth. I was early—it was twenty minutes before nine—but Godzilla had already dragged the youngster into the courtroom.

He looked good. The bandage over his hand had been reduced to a simple dressing, and the sling was gone. He wore the gold-colored shirt he'd had on before, and brown trousers. Except for the expression on his face—that of a scientist consumed in an experiment—he looked like Goliath.

Mad Dog sat in the back of the courtroom like a lizard made up to look like a man. He favored me with a nod when I broke through the door, and I nodded back. He looked away quickly, which suited me fine. Any time I can avoid talking to Mad Dog is time well spent.

Keane wanted to chat, however. The hacks in his party

were right: He looked too young to be the attorney general. His face glowed with wholesomeness, and his eyes glinted with zeal, like Ollie North's. "Got a few?" he asked.

I dropped my briefcase on the counsel table, and we went out in the hall. Mrs. Cattle was there with Tiki, both of them wearing nice clothes. I'd warned them not to talk to or even look at any of the jury, because jurors resent it—especially if somebody made an issue out of it and held a hearing. Their job was to show support for Drusus and to look like decent people. Part of the game. Keane and I found a bench in front of Courtroom L.

Whitney moved down the hallway. LuAnne Jones, whom I'd met the day before, walked beside him. An attractive woman wearing a business suit, her high heels pecked away at the floor like a dancer. Keane watched them sit down. "A mystery witness?" he asked.

"What have I got to lose?"

"A lot," he said. "Time's up. Take the deal this morning or forget about it."

"If Drusus goes to prison, he'll get killed."

"No kidding." Keane laughed. "Are you trying to tug at my heartstrings? If *that* happens, your appeal would be dead, too." He smirked at me. I wanted to hit him. "You'll have to do better than that, old man. Take the deal. They could stick him with the K-9s and keep him safe."

I looked at my shoes. They glistened—parts of them, anyway. Erin makes me polish them; Robyn never did. I entertained myself a moment by pondering the control women have over men. "He won't do it, Keane."

Keane considered my answer. "How hard did you try?" He didn't sound desperate, only curious.

"Harder than I thought I would."

"I'd be willing to ask Ida to give you another hour, Jack, if you think it will do any good." He looked at Tiki. "His sister's a real stick-twitcher, you know? Dark skin, green eyes, European features. She'd look great on a magazine cover." He turned back to me. "Does she know about the offer?"

"I don't know," I said. "Not from me."

"Do you want another hour or don't you?"

I guess I just didn't want to begin. "You don't know him, Keane. You ought at least to know the people you try to kill."

He got up. Young men make it look easy. "Spare me the details," he said, walking away.

LuAnne Jones sat in the witness chair as rigid as an icicle. She had skin the color of cardboard and features that were more Asian than African. When I had her spell her name for the record her expression was that of a wild animal who doesn't know whether to freeze or bolt. "Do you live in Los Angeles?" I asked.

"Yes. Hollywood."

The prospect of testifying in court terrified her, apparently, which surprised me, because she had been so easy to talk to the day before. "What do you do for a living?" I asked, smiling. In my eagerness to put her at ease I stumbled into the lectern, bumping over a glass of water. "Uh-oh." It drenched my tie, and a few people laughed.

"I'm a tour guide," she said, watching me make a mess of things as I tried unsuccessfully to mop up.

"A tour guide?" I made a display of wringing the water out of my tie. "You don't happen to have some extra Kleenex?"

She laughed. It works every time, although you can only do it once a trial. "No, sir." She was pretty, but not different or startling enough for Hollywood. I had a vision of her chasing a dream that would never come true.

"Do you know the defendant in this case, Miss Jones? Drusus Church?"

"Yes, I do." She glanced at Drusus and smiled.

"How do you know him?"

She blushed, not certain what was expected of her. "Well—not intimately, you know." Her color deepened. "Just friends."

"When did you first meet him, and where, if you recall?"

"It was about a year ago." She wasn't afraid anymore. She wouldn't run. "I was dating a friend of his, and we

245

went over to Drusus and Vera's apartment for dinner and to socialize, you know.''

Keane realized who the mystery witness was: Jim-Jim Joslin's girlfriend. "Objection, Judge," he said, standing quickly. "I object to any further testimony from this witness on the grounds of relevance."

Iron Pants had figured it out, too. "Yes. Mister Bard, I'm not going to allow you to relitigate the guilt issue, sir. Is that your purpose?"

I could grandstand and possibly make a few points with the jury, or do it right and stay out of jail. I decided to do it right. "Approach?"

"Very well."

We huddled around the court reporter for the umpteenth time. When I spoke—in a low whisper—I stared at the top of her head. "Judge, this is a witness we've been looking for since the day I got the case. My investigator found her Thursday. She was with Drusus Church, Vera Byrd, and Jim-Jim Joslin the night Kingsley Rhoades was murdered. This is newly discovered evidence. I anticipate that what she says here will be part of my motion for new trial, if I have to make one. I hope I won't have to. I'm going to ask you to reopen the guilt phase so this jury can reconsider its verdict of guilt."

Both of them started whispering, but when Keane heard Ida he stopped. "That is the most inane and absurd request I've ever heard," she said, drilling me with hostile rays from her eyes. "You must know perfectly well that I can't do that!"

"Yes you can, Judge. This trial is yours, and you have the power to reopen. Where does it say you can't?"

"After a verdict? Jack—" She stopped and started biting her tongue. "This is—" She stopped again. "Do you have any other comment?"

"Yes. Even if you disallow those motions—and I haven't made either of them yet, but in fairness to the Court and to the prosecutor, I thought I'd warn you that I intend to— the defense has the right, in the penalty phase of a capital murder case, to put on evidence that questions the verdict

246

of guilt. We have that right, Judge. What she has to say is relevant to that issue."

Her smile was not an object of beauty. It was as thin as a violin string. "Do you have some law?"

"Yes. It's an old case, *People v. Terry*. It creates the law of lingering doubt."

"God." She drummed her fingers. "We'd better get the jury out of here. This could take the whole goddamned day."

Keane and I went back to our chairs. "Ladies and gentlemen, a problem has come up," Ida announced to the jury. She's a pretty good old sport for an ex-prosecutor, and when she smiled she really tried to put her heart in it. "It will require a short recess. As you know by this time, such things happen in the course of a trial." Ivan the bailiff led them out.

We took a half-hour recess to give the prosecutor a chance to look up the law. He and Wink trotted out of the courtroom with Mad Dog running interference, but I noticed—when they reached the hall—that Keane went one direction while Wink and Mad Dog went the other. Forty minutes later Keane came back—alone.

The argument chewed up another half hour, which was longer than it needed. Ida ruled in my favor, but for the wrong reason. She used some language in Penal Code 190.3, which was there for another reason, instead of the *Terry* case. "Judge, the effect of this ruling will be to open that whole can of worms that was sealed when the jury rendered its verdict!" Keane fumed in a futile effort to get her to change her mind. "Do I have to start over, too?"

"Mister Williams. You will have an opportunity to rebut whatever evidence Mister Bard puts on." She turned toward me. "Are we ready?"

LuAnne was in the hall, and Wink hadn't come back. "I'll get my witness, Judge," I said, pushing through the gate. "But what about Wink?" I asked solicitously. "Should we wait for him?" I wanted to know where he was.

"No, he could be out a while," Keane said.

I hope you are clean, my dear, I thought, watching Lu-

Anne climb back in the box. If you are not, as soon as Wink returns Keane will have all the dirty gossip.

Ivan brought the jury back, and LuAnne watched them sit down. She had her confidence now and offered them a nice smile. I'll bet she's a great tour guide, I thought.

When she testified she talked easily, as though used to being the focus of attention. She remembered going over to Drusus and Vera's the night Kingsley Rhoades was shot, she said, because she could relate it to other events in her life: the way Jim-Jim Joslin dropped out of her life, which happened a day or two later, and quitting her job in San Pedro to move to Hollywood. She'd been offered a tryout for a role in a movie and thought some things in her life had turned around, but they hadn't. She didn't get the part. Since that time she'd found a job "performing" as a tour guide.

"All this took place around April fourteenth of last year?"

"Yes, sir, it did."

"I don't remember how far we got before the recess," I said. "I may be repeating myself. On the night of April fourteenth, were you with the defendant Drusus Church and his friend Vera Byrd in their apartment in Long Beach?"

"Yes, sir."

"And you were with Jim-Jim Joslin?"

I was leading her all over the block, but Keane didn't cut the string. He knew it would come in anyway. He sat there like a graduate student taking notes. "Yes, sir."

"And the occasion was just to socialize?"

"Yes." She smiled and glanced at Drusus. "The way Jim-Jim explained it to me, he and Drusus had been friends forever. We went over for a late dinner and to watch movies."

"Did anything unusual happen?"

"*I* thought it was unusual." Her expression showed some disdain.

"What happened that you thought was unusual?"

"Somebody shot a gun off. Somebody said it happens in that neighborhood all the time, but it surprised me."

"What did you see and what did you do?"

"Vera jumped up like they were shooting at her, and the men looked at each other—you know, questioning looks—and I said, 'What was that?' "

"Do you remember what time this happened?"

"It was right around midnight. I think a little before."

"Where was the defendant, Mister Church, when you heard the shots fired?"

"Sitting right in his living room with the rest of us. We'd just seen one movie and were kind of resting up for the next one."

I asked her to describe the gunshots, and she did: two of them, loud explosions. "The men knew right away what they were." Jim-Jim wanted to go see what had happened, but they talked about it, and—

Keane objected. "Hearsay."

"Sustained."

"Did anyone go outside?"

"No."

"What did the four of you do?"

"We put on the other movie."

Wink came back, looking like he'd just filled a straight but wanted to keep the joy off his face. He put his notepad where Keane could see it, and I caught a glimpse of blue-backed paper. It was a rap sheet. Oh, dear, I thought. Who or what did this sweet young thing do? "Miss Jones, do you remember what the living room looked like?"

"It was very nice," she said. "In fact, that whole neighborhood kind of surprised me. The street looked real bad, but here were all these nice apartments off a courtyard. There was this high iron gate protecting everything, but that's just the way it is." She smiled. "It was like a different little world once a person stepped off the street and into that courtyard."

The answer was not particularly responsive, but Keane kept to his chair, and I nudged her back on the path. "And the living room, Miss Jones, how was it furnished?"

"I remember how big it was. Some nice paintings on the walls, you know, a kind of cream-colored couch with lots of fluff in the pillows, long enough to sleep on, and a real nice stereo against a wall that had bookshelves above and coming down the sides"—her hands drew lines in the air indicating how they looked—"and lots of books. They looked like they'd been read, too."

Keane had started smiling one of those evil little prosecutor smiles. "Objection, Judge." His tone and attitude had switched to arrogance, as though the witness was not worthy of respect. "How can a book look like it's been read?"

"What is your objection, Mister Williams?"

"She's stating as a fact something that can't be a fact. The last part of her answer."

"Overruled."

Keane hooked his arm over his chair in an overly casual manner, his back to the witness. It invited the jury to regard her with suspicion. That kind of posturing goes on all the time. I've even been known to indulge in it on occasion. I considered drawing attention to it, but—like a waiter who chews gum—it's the kind of thing you can't be too sensitive about. "Do you remember any of the book titles?" I asked.

"Yes, sir, I do." LuAnne had that incredible sixth sense that some people are endowed with. She immediately picked up on the prosecutor's contempt. A thin ray of fear began limiting her answers.

"Can you name some of them now?"

"I think so." She cleared her throat and glanced anxiously at Keane. "They had books by black authors, like Alex Haley and Langston Hughes, and dictionaries and an encyclopedia, and on one shelf a whole set of books by Donald Goines."

"He's also an African-American author?"

"Yes, sir."

"Now, this was a year ago. Can you explain to this jury how come your memory is so good?"

Keane made a face. If he'd known what the answer was going to be, he'd have objected. "The next day, or maybe two days later, the police asked me about it."

"Did that conversation affect your memory in some way?"

"Yes, sir. It made me remember what it was like."

I saw some frowns on juror's faces. A couple of them—Seven and Ten—leaned forward, paying close attention. "Did you see anything else in those shelves of books around the stereo, other than books?"

She struggled with that one. "Well, you know, like some knickknack items, I think, and maybe a vase or two, and bookends . . ." Her voice ended, and she looked at me as though hoping she'd given the right answer.

You don't make points by being subtle, old Charley used to tell me. Don't use a hammer, use a sledge. I wanted the jury to start adding it up, but that meant they needed more numbers. "Did you see a pouch or a purse of any kind in front of the books by Donald Goines, or anywhere else?"

"No, sir."

"And so that night you did not see a pouch or a purse near the books by Donald Goines?"

Keane thought about objecting but didn't. "No, sir."

"Did you ever go back to the apartment?"

"Yes, I did. It was either the next day or the day after."

"Why did you go back?"

"I was looking for Jim-Jim. He told me he'd help me move, then he was gone. I didn't like him treating me that way. I thought Drusus or Vera would know where he was at." She blushed. It was possible she'd had more on her mind.

"This second time, did you go inside the apartment?"

"Yes, I did."

"Did you look at the bookcase?"

"I probably did, you know, just to see if it was all the same."

"To the best of your recollection, was it all the same?"

"I sure don't remember anything different."

I wanted to tie it tighter. I requested permission to show her the purse that belonged to Kingsley Rhoades. It was still an exhibit and should not have been hard to find, but it was no longer in the courtroom, and it took no-name ten minutes to locate it. "Have you ever seen this before?" I eventually asked.

She took it in her hands. "No, I haven't."

"The night you heard the shots fired, did you see it that night?"

"Objection, Judge," Keane said wearily. "Asked and answered."

"Not exactly," Ida said. "I'll allow it."

LuAnne said, "No."

"And the day you went back, either the next day or the one after, did you see it that day?"

"No, sir."

I thought I'd piqued the curiosity of a couple more jurors, but you never know. Changing a mind that has already formed an opinion is tough. Changing one that has formed an opinion and then announced to the world what that opinion is, as in finding a person guilty of murder, is like changing a papal decree. Keane maintained that smirk. I would have liked to have known how much of it was an act. But Ida seemed to have a question or two in her mind. I felt like an artist putting the final touches on a painting. "You said something about the police asking you about the apartment?"

"Objection, Judge. That's clear hearsay."

"Sustained."

Good, I thought. Make me work for it. Let me give the jurors the impression that the prosecution has something to hide. "Very well." I dug out a photograph of Dave Kincaid, the one Whitney had talked the Long Beach Police Department public relations office out of. He'd already shown it to her. "Can I approach the witness?" I asked.

"You may."

"Let me show you this photograph, which has been marked for identification purposes as defendant's exhibit Q, I think." I turned it over. "Yes. Have you ever seen the person depicted in that photograph, Miss Jones?"

"Yes, I have." She looked uncomfortably at Keane.

"When did you see that person?"

"It was one or two days after Jim-Jim and I were over at the apartment and heard those shots. Like I said."

"Where were you when you saw the person depicted in this photo?"

"At where I worked then. In San Pedro."

"Do you remember the name of that place?"

"Whisky Pete's. It was a restaurant." She blushed.

"What time of day?"

"It was in the late afternoon."

"Was that person with anyone?"

"Well—he was with me."

"Anyone else?"

"No, sir."

"Did he tell you who he was?"

"Yes, sir."

"Now you can't tell us what he asked, because that would be hearsay, and the prosecutor won't allow that. But—"

"Objection, Judge!" Keane stormed. "It's the law that won't allow it!"

"I'll rephrase," I said. "Miss Jones, you can tell us what the man did and what you said, but that's all. Do you understand me?"

"Yes, sir."

"Did he show you any identification?"

"He showed me a badge."

I touched the rim of my glasses. "Your Honor, with the Court's permission, may I request Officer Wink Barrett of the Long Beach Police Department to let me borrow his badge for a moment, for demonstration purposes only?" Iron Pants doesn't like to tell cops what to do. She hesitated a moment. "Or let me suggest this, Judge," I said. "Let me interrupt the testimony of this witness for a couple of minutes, long enough to put Officer Barrett on the stand. I'll need him to identify this photograph of a fellow officer anyway."

Keane stood up. "Approach?"

"Yes."

The boy wonder was a bit more reasonable at the sidebar. "What will she testify to?" he asked me in a low whisper. "Maybe we can stipulate."

"She'll testify that the man in the photo—Dave Kincaid—told her Jim-Jim had been picked up by the police and questioned about the Rhoades killing. Jim-Jim used her as an alibi, told him he'd been with her at Drusus and Vera's apartment, and that Kincaid was checking it out. She'll testify that Kincaid got her to tell him what the inside of the apartment looked like, saying it would corroborate Jim-Jim's alibi. And she'll say that's what she did."

"She did what?"

"Told Kincaid what the inside of the apartment looked like. Told him about the bookshelves and the set of books by Goines."

Keane nodded. I had the peculiar feeling that he wasn't surprised. "I'll still object to the hearsay, Judge," he said. "But we'll stipulate that the man in the photograph is Dave Kincaid and that he carries a badge with him. I don't know where this witness came from or anything about Kincaid talking to her, so I'm still going to make them prove it. They can call Kincaid."

"In a pig's eye we can," I said. "He's retired. He's gone. *You* guys could get him here tomorrow if you wanted to. But I can't, and you know it."

Keane's face started looking more and more like a skull. All I saw was bones. "What you are trying to do here is contemptible, Bard," he said. "You won't get any help from me."

I didn't, either. But the jury got the picture. We stipulated that the photograph was of Dave Kincaid, who on that date was a homicide detective with the Long Beach P.D., and that he did in fact carry a badge. In a voice that kept getting higher and thinner she said the man with the badge asked a lot of questions she thought she was supposed to answer. She did the best she could. She told him Jim-Jim Joslin had been with her the night she'd heard the shots, that they were at the apartment of Drusus Church and a girl named Vera. She went on to say that in response to a question she described the living room to the officer.

She remembered particularly telling the man about the books by Donald Goines on the bookshelf.

Throughout her testimony Keane looked like an enraged crusader. His expression and attitude said to the jury, "Wait. I will expose this pack of lies." "It doesn't hurt to be paranoid when you do a criminal defense," old Charley always said. "It helps."

"Miss Jones, when did you find out that Drusus Church had been charged with the murder of Kingsley Rhoades?"

"Last week," she said. "That big man, Whitney? He told me."

"Are you referring to my investigator, Whitney Lee?"

"I think so."

"From the night in the apartment until the present time, have you seen Drusus Church?"

"No."

"What about Jim-Jim Joslin?"

"Him either."

"Vera Byrd?"

"Just that one time, looking for Jim-Jim."

"Have you had any connection at all with this case—been re-interviewed by any officer with the Long Beach Police Department or anyone else—other than what you've testified to?"

"Just—I talked with your investigator, and then with you yesterday, and that's all."

"Did you know that Drusus Church was in all this trouble?"

"No, sir. Not until last Thursday. I didn't know."

"Thank you, Miss Jones. Your witness."

The expression on Keane's face—too civilized for a sneer, but conveying the same message—reflected off the faces of at least half the jurors. He didn't even bother to say hello. "Of course, if you had known that Mister Church was in so much trouble, you would have come forward immediately with this information, wouldn't you?"

You play them to a jury, so I didn't object. "Yes, sir," LuAnne answered.

"You would have done that to clear him, isn't that right?"

"Yes."

"Can you read?"

"Yes, sir."

"Do you ever watch the evening news?"

"Yes."

"Listen to the radio?"

"Sometime."

"Take the paper?"

"I used to. And have, off and on, you know."

"Yet you did not read, or see, or hear anything about this case. Is that right, Miss Jones?"

"No, sir, I didn't."

Neither had any of the jurors. It was hardly a high-profile case. I would have to remind them in argument, when I tried to change their minds.

"You have lots and lots of friends, don't you, Miss Jones?"

She smiled and shrugged. "I know some people."

"And these are people who know Vera Byrd and Drusus Church?"

"Not really. Can't think of anybody." But she understood the drift of his questions and looked furtive, as though fearful someone might think she was making it up. At least that's the way she looked to me. To them, she probably looked like a liar.

"You were good friends with Vera and Drusus, weren't you?"

"No, sir. I didn't know them at all."

"That isn't what you told us earlier, though, is it?" Keane asked, moving away from the lectern.

"I—isn't it?"

"Do you remember when you were first testifying, after Mister Bard spilled water all over his tie?"

Her hand covered part of her mouth, a gesture some people associate with lying. "Yes, sir. He wanted to know if I had some Kleenex."

"He also asked you if you knew Drusus Church, and

you said something about you had not been intimate with him, but you were pretty good friends. Didn't you say that?"

"I—well—that isn't what I meant."

"But that is what you said."

"Yes, sir."

"That you had not been intimate with the defendant."

What should I do? I wondered. Object on the basis that he's creating a false impression, so he can say "Let the jury be the judge"? Instead I did some posturing of my own. I looked appalled.

LuAnne's posture wasn't an act. She looked distressed, like the victim of a date rape who doesn't think anyone will believe her. At least, that's how she looked to me. I couldn't read the jury. "Yes, sir."

"Then I take it you became very good friends with him on the basis of that one night?"

She flew away. I've seen it happen before. It's the way some people handle pressure. Their bodies remain in plain sight and their mouths continue to work, but all you have to do is look in their eyes, and you know they're gone. "Yes, sir." The shell she left behind will agree with anything he says, I thought.

So by agreement, LuAnne Jones backed away from much of what she'd said. She must have heard something about the case and couldn't really explain why she hadn't come forward with information. She wasn't all that sure what the living room looked like, either. After all, it had been a year, and she'd been in lots of living rooms since and couldn't remember what they looked like—although she continued to remember the books by Donald Goines. She could even have known Drusus and Vera before, too. In fact, she had to agree it would have been hard not to have seen them someplace.

The conversation with the cop? Keane was gathering up his notes as though getting ready to leave when he asked her about it. "Why don't you admit it, Miss Jones?" he asked. "You made that up, didn't you?"

"I did?" She asked the question as though she hoped he could tell her. "I—I don't think so."

"You made it up in a misguided effort to help a friend. Didn't you." It wasn't a question; it was an accusation.

"No," she said, her hand near her mouth.

"Incidentally, you've been convicted of two felonies, haven't you, Miss Jones?"

She smiled at him as though he had complimented her about something and nodded her head.

"You'll have to say 'yes' or 'no,' Miss Jones. The court reporter can't record it when you shake your head."

"Yes."

"One was for possession of an illegal substance with intent to sell, and the other was for fraudulent checks, wasn't it?"

"Yes."

"In other words, lying about the status of your bank account?"

I jumped up so fast my chair fell over. "Judge, objection!" I sputtered. "He's—"

"I'll withdraw the question," Keane said, walking away.

23

Boxers fight with their fists. Soldiers use rifles. Lawyers unload on their opponents with their mouths. But the object is the same in all situations: incapacitate the opposition. Lawyers last longer, of course, because their bodies aren't at risk. The other professional duelists resent the lawyers because of it. Although some of my brothers get personally involved in their work, then wind up in a puddle made of their own juices.

I sat there listening to Keane Williams batter me with his mouth. Until that morning I had thought he would have a long and distinguished career. But maybe I had shortened it a little. He had just started to take this one personally.

"—because none of the cases cited by Mister Bard even come close to supporting the extreme position he wants this Court to take. If this were a civil matter and a lawyer had brought a motion as frivolous as this one, the Court would be justified in imposing costs—" da da da da. It cheered me up. Throughout the trial he had kept his cool, and tomorrow he would have it back. But I'd finally tickled him with my feather stick. At that moment he frothed at the mouth.

I had rested my case after LuAnne Jones floated off the stand. As bad as she'd been hit in cross-examination, I didn't think all the raw-meat-eaters on the jury would be able to digest Keane's assertion that she lied. Keane hadn't thought so, either. He told the Court he had not planned to put on any rebuttal, but following the testimony of the last witness, he had no choice. He would call former Detective Dave Kincaid. "Can you have him here tomorrow?" Ida asked.

"I'm sure we can, Judge," Keane had said, avoiding my gaze.

So Ida sent the jury home, telling them to be back at nine o'clock the next morning. But she told the lawyers to stick around.

We had taken a short recess, and I talked to LuAnne Jones in the hall. She wanted some strokes, so I gave her some—enough, I hoped, so she could get back in her body. "You did fine," I lied. "You helped a lot."

"I hope so," she said—and from the anguish in her eyes, I knew she was back.

Naturally, Iron Pants wanted to utilize every available second. I'm all for that in a judge, except when it applies to my case. "Mister Bard," she said when we started up again, "you told us at the sidebar you would file a motion to reopen the guilt phase. I suggest we dispose of it now."

From the tone of her voice I knew it wouldn't take her long to dispose of it. My worthy opponent, the future attorney general, was in the process of destroying it as I listened in.

"—preposterous to suggest that Penal Code Section 1094 gives the Court the power to reopen a case *after* it has reached a verdict! It's as stupid as if I had filed a motion during the guilt phase demanding that the defendant take the stand. I believe you should give *this* motion the same treatment you would have given that one."

My, I thought, watching him sit down. He has a boiling point. "Mister Bard?" Iron Pants said.

"I didn't think it was that bad," I said when I got to the lectern. "On a scale of one to ten, I'd give it about a—I don't know—"

"A three?" Ida asked. She had a little twinkle in her eye.

I'll be damned, I thought. She isn't as sore as I thought she'd be. Of course, none of the judges can stay mad at me for very long, I added in my thoughts, because I'm such a fine fellow. "At least a three. Judge, consider this, for example. There aren't any cases that say you can't."

She laughed. "I know. The reason is obvious. The appellate courts haven't had the opportunity to reject the argument, because no other lawyer in California—where lawyers are known for trying anything—has tried it."

"That's possible. But—"

"Mister Bard, I don't believe we need any more comment. What you have presented here—the testimony of Lu-Anne Jones, an additional alibi witness—should be considered, if at all, in a Motion for New Trial. But I'm not going to reopen the guilt phase of this case. Your motion is denied." The woman really does have a nice smile. "Now. Shall we argue instructions?"

But doesn't she know when to quit?

I didn't want the next day to begin. I hadn't seen Dave Kincaid since the Motion to Disclose, early in the summer of the year before. We could look at each other then, but I couldn't look at him now, and he couldn't look at me.

He will lie, I thought as the jury came in. The former lineman at Long Beach State will lie through his teeth. It isn't only that he has to, to save his skin. He believes he is above the law he is supposed to uphold. He thinks that because he's a cop, he has the right, and the duty, to lie. And the awful part is that half the citizens in Long Beach agree with him.

A few minutes later Dave got on the stand. He'd put on a few pounds—his belt was all the way to the end, and some stomach hung over it—but he looked as righteous as King Richard mounted on a charger, off to fight the infidel. He didn't try to button his coat, a blue blazer I'd never seen. The glint in his eyes matched the steel gray of his hair.

I could look at him now, and he had no trouble returning my stare. The boy wonder rushed him through the preliminary introductions to the jurors. "I retired nine months ago from the Long Beach P.D.," he said. "Homicide detail. A lot of stiffs."

The impression he generated was that of a man who didn't care what anybody thought of him. Perfect for the prosecution, I thought, because jurors think such men don't lie. "In that capacity, in April of last year, were you assigned to investigate the murder of Kingsley Rhoades?"

"No," he said, as though angry at something. "That wasn't my case."

"Did you participate in the investigation?"

"Yes."

"What did you do?"

"I signed the affidavit for the search warrant. I assisted in the execution of the search warrant and the arrest of the defendant."

"It sounds to me like you did quite a bit," Keane said, as though trying to compliment the witness.

"I helped out."

Keane nodded his understanding, then wandered toward the far end of the jury box, near the chairs occupied by the alternate jurors. You couldn't see the line that ran between the examiner and the witness, but you could feel it. Keane had deliberately drawn it close to the jury, so that they, too, could feel the heat of Kincaid's righteous anger. "Yesterday a woman whose name is LuAnne Jones testified about a conversation she claims she had with you," the boy wonder told the witness. "She said it took place at Whisky Pete's in San Pedro a couple of days after Kingsley Rhoades was shot to death. Do you remember such a conversation?"

"Yes, I do."

At least the jurors were awake. "Was anyone else there?"

"People in the bar. Nobody with us, though. It was just the two of us."

"Did you identify yourself to her?"

"Yes. I showed her my badge."

"Why did you question her?"

I felt like the man in the barrel floating toward Niagara Falls. All you can do is hold your breath. "Detective Barrett wanted me to. He said she was possibly a witness."

"By that do you mean someone who saw the shooting?"

"I didn't know what he meant. To me, just someone who possibly had some information."

Keane nodded, as though he wondered what that information could possibly be. "And so you asked Miss Jones some questions?"

"Yes." His angry gaze slid off Keane's face and confronted Drusus. The youngster returned the heat with a look of expectation, like a spectator at a baseball game.

"What were the questions you asked, and what were her answers?"

"I asked her if she knew Drusus Church, and she said she did. I asked her if she'd seen him recently, and she said she had. I asked her when, and she was somewhat uncertain. The best she could remember, it had been a few nights before at his apartment in Long Beach."

"Mister Rhoades was shot on April fourteenth. Did you ask her the date she had seen Mister Church?"

"Yes, sir, and she could not say. She thought it was ahead of the fourteenth by two or three days."

"She told you that?"

"Yes."

Drusus frowned and looked at me, a big question mark on his face. Some of the jurors saw it, but most of them had tight mouths and were nodding their understanding at the witness. Keane let them soak in the impression—the first impression—he was creating.

"Did you ask her why she was there?"

Kincaid's large face swung back to Keane. "I think I did, but I don't remember what she said."

"This was a year ago. Is that why you don't remember?"

"Yes."

"What else do you remember of the conversation?"

"She told me who was there: a subject whose name was Vera, Jim-Jim Joslin, who I knew, and Drusus Church. She also told me Drusus took a telephone call about eleven, then went out. She didn't see him again that night.''

"Wasn't any telephone call," Drusus whispered to me in anger.

"Did you question her about the telephone call?''

"Yes, I did. She couldn't tell me anything about it.''

"Did she say anything else?''

He shrugged. "Said after a while—I don't remember what time she used—she and Jim-Jim departed the premises. She said they left before Mister Church came back.''

"Did she say anything about hearing gunshots?''

He glared at Keane. "Not to me.''

"Shortly after that conversation, you yourself were in the apartment, weren't you, Mister Kincaid?''

He smiled. "You know, I like it when you call me 'Mister Kincaid.' Yes.''

"When was that?''

"April eighteenth, when we searched the defendant's apartment and arrested him.''

"The apartment was one of many around a courtyard, right?''

"That's right. On the second floor. It had a balcony.''

"Was it next to the alley?''

"No.''

"Could you hear the sounds of traffic inside the apartment?''

"I couldn't.'' He glared at me, as though challenging me to find fault with what he said.

"Miss Jones said it was like being in another world once you entered the courtyard. Would you agree with that?''

"I don't know about another world. But it's better than the street.''

"How long were you in the apartment?''

"I believe about an hour.''

"In that period, did you hear any sounds from outside the apartment—or from the alley, or the street?''

"No.''

Keane checked the jurors. A couple of them—Four and Seven—gave him those bare little nods of approval. "Did you talk about anything else?''

"No, sir. That was it."

"Miss Jones testified that you asked her to describe the inside of the apartment. Did you ask her that question?"

"No," he said angrily.

"She said she told you where the bookshelf was that held the books by Donald Goines. Did she tell you that?"

"She did not."

Keane frowned, as though trying to understand the discrepancy, then shrugged, as though to say, "There you have it." "Did you take any notes, Mister Kincaid?"

He smiled again, and several of the jurors smiled with him. "Love it. No, sir."

"Why not?"

"She didn't say anything. She was a big waste of time." He continued staring with ferocity at the prosecutor. "I mean, why clutter up a file with garbage like that?"

Keane walked away from the lectern toward his chair. "I have no further questions."

"You may examine, Mister Bard," Iron Pants said.

My stomach was in my heart, and my heart was in my throat. As I got up I tried to let my anatomy rearrange itself. "Hello, Officer," I said, standing behind the lectern.

"Mister," he corrected me.

Some of the jurors smiled. "All right. You knew Kingsley Rhoades, didn't you, sir?"

"I knew him."

Keane stood up, as though in warning, but didn't say anything. "You knew he was a drug dealer, right?"

"May we approach, Judge?" Keane asked.

"Yes."

He had regained the cool he'd dropped the day before. Every hair on his brushed and scented head was in place, as was his smile. "Your Honor," he whispered, "the witness testified only to the conversation he had with LuAnne Jones, and Mister Bard's cross examination shouldn't be allowed to go beyond that. Yet here he is asking about Kingsley Rhoades. It's clear he's off on some other mission."

"I tend to agree. Mister Bard?"

"He opened the door when he talked about the murder of Kingsley Rhoades, Judge," I whispered, keeping my head down. "I can go into anything he opened the witness up to, as long as it's relevant to an issue in the case, which it is: lingering doubt."

"Come on," Keane whispered heatedly. I'd like to know how you do that, I thought. He was pissed as hell but still looked cool. "You rested, remember?" he hissed. "Your turn is over. This is rebuttal."

"I'll ask the judge to reopen, then." I looked at her. "Judge, this time I mean it. They kept Kincaid off the stand during the guilt phase, even though he is the one who signed the affidavit on the search warrant. I haven't been able to cross-examine him at all."

"Jack, I've already denied your motion to reopen, and I'm not going to change my mind! Now let's get going."

"That was a motion to reopen the guilt phase, Judge, and I'm not asking for that. I'm asking you to let me reopen my case in the penalty phase."

"But you've rested, and we've started rebuttal."

"I realize that, Judge. But we've only just started, and I rested yesterday. It's not the same."

She glared at me. Her mouth had shut so hard her teeth should have fused together. "Damn it." I don't know where the sound came from—through her nostrils, maybe. "I'll allow it."

Keane couldn't believe it. "Judge—"

"Enough, Mister Williams. Now, I'm not going to make an announcement to the jury. They're confused enough as it is. But he's your witness, Jack."

"A hostile witness?"

She shut her eyes. Everything I was asking her to do went contrary to the true-blue prosecutor's heart that beat in her chest. But by God, that day she was a judge. "Yes."

What it meant was that I could take Kincaid as far as I could take him to prove lingering doubt. And I could ask leading questions to get him there. "Thank you, Your Honor."

Keane was in his chair before I got back to the lectern,

smiling and looking cool. I hoped he was burning up inside.
Dave had no clue as to any of it. "Officer—pardon me.
Mister Kincaid," I said, "you knew that Kingsley Rhoades
was a drug dealer, right?"

He glared at Keane, then turned toward me like an angry
lion. "Yes, I did."

"As a matter of fact, Kingsley Rhoades was a person
you had quite a file on, correct?"

"No. I didn't have no kind of file on him whatsoever."

"The Long Beach Police Department had a file on him,
then. Vice, or narcotics, or however you divide it up?"

"I don't know about that at all."

It's never as easy as it ought to be. That's what makes
it so much fun. "All right. You knew he was a drug dealer,
but you don't know if the department you worked for maintained a file on him, and you yourself have no knowledge
whatever of a file on Kingsley Rhoades. Is that a fair
statement?"

He shifted his weight uncomfortably. "Close enough."

"I don't want to be 'close enough,' Mister Kincaid. This
isn't horseshoes. Is that what you are testifying to, or isn't
it?"

"Yes."

"Fine. Now, you knew Mr. Rhoades didn't even live in
Long Beach, didn't you?"

"What's that got to do with anything?" he demanded.

Keane was on his feet. "I was about to ask the same
question," he said, a big smile on his face. "Objection,
Judge. Irrelevant."

"What is your purpose, Mister Bard?"

Keane screwed up. He should have asked for a sidebar
huddle but didn't. Defense lawyers don't get chances like
that very often, and I made the most of it. "Relevant to
the issue of lingering doubt, Judge. My purpose is to suggest that Mister Kincaid, and possibly others in the Long
Beach Police Department, had a motive—"

That was as far as I got. Her gavel came down. For
a minute I thought my head was under it. "Ladies and

gentlemen," she said to the panel of jurors, "I'm going to excuse you for a few minutes. This shouldn't take long."

It didn't, either. While they waited in the jury room I stood in front of the bench with my head bowed while Ida stroked my neck with a hatchet. I didn't blame her particularly. I'd earned it. I appeared contrite and subdued on the outside, but on the inside my heart and stomach were doing a happy little dance.

Kincaid stayed on the stand during the flogging exercise, grinning the whole time. But when the jury came back and he discovered he had to answer the question, his grin disappeared. "Yeah, I knew," he said sullenly.

"This was knowledge you had about this known drug dealer, even though the department you worked for did not, to your knowledge, maintain a file on him?" I asked, driving the same nail in deeper.

"Yes." Dave has always been fun. His face burned, and so did his eyes. I thought the lectern would combust from the heat.

"He lived in Palos Verdes, didn't he, Mister Kincaid?"

Kincaid frowned. "Yeah. So what?"

"In a very expensive house with a swimming pool, sauna, and tennis court?"

"So I understand."

"He supported himself with illegal drug money from that crack house in Long Beach—a fact known to you, at least. But neither you nor the department you work for could do anything about it, right?"

Kincaid leaned forward in the manner of a man who has had enough. "You're asking questions here that could compromise ongoing drug investigations," he said.

"Of whom?" I asked. "Isn't Kingsley Rhoades dead?"

Kincaid looked at the judge for support, but none was offered. He sat back in his chair. "Yes."

"The crack house he operated. Is it still in operation?"

"Your Honor, please," the boy wonder implored. "This has gone on long enough."

"You've made your point, Mister Bard. Move on to something else."

"Thank you," I said. What a game. "Mister Kincaid," I said, turning again to him. "You signed the affidavit for the search warrant, did you not, sir?"

"That's right, Counselor."

"And that was on the basis of information supplied to you by a so-called confidential informant?"

"Yes."

"And that person told you exactly where the purse"—I walked over to the exhibit table and picked it up—"this object here, and I'm referring to People's exhibit 8," I said, lifting it and showing it to him, "was located in the apartment of Drusus Church and Vera Byrd. Right?"

"She told us a lot more than that." He spoke with deadly sincerity, and he knew he had scored with the jury.

" 'She'?" I asked. "The informant was a woman, then?"

Keane saw what had happened to Kincaid. The man had become a loose cannon, and one shot could blow their case to bits. "Before the witness answers, Judge, may we approach?"

"You may."

"Your Honor," he whispered earnestly, "we are way, way too far afield here. This witness cannot under any circumstances be made to reveal the name of a confidential informant. That matter was resolved earlier at another hearing."

"I agree totally. Jack, that's enough along this line."

"Can I respond, Judge?"

Her patience was so thin that if it had been skin, she'd have been bleeding. "Go ahead."

"It may no longer be necessary to maintain the confidentiality of the informant. If it isn't, then in the interests of justice, that name should be disclosed now."

"No."

"Judge, all I'm asking is that you hold another *in camera* hearing to make your own determination—now—as to whether or not circumstances have changed enough so that there would be no danger in disclosing the alleged informant's identity. It's been a year!"

"Absolutely not," she said. "Now, I've given you far

more latitude in this case than I should have." Uh-oh, I thought. Maybe she's suffering withdrawal symptoms from her brief sojourn as a jurist. "I am not going to interrupt this trial to second-guess another judge."

"It wouldn't be a second guess, Your Honor. It would—"

"Enough, Jack!" I felt her anger like a punch in the stomach. Then she smiled. "Do not pursue that line of questioning. Do you understand me?"

I nodded. "For the record, Judge, I object."

"Noted. Let's move on."

When you get that close, only to get turned back, it's hard to move. I walked slowly back to the lectern. If I could have toyed with the loose cannon a few minutes more, he might have blurted out who the CI was: Vera Byrd's mother. Then I'd have proved she didn't have one, and truth and justice—meaning my side of the case—would have had a chance to surface. So close, I thought.

I looked at the clock on the back wall of the courtroom: almost eleven. And there was old Charley, grinning at me from behind the face of the clock. You're doing fine, laddie, he said.

24

Kincaid sat in the box with his arms crossed, glaring at me with that misunderstood look cops are born with. I should be fair: not all of them wear it, only ninety percent. They aren't born with it, either. They learn from each other that they are right and the pukes are wrong and there is no middle ground. They put it on their faces when they discover—from each other—that most of the world is inhabited by pukes.

What do I do now, Charley? I asked my old dead mentor.

Open your mouth, laddie, he said. It will think of something.

"Officer Kincaid—"

"Mister."

Charley was right. Once my mouth got going, it didn't have any trouble. "Sorry," I said to Kincaid. "Old habits die slow. We've faced each other in a lot of courtrooms over the years, haven't we, Dave?"

He was not receptive to charm. "That's right, Counselor. And it's still Mister."

I raised my eyebrows for the benefit of the jurors but didn't tease him about it. "Fine. Let's go back to the night, or the early morning, that Drusus Church was arrested for the murder of Kingsley Rhoades. That was April eighteenth last year, wasn't it?"

"Yes."

"About three o'clock in the morning?"

"Correct."

"You told Mr. Williams you were there about an hour, right?"

"Yes."

"In that period of time you didn't hear any sounds of traffic from the street or the alley. Isn't that what you said?"

"Nothing. Not even a garbage truck."

He is getting smarter in his retirement, I thought, considering his answer. "Of course, there wouldn't be much to hear at three o'clock in the morning, would there be?" I asked.

"Objection, Judge, calls for speculation," Keane said.

"Sustained."

The jurors were probably bored with the line of questions anyway, I thought. It might entertain lawyers, who could ooh and ahh over a clever trap revealing that gunshots might have been hearable after all. So I smiled and nodded agreeably—standard procedure in such situations—which doesn't fool anybody either. "Who were the officers with you, sir?"

"Detective Barrett, Detective Danforth, and Officer Morschy."

"You flattened the door going in, right?"

"We broke through the door. It was not a situation where we wanted to hazard advance warning."

"Who was in the apartment?"

"Hammer—that's the defendant, Drusus Church—and his girl, Vera Byrd."

"Where were they?"

"In bed."

There is a standard rule in cross-examination: never ask an open-ended question unless you know the answer. But when the witness is a loose cannon who wants to shoot you to death, and who in the process might blow over his own fortress, you can take chances. "What happened immediately after you broke through the door?"

"Hammer met us in the hall of his apartment, where he was subdued."

He should have looked at Wink, who sat quietly next to the boy wonder. Wink had on an interesting expression. "Go on," I invited.

"I was pumped, things happened fast. Took three of us to get him down is what I remember." Then he glanced at Wink.

"You had to wrestle him to the floor?" I asked.

He became uncertain. "That was a year ago."

I didn't press him for an answer because it was obvious to me he'd seen his mistake. "Detective Wink Barrett testified during the guilt phase of this trial about the same situation," I told him. "He told this jury that the defendant offered no resistance whatever and that he was arrested while he was in bed. Was Barrett wrong?"

Kincaid's large hands opened, and he smiled. "Not Wink," he said. "He writes things down."

"You don't, however, do you, Mister Kincaid?"

"I put down what's important."

"And the important thing here was that Drusus Church was arrested?"

"Right."

"The manner of his arrest in your mind was just a detail?"

"That's all it was to me."

I nodded pleasantly. "So when you are questioned about a detail that you don't make a note of, what you do is make it up?"

"Objection," Keane said quietly. "Argumentative."

"Sustained."

"If it please the Court—"

"Continue with your examination, Mister Bard," Iron Pants said. Uh-oh, I thought. As far as she's concerned, I'm back in jail.

But I had enough to work with. "Who found the purse?"

Kincaid glanced hopefully at Wink, but Wink knew better than to flash a sign. "I'm not sure, sir."

"Is that a detail you didn't make note of?"

273

"It's something I don't remember."

"Officer Barrett testified during the guilt phase that you found the purse. Would you dispute that?"

"I guess I found it, then," he said, smiling broadly.

I took my time with the next question. "So you were the person who talked with the confidential informant, and who signed the affidavit which described the precise location of the purse in the apartment, and then you found the purse yourself. Is that right?"

"I know what you're tryin' to pull here, Counselor," he said, menacingly.

Good, I thought. The loose cannon was pulling on the trigger. "Then your answer to my question is, you know what I'm trying to pull?"

"Objection," Keane said coolly. "Relevance."

"Judge, this is cross-examination," I said quickly before she could swat me again with her gavel.

She hesitated. "Overruled."

I smiled at Kincaid, who glowered back. He didn't say anything, however. "Do you want me to repeat the question, Mister Kincaid?" I offered nicely.

"You are trying to make it look like I put that purse there, Counselor. I didn't. I found it there."

"Did anyone see you?"

"Yes! I think so. Danforth or Barrett, I don't remember. Somebody did."

"Is that a detail, or did you make a note?"

He whipped his head angrily toward the judge. "Do I have to answer that question?" he asked.

"Answer the question," she said.

He looked betrayed, as though he suddenly realized that the judge was one of the pukes. "It wasn't my case," he said. "I was along for the ride."

Some cross-examiners always insist on an answer. But I had a loose cannon. The jurors were watching him now. I thought it would be better to keep moving him around because it's hard to aim a moving cannon, and the ball could hit anything. "It was your affidavit, however, wasn't it?"

"That's right."

"It was also your confidential informant?"

"She came to me, yes."

"So you were interested in the outcome, weren't you?" He shrugged. "I get paid either way."

I glanced toward the jury. Four and Eleven, who I believed were hard-asses, had slumped in their chairs. The vibe I got was they were embarrassed by the witness. Probably I'll find out later, I thought, that they were asleep. But Kincaid's answer sounded to me like obvious bullshit, so I left it alone. "And you discovered the purse?"

"I'd forgotten that," he said.

"How much more do you have, Mister Bard?" Iron Pants asked.

Sometimes I think judges who were prosecutors get hooked up with invisible wires to deputy DAs. That way they can send messages to each other without anyone knowing about it. "Not much more, Judge." I didn't want a recess now. I didn't want Keane to have the chance to straighten Kincaid up.

"I have to leave a bit early this morning," she said. "Would this be a convenient place to break for lunch?"

"Fine with me, Your Honor," Keane said, closing his notepad as though we had adjourned.

"I think I'll be done in about ten minutes," I lied. "It's only eleven-twenty. Should we make the jurors eat before they are hungry?"

She blessed me with one of those thin smiles. "Very well. But we'll have to stop at eleven-thirty, Mister Bard. Even if you're in the middle of a question."

Ten minutes, I thought. Here goes. "You were the detective in charge of the investigation into the murder of Tommy Sherman, weren't you, Mister Kincaid?"

"Correct."

I was on very thin ice. One little misstep and the door could swing open wide enough to float a battleship through. I would then go crashing into very cold water. "Salvadore Mira witnessed that shooting, didn't he, sir?"

"Salvadore reported it," Kincaid said. He had the patronizing habit of calling witnesses by their first name, as though to control them. He also seemed unwilling to admit that Salvadore was a witness. "He seen something, but my recollection, the man was very nervous. He wasn't clear about what he saw."

"That didn't stop you from showing him a mug-shot folder with the defendant's photo in it, however, did it?"

"No. We put one together and showed it to him."

I wandered over by Wink, as though—for the moment—he and I were on the same side. "Mira did not identify the defendant as the shooter, did he?"

Kincaid shifted around in his chair. "My recollection, he wasn't certain."

"Well, it's true, isn't it, that if Drusus Church had been identified at that time by Salvadore Mira, you would immediately have gotten a warrant out for his arrest?"

"Sometimes factors get in the way," he said.

This time I pressed. "Do you mean to say that if you had an eyewitness to a murder who could identify the murderer, that you would have waited to get out a warrant?"

"Not if you put it that way."

That's good enough, old Charley whispered in my ear. I stayed near Wink and took one of those mighty leaps. "When you showed the mug-shot folder to Salvadore Mira, you already had another witness, didn't you?"

His eyes lit up. He got ready to shoot again. "We had *two* other witnesses."

I smiled nervously. "Just so we are clear on who those other witnesses were. One of them was Larry Walker, right?"

"That's right, Counselor." He blasted Drusus with a glare.

Old Charley taught me to make sure the jurors keep up, so I asked him a question for their benefit. "Larry Walker gave a statement to Detective Danforth, and Danforth testified about it last week. Were you aware of that?"

"I heard about it, yes."

"And Salvadore Mira identified a picture of Larry Walker also, as one of the three people he saw that night. Were you aware of that?"

"No. That's news to me."

I walked back to the lectern. Now for the tricky part, because I had to lock him in. "You said two witnesses, right?" I asked, then immediately cleared my throat, as though—if I could—I'd take the question back.

He looked amazed for a moment, as though he couldn't believe my stupidity. Then he made the most of it. "The other gentleman's name was Archie Dock."

I finished clearing my throat. "I didn't ask for his name," I said angrily, standing at the lectern, trying to compose myself. "Which name did you get first—Walker or Dock?"

He leaned back with satisfaction. "We got the names of both individuals together."

"But this was after you put together the mug-shot folder, wasn't it?" I asked, a bit desperately.

"No, Counselor. It was before."

"In other words, you knew who shot Tommy Sherman before showing that folder to Mira?"

"That's right."

"And that's why you put Mister Church's photo in. Correct?"

"Correct, Counselor. Because by that time we knew it was him."

"And of course you expected Mira to confirm what you already knew by picking Drusus Church's photo out of the folder?"

He nodded. "That's right. We had not expected Salvadore to be so nervous, but it will happen."

He was locked in. Well done, laddie, old Charley said. "You didn't get the names of Walker and Dock from Mira, did you?"

"Oh, no."

"Then where did you get them?"

He still didn't know what had happened to him. My big regret was that Whitney wasn't there to watch. It was the question he had wanted an answer to a hundred years ago, after our session at the Long Beach Police Department.

"We had some intelligence."

"You had in informant. Right?"

"It was all over the street, Counselor. Everybody knew."

"Everybody knew what?" I demanded.

"Everybody on the street knew that Drusus Church had shot Tommy Sherman."

"That isn't the question, Mister Kincaid. How did you know that Dock and Walker saw it happen?"

He shifted in his chair and looked toward Wink, then back to me. "Somebody must have told us. I don't remember."

"That 'somebody' was an informant, wasn't he? Just as you had an informant for Kingsley Rhoades, you had one for Tommy Sherman, didn't you?"

"The informants on those murders are apples and oranges, Counselor. They can't be compared whatsoever."

"But there was an informant in both cases. Right?"

Getting a straight answer out of Kincaid was like sticking a pin in a greased pole. "The person who told me about the purse was a confidential informant. That other was more in the nature of intelligence."

"Whatever you call him or her in the Tommy Sherman case, someone told you not only who the shooter was, but who the witnesses were. Isn't that true? Isn't that how you got the names of Larry Walker and Archie Dock?"

He hesitated—in part, I suspected, because he didn't know what I had, and he was looking pretty stupid. "I don't remember."

Good, I thought. If he doesn't remember, it could have been anyone. "It was Kingsley Rhoades, wasn't it?"

I was right! The question jolted him, and he followed the jolt with a shrug. "Could have been, I suppose."

"You talked to Rhoades, didn't you?" I asked, knowing how he'd have investigated the case.

"I didn't myself, no."

"Well, someone did, didn't they, Mister Kincaid?" I made him look at me. "You aren't going to tell this jury that if a person got murdered right in front of Rhoades's crack house, no one from the department would have questioned him about it?"

"It is certainly possible that someone did." He managed a knowing smile. "Kind of a shame we can't ask Rhoades, ain't it?"

My God, I thought suddenly. My mouth opened, and I couldn't seem to get it going. "Mister Bard, it's eleven-thirty," Iron Pants said, filling the void. "Do you have anything further of this witness?"

"Yes, Judge." Will that work, I wondered? "I'll need another ten minutes."

"You'll have to wait until after lunch, then," she said.

Iron Pants gave her usual admonishment to the jurors, then told them to be back at two. Before leaving she looked long and carefully at Drusus. I would have liked to have been plugged in to her mind.

I told Drusus not to eat too much. He grinned as Godzilla wrapped all that iron around him. I waited long enough to see Keane leave with Kincaid, then got to a telephone as quick as I could. If I was lucky, Keane would be too busy to send the cops. "Mouse? Put Carlotta on."

"Hi, Daddy. She isn't here. She'll be back at noon, because that's when you always call."

"What about Whitney?"

"He left a few minutes ago."

I hated to dump something as big as this on my darling daughter. "Okay. Drop whatever you are doing and get a hold of Salvadore Mira. I need him in court this afternoon, but the cops could be looking for him, too. You've got to get him before they do."

"How can I do that?" she wailed helplessly. "I barely know who you're talking about!"

I took a deep breath. What could I expect of a mere college graduate? "Okay, don't worry," I said. "I'm on my way. If Carlotta shows up, don't let her go anywhere."

That day it would have been faster to walk from the courthouse to the SeaFarer Hotel than to drive. It doesn't happen often, but now and then Ocean Boulevard will plug up like an old drain. When I blew through the door to my office twenty minutes later I decided that Carlotta was right: time for me to put a telephone in my car. I'd put an extension in the bathroom when I got to be fifty and started spending extra time on the pot. I guessed now it was time to louse up my car with one of the goddamned things.

No one was there. Not even Mouse. I found a note in Carlotta's typewriter: "Hi, Beast. Had to go. Daddy called early and needs a witness. I *found* him! Isn't that great? He sounds like a heavy breather on the telephone, but I'm so horny it sounds nice!" (My little Mouse?) "Tell him not to worry, okay?" She signed it "Beauty."

I heard Carlotta's heels clicking down the hall, and the door opened. "What are you doing here?" she asked when she saw me. "Where's Mouse?"

I showed her the note.

"You weren't supposed to see this."

"Girls don't get horny, do they?"

"Are you kidding?"

At five minutes after two o'clock I watched Dave Kincaid climb back into the witness box. I tried to read the faces of the jurors, but they were blanks.

The remnant of what had once been a huge and lusty stomach had turned inside out, emptying the coffee I'd had that morning somewhere. I didn't want to think about it. The reason that my stomach had done its flop was that Mouse and Salvadore Mira had disappeared.

Carlotta had dispatched Whitney to the shoe store on Broadway where Mira worked, only to find that Rory Danforth was already there. Danforth told Whitney that Mira was out to lunch, and not to interfere when the man returned. "Official police business. You get in the way, dude, and you're under arrest."

I rubbed my stomach, trying to ease the pain. "Mister Kincaid, you are still under oath," Iron Pants said. "Mister Bard, we interrupted your examination. You may proceed."

It was a different Dave Kincaid. His coat was buttoned, and his expression no longer burned with righteous resentment. He even tried a nice little smile. It was obvious to me that the special prosecutor had worked over the lunch hour with the latest addition to his cast of characters. "Mister Kincaid, you don't deny talking to LuAnne Jones at Whisky Pete's in San Pedro, do you?"

"No, we talked all right, sir."

"Did you make a tape recording of the conversation?"

"No, sir, I don't do that without asking."

"And you didn't take notes?"

"As I explained to Mister Williams, there was no need to take notes. Miss Jones didn't say nothing worthwhile whatsoever in my judgment."

"You only put down those things which in your judgment are important, correct?"

"Yes, sir."

"You don't record details?"

He smiled at the jury. "Hardly ever."

"And that leads to mistakes, doesn't it, Mister Kincaid?"

"I ain't perfect."

"You will admit that you are not like Detective Wink Barrett, who writes things down, then?"

His smile had thinned out. "I'd have to agree that Wink is better in court than me."

The macho implication was clear. I didn't do anything for a minute, hoping the jurors would pick it up. The trouble is, probably half of them would like him for it. "When you say that Officer Barrett is better in court than you are, I take it you mean that he is more accurate than you in court because he takes notes?"

Kincaid cleared his throat. "Yes."

I took a deep breath, like a skydiver before a jump. Good luck, laddie, old Charley said. "Mister Kincaid, let's shift gears here," I said—not for his benefit, of course. I did it for the jury. "In the course of your investigation into the murder of Tommy Sherman, did you show a picture of Kingsley Rhoades to Salvadore Mira?"

He rolled his eyes up, then caught himself, remembering his new image. "No, sir."

"Why not?" I asked.

"Because that would have been a waste of time, sir. We knew it was not Kingsley Rhoades. We knew who it was."

"Salvadore Mira described the killer as a big black man. Didn't that description fit Rhoades?"

"You don't understand, sir. Rhoades owned the crack house. The man had a degree from college, it was his business. If he wanted somebody done, he'd give an order, he wouldn't do it himself. No way would he shoot and kill somebody on his own doorstep."

"But just to eliminate him as a suspect, wouldn't you show Salvadore Mira his picture?"

He shrugged, then smiled. "In this case, no, sir. You make up a mug-shot folder from mug shots. We didn't have any of Mister Rhoades because the man didn't have no record of any kind whatsoever."

I nodded, wondering what the jurors were thinking. "Thank you, Mister Kincaid." I sat down.

"You may proceed, Mister Williams," Ida allowed.

Keane stood easily at the lectern, projecting confidence and sincerity at the witness. Like a mirror, Kincaid reflected it back. With Keane, an actor's performance; with Kincaid, the result of skilled coaching.

"Forgive me if we cover some of the same ground, Mister Kincaid," Keane said. "I know you're retired and don't need this."

I didn't need it either. "Judge, would it be out of line for me to suggest that Mister Williams should get to the point?"

Ida is a good woman, but her prosecutorial heart had reasserted itself. She had a stone face when she looked at me, which somehow turned into skin when she looked at anyone else. "Thank you for the suggestion, Mister Bard," she said. "Proceed, Mister Williams."

Keane coated himself again with the righteous fervor the white hats put on from time to time. "How long were you with the Long Beach Police Department, Mister Kincaid?" There was an extra throb in his voice.

"Twenty-five years."

I got up as amiably as possible. "Excuse me, Judge, we've already heard this. The jury knows who Mister Kincaid is. The prosecutor took us through his qualifications and career and so forth earlier."

"Mister Williams?"

"Approach?"

At the sidebar Keane got serious. "This man's character, credibility, integrity—all of the things that really matter to him—have been viciously attacked," he whispered. "I had not expected anything like that when I first put him on. I thought he would only be a rebuttal witness to a conversation, but Mister Bard cleverly opened him up to a lot more. That changed everything. I think I have the right to go back over his qualifications, to bring out more of his background, to do what I would have done had I known he was going to be challenged in such a high-handed manner."

"Mister Bard?"

"There was nothing high-handed about any of it, Judge. That isn't the point anyway. Mister Williams had his chance to bring all this stuff up and didn't," I whispered. "He should have to live with it."

"I let you reopen your case, didn't I, Jack?" She smiled at me. "Don't you think I should allow him the same courtesy?"

I rubbed the back of my neck, trying to think of a good argument. "Judge, according to Mister Williams, that was a mistake." So I lost the argument, but it gave me the chance to grin all over the place as I sat down.

When Keane got going I drummed my fingers on the table, shifted my weight around, shuffled papers, and whispered to Drusus. It didn't keep the boy wonder from expanding on the image of Dave Kincaid. Over the years he'd picked up seven citations for bravery and courage, four awards for meritorious service, and several letters of commendation. He had also been active in the community, working with youth—in particular, the Police Athletic League—coaching football. He had seen young men turned around, he said with a hitch in his voice, which gave a whole lot more pleasure than slamming the steel-bar door of a cell in their faces.

I'll bet Dirty Harry feels the same way, I thought, but I decided not to comment.

Carlotta came into the room. She can stop a jet airliner in flight, and Keane was no match for her. The courtroom world shut down long enough for her to stick a note on the table in front of me, nod apologetically at the judge, then leave. I read the note. "SM is in the cafeteria drinking coffee with Mouse," it said. "He doesn't know why he's here. Whitney and Danforth are at the shoe store waiting for him and staring at each other. I'm in the hall if you need me."

My fingers tingled, and so did the soles of my feet. I kept wondering if my little scheme would work, and whether it was worth the risk. "Let's go to the murder of Kingsley Rhoades, Mister Kincaid," I hear Keane say. "That is the killing which this jury has already found the defendant guilty of. Are you with me, sir?"

Kincaid nodded eagerly, as though he would like nothing better than to answer questions about it. "Yes."

The boy wonder pointed at me. "The defense lawyer has implied that you planted the purse belonging to Kingsley Rhoades in his client's apartment. My question to you, sir, is this: Did you?"

"Absolutely not." His voice trembled with righteous indignation.

"If you take that implication one step further, the defense lawyer has implied that you murdered Kingsley Rhoades." I shuffled my feet. I didn't know whether to object or not. "My question to you, sir, is this: Did you?"

"I did not." He gave it the same intensity.

"Do you feel as though the defense lawyer has put you on trial here, sir?"

"Yeah. And it hurts." There was no mistaking his sincerity.

"Why does it hurt?"

Maybe you should have objected, laddie, I could hear Charley say. "I know Jack Bard, known him all my life, went to high school with him." He stared at me with a sad look of betrayal. "For him to do that . . ." His lip trembled, and he jerked his head around. "For him to do that."

Keane let the jurors feel the man's anguish. "No further questions."

"Do you have any questions, Mister Bard?" Iron Pants asked.

I couldn't leave it there. Not with all the wet eyes in the courtroom stabbing me like I was Judas. I stood up but didn't go over to the lectern. "Were we that tight in high school, Dave?"

"I don't know. I always thought so."

Maybe he had been. "Those were the days, right, when Long Beach was a town and things were simple?"

"Mister Bard," Iron Pants said, "I don't think we need this, sir."

I nodded. She was right. We didn't. "Mister Kincaid, just before we broke for lunch you said something to the effect that it was too bad we couldn't ask Kingsley Rhoades anything more about Tommy Sherman. Do you recall that statement?"

Keane stood up. "Judge—"

"I agree. Mister Bard, the questioning of this witness has to end sometime. Do you have any proper—and let me emphasize the word proper—re-direct?"

I hate taking a shot like that, especially in front of a jury. "Let me see if I do, Judge. Mister Kincaid, Larry Walker worked for Kingsley Rhoades, didn't he?"

"Again, Your Honor, this is beyond the scope of my redirect," Keane said.

"I'm going to allow it," Ida said. "Mister Kincaid, answer the question, please."

He opened his palms. "No secret there. He did."

"Archie Dock did, too, didn't he?"

"Yes."

"That's all, Judge."

"Fine." She smiled at the witness. "You are excused, Mister Kincaid. Enjoy your retirement."

He looked retired all right, like a man with no place to go. I had an inspiration. "Maybe Mister Kincaid would like to stay in the courtroom, Judge and watch the rest of the trial," I said, watching him lift himself out of the witness box and amble toward the aisle.

"I see no problem with that," she said. "We're done anyway, aren't we? Will either of you recall him?"

"No."

"No."

"Stay if you'd like, Mister Kincaid," Ida said, "and thank you for your testimony."

Kincaid smiled at us like we were family and took a seat toward the back with the court watchers. Iron Pants smiled, too. "We are done, aren't we, gentlemen? Do both sides rest?"

"Judge, I have one more witness," I said. "It won't take long."

"Who?"

"Salvadore Mira."

25

Carlotta opened the door to the courtroom, ushering Salvadore in. I watched them come down the aisle. He wore a coat and a tie and a new pair of shoes, and as he approached the witness box Carlotta—in a whisper—asked me what I wanted her to do. "Go sit by Kincaid," I whispered back.

"You were previously called as a witness, Mister Mira, and sworn to tell the truth. You are still under oath, sir," Iron Pants said. "Do you understand?"

"Yes, ma'am."

I peeked at the clock on the back wall as he sat down—not because I cared what time it was, but to see Charley. It was almost three, but he'd gone. Over here, laddie, I heard him say. But I couldn't find him. "Where?" I asked, turning around. Careful, my boy, he said, appearing on the exhibit table, the size of a doll. They'll think you're barmy.

"Did you say something Mister Bard?" Ida asked, curiously.

"I might have mumbled something to myself, Judge."

"All right." She smiled at me. "You may proceed."

I stood at the lectern, trying to decide the best way to go about it. "Mister Mira, do you have any idea why you are here?"

"No, sir, I don't." He didn't sound upset. Just curious.

"I already told you everything I know." That daughter of mine had done a good job.

"Have I talked to you since you testified, in person or on the telephone or in any way?"

"No, you haven't."

"What about my investigator, Whitney Lee?"

"Him either."

"But you talked to my daughter today, didn't you? She took you to lunch?"

His face reddened. "Was that your daughter?"

I didn't like him blushing about it. "Did you have lunch today with a woman from my office?"

"Yeah, Mister Bard, but I didn't know—"

"It's okay. Did she tell you what her name was?"

"Yeah, but it wasn't Bard. She told me to call her 'Mouse.' "

"Gifford?" I asked. "That's her married name."

"Yeah." He relaxed a little. "I mean yes, sir."

"What did you talk about at lunch?"

His color deepened. "Just talk. You know. I asked her if that other girl, you know, Carlotta, who speaks Spanish? Did she quit?"

"All right. Did you talk about the case at all?"

"Not really. I asked her how it was goin', and she said she didn't know, just that I might be needed again, but she didn't know why."

"Can you think of anything else you said about the case?"

"No."

Keane had not objected, but Iron Pants decided to put her two cents in anyway. "What is the purpose here, Mister Bard?"

"Just to show no taint, Judge."

"You've made your point. Move on, please."

"Thank you." I walked over to the jury rail and stood near the alternates, down at the end. "Do you recall the early morning of March eighteenth of last year, that being when you witnessed a murder?"

He chuckled. "I sure do."

"You've already testified to that, right?"

"Yes, sir."

When I was a kid, we had an expression: scared shitless. As the language evolved the expression became: tight asshole. That's the way I felt now. "Did you get a clear look at the killer?"

He nodded slowly, his eyes alive with memory. "I could see it happen, man."

"Afterwards, did you provide the police with a verbal description of the man you had seen?"

"Yes."

"What did you tell them?"

"I said a big man"—he gestured with his hands and arms—"black, no older'n me, built like a boxer."

"Have you seen that man since?"

"No, sir."

"Do you see him now?" He looked toward Drusus. "Stand up, Mister Church." I couldn't breathe, watching the youngster climb out of his chair. "Your answer, Mister Mira. Do you see him now?"

He looked at me with harshness, as though to say, Why do you want me to say it's him? "No, man, he ain't the one."

I exhaled. "Would you recognize the killer if you saw him?"

Mira was slow to answer. Then he nodded in the affirmative. "Yeah. I would."

I walked over to the exhibit table. Charley kind of guided my hand and steadied it as I picked through the People's exhibits, searching for a particular photograph. "Approach the witness, Judge?" My knees were shaking like I had palsy, except that isn't what they call it now. That's okay, laddie, Charley said. I don't hear a thing.

"You may."

"I'm handing you People's exhibit number twelve. Have you seen this person before?"

Salvadore's expression evidenced immediate and unmistakable recognition. "Yeah. Yeah!" He looked up at me with wonder and relief. "He's the one, man."

"Is that a photograph of the man who you saw doing the shooting that night?"

"No question. He's the one."

"For the record, Judge," I said, barely able to keep my feet on the ground, "I have shown the witness a photograph taken by Doctor Graham Wallotan, the pathologist. It is of the upper waist and face of the body of Kingsley Rhoades."

Keane did what he could to destroy the witness. He had Drusus talk again and reminded Mira of what he had told the jury earlier. He did his best to make the early morning of March eighteenth as dark as the inside of a closet and got Mira to agree that—in the dark—he could identify a voice better than a face. But Salvadore knew. You could tell it was a relief for him to know. Even the hard heads on the jury—Four, Seven, and Eleven—were pulling at their faces.

Kincaid knew, too. Carlotta told me later he'd jumped like he'd been touched with a hot wire.

We adjourned for the day. Iron Pants had some questions about the instructions we'd approved the day before, but it didn't take long. When we were done I went down to 3D to see the youngster. It was crowded; lard-ass lawyers on my side of the glass wall, sitting on the dish seats with their elbows on the platform and their jowels hanging down, talking in low tones through the heavy wire to young black men, mostly, with thin faces. I had to wait a few minutes until Betty Bitler could clear out a cube in the middle of the row.

Drusus beamed a huge, wide grin at me as we pressed palms. The chains over his wrists dragged along behind his hands. "Man, I didn't know what you were doin' today!" he said. "I thought when you brought up all that talk about how everybody see it go down and it's all over the street and they got Larry Walker watching and Archie, too, I thought, hey, my lawyer's the prosecutor!"

"How do you feel now?"

"Great, Jack. Like, I can taste freedom. Go someplace

with a girl, you know, and I'm wondering if you'll let me use your Mazda!"

I was afraid of that. "Drusus, it won't be that easy."

He smiled. There were lines around his eyes, and a softness and a hardness that was a thousand years old. "Yeah, I know." A slight movement behind him, and catlike, he stood in a crouch and faced around. Cautiously, with his face turned so he could watch his back, he sat down. "I just like to think about it."

"Hang in, youngster," I said. "The judge won't reopen. But I'm betting she'll give us a new trial."

"How long I have to wait to find out?"

"I'll move for it as quick as I can. But it'll take time to put the motion together."

"A year?" His eyes looked to me like they were full of visions.

"Nothing like that. Thirty days max on the motion. Then if we get a new trial, another four to six months."

"I'd stay in the county jail?"

"Yes. You don't go to prison until you've been sentenced."

"Jack, I don't like it down here today," he said, turning around. "Too crowded." He stuck his palm against the wire, so I pushed mine against it. "I'm glad you're my lawyer, man. I better go."

"You watch your back, youngster."

"Don't worry about me."

We started on time. In Ida's court you usually do. She greeted the jury after they'd taken their chairs, told them that all the evidence had been produced, and that final arguments from the lawyers would take place next. She said it wouldn't be the same as it had been in the guilt phase. There would be four arguments instead of three. The prosecutor would start, but the defendant would have the final statement. As Keane approached the lectern I made a note on my pad: "Wednesday A.M., 9:07."

I didn't know who to watch: him or them. You try to be God so you can see and hear it all. Then you realize you can't and concentrate on what is being said. By the time

I'd put myself through that drill, Keane had greeted them and thanked them for their patience and had gotten down to it. Should he live or die? "It's a tough call."

I like the way prosecutors think. They will toss a decision having to do with a human life into the metaphor of a baseball game.

When he launched into his argument it rolled out smooth and neat and well-rehearsed, like off a reel. We do that now. Lawyers have become high-tech image packagers who take courses where their performances are taped and critiqued by experts. The knights of today take acting lessons instead of learning martial arts.

"You must cleanse your mind of the way you worked during the guilt phase," he told them, waving his hands like erasers, wiping chalk off a blackboard. "The penalty phase is altogether different. Back then the issue was guilty or not guilty. Now it is life without possibility of parole or death. But it's more than a new issue. The way you work is different, too.

"In the guilt phase there was the presumption of innocence. The People"—he touched his chest—"had to overcome that presumption with evidence. Your job was to give him the benefit of that presumption, and to find him guilty only if you believed—beyond a reasonable doubt and to a moral certainty—that he did in fact murder Kingsley Rhoades. In other words, the scales of justice"—and he held out his hands, palms up, like a pair of scales—"were tipped, at the outset, in the defendant's favor." He indicated what he meant by dropping his left hand and raising his right. "But in this, the penalty phase, the scales start even."

He held his hands at eye level, along a horizontal line, to show the difference. "The defendant doesn't get the benefit of a presumption of innocence. Instead, our law provides you with a list of statutory factors, some in aggravation and some in mitigation. If you determine that the factors in aggravation outweigh the factors in mitigation—even by so much as an ounce"—he let his right hand drop an inch and lifted his left, to demonstrate—"then the proper call, the legal call, is death."

He followed with standard prosecution rhetoric. "Don't *you* feel guilty over having been put in this position, ladies and gentlemen. *He* is the one"—pointing at the youngster, who watched with his customary appearance of absorbing interest—"who has put you there. Make no mistake about where the responsibility lies. If he had not murdered Kingsley Rhoades, you would not have to make this call."

Then he put his spin on the instruction that usually causes all the trouble. "You should also bear in mind that the weight to be given to these factors comes only from you, the jurors. Example: The murder of Kingsley Rhoades is an aggravating factor. Let's assume you decide that one weighs ten ounces." He held his hands like scales, letting his right hand fall as his left one went up. "Sympathy for the defendant is a mitigating factor. For the sake of the example, let's say twelve ounces." He adjusted the scales accordingly in the defendant's favor. "Terrorizing the Greer family is an aggravating factor. Let's assume you give that one a mere five ounces." The scales unbalanced again, in favor of death.

His hands came to rest on the lectern. "My point is this: Each of you—individually—has to decide how much these factors weigh. In all likelihood you won't agree on those weights or amounts, but you don't have to. Where your verdict has to be unanimous is this: All of you must agree—with each of you using your own set of weights—that the scales weigh heavier on one side"—he tossed his hands like a juggler—"or the other."

The first factor he asked them to consider was the murder of Kingsley Rhoades. "Probably you know more about that one than anyone in this courtroom, except the man over there"—he jerked his head at the defendant—"who pulled the trigger. Because you not only heard the evidence, you deliberated on it. The collective wisdom of twelve minds now belongs to each of you, so I won't try to tell you what you already know."

He then belabored it for all it was worth. He talked about

the due process they, the jurors, were bound by law to give the defendant; and he told them how that had been done. Then he asked rhetorically if the defendant had given due process to Kingsley Rhoades. "No. April Tillman told you how he grinned—remember?—as he ripped the purse off his victim's neck. Where was the due process in that? My friends, he can kill another person as easily as you or I can step on a bug. I ask you: How much weight should you give to that factor?"

He introduced the next factor to them by reading the instruction. "It comes to this," he said, setting it down. "Other acts of violence are factors in aggravation. In this case, there are two." Of course, they have to be proved beyond a reasonable doubt—he paid lip service to the notion—then explained how that had been done. "We know he killed Tommy Sherman, just as surely as everyone in the neighborhood knew right after he'd done it. The news was all over the street! News like that spreads quickly, like fire in a dry forest. Furthermore, Larry Walker saw it happen. Remember Mister 'no comment,' and how he squirmed on the witness stand? But in spite of his refusal to tell you what he saw, is there any doubt about it? Then yesterday we learned the name of the other witness: Archie Dock."

He sipped from his glass. "Don't be confused by poor Mister Mira. In the first place, you know from your own experience how much, and how little, a person can see at night. You also know what happens to anyone, except for battle-hardened veterans, when bullets start to fly. The average person will duck. Frequently he will get it wrong, often imagining something that has been suggested to him. But you also know that the sounds of voices are as distinct and different as faces. In the darkness, when a person is ducking"—he dropped his head—"sounds will stay in a person's mind."

Keane raised his voice in emphasis. "Larry Walker is a battle-hardened veteran who knows what happened. But Mister Mira was nervous, perhaps as any of us might have been. Mira heard, but you know he was too busy to see.

You can trust what he told you about what he heard. But you can't have any faith at all in what he told you he saw."

More water. Good, I thought. At least he has the decency to have a dry throat. "This man"—he glared at Drusus—"killed Tommy Sherman with the same terrible casualness, the same lack of due process, the same ease that others feel when they step on ants. And I ask you again: How much weight do you give that factor?"

Keane went on and on and on. He reminded them of the burglary committed in Compton, the terror generated in those little girls who hid with that brave woman, Mrs. Greer. "He made it sound like a prank that went haywire, but do you think she thought it was funny?" He asked them how much weight they should assign to that factor. "It has to weigh something. And the burglary conviction—another factor in aggravation. What will you give it? How many ounces? Did he learn from it? Obviously not. Because after doing his time he killed two men! So add it in, too."

Then he told them he really didn't know what I would talk about. Sympathy? What else did I have? "After adding all this up, if you feel that the single factor of sympathy outweighs two murders, a burglary conviction, and the terrible invasion of a home at night with a gun, and the horror of nightmares that have followed that family since . . ." He paused. "Can any of you do that? Wouldn't you rather be able to look at yourselves in the mirror and tell your friends and your children that yes, I had the courage to follow the law?" He found as many eyes as he could. "It's never easy to sentence a person to death. But in this case it's the correct thing to do. It's the right call. And it's clearly the law—the law you took an oath to uphold. Don't back away."

"Mister Bard?" Ida asked once the boy wonder was in his chair.

I thought of all the stuff Keane hadn't even mentioned, like LuAnne Jones and Dave Kincaid, and the photo identification of Kingsley Rhoades as Tommy Sherman's killer. He's been there before, I said to myself. He's trying to control the argument by talking only to his strength, then he hopes to dismiss mine in rebuttal.

I started too quick, like I was on "L.A. Law" and had only five minutes before a station break. "He's asking you to make a 'call,' like 'you're out,' or 'safe,' or 'stee-rike!' He wants you to think it's easy, like a baseball game!" I carried on long enough to let them know I was offended. But I didn't get much in the way of feedback. They might have thought, "Good! If the defense lawyer is pissed, that's a step in the right direction!"

So I stepped away from the lectern and paced back and forth in front of them, and I told them what was in my heart: how it's never easy to beg for a man's life, especially when the man is someone you have come to know and respect. "You know him, too, don't you? During the guilt phase he exercised his right not to testify, and so all you had was his face and the words of others. But you *know* him now. You've heard him talk. Maybe some of you were close enough to feel the heat from his body, to get a real sense of him. Is he who you thought he was then? This ghetto kid—a former gang member—who was on his way out of both the ghetto and the gang?"

I reviewed the evidence that proved my belief: Sarah Perkins, the social anthropologist; William O'Rourke and multiple marginality; his grandmother, his sister, the teachers who believed in him—"dismissed by the prosecutor as 'sympathy,' stuff that doesn't add up to anything when you make your call."

They were watching me, at least, which didn't mean much. People watch tennis balls, too, because they are moving. I didn't know if they were listening. "Now that you know him better, I wonder if you don't have a doubt—a lingering doubt—as to his guilt."

I stopped behind the lectern and watched as most of them ducked away from my gaze. "A lot of new stuff came in during the penalty phase, evidence that could have made a difference if you'd known about it sooner."

I asked them to take another look at what they had done during the guilt phase in convicting Drusus Church of the murder of Kingsley Rhoades. "You'll say, 'Come on, Mister Bard, don't ask us to beat a dead horse! We've already found him guilty beyond a reasonable doubt!' " You got it, Juror Four's face said. "My point is this: There is a space between reasonable doubt and absolute certainty. It's called 'lingering doubt.' I'd like you to take a fresh look at his guilt—not to acquit him, because that's already been decided. But with all you've learned since the guilt phase, I wonder. Isn't there a lingering doubt now as to whether or not he did it at all?"

I tried to coat it with enough sugar so they could swallow it. I laid out a brand-new scenario, courtesy of evidence developed during the penalty phase: how it showed beyond all question—not that the defendant did in fact kill Tommy Sherman, but that the police believed he did. "They had two witnesses, an informant, and all that gossip on the street. Can you blame them? But they couldn't use any of it"—I explained why—"so they had no case! Can you imagine their frustration? Can you feel what they felt? Like here was a man who was getting away with murder!"

Then I asked them what they thought a man like Dave Kincaid would think of Kingsley Rhoades. "You know Rhoades better now, too. He dealt misery in Long Beach and used the money from his business to pay for a mansion in Palos Verdes. A perfect example, to this first-class cop, of the adage: Crime pays."

Some of the jurors saw where I was taking them, and the vibe I got was: Do we have to go there? So I sautéed the pill in more sugar. "You didn't know any of this two weeks ago. But now you do. Again, I'm not asking you to acquit Mister Church. I'm only asking this: Does this new evidence generate in you a lingering doubt?"

I took them over the testimony of LuAnne Jones. Could that be how Kincaid learned what the inside of the defendant's apartment looked like? "Take this from the point of view of an honest, hardworking cop," I said, "someone who sees on a daily basis the misery in the ghetto and knows nine tenths of it is caused by drug dealers and other forms of vermin like Kingsley Rhoades. How will a cop—

not all of them, but some of them—regard his summary execution? Murder or street justice?" My eyes caught on the hard face of Juror Four. "What do you think?"

I turned away, wandering down the rail to the end. "I don't know, and I'm certainly not prepared to accuse a cop of having murdered Kingsley Rhoades. But from their point of view, what could be more poetic than to pin it on someone who had gotten away with murder? I'm not asking you to believe it. But does the possibility raise, in your mind, a lingering doubt?"

Sit down, laddie, I heard old Charley say. You'll be back, my boy. Save the rest for later. So I sat down.

It took a moment before Ida reacted to the fact that I had taken my seat. She snapped awake, as though she had been in a trance. "Rebuttal, Mister Williams?"

When Keane got up he looked at the clock. The expression on his face showed more concern for the time I'd taken than for my argument. "So now we know where he's coming from," he told the jurors. "An interesting scenario. Do you know what it puts me in mind of?" His face took on a look of betrayal. "Mister Bard's high school friend, Dave Kincaid, said it best when he testified yesterday." He searched through his notes. "Here it is." He read from a piece of paper: " 'For him to do that.' " He flung the paper down and did his best to choke back his anger.

The boy has a future in this business, old Charley muttered in my ear.

"Unfortunately for Mister Bard and the defendant, the scenario they have concocted depends on the credibility of LuAnne Jones and the complete lack of credibility of Dave Kincaid!" Then he charged around in front of them, using hyperbole and rhetoric and punctuating his points with angry, stabbing gestures. Do you take the word of a convicted felon, he asked—bad checks, a crime involving deceit—over the word of a man who spent his life in Long Beach, serving the community? "I hope his citations and commendations and awards mean more to you than that."

And as long as Bard put us in the scenario-concoction mode, he suggested one of his own: that LuAnne Jones was part of a cleverly orchestrated strategy designed by the defense to put doubts in the minds of the jurors and to deflect them from their obvious duty. "What about April Tillman?" he asked. "She *saw* the defendant shoot and kill Rhoades. And now, for him to do that."

He shook his head, obviously saddened by my conduct. "Ladies and gentlemen, nothing Mister Bard has said can change the law. Listen carefully to the instructions you get. Read them in the jury room. See if the words 'lingering doubt' appear in them anywhere. I can tell you this: They don't. This so-called 'lingering doubt' is not a factor in this case. It simply is not a mitigating factor. The *only* mitigating factor the defendant has given you is sympathy."

He prepared to sit down. "Add it up," he said. "Then put it on the scales. Does that one factor weigh more than two murders, a night of terror that still lives in the minds of two young girls, and a burglary conviction?"

When I got up I was tempted to look at the lad and say: Give up? "The scenario I 'concocted' "—I held my fingers up, indicating quotes—"depends on more than Mister Williams told you. It depends on the absolute and complete belief, held by the police, that Mister Church had gotten away with the murder of Tommy Sherman. The irony, ladies and gentlemen, is this: They were wrong.

"If they were absolutely certain that Drusus Church killed Tommy Sherman, then it could, in their minds, justify a frame. But you *know* they were wrong!" I hit the lectern with the heel of my hand.

I told them how the police had investigated Sherman's murder: by going to Rhoades! Good police work, possibly, because they knew Rhoades was too smart to kill a man himself—and they also knew Rhoades would know who had done it. "Get the word out on the street? Archie Dock and Larry Walker, the two men who walked with Tommy Sherman that night. And who did they work for? Kingsley Rhoades! Isn't it possible that the police simply bought it, hook, line, and sinker?

"Listen to me." Cool it, laddie, old Charley said. You're too intense. Fuck off, Charley, I told the old ghost. That's how I feel. "No amount of trial technique or cross-examination genius or persuasive argument can erase that shock of recognition on the face of Salvadore Mira when he saw the picture of Kingsley Rhoades. He knew! It was a relief for him to know. And *you* know, ladies and gentlemen. *You* know, too!" I picked up a couple of sets of eyes and a few heads among the jurors. They didn't want to agree, but I felt that they did. All Keane could do was sit there and take it.

It can be fun pummeling your opponent in a court of law. It's what old guys who like to fight are reduced to, because fistfights hurt, even when you win. And I was proud of the clever way I had managed the argument. I had the last word.

"Mister Williams also mentioned April Tillman, as though her testimony in the first part of the trial settled the issue. But let me ask you this: Would any of you have convicted anyone on this earth of capital murder on the basis of that poor derelict's testimony alone? No!" Worse things than that have happened, but—as the person with the last word—I could afford to appeal to their better instincts. "You needed more, and you had it: the purse."

Now and then you stop. Now and then you are overwhelmed with the majesty and the tragedy of life, and your part in it. I stopped. But then my mouth started flapping again. "The prosecutor wants you to believe that any lingering doubts you have about Kingsley Rhoades should be ignored. He says lingering doubt isn't a factor in mitigation and can't be considered. Hogwash. That's like asking you to give up your soul. Turn yourselves into machines, he says, that do nothing except add things up."

I felt like I was in a trance. My spaced-out eyes might have been misunderstood, but there wasn't anything I could do about that. "You are a jury. You are not robots. Listen to the words of one of California's great jurists—Justice Tobriner—and see if they don't ring in your mind as they ring in mine." They did, too. I didn't have to read the words because I could hear him say them. " 'Only the most fatuous would claim the adjudication of guilt to be infallible.

A Lingering Doubt

The lingering doubts of jurors in the guilt phase may well cast their shadows into the penalty phase and in some measure affect the nature of punishment.' '' I caught a soft smile on Juror Ten's face. "That kind of eloquence is rare," I said. "But it is at the heart and the soul of our law.

"Listen to me. I'm not asking you to believe that Dave Kincaid murdered Kingsley Rhoades, then took his purse and planted it in Drusus Church's apartment. It's too late for that. But you know more about this case than you did two weeks ago. I'm asking you—I'm pleading with you—to take another look. You owe it to yourselves, and to my client, and to Justice Tobriner. Maybe you can't acquit him. But you can have a lingering doubt."

The boy wonder wanted to shake hands and down a few beers at Redheads while we sweated out the jury, but I didn't feel like it. I shook his hand and endured his compliments, floated out a few of my own, but the truth is, I had trouble staying in the same room with him. I talked to Drusus a few minutes until Godzilla laced him up and took him away, then went to my office.

It's hard not to let down when a case goes to the jury. But I wanted to file the motion for a new trial as soon as possible, before Iron Pants cluttered up her docket with other people's problems. I also thought I'd seen questions in her eyes when she looked at the youngster, which she seemed to be doing more and more.

By four-thirty that afternoon I had a good outline. No verdict, so the judge let the jurors go. I was pumped and worked until ten, then called Erin and woke her up. She said I could come over and get in her bed as long as I soaked my hands and feet in hot water first. That shocked me. I didn't know they felt cold to anyone else. But I did as she asked, and she let me huddle with her against the night.

She was gone when I woke up the next morning. I found a note by the coffee machine: "Plug it in, help yourself, then *turn it off,* okay? If you ruin another pot, you will definitely have had it!"

When I struggled into the office that morning I tried to remember whether I'd turned the damn thing off, then decided I must have because I always do when I sweeten the coffee with a shot of cognac. And I had a distinct recollection of dumping in a shot of Courvoisier. Carlotta and Mouse were already there, bouncing off each other like atoms getting ready to explode, so I hid out in the law library, refused a few calls, and got lost in what I was doing.

I took a conference call with Keane and the judge at three that afternoon. "I didn't think it would take this long," Ida said in her most neutral voice. "They haven't asked for anything, and I can't imagine what the problem is. Shall we let them work longer tonight than four-thirty? See if we can't get a decision out of them before the weekend?"

Neither Keane nor I wanted to push, so she agreed to let them go at the usual time.

Before anyone could hang up I brought up the subject of my motion for a new trial. "I'll have it finished this weekend," I said, "but it only goes to the guilt phase." I asked Ida if she'd be willing to hear a guilt-phase motion first and let me do a penalty phase motion later if it was needed.

"I don't believe it, Jack," she said. "You are going to be ahead of time?"

So I took some abuse. She said she'd think about it. She couldn't hear it until after a verdict, but if I was in a hurry, she'd do everything she could to accommodate. "What do you think, Keane?"

"Personally, I don't care," he said. "I do trials. The DA's office will do the motion."

I wondered if that meant Mad Dog would plug back in. I hoped so.

At four-thirty they still hadn't reached a verdict, so she let them go. She told them to report back Monday.

On Monday I gave Ida and Keane a copy of the new trial motion. "You can file it when you get a verdict," Ida said, "assuming we get one. We may have a hung jury." On Wednesday, after lunch, she decided it was time to do something about it. "We'd better find out what's going on," she said, ordering us into court. She brought the jurors in. Then she asked the foreman, Mrs. Stewart, if they were near a verdict.

Mrs. Stewart didn't think so.

"Well," Ida said carefully, "has the jury voted on the issue before it?"

"Yes, Judge, several times. It—"

"Excuse me, Mrs. Stewart, I don't want in any way to influence your deliberations or to know how you stand at this point. But apparently there is some disagreement at this point in time. Is that correct?"

"Yes," Stewart said, smiling at some of her fellow jurors. Two of the men were slumped in their seats, but most of the others nodded their heads and watched attentively.

"I see," Ida said with caution. "Now, please pay close attention. I do not want to know how many of you have voted for life or how many have voted for death. But it could be helpful for me to know the numbers. Do you understand what I'm saying?"

"I'm not sure."

"Let me try again. There is a split of opinion among the twelve of you. I don't want to know how many votes are for death or how many votes are for life. But I do want the numbers. For example, if three of you go one way and nine the other, then I just want the numbers. Not how many are for life or for death. Do you see what I mean?"

"Yes."

"Then what are the numbers, Mrs. Stewart?"

"Eight, one, and three."

"Pardon me?" Ida asked, surprised. "How can that be? Strike that!" She smiled at the pleasant-looking woman. "The numbers are eight, one, and three?"

"Yes, Judge."

We sat around in her chambers, trying to figure out what it meant. How could there be a three-way split? We weren't on the record, so no one had his guard up. I brought the conversation around to my motion, and Ida said, "I find it very persuasive."

"It's good," Keane said, smoothing out the wrinkles in his pants. "But I hope you won't act hastily, Judge. The DA's office is drafting an answer, and it's great."

I felt like dancing. I knew this particular judge better than the boy who would be attorney general, and I thought she smelled a dead rat. If Iron Pants had that odor of putrefaction in her nose, the hunt was over. There'd be a new trial!

At four o'clock she decided to call a mistrial on the penalty phase, unless there was some indication that positions were shifting. She brought the jury back in, but nothing had changed. She went into the routine spiel she delivers on such occasions, thanking them for their service and assuring them that justice is served even when they don't agree. Then she declared a mistrial due to the inability of the jurors to reach a unanimous verdict.

"Now that it's over, the lawyers may want to talk to you about the case," she said. "Very often they like a critique of their performance, which would be helpful to them in the event of a new trial. There is nothing illegal or improper in talking with them, but you don't have to if you don't want to, and if you think you are being pressured, let me know and I'll put a stop to it."

That's the way, Iron Pants, I thought. Make it easy for us.

I talked to juror four, the hardheaded engineer I'd been fighting with all through the trial. He told me it hung eight for life, one for death, and three who wanted to redo the guilt phase and acquit! Old Charley did cartwheels and handsprings. Get affidavits, laddie, he said. Supplement your motion. You won't lose it now.

As soon as Keane knew how they'd hung, he worked them like a crowd of voters, shaking hands and talking about the tough call. "Sure I'm disappointed," he said, wearing a lopsided Jimmy Stewart grin. "But you know, I never second-guess. And I'm proud to be a part of the judicial process." He even stuck his hand out to Drusus, who stared at it. "Good luck."

"Huh."

"Jack S," he said to me, smiling with what appeared to be real and sincere pleasure, "it's been an experience." Then he grabbed my hand and pumped it with enthusiasm. "If the judge grants your motion, I don't know who Trigge will send out to try it, but it won't be me. I'll be knee-deep in blood splatters! Ciao."

"Where's Betty?" I asked, standing in the cage at 3D. There were three sheriffs sitting at their desks. I'd seen them but didn't know their names. None of them heard me. "She never made me wait." I smiled, thinking how I probably came across like an old salt.

"Betty Bitler?" the male deputy asked. "Who's she? Didn't she get fired for consorting with the enemy?"

"No," one of the two uniformed women said, picking up the telephone. She was Korean. "Indecent exposure."

"You're just jealous," the other woman—a heavy Mexican—said. "Everything Betty puts on is indecent."

I'm making progress, I thought. At least they're treating me like we're in the same room. "Come on, folks. Where is she?"

"Pull Drusus Church, okay?" the Korean said into the telephone, then she put her hand over the mouthpiece: "They made her a lieutenant."

"Good for her!"

"You can go in, Mister Bard."

"Thanks."

Two other lawyers' butts were hanging over the platter seats in the bubble. I didn't recognize either ass. I walked to the end and sat down, waiting for the youngster. I really felt great. Mad Dog wanted a month to file a response to my motion for a new trial, but Ida had impatiently cut him off in the middle of his pitch and told him he had two weeks. I knew the signs.

Drusus shuffled in wearing chains and bracelets. They still carried him as a gang member on a capital beef, which meant the shackles, even though none of the other inmates had to wear them. From his side of the glass wall he saw where I was sitting and let his face spread into a big grin. I watched him come over slowly, like a lion pushing his way through a herd of elephants. He saw where everyone was, then sat down. "Where's Mad Dog?" he asked, reaching up with both palms and pressing them against mine. His hands stayed high, exposing his back. "How come he don't ever come down—uh."

Suddenly something went wrong with his face. He sagged toward me, then savagely jerked around and staggered to his feet. "Mother ff—!"

"NO!" I shouted. I could see the bristles of a toothbrush. It looked like it had been pasted on his back and filled with blood. "GUARD! HELP!" I looked past Drusus at the prisoner who had come up behind him. The hard young face changed from satisfaction to confusion. Then it was gone. "GUARD! SOMEBODY! HELP!"

No one on the prisoner side of the glass did anything except move out of the way. The youngster sat down on the floor, then fell forward.

I found out later that the long plastic handle of a toothbrush, sharpened and barbed like a fishhook, had been shoved between his ribs. It poked all the way into his heart. That huge muscle couldn't handle the insult, and it stopped.

Two days later I was still in the bag. But I've had practice. I wasn't so deep inside that I couldn't see out. The trouble was, Annie wanted to cut me off. She said I'd have to wait until noon for another carafe.

That made me mad. "Damn it, Annie!" I yelled, trying to stand up. "Where's the Redhead? Bring me the fucking Redhead!" I quit trying and sat down. "I'm gonna buy this shithouse and then fire your ass!"

An attractive woman slid into the booth across from me. I didn't recognize her for a minute, but her presence kind of toned me down. "Ida?"

"Yes." Damn it. She smiled at me, and I started to cry.

"Carlotta told me I'd catch you here," she said. "I hope you don't mind."

"No."

She put her hand on top of mine. Her face looked like it was on the other side of a waterfall. "What about some food, Jack?"

"Can't. I've only got part of a stomach, and it's full of wine."

She just sat there across from me with her hand on mine and let me cry. Damn woman. It seemed awfully quiet for Redheads. I grabbed a napkin, wiped off my face, and blew my nose.

"I guess you heard about it," I said, which ought to qualify for the dumbest remark of the decade.

She nodded. She let go of my hand and reached in her purse. "Mind if I smoke?"

"That's okay." I pushed the ashtray toward her.

I watched her light up and flick off an ash. "My timing is terrible, Jack. Could you use a partner?"

"What?"

She exhaled a whole yard. "I've been on the bench for nine years. That's too long. I'm getting jaded."

"You're thinking about quitting?" Which qualifies as the second dumbest remark of the decade.

"It isn't the same. I never thought I'd feel like this."

She is a very attractive woman, I thought. She looks great in a dress, and her hair has a nice wave. The lines in her face show character, too. I tried to show my enthusiasm. "We'd be great, Ida," I said. "What about Haralson? Isn't that your husband's name?"

"He wouldn't care. He wouldn't even notice." She tapped off an ash. "Will you think about it?"

"Listen to me," I said.

"I'm listening."

"You come down any time you want." But I couldn't help myself, and I looked away from her. "We'd make a great team," I said, trying to sound enthusiastic. "We'd make more money than is decent, take a criminal case once in a while and rip those bastards. Then we'd howl at the moon.''

She nodded coolly and inhaled deeply on her cigarette. "You'd rather I didn't. Am I right?"

How did she know that? "I don't know."

"I am so disgusted and disappointed with the judiciary in this state, Jack. You have no idea. I thought once how wonderful it would be to be a judge. But it's changed so much in the last few years. It's awful."

"The trouble is, you're good at it."

"What about your young man?"

"You didn't kill him."

She butted the cigarette. "So the answer is no?"

"Wrong. The answer is yes. Except I kind of hope you won't do it."

"This sounds like one of those three-way splits."

Old Charley was caught in the wine bottle. I watched him try to climb out. "You're a good judge, Ida," I said. "You still make a lot of mistakes, and you're way too impatient. You're about as flexible as a steel rod, which is why they call you Iron Pants." I looked at her and grinned. "*I* don't, but I've heard others."

She started smiling again. "You'd rather I stayed on the bench?"

"Yeah. I would." I looked at my watch; it was five past noon. "How about a glass of wine?"

The Author

Warwick Downing was born and raised into the law. His father was a lawyer, as was his grandfather. Both his brothers are lawyers, and his sister is married to one.

Downing is a former Deputy District Attorney (Merced, California), Assistant United States Attorney (Denver, Colorado) and District Attorney (22nd Judicial District, Cortez, Colorado).

He is also a novelist. In addition to the NASP series, he has written three suspense books and one book for young readers.

He presently lives in Denver.

WARWICK DOWNING

"Warwick Downing has to be the finest mystery writer in the country today. His remarkable talent for probing the dark side of the street has established him as the master of the mystery genre. He is the perfect author to read late at night." —Clive Cussler

---

A CLEAR CASE OF MURDER

THE WATER CURE

A LINGERING DOUBT

Available from Pocket Books